The Explosive
Autobiography
of the Controversial,
Death-Defying Founder
of the U.S. Navy's
Top Secret
Counterterrorist Unit
SEAL TEAM SIX

"Fascinating....
Marcinko...
makes Arnold
Schwarzenegger
look like
Little Lord
Fauntleroy."
—*The New York
Times Book Review*

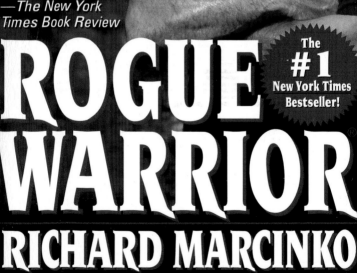

The #1 New York Times Bestseller!

ROGUE
WARRIOR

RICHARD MARCINKO
with JOHN WEISMAN
Authors of *Detachment Bravo*

READ THESE ROGUE WARRIOR® BESTSELLERS
FROM POCKET BOOKS!

By Richard Marcinko
VIOLENCE OF ACTION

By Richard Marcinko and Jim DeFelice
VENGEANCE

By Richard Marcinko and John Weisman
DETACHMENT BRAVO
ECHO PLATOON
OPTION DELTA
SEAL FORCE ALPHA
DESIGNATION GOLD
TASK FORCE BLUE
GREEN TEAM
RED CELL
ROGUE WARRIOR

"Outstanding . . . a short course in
special operations techniques and weapons."
—Col. Calvin G. Bass, USAG [Ret.],
Tulsa World (OK)

More Pocket Books by Richard Marcinko
*THE ROGUE WARRIOR'S
STRATEGY FOR SUCCESS*
A Commando's Principles of Winning

*LEADERSHIP SECRETS OF
THE ROGUE WARRIOR*
A Commando's Guide to Success

THE REAL TEAM
True Stories from the Real-Life SEALs
Featured in the Rogue Warrior Series

VIETNAM, 1968: Leader of a SEAL platoon, Marcinko became an expert at guerrilla war. When the Viet Cong overran Chau Doc, he and his men defied a spit-and-polish colonel's orders and fought street to street, house to house, to rescue trapped civilian women. . . .

CAMBODIA, 1973: Marcinko was training Cambodian Navy officers when the trainees disappeared, leaving him floating in a river above forty pounds of C-3 explosive rigged to explode—with Khmer Rouge gunners shooting at him from both shores. . . .

WASHINGTON, D.C., 1980: In a Special Classified Intelligence Facility in the Pentagon, Marcinko and others listened helplessly as Delta Force commandos attempted the ill-fated rescue of the American hostages in Iran. . . .

VIEQUES ISLAND, 1981: Nineteen thousand feet above the Caribbean island, Marcinko's first parachute failed. His backup chute collapsed too. He was spiraling wildly in the blackness toward a target he believed held armed terrorists, a hostage, and a hijacked nuclear weapon. . . .

THE NORTH SEA, 1982: In freezing water with waves that flipped Boston whalers like pancakes, Marcinko led SEAL Team Six and German GSG-9 commandos in an anti-terrorist training exercise, storming an ice-encrusted oil rig. . . .

CALIFORNIA, 1985: Marcinko and his Red Cell team staged a successful mock-attack on Air Force One, outwitting the Secret Service, a special SWAT team, an Air Force security detail, the FBI, Marine guards, Navy Security sweeps, Department of Defense police, local rent-a-cops, and the Point Mugu Naval Air Station's fire department. . . .

The Rogue Warrior® series by Richard Marcinko and John Weisman

Rogue Warrior
Rogue Warrior: Red Cell
Rogue Warrior: Green Team
Rogue Warrior: Task Force Blue
Rogue Warrior: Designation Gold
Rogue Warrior: SEAL Force Alpha
Rogue Warrior: Option Delta
Rogue Warrior: Echo Platoon
Rogue Warrior: Detachment Bravo

Also by Richard Marcinko

Leadership Secrets of the Rogue Warrior
The Rogue Warrior's Success Strategies
The Real Team

Also by John Weisman

Fiction

Blood Cries
Watchdogs
Evidence

Nonfiction

Shadow Warrior (with Felix Rodriguez)

Anthologies

Unusual Suspects (edited by James Grady)
The Best American Mystery Stories of 1997
   (edited by Robert B. Parker)

For information regarding special discounts for bulk purchases, please contact Simon & Schuster Special Sales at 1-800-456-6798 or business@simonandschuster.com

ROGUE WARRIOR®

RICHARD MARCINKO

with
John Weisman

POCKET BOOKS

New York   London   Toronto   Sydney

POCKET BOOKS, a division of Simon & Schuster, Inc.
1230 Avenue of the Americas, New York, NY 10020

Copyright © 1992 by Richard Marcinko
Foreword copyright © 1992 by John Weisman

ISBN -13: 978-0-671-79593-1
ISBN -10:   0-671-79593-7

First Pocket Books paperback printing March 1993

40 39 38

POCKET and colophon are registered trademarks of
Simon & Schuster, Inc.

ROGUE WARRIOR is a registered trademark of Richard Marcinko

Cover photo by Roger Foley

Printed in the U.S.A.

To the shooters—
who have been,
and always will be

To avoid compromising special operations sources and methods, certain names, locations, and time frames have been modified. Tactical details and chronological sequences have also been altered so as not to betray current SpecWar techniques.

It's not the critic who counts. . . . The credit belongs to the man who actually is in the arena, who strives violently, who errs and comes up short again and again . . . who if he wins, knows the triumph of high achievement, but who if he fails, fails while daring greatly.

—Theodore Roosevelt

If we weren't crazy, we'd all be insane.

—Jimmy Buffett

Foreword

IN THE HISTORY OF THE U.S. NAVY THERE HAS NEVER BEEN an unconventional warrior quite so unconventional as Dick Marcinko.

Perhaps the best indication of his capabilities was that in August 1980, at the age of thirty-nine, Marcinko, then a commander, was picked by the Chief of Naval Operations, Thomas Hayward, to design, build, equip, train, and lead what many believe to be the best counterterror force in the world, SEAL Team Six.

His route to the command of Six was circuitous. A renegade high-school dropout from a broken home in the Pennsylvania coal fields, Marcinko made the Navy his career and special warfare his obsession. As a gung-ho young SEAL officer in Vietnam, he operated behind enemy lines. While others dug in behind barbed wire and sandbags, Marcinko and his platoon—in black pajamas and barefoot, using captured Soviet weapons and ammo—hunted the Viet Cong deep inside their own turf.

During one six-month period, Marcinko's SEALs performed an incredible 107 combat patrols, with more than 150 confirmed VC killed and 84 captured. During two tours in

Vietnam, Marcinko won the Silver Star, four Bronze Stars with Combat "V," two Navy Commendation Medals, and the Vietnamese Cross of Gallantry with Silver Star. As a Naval attaché in Cambodia in 1973 and 1974, Marcinko's exploits included body-surfing behind a patrol boat on the Mekong River during a Khmer Rouge ambush. He spent 291 days in combat in Cambodia, and was awarded the Legion of Merit for his actions.

The Navy was Dick Marcinko's life. It gave him an education—a high-school diploma, a B.A., even a master's in international relations. It also gave him a deadly trade: unconventional warrior. Ambushes, booby traps, exotic weapons, high-altitude parachute drops, underwater infiltrations— Marcinko is a virtuoso of them all.

The day he assumed command of SEAL Team Six, CNO Hayward's orders to Marcinko were brief—almost to the point of curtness. He was told he had less than six months to bring the new unit "on line." He was ordered to get the job done, whatever the personal or professional cost. "Dick, *you will not fail*," is what Hayward said.

To achieve that goal, Marcinko rewrote the rule book on unconventional warfare, and its training. He cut corners. He stepped on toes. He wheedled and cajoled. He threatened— and occasionally he terrorized. His sin was that he believed the end was worth the means; his hubris, that he thought he could get away with it.

Indeed, if we're talking heroic here about Dick Marcinko (and I believe we should be), he is heroic in the classic sense of the word: Dick's warrior hubris was too much for some of the Pentagon's Olympians, and so a few Navy technocrat "gods" brought him down as an example to others.

The specific tragic flaw that caused Marcinko's fall was one of his most gallant qualities: loyalty. His loyalties always lay with the men under his command, rather than with the Navy system of which he was a part.

Marcinko has never been reluctant to admit as much. Soon after we met, I asked him if the litany of transgressions against the system the Navy accused him of committing were true.

"Absolutely," he said. "Guilty as charged. Guilty of preaching unit integrity above other values. Guilty of putting my men before bureaucratic bullshit. Guilty of spending as much money as I can get my hands on to train my men properly. Guilty of preparing my men for war instead of peace. Of all these things am I indeed guilty. *Mea culpa, mea culpa, mea maxima* fucking *culpa.*"

Dick Marcinko's story is as exciting as any piece of fiction—but it is more than that. It is the provocative chronicle of an American hero—a warrior whose legacies still live on, through the men he trained, and led, and inspired.

—John Weisman
Chevy Chase, MD
October 1991

Part
One

GEEK

Chapter

1

January 1981

IT WAS A BIG FIRST STEP—NINETEEN THOUSAND FEET BE-tween the soles of my boots and the scrubby jungle—but I didn't have time to think about that. The green light was on and the jumpmaster was pointing vaguely in my direction, so I blew a polite kiss at him and went out for a walk—took a stroll off the deep end of the C-130's greasy ramp and dove into the nighttime sky. Just the way I'd done it more than a thousand times before.

The ice-cold slipstream punched at me as the blacked-out plane disappeared overhead. I looked down. Nothing. Almost four miles to the ground—too far to see anything yet, or for anyone down there to have heard the plane.

I looked around me. Zippo. What had I expected? To see my men? That would be impossible, too, of course. We were showing no lights, carried nothing reflective, and were all dressed in dark camouflage tigerstripes, invisible in the black-ness above our objective, Vieques Island, in the Caribbean far below.

I clenched my fist and tucked my elbow in silent triumph. Yes! Right on! The first eight seconds of this operation had gone absolutely perfectly. So far, we were ahead of the curve.

I checked the altimeter on my wrist then pulled the rip cord. I sensed my chute slip out of the backpack and felt it separate.

I was yanked skyward by the harness in the bungee-cord way you're always bounced by a chute. Then all of a sudden I veered sharply to my right and began to spiral wildly, uncontrollably, toward the ground.

So much for perfection. I looked up. One of the cells of my sky-blue silk canopy had collapsed in the crosswind. I tugged on the guidelines to shake it out and fill the chute with air, but couldn't make it happen.

It didn't help that I was carrying almost a hundred pounds of equipment strapped to a specially built combat vest or attached to my fatigues. The weight was a problem in the thin air during HAHO—high altitude, high opening—jumps. Most of what I carried was lethal. There was my customized Beretta 92-SF in its thigh holster, along with eleven clips of ammo—165 rounds of hollow-point Hydra-Shok, custom-made hot loads that could literally blow a man's head off. Hanging from a strap attached to my shoulder was a specially modified HK—Heckler & Koch—MP5 submachine gun and 600 rounds of jacketed hollow-point in 30-round magazines.

Then there were the other goodies: flash-bang grenades and thunder-strips to disorient bad guys; strobes and light-sticks for guiding choppers into a drop zone. Wire snips for cutting through fences. And I carried a selection of the miniaturized communications stuff we'd developed—strapped to my waist was a secure Motorola walkie-talkie (it came with lip mikes and earpieces so we could talk and listen to each other while moving. No Secret Service whispering into our shirt cuffs for us).

In the upper right-hand pocket of my combat vest was a satellite transceiver, a SATCOM unit about the same size as a cellular phone. On it I could talk to my boss, Brigadier General Dick Scholtes, who ran the Joint Special Operations Command, back at his Ops Center at Ft. Bragg, North Carolina, as clearly as if I were in the next room instead of almost two thousand miles down the road.

I laughed out loud. Maybe I should punch up Scholtes now. "Hey, General, I'm calling about this little momentary snag that's developed. Dickie's about to go squish."

Another two air cells in the parasail collapsed and the chute folded in half. Okay, so it screwed up. No problem. I'd rehearsed this move maybe eighty, a hundred times during practice jumps. I did a cutaway, jettisoned the faulty canopy, then resumed free-fall. Fifteen thousand feet and cruising.

Five seconds later I yanked the cord on my second chute. It started to open nicely. Then it developed a fissure, folded in half, and collapsed just like number one, and the crazy corkscrewing began all over again.

I didn't have any more backups.

I tore at the lines with both hands to open the parasail to its full width, screaming profanities into space.

It came to me in the absolutely clear way things come to dying men that I had been the thirteenth jumper to exit the C-130. This was a bad joke on Dickie. This wasn't the way it was supposed to happen. Down there—where I was about to splatter myself into strawberry-colored goo—were, according to what we'd been told, thirty to forty armed terrorists, a hostage, and a hijacked nuclear weapon.

This clandestine airborne assault was the culmination of five months of bone-wrenching, take-it-to-the-limit training —eighteen hours a day, seven days a week. I was spiraling wildly in the blackness because the U.S. Navy, in its infinite wisdom, had chosen me to design, build, equip, train, and lead what I now believed to be the most effective and highly secret counterterror force in the world—SEAL Team Six.

Admiral Thomas Hayward, the chief of naval operations, gave me the order to create the unit himself, not ninety days after our disastrous April 1980 rescue attempt of the American hostages held in Tehran.

What the CNO had said to me was unequivocal: "Dick, you will not fail."

I took his words to heart. SEAL Team Six trained harder than any unit had ever trained before, waiting for the opportunity to show the skeptical bureaucrat-sailors and dip-dunk bean-counters prevalent in Washington that it was possible for the U.S. Navy to fight back effectively against terrorists. I had cut more than a few corners and stepped on a shoe store full of toes carrying out Admiral Hayward's order.

And I hadn't failed—until now, it seemed. Was it now all going to come to this? Dickie gets slam-dunked and misses all the fun while the rest of the guys get to kick ass and take names?

No way. I was only forty—far too young to die. I yanked on the guides again. No fucking way I was going to buy it. Not like this. Not because my outrageously expensive, personally selected, ingeniously modified, packed-by-my-own-loving-hands, goddamn fucking parachute didn't work.

I dragged at the lines with as much force as I could muster. Finally, the two far right-hand cells filled with air and I began a controlled descent, spiraling in lazy circles as I hung in the harness, sweating, and tried to figure out where the hell I was.

Where I was, was about three miles out over the ocean, the speed of the C-130 and the free-fall having carried me way off my original flight path. I could see beach below, so I checked my compass and altimeter and changed course, parasailing back toward the prearranged 300-square-yard landing zone, a little airstrip cut into the rough countryside about half a mile from where the terrorists were holed up. We'd chosen it as our assembly point from an ultra-high-resolution NSA satellite photo that had been faxed to us during our flight down from Norfolk.

I was at eleven thousand feet now, and by my best guess-timate I had about ten miles before touchdown. I watched the breakers wash ashore more than two miles beneath my feet, phosphorescent white crescents moving in rippling, parallel lines. Beyond the sea was the jungle. It was, as I knew from the intel pictures, scrubby jungle, the kind common to much of the Caribbean and Latin America. Not rain forest, thank God, with its treacherous high canopy of trees that made parachute landings a bitch. If it'd been rain forest we'd have had to jump way offshore and land on a narrow strip of beach, or come in by sea, swimming from a mother ship, an innocent-looking, apparently civilian vessel that passed far off the coast, or landing in specially modified IBSs—rubberized inflatables that, along with us, were dropped by ships or low-flying planes.

I looked up. No stars. No moon. The chute was now working perfectly, and from the way the wind was blowing, I knew I'd make the landing zone easily. I had a twenty-minute glide ahead of me, and I decided to sit back and enjoy the ride.

I figured I could. Surprise would certainly still be on our side. All the intelligence we'd received during our flight from the States indicated the bad guys wouldn't be expecting us. Not so soon. That's what made SEAL Team Six so special. We were unique; a small, highly mobile, quick-reaction team trained to do one job: kill terrorists and rescue hostages, and do it better than anybody in the world. Nobody could move as fast as we could. No other unit could come out of the water, or the sky, with equal ease.

Delta Force, the Army's hostage-rescue unit originally commanded by my old colleague and sometime rival Colonel Charlie Beckwith, was good. But it was also big—more than two hundred operators—and it was cumbersome as a bloody elephant to move. My entire unit numbered only ninety, and we traveled light. We had to go that way: often, we had to swim to our objective with everything we'd need in tow.

Tonight, fifty-six SEAL Six jumpers parachuted off the ramps of two C-130s that had taken off from Norfolk, Virginia, six and a half hours previously. If my chute was the only one that had screwed up, they'd all be on final approach to the LZ by now, gliding into circular formations of seven, then dropping onto the ground by quickly pulling up, or flaring, just before their feet touched. It kept you from being dragged by your chute and making a furrow with your face.

Normally I'd have been a part of the pattern, but I'd been unavoidably detained and wanted to get onto the ground fast, so I flew a straight approach into the LZ. As I came in, I could hear ambient canopy flutter all around me, and I knew the team was S-turning to eat up ground speed, then corkscrew circling and landing just as we'd trained to do. As for me, I came in fast and high—I didn't brake as I was supposed to, never flared, and took out a small tree at the end of the overgrown runway. I never even saw it coming. I was at maybe fifteen feet or so and then—*blam*—took the trunk smack in the face.

It was a good hurt. The kind that made me feel I was alive. I left the canopy up in the foliage, hit the deck, and started to assemble the teams.

We did a fast count. I was ecstatic. Every man had made the LZ with equipment intact. I called JSOC—the Joint Special Operations Command—on the SATCOM and reported we were fifty-six out of fifty-six on the ground and were about to move.

Paul Henley, my XO—Six's executive officer, who I'd nick-named PV because of his Prince Valiant haircut—and I formed the teams into four prearranged assault groups.

I punched Paul on the upper arm. "Let's go hunting."

Following our NSA maps, we moved off silently into the jungle to the southwest, single file, weapons at the ready. We functioned entirely through hand signals, the way I'd done in Vietnam more than a decade earlier. Our moves were cho-reographed into a deadly sort of ballet—*pas de mort*—we'd worked on for months. No one spoke. No one had to. By now, PV and I thought alike. He'd been the first man I'd chosen for Six, a bright, energetic, capable young SEAL of-ficer who could jump and shoot and party with the best of them.

Moreover, unlike me, he was an Academy grad, which gave Six some cachet with the bean counters. The Navy's caste system has the reputation of being about as rigid as any in the world. The first thing most Navy officers do when they meet you is look at your hands to see whether or not you're wearing a Naval Academy class ring. If you do, then you're a part of the club. If you don't, then you're an untouchable. I was the original untouchable. The only things I wore on my knuckles were scars. But I loved my work and was uncom-monly good at it, and in a few rare cases—mine included—the Navy establishment rewards ability almost as nicely as it does jewelry.

I checked my watch. Twenty-one seventeen. Two minutes behind the schedule I kept in my head.

We'd gotten the word to move twenty-seven hours before-hand. It came from JSOC. The first info was pretty sketchy: a Puerto Rican terrorist group called the Macheteros, or "machete wielders," had broken onto the National Guard airfield just outside San Juan and destroyed $40 million worth of planes and equipment. That much of the story would make it into the newspapers.

What wouldn't be reported, according to JSOC, was that during the attack the Macheteros—we commonly referred to terrorists in the radio phonetic term as Ts, or tangos—took a hostage, and a pallet load of equipment. Including, it was believed, a nuclear weapon. No one was sure. Don't ask how no one could be sure whether or not an A-bomb was missing. This was the United States Air Force after all—home of $600 toilet seats and $200 pliers.

Anyway, the Macheteros, I was told, had managed to evade police dragnets, roadblocks, and SWAT teams and disappear. Except that U.S. intelligence tracked them to Vieques, a small island due east of Puerto Rico, where they had a clandestine training camp. That was where they were now.

I knew Vieques Island. I'd trained there as a member of Underwater Demolition Team 21 two decades ago. It seemed somehow incongruous that a bunch of tangos would choose for their clandestine base an island that normally crawled with U.S. military personnel.

Moreover, we'd had so many false alarms, I was suspicious that this scramble was just another cry-wolf operational drill, or another training exercise to be done in "real time," known as a full mission profile. Indeed, we'd been scrambled by Dick Scholtes before, only to find out while we were in the air on the way to the "target" that we were part of some goatfuck war game JSOC had based on a real incident, to make us think we were playing for keeps.

Game or not, I was willing to play along. We had never performed a massed night jump over a hostile target. We'd also never coordinated so many elements at once—clandestine insertion, taking down the target, snatching a hostage and a nuke, and synchronizing an extraction from a hot landing zone was as complicated a series of tasks as SEAL Team Six had been required to perform in its short history.

The call-up had gone right according to schedule. Each man at Six carried a beeper at all times. When it went off, he had four hours to show up at a prearranged location with his equipment.

During the initial hours, while the crews were assembling, PV and I called in my ops boss, Marko, and Six's master chief petty officer, Big Mac, and we began putting together our basic strategy. That's the way it worked at Six. Officers, petty officers (Navy noncoms), and enlisted all had a say in what went on, although I made the ultimate aye-or-nay decision on everything.

We realized from the start that a seaborne operation was out of the question because it would have taken too long to land from a mother ship. That meant we'd be launching an air strike. And given the location of the terrorist camp, it would be easier to go straight in than drop us eight or ten miles offshore with our boats.

The first intelligence we received came from a guy I'll call Pepperman, a former Marine lieutenant colonel who was working special ops assistance at the National Security Agency at Ft. Meade, Maryland, out of a room five or six stories below ground. That basement room was the hub for covert and clandestine operations all over the world, and my old friend Pepperman sat there like a balding Buddha, watching and listening as things went down.

Pepperman—I called him that because he grew his own incredibly hot Thai peppers in the backyard of his suburban Maryland home, a culinary holdover from his special ops days behind the lines in Southeast Asia—was one of those wonderful, ex-military scavengers who could get you anything, anytime. In Vietnam he'd probably been the type who could lay his hands on a bottle of Chivas or a case of beer even though he was six days into a ten-day long-range patrol behind the Green Line in Cambodia. Now, he was in the code-word-secret classified-information business, and there wasn't much he couldn't come up with, *if* you were a friend in need—and *if* you had the proper clearances, which I did.

He immediately supplied us with the kind of info that allowed me to outline our basic strategy: a thumbnail of who the bad guys were, their history, modus operandi, and basic political and military objectives. It didn't take long to reach the bottom line: these people weren't nice.

The Macheteros had been active since 1978. They were a small, well-financed, tightly organized guerrilla force of ultranationalists. Their objective was to wage a terrorist war against what they called "U.S. colonialist imperialism" in the broadside "communiqués" they distributed following dozens of attacks. They'd received training in Eastern Europe courtesy of the KGB—and they'd learned their deadly lessons well. The Macheteros had staged a number of lethal, effective attacks. Half a dozen Puerto Rican policemen had been shot, and in the fourteen months before the current raid, they'd murdered two U.S. sailors and wounded three other American military personnel in separate ambushes.

About an hour into the planning, my jumpmaster, a boatswain's mate I called Gold Dust Frank, showed up. I gave him a quick rundown of what was going on. Then he and PV, who had been a member of the Navy's parachute team, began to work out the intricacies of a 56-man clandestine jump and a ten-nautical-mile glide, given the approximate load each man would be carrying, the topography of Vieques Island, and the sort of landing zone we'd be dropping into.

Another pair of SEAL Six petty officers, Horseface and Fingers, showed up. They were my top demolition experts, and they started to assemble the explosive bundles necessary to take down an armed installation. Except they had a question or two I couldn't answer.

Like: "How thick are the doors, Skipper? And are they wood or metal?"

"What am I, a goddamn clairvoyant?" I punched up the all-knowing Pepperman in his NSA basement.

"Pepperman, Dickie here. Can you give us an info dump on door thickness and material?"

He laughed out loud. "That's always Delta's first question, Marcinko, you dipshit asshole. What's the matter, can't you be original?"

I loved it when he talked like that. "Screw you, shit-for-brains." I asked him to fax us a quick flick of the target area—the terrorist camp—so Horseface could determine the approximate size of a charge that would breach the door without blowing up the hostage inside. Meanwhile, Fingers (he was called that because he'd lost a couple doing demolition work) began building the other explosive charges—the ones we'd use to destroy the nuclear device if it couldn't be brought out with us.

"I got a Blackbird working, Dick," Pepperman said. That was good. It meant he'd already scrambled an SR-71 spy plane and its cameras were snap-snap-snapping away from 85,000 feet. At that height the bird was invisible to the normal eye —even to most binoculars. We'd have pictures in a couple of hours at most. "And we'll start getting full imagery in seven, eight hours," Pepperman continued.

"Full imagery" was the stuff from one of the KH-11—for

Keyhole-11—spy satellites that NSA operated in conjunction with the CIA and the military. "Sounds good. Keep me posted, cockbreath." I rang off before he could insult me back.

Our communications maven—I called him Ameche, after Don Ameche, who played Alexander Graham Bell in the thirties movie—reported for work. He began getting the SATCOM relays up and working. We don't like to go through the operator in SEAL Team Six; we're much more a direct-dial outfit. Our portable phones were called PSC-1 manpacks, which in Navyspeak translates as Portable Satellite Communications terminals.

PV and I worked the phones, negotiating with the Air Force to set the pickup time so Six, the hostage, and the nuke could all be exfiltrated by HH-53 choppers flown from the Air Force's 20th Special Operations Squadron at Hurlburt Field, located on the western edge of the Eglin Air Force Base complex in Florida. Coordination was important: the four HH-53s had to be refueled in flight by a pair of MC-130E Combat Talon aircraft; moreover, they couldn't arrive too early because they'd give our position away. If they kept us waiting, they'd leave us vulnerable in hostile—potentially deadly—territory. Once airborne, they'd sprint us from Vieques to a friendly airfield on the main island, about eleven minutes away. There, we'd rendezvous with a C-141 StarLifter out of Charleston, South Carolina, which would in turn move us and our packages back to CONUS—the CONtinental United States.

The team started to arrive midevening; guys drifting in from all over the Virginia Beach area. We looked like a bunch of dirtbags. The Navy called it "modified grooming standards." I called it ponytails, earrings, beards, and Fu Manchu mustaches, biker's jackets, tank tops, and T-shirts.

The guys' cars and pickup trucks were crammed to overflowing with gear, covered with tarps or canvas. I'd bought them the best of everything, from mountaineering equipment to Draeger bubbleless underwater breathing apparatus. And until we were able to build each team member his own personal equipment cage, they had to bring everything with them each time there was a call-up. Who knew where we'd be going.

We went wheels up at 1400 hours. The guys looked tired

but ready as they settled as comfortably as they could in the canvas cargo sling seats that ran up and down the sides of the C-130's fuselage, or sacked out on the cargo pads that lay strewn on the greasy floor. Our shrink, Mike the Psych, wandered up and down, making sure nobody got too apprehensive. We'd learned from Delta that an SOB—Shrink On Board—was a good idea. First, you didn't want a guy who'd go bonkers on you jumping with the team. Mike knew these men—if he sensed there might be a problem, I trusted him to let me know immediately.

Once we got airborne, I'd formulate our final plans based on the information and pictures that would start arriving on our scrambled fax machines. PV and I were on separate aircraft, but we could talk on secure phones and share information, or consult with Dick Scholtes at Ft. Bragg or call Pepperman in his Maryland basement for advice if we needed to.

I climbed the ladder to the cockpit and peered through the windshield, watching the sky darken. Pretty soon we'd refuel, a pair of KC-135 tankers lumbering above us at four hundred knots while the pilots nudged our C-130s up to the trailing fuel drogues, plugged up, and sucked gas. Absentmindedly, I dropped the clip out of my Beretta and popped a round into my palm. The clip—in fact, every round of ammunition carried tonight by SEAL Team Six—came from a special section of the base ammo lockers. It had been preloaded into magazines for our Berettas and HK submachine guns. Its release had been authorized by JSOC just prior to our departure.

Something was awry. The weight was wrong—lighter than the custom load I'd helped design. I dragged my fingernail across the dull lead hollow-point and left a track. It was a compound bullet—a goddamn training round. They were sending us on another pus-nuts exercise—a full mission profile.

Goddammit—the Macheteros were real enough, why the hell not let us take 'em on? We'd designed a good mission, based on real intelligence—and were executing it according to the numbers. Why the hell didn't they let us do what we'd been trained to do? A decade and a half ago, in Vietnam, I'd learned firsthand what SEALs did best: hunt men and kill them. But even in Vietnam, the system kept me from hunting and killing as many of the enemy as I would have liked. Since Vietnam, no one had given me the chance to do that job again—until I'd been ordered to create this team of men whose only job, I was promised, would be the hunting and killing of other men.

Now the system was at it again. We were ready. Capable. Deadly. Why the hell weren't we being used? I'd never considered SEALs strategic weapons—expensive systems that you keep in your arsenal as deterrents, but don't use. SEALs are tactical. We want to be sent on missions. We wanted to shoot and loot, hop and pop—do all the wonderful, deadly things that SEALs are supposed to do.

I'd begun to believe we were finally getting our chance. The bullet in my palm told me otherwise.

Furious, I started for the secure radio to call Paul and tell him this was just another in the series of games our command structure was playing on us. Halfway down the ladder I stopped. Dickie had a better idea. I'd play out this little charade as if I didn't know any better and turn it into my *own* war game.

I probably had more unanswered questions than JSOC anyway. Like, how would my men perform during this complicated series of tasks? They were all good—but which ones would become great under the pressure of keeping to a tight combat schedule? Would any of them realize we weren't doing this for real—and if they did, what would their reactions be?

I wanted to learn which of them I could order to do a job—even though it might mean their deaths. Being cannon fodder was part of the assignment. Every man who'd volunteered for SEAL Team Six knew he was expendable—from me, right down to the youngest kid on the team. This was an opportunity to test that resolve—to see which ones would play for keeps, and which ones would, at the last instant, hold back.

That's what SEAL Team Six was all about, anyway—playing for keeps. Oh, sure, the goddamn technology of war was almost beyond comprehension—and it wasn't just air-refueling or high-tech satellites either, anymore, but micro-burst transmitters and stealth aircraft and hundreds of billions of dollars invested in technotoys—laser-guided, shoulder-fired missiles, computer-assisted antitank guns, "smart" bombs, and a whole collection of weapons that the assholes in the Pentagon were quick to tell you could think for themselves.

Today you could sit in a fighter, press a missile launch button, and kill an enemy twenty, thirty, forty miles over the horizon, watching his plane explode on a TV screen, just like the video games my kids played.

And yet, what it really came down to, after all the bullshit and the computers and the video, was the very basic question embodied by the bullet in my hand. Could one of my men look another human being in the eyes, then pull the trigger and kill that person without hesitating for an instant?

In Vietnam, I'd discovered who could kill and who couldn't in combat. But that was fifteen years ago, and less than half of SEAL Team Six had ever been in combat. So there was only one way to find out who'd pull the trigger, and who'd freeze—which was to play this thing out and see who did his job and who didn't. War, after all, is not Nintendo. War is not about technology or toys. War is about killing.

Chapter

2

ENSIGN INDIAN JEW, THE POINT MAN, SIGNALED. HE WAS half Yakima and half Brooklyn, hence the moniker. I used to kid him about growing up spearing and smoking salmon up on the Columbia River—but never being able to find any bagels or cream cheese.

I squinted in the darkness, barely able to pick him out against the foliage in his tigerstripes and camouflage war paint. But I'd seen him put his hand up, palm flat. Now he was clenching his fist. Enemy ahead. I moved up the line slow and easy, the MP5 in my hand. We'd covered about six hundred yards, making a hell of a lot more of a racket than I wanted to. If the bad guys had pickets out or they'd deployed electronic sensors, they'd surely know about us. That was something we hadn't had a chance to work on—moving in large groups. Usually, SEALs operated in squads of seven, or in 14-man platoons. Frankly, I was uncomfortable at having to move so many men in one group because of the noise. But it couldn't be helped. I felt lucky we hadn't been observed so far.

I drew abreast of Jew and knelt next to him. He was one of the best I had—a former enlisted man whose capacity to learn fast was boundless. Jew epitomized the future of Navy Special Warfare—SpecWar in Navyspeak. He was big, smart, tough, too handsome for his own good, and ingeniously adroit when it came to the deadly arts.

I pulled my NV out. I took a look. The blackness became oscilloscope green; the foliage turned dark against the brightness. Two hundred feet ahead I could see a chain-link fence about eight feet high with a yard of barbed wire coiled on top. Beyond were two warehouses, as well as three other low, barracklike buildings. There were no lights. So much the better. The grounds were unkempt—a lot of cover for us to move behind. It looked just like the satellite picture that was folded in my pocket.

I mimed a man with a rifle to Jew. Any sentries?

He shook his head. No.

I gave him thumbs-up. I pointed at him. I snipped the air with index and middle finger. I mimed peering out.

He nodded. He'd cut through the wire and do a fast sneak and peek. We'd wait.

He slithered forward, moving with a slow, practiced crawl until he melted into the underbrush. Like so many of my guys he was perfectly at home in the jungle. He was too young to have served in Vietnam, but he'd adapted well to SEAL training in Panama and Florida and was one of the best scouts the unit had.

That he was an ensign didn't matter. In Six, officers and men were interchangeable. No caste system for us.

I edged back and signaled the men to drop. They disappeared into the darkness. I lay back and stared at the sky, listening for anything out of the ordinary. I perceived nothing. The silence was good. You could hear the jungle's natural sounds—insects, birds, whatever, resuming their normal activities. I smashed something small and winged and sharp that had decided to take up residence on my earlobe. Moments passed.

Jew came back. "Nothing, Skipper," he whispered. "A second perimeter line of wire fences by the barracks there." He pointed to the southwest. "And the warehouses east of the barracks, just like on the picture. I heard some noise— maybe they're having a few cold ones."

I punched him with my elbow. "Nice job." I took a recon

photo from my pocket. I motioned to PV and an officer I called Lieutenant Cheeks because his jowly face looked like a squirrel hoarding acorns. The three of us huddled over the picture as I illuminated it with a red-lensed pencil light. I showed them what I wanted done. They nodded and gave me thumbs-up.

I circled wagons with my index finger. "Let's go to work."

We would move in four 14-man platoons. PV would go south with two of them, work around the perimeter, and cut through the fence closest to the barracks. He'd lead one of his platoons and hit the storage area, where we believed the hostage to be. The other—Cheeks'—would neutralize the barracks.

I'd take down the warehouse where the nuke was, with my platoon. The last platoon, split into two seven-man boat crews, would act as flankers. They'd sweep up any bad guys who got between us and the gate. As we withdrew, they'd join up with Cheeks' platoon as the blocking force, shielding our escape north and east, back to the LZ.

I pulled the headset onto my head, securing it with a lightweight knit cap. Then I fitted the earpiece snugly inside my left ear, adjusted the filament microphone so it sat on my beard just below my lower lip, ran the wire down the back of my neck, passed it through a slit in the shirt, and plugged it into the Motorola. I pressed the transmit button for an instant and *tsk-tsked* twice into the mike—radio-talk for affirmative. I heard PV do the same thing. Then I heard Cheeks and Jew. We were all on line and ready to go. And if the bad guys had scanners on, we hadn't given them very much to scan. At least not yet.

I swept my arm left, then right. The SEALs moved into the shadows. I moved forward, following the path Jew had left me, until I came to the chain-link fence. I found the slit he'd made, took my snips and enlarged it slightly, then pulled myself through.

Once on the other side I slipped behind some scrub, took out my night-vision glasses, and secured the strap tightly around the back of my head. I didn't wear them all the time because they tend to narrow your field of vision when you're moving. And they made me slightly top-heavy, but now, when

I needed to see inside a darkened building, they'd give me a terrific advantage.

I had a look around. All clear. I moved out, the MP5 cradled in my arms as I scrunched across the ground, moving silently from tree to tree to take the best advantage I could of the natural cover. Scanned the perimeter. Clear—nothing. No muzzles pointing from any of the roofs. No signs of life at all. I liked that.

Fifty feet from the warehouse I flicked the MP5's safety downward to full fire, rose into a semicrouch and ran to the cinder-block wall.

The building was perhaps a hundred and fifty feet by sixty, topped by corrugated metal roofing that sat on exposed metal trusses, which allowed air flow in the tropical heat. Back and front entrances were heavy, fifteen-foot-wide, sliding, segmented metal doors that sat in tracks. On the side was a two-step, roofed porch and a metal, windowed door that led to some sort of office. There was light inside. On each side of the door were windows. In the left-hand one a rusting air conditioner wheezed and dripped water slowly, steadily, into a sizable puddle. That told me it had been turned on for some time.

I worked my way around the back end of the warehouse and snuck a look. It was all clear. I did a 360. Nothing. This was like stealing—no, this was better than stealing. I slowly edged up to the big, tracked door, moving a fraction of an inch at a time so as to make no noise. There was a small space between the segments, and sucking ground like a snail, I approached slowly, slowly, and had a look-see. For all I knew the Ts inside had NV glasses, too, and I didn't want 'em screwing with me.

I let my eyes get accustomed to the interior. It looked quiet enough. The place was empty except for some 50-gallon drums piled along the wall to my left, and what looked like a three-quarter-ton Army truck parked close to the tracked doors opposite where I was. There was a scaffolding around the outer wall perhaps ten feet up, six or seven feet below the ventilation break where the walls stopped and the roof began.

Sitting on a wood pallet close to a door under which a crack of light escaped was a wooden crate about the same size a 2,000-pound bomb came packed in. That had to be the nuke.

Something was . . . not right. It was too quiet. I crushed my face into the hard ground to get a better look. It was impossible they'd leave the jewels unprotected, unless they didn't know what they'd taken.

No way. It was a trap. Had to be a trap. I waited. Plotted. Schemed. Laughed silently at these assholes. It was a game of patience. It all came down to patience: would I move first, or would they.

I knew they were in there. I could sense 'em. Almost smell 'em. I controlled my breathing, slowed my whole system down the same way I'd done when I'd learned I could sit on the bottom of Norfolk harbor for three and a half minutes at a stretch during UDT training.

Oh, the fucking instructors—they loved me when I ran *that* game on 'em.

During E&E—evade and escape—training, they'd make us play hide-and-seek. They'd dump us in the water and then put boats out to search for us. It was like shooting fish in a barrel—you can't swim fast enough to get away from boats with lights, and you gotta surface to breathe. To make it more interesting (and to give us some added incentive), the instructors usually pounded the crap out of you when they caught you, and they were tough sons of bitches, too.

So I cheated. That's what E&E's supposed to be about, anyway. I lost 'em by swimming like a bat out of hell until I was just off the slip of the Kiptopeake-Norfolk ferry—on the far side, so the ferry would come between them and me. Timing was everything. I waited until the ferry got real close, then made a lot of noise in the water. When they caught me in the lights, I dove. I swam underwater about thirty yards to the slip and sucked mud while the ferryboat docked, sitting on the bottom holding on to a filthy, greasy piling with the big screw churning eight feet above my head *chunka-chunka-chunka.* Then I came out of the water, checked to see if the instructors were anywhere close. They weren't. So I chucked my mask and fins, climbed up over the port side of the stern onto the ferry, stole a set of mechanic's overalls out of a locker, and walked right out onto the dock. Nobody noticed I was barefoot.

I studied them as they crisscrossed the harbor, searching for me for about half an hour. Then I ambled off the slip, bought a quart of beer with some change I found in the coveralls, came back, and drank almost all of it dockside. Then, when I was good and ready, I whistled and waved 'em over. I let them watch as I drained the last of the beer and tossed the bottle into the harbor. Oh, they loved me for that. I don't know what made 'em madder—that I got away, or that I bought beer and didn't share it.

Something moved. Behind the drums. Something back there. I waited. Looked intently at the truck. Something there, too. One or two in the back, muzzles protruding just over the back gate. M16s probably. Combat-scoped? Maybe. Just inside the door I heard a scrape-scraping. Just a little something—the shifting of a foot or a rifle butt on the door. I froze. No breathing. *Chunka-chunka-chunka*. Wait the sons of bitches out.

Only after some minutes did I withdraw the way I'd come, silently, inch by inch, careful not to leave tracks behind. I made my way around the side of the warehouse, did another 360. It was still clear. I slid myself along the wall to the window with the air conditioner, went under it, around the two-step porch, removed my goggles, and let my eyes adjust to the night again. Then I peered inside.

A middle-aged man with dark skin, dressed in a bulky, short-sleeved sweatshirt and greasy khaki trousers sat behind a desk facing me. He was wearing wraparound plastic shooter's goggles—a giveaway that this was Memorex, not real—and he wrote intently in a spiral notebook with the stub of an old pencil, his thick lips moving as he formed the words. A bottle of Bud sat sweating at his left elbow. A blue steel .45 automatic lay next to it. He looked up from the page, ran a hand over thinning, kinky, salt-and-pepper hair. A broad face. A nose that had been broken too many times. Slit, yellowed eyes. Maybe fifty-five or so. Powerful, workingman's hands that were obviously uncomfortable with the pencil.

I dropped back down onto my haunches and withdrew to the underbrush cover where I'd left the platoon. I briefed the squad leaders about the ambush. Everybody had night-vision equipment. They'd hit the doors simultaneously, working opposing fields of fire so they wouldn't shoot each other. One squad would go left and high, working the truck and catwalk, the other would mirror—left and low, taking down the oil drums and opposite catwalk. I'd take down the guy in the office and come out by the nuke.

I pressed the Motorola's remote transmit button that was clipped to my vest. The radio could be used either in an on-off mode, or switched to continual transmission. "One set," I whispered.

I heard PV's voice. "Two set." The hostage snatch team was in position.

Cheeks checked in. "Three set." Barracks sweepers were ready.

"Four set." Jew's blocking force was primed.

I looked at my watch. We'd been on the ground for forty-seven minutes. The operation was scheduled to last ninety, so our four choppers were already in the air, being refueled, and just under three-quarters of an hour away from touch-down. That gave us a slim, but acceptable, margin for error. I turned the Motorola on. "Six minutes. Then go." Plenty of time to set up.

I gave hand signals and watched the squads move out. They knew their jobs. Each had become a superb shooter over the past five months. We didn't train with regulation targets at SEAL Team Six. We used three-by-five-inch index cards pasted onto silhouettes. You had to be able to hit the card with a double-tap—that is, two shots in rapid succession—whether you were coming out of the water with the stainless Smith & Wesson .357 magnum pistol, or breaking through the hatch of a hijacked airplane with the Beretta.

Right-handed, left-handed, one-handed, two-handed, we shot in every conceivable manner. In fact, I didn't care how my guys shot, just so long as they hit tight, man-killing groups every single time. No concentrating on fancy angles or head shots. Those techniques are what you see in movies, not Six. We used heavy loads that would knock terrorists down no matter where we hit them. Head, chest, arm, leg—it didn't matter. In sniping—at ranges of six hundred and eight hundred yards—we were still a little behind the curve. But overall, my shooters were better than any in the world today, including Delta's much publicized pistoleros.

I knew PV was in position. Six of his shooters would take out the bad guys holding the hostage; the others would clear any remaining terrorists. He had two medics with him in case the hostage was injured or hurt. Cheeks' two squads would hose the barracks if the tangos inside got restless. My guys had a somewhat tougher job. They'd have to set up and blow the doors, then hit the ambushers in the dark, while I took out the guy in the office. After that we'd have to figure out a way to move the nuke back to the LZ—or render it unusable.

The digital timer on my watch was running. It showed one minute forty seconds elapsed. I was just under the air conditioner now, cool water dripping onto my shoulder. It felt good. My mind's eye had a picture of the tango behind the desk. I'd catch him in the chest. The Beretta was in my hand, ready. In my earpiece I could hear PV, Cheeks, and Indian Jew's breathing on the open lines. They could probably hear me, too.

A minute fifty. Four minutes, ten seconds to contact.

Suddenly automatic weapons fire broke out to the southwest. At the same time I heard PV's voice: "Shit—early contact, early contact—everybody go."

There was no time to lose. I rose, swiveled, and kicked the door just below the handle.

It burst inward. The dark man in the sweatshirt was already standing, pistol in his hand, as I came through low, Beretta in a two-handed grip. Before he could react I hit him with half a dozen shots in the chest. I fired so quickly the 9mm sounded like a submachine gun.

The loads punched him back against the wall. His .45 went flying. A dark stain spread from the center of his chest. I ejected the clip and slapped a spare, from a mag-holder taped to my right wrist, into the Beretta's rubber-clad grip.

I looked up as I heard two explosions in rapid succession behind the office. The other two squads had initiated.

I grabbed the spiral notebook and did a cursory search for documents. There were three manila files in a desk drawer and I took them, too, rolling them and stuffing them into the cargo pocket of my fatigues. I hit the office lights to get my eyes ready for the NV goggles. I took out the SATCOM and told JSOC we'd initiated contact early, and to expedite the snatch. Four minutes may not seem like a lot of time, but on a hot LZ it's an eternity.

I strapped my NV on and slid through the door into the

warehouse, Beretta in my right hand. In my earpiece came the sound of heavy automatic weapons fire, followed by Cheeks' raspy voice, "Well, *get* the mothers, already!"

The front and back doors had been blown open, and smoke grenades were filling the warehouse with opaque, white fog. I could hear my guys working the room and the staccato buzz-saw *brrrrrp* of return fire from M16s.

It was easy to tell who was who. The SEALs fired their MP5s in controlled, three-shot bursts. The bad guys were letting whole mags go at once.

I crawled to the pallet and reached left-handed into my vest for an atomic detection device. There was movement behind me, and it wasn't one of us. I swiveled and fired at a shadow in the smoke, then rolled back toward the pallet.

The indicator told me whatever was in the crate was nuclear.

I heard PV's voice in my ear. "Hostage clear. Alive and well."

"Okay. Cheeks?"

"Call you back."

"Jew?"

"A-okay."

From my left I heard the Alpha squad leader, Fingers, shouting, "Alpha side clear."

There was another long M16 burst from the far side of the warehouse, then six shots in rapid succession from a Beretta, then silence. Gold Dust Larry, Bravo's squad leader, called out, "Bravo side clear."

I pulled off the night-vision goggles and stowed them.

"Anybody down?"

"Not us, boss."

"PV?"

"Nope."

"Cheeks?"

"No."

"Jew?"

"Ain't seen no action yet, Skipper."

"You won't be disappointed." I looked at the timer. Seven minutes, ten seconds.

I pulled SATCOM from my vest. "Six—all sites clear. Hostage and package under control. Nobody down but bad guys."

That was because we were all firing blanks—but even so, it was damned good work by my guys. I stood up and secured my Beretta, windmilling my arms in the opaque, white smoke that still obscured much of the warehouse. "Anybody see a fan to get this smoke outta here? Let's get on it." I slapped the wood crate and called over to Gold Dust Larry, "Somebody get the three-quarter started. Let's get this goddamn thing loaded and moving."

"Aye-aye, Skipper."

"PV—"

"Boss?"

"ETA to the LZ?"

"The hostage is pretty shaky. We're gonna have to carry him out. Tangos were working him over when we arrived—nothing serious, just harassment, but he's not used to it. I'll be ready to up and out in six, seven minutes."

"Ten-four. Cheeks?"

"I'm getting some hostile action here. I'll withdraw clean in four to five minutes. We got a shitload of intel, Skipper."

"That's what I like to hear." I heard a satisfying roar as Gold Dust Larry revved the truck's engine. "Gotta go. See you at the LZ."

The smoke was finally clearing out of the warehouse. "Somebody find a couple of two-by-fours or pieces of pipe. Let's get this thing moved."

I checked the Casio again. Elapsed time: sixty-three minutes. Twenty-seven minutes until the choppers touched down.

God, how time flies when you're having fun.

We slid three rails under the crate. Four men to a rail, and two to stand guard. I showed them the atomic particle counter. They watched as the indicator moved into the red zone. "This shit is radioactive, so any numb-nuts dumb enough to drop it is gonna suffer. On three, heave and up."

It was like the weightpile, but easier. The average Six bench press was just under four hundred pounds. It wasn't going to take twelve of us to lift a 2,500-pound container, but I wanted everyone to have a piece of the action.

I watched them load while I checked the recon photo in my pocket. I'd marked an escape route with crayon. That was a stupid thing to do. What if I ate a bullet and the bad guys pulled the map out of my pocket? I rubbed the photo on my fatigues until I'd obliterated the red line. I knew where the hell we were going.

Gold Dust Larry rolled the balaclava hood down onto his neck, revealing a crooked, gritty smile on his mustached face as he held the truck on course. I hung off the passenger-side running board and navigated. As we came to the gate, I saw Horseface, who'd just cut the locks. As he waved us through, I heard firing from the barracks area. "Just keep moving."

It took us a little over ten minutes to make the LZ where we'd touched down. We parked the truck at the side of the old runway, set up a perimeter, and waited. About five minutes later PV's platoon arrived, he and one of the petty officers supporting a thin, gray-haired man well past middle age, in a filthy white shirt and stained gray trousers, and a pair of heavy-framed eyeglasses worn with an elastic band to keep them on his head. I went over to him and shook his hand.

"You all right, sir?"

He nodded. "A bit shaky, Commander."

The accent was pure Deutschland. I wondered where they'd found him. It didn't matter. I role-played as if I didn't know we were all following a script. "German?"

"Yes. Thank you for coming for me."

I did an exaggerated Three Musketeers bow. "Commander Otto Von Piffle at your service," I said in a passable Otto Preminger accent. "It vass mein pleasure to koming to der rescue because zay heff vays of making you talk, you know."

The hostage's eyes went wide.

PV spoke a burst of rapid-fire German. He'd learned the language during a 26-month stint with the *Kampfschwimmerkompanie*—the combat swimmers who were the West German equivalent of SEALs. The hostage laughed.

"What'd you tell him?"

"I told him, 'What the commander meant to say is that he's glad you're okay.' Then I added that you're not as stupid or ugly as you might appear at first sight."

PV's two squads reinforced the perimeter. The watch said nine minutes until the choppers arrived. Cheeks and his two squads showed up moving at a trot. Four or five of the SEALs carried boxes on their shoulders.

"Intel goodies," Cheeks said. "All sorts of stuff—plans, maps, receipts. And diagrams—bases in Puerto Rico and on the mainland, too. The DIA dip-dunks'll have a field day with it all."

I threw an exaggerated salute at Cheeks. "I do love it so when you make the dip-dunks happy, Lieutenant. It keeps 'em off my back."

Cheeks returned the gesture. "You're welcome, sweet cakes."

Automatic weapons fire from the rear. "Let's be careful out there," I shouted. "No time to start losing people now." I'd been about to light the flares to guide the choppers in, but it didn't make sense to tell whoever was shooting at us precisely where we were.

I saw Jew emerge from the scrub at the far end of the clearing. I waved him over.

"Jew, what's up?"

"They must have had more people than we knew about— or some of those guys we shot just got up and walked away. We're taking fire."

The kid was good. He was right about the tangos just walking away—except he just didn't know it. I gave him a concerned look. "Anybody hurt?"

Jew nodded. "Two—nothing serious. One sprained ankle on the path, one ran into a thorn bush in the dark."

"Just keep the tangos out of our hair until the choppers get here."

"Aye-aye, Skipper." Jew melted back into the jungle.

It was time to illuminate the LZ. We set out six white strobes and three red ones. To guide the choppers in on final approach we had neon-green light-sticks.

The firing got closer. I looked skyward anxiously. The goddamn Air Force was probably taking a coffee break. That's how they worked—like union bus-drivers—most of the time. Six or seven hours of flight time (not to exceed this or that altitude, of course), and then it was bye-bye for a didy change, a nap, and a cup of cocoa.

We could run for a week with no sleep, then do a 35,000-foot-jump hop-and-pop exercise, pick ourselves up, and do it all over again. Not fly-boys. I checked my watch. They were now late.

I called JSOC. "Where the hell are our choppers?"

"They're on the way. Relax."

"Relax?" Who the hell were these idiots, anyway? I put the German under the truck and hunkered down with PV. It seemed like an eternity until we heard the sound of rotors. They'd kept us waiting eighteen minutes. On a hot LZ, you can lose your entire force in eighteen minutes.

The quartet of choppers, their long refueling nozzles projecting from the noses of the aircraft like knights' lances, circled the LZ lazily to pick the spots where they'd set down. Unbelievably, they were doing an admin—administrative—approach. That is, they were landing as if they were coming into a runway at an Air Force base. To them, this was only an exercise—so why the hell should they put themselves out? Assholes—I'd kill the sons of bitches after we got out of here.

I shook my light-stick at them to drop quickly. This was supposed to be a hot LZ. They were supposed to fly as if there were ground fire. Their job was to come in, drop their ramps, scoop us up, and get the hell out. I waved my arms like a madman. The pilots were oblivious. They settled in as if they were landing on the White House lawn—and started to cut their engines.

"No no no no no. Keep 'em revved up. Move it," I screamed, windmilling my light-stick. I pointed PV toward the nearest chopper, which was dropping its aft ramp. "Get the hostage on board." I watched while PV and his crew hustled the German up the ramp. That was fourteen plus one. I ran the light-stick in a circle at the pilot. "Get the hell outta here."

He gave me a thumbs-up. The six rotors started up again, the jet turbines reached full thrust, and he lifted off. Three to go. Cheeks was loading the intel in one bird while my platoon ran the nuke into the second. As soon as they'd strapped it down, I tossed Alpha squad aboard and waved the chopper into the air. That was two. Twenty-one SEALs airborne.

I stuck my head into the third chopper's forward hatch and screamed at the pilot. "Rev it up—I'll tell you when to go." I ran to Cheeks' position on the perimeter and pointed toward the chopper. "Get the strobes and the chutes and take my Bravo squad, then get the hell out of here. I'll ride with Jew."

"Affirmative." He got his guys working. One group collected the lights and heaved them onto the chopper while the other retrieved our chutes from the underbrush where we'd concealed them and threw the piles of silk up the ramp, past Cheeks, who stood at the top, his HK pointing skyward, waving men on, counting. "Let's get moving."

When I saw they were all loaded and aboard, I pointed at the pilot. "Go!"

Another twenty SEALs gone. That left Jew's fourteen—and me.

I shouted for Jew into the Motorola mike. No answer. "Jew, goddammit—" I realized I'd pulled the plug out of its socket. I fixed it and shouted his name again.

"Coming, Dickie."

I waited as Jew's platoon emerged from the darkness, running in leapfrog pattern, their route punctuated by short bursts from the MP5s. I grabbed a couple of them by the vests and threw them toward the chopper. Jew and I were last on board. As the ramp shut, we gave the LZ a good burst of submachine-gun fire. "Move it!" I shouted to the crew chief.

Then we were airborne. Mission perfect. Rehearsal or not, I was one happy goddamn SEAL CO. I checked my watch. I slammed my palm into Jew's chest, knocking him ass over teakettle into a startled Air Force master sergeant. I perused my SEALs. "You guys are wonderful."

I could see the C-141 StarLifter's huge, black fuselage as we banked into the air base on the main island. I hoped the flight crew had some cold beer on board—we were going to need it. The first of the choppers was already on the ground, disgorging SEALs and the hostage. The second and third were just settling in. I felt so good I forgot about putting the chopper pilots in the hospital for their 18-minute delay and admin approaches back at Vieques.

We set down. I was first off, hitting the ground before the ramp did. I ran to the StarLifter. Yeah—there was beer on board. Terrific—we were going to party on the way home. I loped over to PV and Cheeks and slapped them on the back. I assembled my troops. "Great job. Terrific. Fuck you all very much, you merry murdering cockbreath shit-for-brains ass-holes."

Oh, I was full of myself. But justifiably, goddammit. Justifiably. Exercise or not—what we'd done tonight had never,

ever, been done before by a military unit. We'd flown three thousand goddamn miles, inserted four SEAL platoons in a clandestine, high-altitude, high-opening, mass, night jump, parasailed ten miles to our objective, landed in a single group on a drop zone no bigger than a couple of football fields, assembled, taken down a bunch of bad guys, rescued a hostage, snatched back a nuke, and hadn't lost a single SEAL in the process.

This is what we'd groomed ourselves for; why we'd busted our asses. We'd practiced each risky element—shooting, jumping, parasailing, clandestine infiltration, hostage snatch, and extraction—separately. But we'd never put all of them together before; never run a real-time, full-tilt boogie war game until tonight.

The German came toward me. "You and your men did very well," he said.

"Thank you. I'm proud of them."

"You should be."

I started to say something else when a Beetle Bailey Army colonel in starched fatigues and half-inch-thick glasses marched across the tarmac. "Commander Marcinko?"

"Aye-aye, sir."

"I have a message for you to call Joint Special Operations Command."

"Sure." I took the SATCOM from my vest and punched up JSOC.

"It's Marcinko." I waited. A familiar voice came on the line.

"Dick."

"Sir—"

"You did wonderfully—better than we expected. The Joint Chiefs are impressed."

I liked that. There had been some real skepticism at the Joint Chiefs about whether or not we'd been ready for a mission. Unlike Delta, which was based on the British SAS and went through an SAS-like administrative certification process, I had refused to let my men be graded by outsiders.

My argument was simple: what we were training to do hadn't ever been done before. So how the hell would some four-star, pencil-dicked Pentagon paper-pusher know whether or not we were good at it?

My conclusion was, they wouldn't. What I'd told the chain of command in no uncertain terms was, "Thank you very much, sirs, but I'll certify SEAL Team Six myself."

But it wasn't to be. The command structure can—and had—imposed its will on us, no matter how I felt. The Vieques exercise was ample evidence of that. The voice in my ear continued, "Dick, this has been a first-rate exercise. I think you and your troops need a couple of days off while we analyze and evaluate."

Analyze and evaluate. Those bureaucratic syllables made me cringe. Ever since Vietnam, even the military's vocabulary had shifted from martial to managerial in tone. Goddammit —we didn't need managers, we needed leaders, warriors, hunters. Instead, we got accountants. It seemed that every time I'd get prowling and growling some three-star asshole would slip a choke-leash around my neck and give it a yank to show he could make me heel. Well, it was time to growl back. Throw a shit fit. Chew the carpet. Play crazy. I owed it to my men. Shit—I owed it to myself. I raised my voice to let them hear as I shouted into the mouthpiece. "Exercise? Analyze? Evaluate? What the fuck, General? Over."

He played his role well, too. "I couldn't say anything until now, Dick. It was imposed by the Joint Chiefs on me." He paused. "And you did great. Six is certified. You're in business—as of right now."

"Well, thank you for that valuable information, sir. I'm sure my men will appreciate your opinion." I wondered whether he caught the irony in my voice. Surreptitiously, I flicked the transmit button on the SATCOM to off and covered it with my hand. Then I continued my "conversation." PV, Cheeks, and Jew drifted closer as my voice grew louder and more disturbed. "You did *what?* You switched ammunition on us in the armory?"

I shouted into the dead SATCOM, "Sir, this was a goatfuck. Goddammit—you can't hang up on—"

The Beetle Bailey colonel was peering into the fuselage of my C-141. He turned toward me. "Commander, you have *beer* in there—that's against regulations."

I started toward him. "Hey, Colonel—how'd you like a new asshole?"

PV tackled me and grabbed my combat vest with both

31

hands, slowing me down like a sea anchor. He's five inches shorter than I am, but he was a boxer at the Academy and he's a tough little scrapper. "Lighten up, Dick." He turned to the colonel. "I think it's better if you leave us alone right now, sir. We're all just a little worked up, and it could be, ah, dangerous for you to stay around."

Paul's heels were dragging on the tarmac. The colonel saw the look of mayhem in my eyes as I pulled my XO toward him, and he beat a hasty retreat.

Paul let go. "He's not worth it, Dick."

"Screw you."

Cheeks and Jew slammed me on the back. "Hey, Skipper," Jew said, "about the Joint Chiefs and all that crap—chill out. It's okay. We knew."

"Knew what?"

"That it was a full mission profile," said PV.

"Had to be an exercise," said Cheeks. "No casualties. Lots of firing and no scratches. Plus—the tangos wore shooting glasses—every one of them."

I was smiling inside. I'd picked these men because I believed they were smart. Goddammit, they *were* smart. "So why didn't any of you numb-nuts say anything?"

"I remembered the sign every SEAL sees the day he begins his training," PV said. "The one that reads, 'The more you sweat in training, the less you bleed in combat.' Besides, we'd never put it all together before, boss—seemed like a good idea to play it out and see if it worked."

He was right of course. I wheeled toward the C-141. "Let's get moving."

PV punched me on the arm, hard enough to hurt. "Aye-aye, boss." He pointed his index finger in the air and drew circles with it. "Come on, guys—load up. Let's go get drunk."

He was right. Screw 'em all. It was time to get drunk and go home.

Chapter

3

GOING HOME IS NOT SOMETHING I'VE EVER BEEN VERY GOOD at. I certainly didn't do it much as a youngster. I was born on Thanksgiving Day, 1940, in my grandmother Justine Pavlik's house in Lansford, Pennsylvania, a tiny mining town in Carbon County—appropriate, isn't it?—just east of Coaldale and Hometown. For the uninitiated, that's about half an hour northwest of Allentown, and a lifetime from Philadelphia. My father, George, and mother, Emilie Teresa Pavlik Marcinko, never made it as far as the hospital delivery room. Typical.

I'm Czech on both sides. My mother is short and Slavic looking. My father was big—just under six feet—dark, brooding, and had a nasty temper. All the men in the family—and virtually every male in Lansford as well—were miners. They were born, they worked the mines, they died. Life was simple and life was hard, and I guess some of them might have wanted to pull themselves up by the bootstraps, but most were too poor to buy boots.

We lived on top of the hill, just around the corner from Kanuch's, where we got our groceries and Old Man Kanuch would lick the thick pencil stub before he wrote down what we'd taken in his ledger book. He'd keep a tab and collect from us on payday. It would probably have been cheaper to shop at the A & P six blocks away, but hardly anybody did. You went where you were known.

If I'm ornery, and there are those who think I am, I probably got it from my maternal grandfather. Joe Pavlik was a cantankerous, short, barrel-chested, shot-and-a-beer, hard-drinking son of a bitch with a square face, and Leonid Brezhnev eyebrows, who worked the mines all his life and never complained about it once. I don't remember him ever complaining about anything. He was a real hell-raiser—one of those archetypal tough guys you see in working-class bars, with big, wide, labor-toughened hands that look as if they were designed to go around old-fashioned beer glasses.

I was always independent. I had my own paper route by the age of five. At seven, I was taking off for a day at a time, running through the mile-long Lehigh Railroad tunnel to swim in the Hauto reservoir. You could get there by going through the old Lansford water tunnel, too, but there were huge rats living in the water tunnel, and besides, it was farther up the mountain. So I took the shortcut—and my chances—with the trains. I got nailed a few times. The first time the steam locomotive bore down on me I thought I'd die. I held my breath and squeezed my eyes tightly, hugging the wet stone tunnel wall as car after car after car went by *ka-chang-ka-chang* about a foot from my nose. My dad, George, beat the crap out of me after I told him what I'd done. Thereafter, whenever I used the railroad tunnel, I kept my mouth shut.

Neither of my parents was big on education. My dad probably dropped out of school around eighth grade; my mother may have gotten as far as ninth or tenth. Neither of them ever put any emphasis on book learning, so school was something I never took very seriously. I was much more interested in having fun—or making money.

Fun, before I discovered women, consisted of swimming at Hauto and summer vacations in the Catskill Mountains—the Jewish Alps—where my uncle Frank and aunt Helen had a boardinghouse. Money was always a problem. The mines closed down when I was in the seventh grade, and after several months of just scraping by, my father finally found work as a welder in New Brunswick, New Jersey. We moved to New Brunswick in 1952. I went through real culture shock. Lansford was a town of maybe four thousand, mostly Czech. In New Brunswick, there were Poles, Hungarians, Irish, Jews, blacks, and Hispanics. That took some getting used to, with the result that I both gave and received more than my fair share of welts and bruises on the walk between school and the small basement apartment we could afford.

Life around the house was not pleasant. My mother's brother moved in with us—three adults and two kids (by then I had a brother) crammed in a three-room apartment. When my parents fought, which was often, my mother's brother would take her side. The result was that my father spent less and less time at home. My younger brother, Joey, who was nine or ten at the time, was close to my mother, so he stayed around the house with her. Me, I couldn't stand the place. So I went off on my own, returning only to sleep or do what little homework I did.

I escaped by working as a pin-setter in a bowling alley, doing whatever odd jobs I could find—even by serving seven A.M. Sunday mass as an altar boy. On the days I decided to show up, I went to St. Ladislaus Hungarian Catholic School, where like generations of students before me, I had my knuckles rapped by nuns hefting wicked rulers. But I never liked classes very much. I cruised through school on autodrive, much more concerned with earning pocket money than A's or B's.

During my sophomore year, for example, I worked sixty hours a week at a luncheonette called Gussy's, just off the Rutgers campus. During the summer vacation I worked there a hundred and twenty hours a week—from five A.M. until ten at night, seven days a week. The hours were long but the money was great: a dollar an hour, off the books. That was a real windfall for a 15-year-old in 1955.

Besides, Gussy—his full name was Salvatore Puleio Augustino, but I can't remember anyone ever using it—treated me like his own family. He took me upstairs, where his father, Old Man Sal, lived, and filled me with pasta and sauce, and sausages and chicken and huge platters of vegetables sautéed in olive oil and garlic, instead of my having to eat meat loaf or Salisbury steak off the luncheonette steam table. Old Man Sal let me watch as he made wine in the basement, and I developed a real taste for Chianti. I even picked up enough

Italian to get by at the dinner table, which Sal's old man just loved. Gussy made a real Czech guinea out of me.

Because I had a lot of money in my jeans for a teenager, I even bought a car, a chrome-yellow 1954 Mercury convertible, as soon as I was old enough to get my driver's license —the day after my seventeenth birthday.

Things were made even more interesting because Gussy's was a hangout for many of the Rutgers fraternity guys, some of whom adopted me as a kind of mascot. I spent a fair amount of time in the Rutgers Greek houses, which ultimately turned out to be a great and enlightening experience. The exposure helped smooth a few of my roughest edges. When most of the kids from backgrounds similar to mine were sporting pegged trousers and motorcycle jackets, and styled their hair like Elvis or Dion, I dressed in button-down shirts, chinos, and Harris tweed sports coats. I learned how to drink beer at an early age, and—more important—how to handle it, too. My fraternity friends also instructed me in some of the finer points involved in the constant search for meaningful female companionship.

The inculcation worked. The summer between my sophomore and junior years—I was fifteen—I met a beautiful and sophisticated young student teacher named Lucette at one of the fraternity parties. We hit it off right away. She was a French major, and I spoke my pidgin Italian, and we clicked. I was big for my age and always had cash in my wallet, and I talked and dressed like I went to Rutgers and acted like I owned the goddamn fraternity house, so she never realized I was a high-school kid.

She found out the hard way. With what the inscrutable Orientals might call a dose of Real Bad Karma, she was assigned to teach a third-year high-school French class in September and saw my beaming face in the third row. *Zut alors!*

By the time I was seventeen I'd gone through a bunch of changes. My parents split up. My mother took a job at Sears, and we—she, my younger brother, and I—moved into public housing. My father rented a furnished room over a Slovak bar called Yusko's, just a few doors down from the luncheonette where I worked. He'd spend a lot of time there and I'd drop by Yusko's to visit. The place could have been transplanted from Lansford, with its pickled pig's feet in big jars, and hard-boiled eggs sitting in bowls, and three or four guys who looked like Joe Pavlik sitting on the barstools from ten in the morning until closing time, drinking steadily and chain-smoking Camels. My old man was happy there because it reminded him of home. George Marcinko never got used to New Brunswick.

Meanwhile, I was spending less and less time in school—cutting classes regularly—and more and more of my time with a young Italian woman who was married to a guy twenty-seven years her senior and in serious need of vigorous humping and pumping, which I was all too willing to provide. I quit Gussy's and went to work as a counterman at a Greek place in the heart of New Brunswick. The money was good —about $200 a week including tips, for about half the time I'd been spending at Gussy's. Moreover, the chefs were willing to teach me some rudimentary cooking and baking skills, so I saw the job as a way to learn a trade. That was a first for me. I'd never really considered what I'd do with my life.

I finally quit school altogether. As I would refer to it some years later in official-sounding language, I "voluntarily disenrolled" in February 1958. Continuing just didn't seem to make any sense. The classes all seemed to be b.s. anyway. And who needed a high-school diploma? There was money to be made, and women to be hustled, and you could drive down to the shore and lie on the beach for a couple of days at a time—I didn't need an education for any of that. So I split.

I also tried to join the military. When President Eisenhower sent Marines to Lebanon, I volunteered. I liked their dress blues and their swords. So I went down to the Marine recruiter, walked in, and probably said something asinine like, "Well, friend, I'd kind of like to go shoot a few bad guys. Where's my rifle, where's the ammo, and when can I leave?"

And the recruiting sergeant most likely restrained himself from reducing me to a pile of rubble and said, "Look, sonny, you gotta go to boot camp before we let you kick any ass, and besides, you're underage and you haven't finished high school. So why not get your diploma, and then we'll talk."

Well, I knew for damn sure that by the time I did all that, the Marines would have the Lebanese problem solved without my help. So I walked away and had a lovely summer on the beach, and I worked on a serious, class-A, surfer-grade tan and got laid a lot. I also spent some time trying to toss a good-looking neighborhood girl named Kathryn Ann Black off the three-meter board of the Livingston Avenue swimming pool (off the board and into the sack). We dated most of the summer, when I wasn't catting around with other women, and discovered that we liked each other. We must have: despite my proclivity toward outside activities, I kept coming back. There was something out of the ordinary there.

Then in September, after I'd had my fun, and Kathy went back to school, I walked into a Navy recruiting office, volunteered for service, and after taking a battery of tests, was accepted for duty. Oh, if they'd only known.

On October 15, 1958, I reported to boot camp in Great Lakes, Illinois. For some inexplicable reason, I felt better about walking through the gates of that camp than I'd ever felt going anywhere in my life before.

I was the perfect MARK-ONE, MOD-ZERO sailor—that's military jargon for the most basic model. Talk about gung ho—I even spit shined the *soles* of my boots. I was the one asshole in a hundred who actually believed the chiefs when they told us, "He who shines only half a shoe is only half a man."

There'd been a cabdriver I'd gotten to know in New Brunswick—Joe something or other. He'd been a sailor, and he gave me his old *Blue Jacket's Manual*, which I'd read by the time I was sixteen or so. He'd taught me how to roll and tie a Navy neckerchief, as well as a bunch of other Navy procedures, so by the time I got to boot camp, I was already ahead of the curve. I volunteered for everything—from the football squad to the drill team—and was even made the acting athletic petty officer for a couple of weeks. There was an incredible amount of b.s. involved in the training, but overall, it seemed like a good deal: I gave the Navy a full day's work, and it gave me a full day's pay—and I even had some fun in the process. I really liked the swimming and the shooting and the marching. The book stuff they could keep.

After Christmas I qualified for radioman training. But there were no openings at the school. Instead, I took a temporary assignment to Quonset Point, Rhode Island, where I helped teach swimming to naval aviators during their survival training.

Then, one night in Rhode Island, I went to the movies and saw a terrific flick called *The Frogmen*, with Richard Widmark and Dana Andrews. It was the story of the Navy's Underwater Demolition Teams in action in the Pacific during World War II. Lots of action. Lots of heroism. Lots of songs. Like the "Marine Hymn" with new words:

> From the halls of Montezuma,
> To the shores of Tripoli,
> We will fight our country's battles—
> Right behind the UDT!

I walked outside afterward and thought, hey—I could do that. I mean, I was a reasonably aggressive sort of person; I'd wanted to join the Marines. So the prospect of "Demolition Dick, Tough-Guy Shark Man of the Navy" was a lot more satisfying than "Fingers Marcinko, Pencil-Pushing Teletype Operator."

The Demo Dick/Fingers Marcinko identity crisis climaxed a few weeks later when I was finally transferred to radio school in Norfolk, Virginia. Norfolk, it turned out, is just a stone's throw from the Underwater Demolition Teams, which were based out of the amphibious base at Little Creek, across the harbor. I saw radiomen close up. I saw Frogmen close up. No contest.

The answer was simple: let's bag this radio crap and go straight to Frogman. So I visited the UDT command and told them what I wanted to do. The news they gave me was like the Marines all over again. I couldn't become a Frogman until I had a permanent assignment. They didn't take applicants from temporary commands—and radio school was a temp. Good-bye, Demo Dick; hello, Fingers Marcinko.

It would take me almost two years to get back to Little Creek. My odyssey meandered through Dahlgren, Virginia, where the Navy ran a space surveillance center to track Sputniks, and Naples, Italy, where I worked as a Teletype clerk at the Naval Support Activity Station.

After five months at Dahlgren I applied for UDT training. I made it through the first step, which in those days consisted of being sent to the Navy Yard in Washington, where they put me in one of those old-fashioned canvas diving suits with the hard-hat helmet and thick air hoses, and dropped me into the Anacostia River to see whether or not I had claustrophobia.

I passed the claustrophobia test and was just about to leave for UDT training when I broke my hand slamming it against something hard—the side of a very stupid sailor's head. It wasn't my fault. He should have ducked. Good-bye, UDT. Hello, Naples.

Naples turned out to be more fun than I'd expected, even though the job sucked. I realized that I was not cut out to be a Teletype operator. The job was a dead end: it required no imagination or ingenuity. Worse, my watch-mate drove me crazy. He was a real sniveler, a pug-nosed, acne-faced momma's boy named Harold who picked his ears all day and complained about everything. I called him The Whiner. Harold's sea daddy was the chief petty officer who ran the Com Center, a self-important s.o.b. black guy in his mid-forties named White, who acted as if he were royalty. Between the two of them, I plotted murder. No jury in the world would have convicted me.

On the other hand, Naples was terrific. I worked and lived in the same apartment house in the middle of the city, not on the naval base. So unlike a lot of sailors in Italy, I actually got to see the natives. The Italian I'd learned from Old Man Gussy got me by. And while my hand healed, I jogged through the Neapolitan hills, lifted weights, did calisthenics and swam.

But I was still a shore-duty, pencil-pushing Teletype operator. And there was still this little voice inside me that kept saying, "UDT, UDT," louder and louder. The question was, how to get there.

I had one immense problem to overcome: my commanding officer. How immense? Two hundred pounds. And the ugliest female I'd ever set eyes on in my life. I called her the Big Female Ugly Commander, or Big FUC for short. Big FUC was also a rule-book creature, and she was shorthanded, a combination that made it impossible for me to leave (I'd made the mistake of signing on for a one-year extension of my assignment in Naples—hoping to transfer to UDT as soon as possible). To Big FUC, a year meant 365 days. *Transfer* was not a word in her lexicon.

Ultimately, I forced her hand. The next time The Whiner pissed me off, I tossed his typewriter out the window. I would have stopped there, but the little son of a bitch just wouldn't let up—"I'm going to put you on report and tell Chief White what a bad person you are."

Something in me snapped, and I busted his face wide open. He was in sick bay for a month. That set the chief off. He was an extra large—six two or so, two hundred pounds—about the same size as my father. He grabbed my ass and hauled me off to the bathroom by the belt and the scruff of my neck and shoved me up against the tile.

"I ought to beat the shit out of you."

I was in the mood for anything at that point. "Hey, Chief, if you're feeling frisky, let's have at it."

He grabbed me with his big ham hands. I stepped between 'em and gave him a knee in the balls. He went down like a bag of cement. He struggled to his feet, came at me again, and I slammed him in the gut—I'd learned my lesson about hitting sailors in the head the hard way—clinched him up close so he couldn't do much, and kneed his groin as if I were stretching wall-to-wall carpet onto a tackless batten, lifting him five, six inches in the air with each pop. When his eyes rolled back, I dropped him on the deck.

He lay there sucking air for a while. Then he rolled onto his knees, crawled on all fours to the toilet, and was sick. "I'll get you," he wheezed at me. "You're gonna be outta here."

Oh, please, oh, please, Br'er Bear, toss dis rabbit into de briar patch.

So the next day, after he'd cleaned himself up, he hauled me in front of Big FUC. Think of a cross between Jabba the Hutt and Roseanne Barr stuffed carelessly into a tight, white uniform. Big FUC read me the riot act. It was full of "The chief wants you out of here" and "I should toss you in the brig." But they were all empty threats. She couldn't bring me up on charges because it was the chief who'd laid his hands on me first—that would cost him his job. Maybe I'd take a demotion or a couple of demerits, but so what?

Anyway, I was anticipating the bitch. I had two transfer request chits in my hand. I gave her the first. "I'll tell you what, Commander—here's a request for transfer to any god-damn ship that pulls into port. I don't care if it's the USS *Lollipop*. Then I gave her the other. "This one's a transfer to UDT training. I don't give a damn which one you do."

She called me back two days later. "Sea duty would be too easy for you, Marcinko. I'm gonna send you where they'll knock all this aggressive shit right out of you." Big FUC put her fat cheeks and all six chins up close to my face and sneered, "You're going Stateside, to UDT training—immediately!"

And people say there is no God.

Chapter
4

LITTLE CREEK, VIRGINIA, IS A MASOCHIST'S DREAM. IT'S THE place where the Navy used to take large groups of mean, aggressive, self-confident, ass-kicking, extrovert volunteer sailors and turn them into small groups of mean, aggressive, self-confident, ass-kicking, extrovert UDT animals during sixteen glorious weeks of torture, madness, and mayhem. I walked through the main gate at Little Creek on June 21, 1961, alongside a skinny little son of a bitch named Ken MacDonald. He was a wiry, 135-pound petty officer second class with the remnants of a Brit accent, whose straight hair was so long he held it in place with a bobby pin. He took one look at me, shook his head morosely, and said, "Mate, you ain't never gonna make it."

I never stopped walking. I just smiled sweetly at him and said, "Screw you, you little faggot." Of course, since we checked in together, they made MacDonald and me swim buddies. We were virtually inseparable the entire UDT training cycle and have remained close friends ever since.

And what an amusing, diverting cycle it was. One hundred and twenty-one of us started it together as members of UDT Class 26. Twenty-four survived—20 percent. Many of those who washed out were so-called SpecWar experts: Green Berets and Army Rangers who wanted to get some maritime training. We also lost most of the officers—they just couldn't take it.

Me? I found it perversely enjoyable—most of it. Today, SEAL training (UDT was phased out in 1983) takes six months. It's called BUD/S (Basic Underwater Demolition/SEAL) training, and it includes parachute work, demolition, and diving we never learned during our 16-week UDT sessions thirty years ago.

I breezed through the first four weeks. I'd worked out regularly in Naples, so the PT (Physical Training—calisthenics and running) and swimming came easily for me, although the sailors who'd come from the fleet were ragged by the end of the first week because they were so out of shape. They ran the hell out of us. Every day we'd cover a five- or six-mile course that included a series of old landing craft on the beach. You'd vault the gunwales—an eight-foot jump, drop six feet down, clamber across, struggle up, over, down, and keep going.

Down behind the rifle range was a big sand dune the instructors called Mount Suribachi. They'd run us up and they'd run us down a dozen times or so. When it rained, they'd run us through the mud. When it was dry, they'd run us through the surf. Remember how those Olympic runners looked in the opening shots of *Chariots of Fire*, all clean and white and shimmery running along the beach? Well, we looked nothing like that at all. We wore green fatigues, heavy "boondocker" boots, red-painted steel pot helmets, and kapok life vests that weighed eight pounds dry and twenty-eight pounds wet, and the instructors always managed to keep them wet.

The instructors, it should be said in their favor, ran with us. Most of them were real Methuselahs—old guys in their mid- to late thirties. I remember one, a flyweight named John Parish. He smoked a pipe as he ran the beaches, or up and down Mount Suribachi. When he'd gone through the bowl of tobacco, he'd flip it upside down and chew on the stem, never losing a step. You learn to hate people like that.

There was no diving involved at first, except for some basic fins-and-face-mask shallow-water stuff. Mostly we were getting accustomed to working in a water environment, learning life-saving techniques, and being instructed in the rudimentary procedures for beach reconnaissance and clearing a beach for an amphibious assault. But we swam a lot. That is an understatement. You swam and you swam right over de dam. We did day swims, night swims—warm weather, cold weather, it didn't matter.

You do not test the water with your toe if you want to be a Frogman.

One night Mac and I were out on a night reconnaissance exercise. We were rolled off an LCPL—Landing Craft/PersonneL—in the Chesapeake Bay, a thousand meters off Little Creek. It's an interesting insertion technique. Lashed to the LCPL on the offshore side (so it's invisible to anyone watching from the beach) is an IBS—Inflatable Boat: Small. You roll over the gunwales of the LCPL onto the IBS, hit it, bounce/roll into the water, and go under. The enemy on shore sees only what appears to be a patrolling landing craft, almost two-thirds of a mile out to sea. The Frogmen, who understand the principle of dramatic irony, know better.

Our objective that night was to identify the correct beach, infiltrate, mark the beach, then swim back the thousand meters into the bay, where we'd be picked up by the LCPL again. (Another interesting technique. You swim out beyond where the boat will pass you and wait. Now, as the LCPL sweeps by at about ten knots, there are Frogmen in the IBS. They are equipped with SNAREs, horse-collar-like devices with which a fast-moving boat can pick up swimmers in the water. You put out your arm, and—slam—you're whipped aboard. If the Frogman doing the SNARing doesn't like you, he may SNARE your neck instead of your arm, which smarts as you are whipped aboard. That is an understatement.)

I knew Mac was feisty, but exactly how feisty I didn't learn until that night. The water was thick with jellyfish, and MacDonald caught quite a few of them across his face mask. The stings brought him to the surface, gasping, more than a few times. By the time we reached the beach he was definitely uncomfortable—I could see dozens of stings on his face and neck.

Just before we left the beach, I called, "Time out," to one of the instructors—Mac was in pain, and I thought he needed attention.

45

"Go to hell you goddamn Polack."

"Come on, man, you've got welts all over your face. You're stung bad."

"Bugger off, Marcinko."

MacDonald staggered back into the water and we swam our thousand yards through the jellyfish again. By the time the IBS snared us he was in a mild state of shock. But he wouldn't quit. He never stopped swimming. It was exactly the sort of tenacity the instructors looked for. Their goal was to build endurance, strength, and a feeling for working as a swim pair—the most basic "Team" portion of UDT. Both the U—underwater—and the D—demolition—would come later, if we made it through the first few weeks.

For a group of sailors I thought we used a lot of wood in training. Wood? you ask. Logs. Big logs. Long logs. Heavy logs. We ran the beaches carrying them over our heads. We vaulted over piles of them. And they were used to build the especially nasty Little Creek Amphibious Base obstacle course, which we lovingly called The Dirty Name.

The Dirty Name was a series of logs of various heights and diameters embedded in the ground. The goal was to progress from one to the next without falling or touching the ground. The logs were spaced ingeniously, so that if you could jump high enough to the next one, you found you couldn't quite jump far enough; when you could jump far enough to achieve the next log, it seemed impossible to go as high as necessary. For the instructors, it was a way of discovering which of us were motivated enough to summon that extra energy or adrenaline that allowed us to complete the course. For us, the motivation lay in trying to get from one log to the next without breaking our necks or legs, or jumping short and laying ourselves open on the splintery edges of the logs.

The instructors also encouraged competition between each of the boat crews. We'd race each other in swimming relays, boat races, and land runs. Unlike SEAL platoons, which have fourteen men, Underwater Demolition Teams were composed of 20-man platoons. The reason for twenty is because that was the number of men needed to do a 1,000-yard string-line reconnaissance of a USMC-battalion-sized landing beach. The 20-man platoon was devised when the first UDT teams were assembled at Fort Pierce, Florida, in the summer of

1943; they continued until 1983, when Frogmen were finally phased out and everyone became a SEAL.

SEALs are leaner: a SEAL platoon consists of two seven-man boat crews—each containing six enlisteds and an officer. The reason behind this number is that one of the most basic SEAL modes of transportation, the IBS, holds seven people and their combat gear. IBSs can be dropped out of planes like rubber duckies or launched underwater from submarines, so they are convenient for surreptitious or covert operations. Other basic forms of SEAL transportation include the STAB, or SEAL Tactical Assault Boat, which is a 28-foot fiberglass boat powered by twin 110-horsepower Mercury engines and armed with .50-caliber machine guns and other deadly goodies; Boston whalers, 16-foot craft that we found useful in SEAL Team Six; and LCMs, or 45-foot Landing Craft/Mediums—Mike boats—which could be armed with mortars and were helpful in Vietnam.

Nevertheless, the lowest common denominator of transport, the IBS, and the basic SEAL boat-crew unit, the seven-man squad, are elements that have never changed since SEALs were commissioned in 1961; they're still in use in SEAL Team Six. Remember these numbers. You will see them again.

The Sunday our fifth week began brought a perceptible change of mood around the barracks. MacDonald and I usually spent our Sundays lying out on the beach and drinking beer. But this day was different. We stayed in, watching as a couple of the guys who'd been through the course before but had dropped out for one reason or another shaved their heads, then applied red dye.

"I wonder what the hell they know that we don't," I said to Ken.

We found out shortly after midnight. We were rolled out of the sack by instructors blowing whistles and pounding on us with paddles, and we didn't sleep more than two hours a night for the next six days. Welcome to Hell Week.

I had a problem with Hell Week: I'd developed a case of the runs. In today's Navy that would probably be enough to get me excused. Not in 1961. They stopped for nothing. The solution was speed: I discovered as they ran me up and down the beach that if I ran fast enough, the smell of what ran down my leg and into my boot got left behind for the next boat crew to enjoy.

The instructors gave us each a gift for Hell Week. Each crew was presented with an IBL—Inflatable Boat: Large— for the duration. We'd use it in our daily "Round-the-World Cruises." Oh, were *they* fun. We'd begin with the IBLs on our heads—the short guys piling a number-ten can on their helmets so they'd bear their share of the weight—while the instructors rode inside, beating on us with a paddle for mo- tivation. We'd run, dump the boats in a series of drainage ditches that ran through the huge base, paddle across, pick the boats up, and run some more, from Gate 5 to the Main Gate to the Mud Flats two miles away, launch the boats into the harbor, and paddle out through the ferry channel onto a course that ran parallel to the Chesapeake Bay beaches. We'd row for a while, then buck the currents shoreward, land, pick up our beloved IBLs and instructors, and run past gawking tourists, taking the beach all the way back to Little Creek— a distance of about twenty-one miles as the Frogman swims, runs, limps, and crawls. It paid to win those races, too. The first boat crew to finish got to rest before the next evolution. The last guys in got to partake in a unique bit of fun and games called The Circus. The Circus was PT until someone quit. You could quit by turning in your red helmet, collapsing, or dying. Dying was easiest—it was the only way you wouldn't be harassed by the instructors anymore.

The harassment was constant. If you fell asleep, they'd pour water on you. On the few occasions we went for chow at the mess hall, we'd have to leave guards with the IBLs, otherwise the instructors would deflate them (and we'd have to blow them up manually). So we'd rush in, a messy, loud, obnoxious group of filthy, grubby, foul-smelling sailors, eat without the benefit of utensils—it's probably where the expression *stuffing your face* was invented—and relieve the IBL guards so they could chow down and grab a few minutes rest before the whole painful cycle started all over again.

The instructors made sure that we were always wet or cold or tired or sore. By day three my feet were a mess: cracked nails, blisters that festered because of the sand and seawater, and splinter-filled hands from vaulting logs. Even my head was sore (we were expected to wear our red steel helmets all the time—about the second day I realized why those guys had dyed their heads red). We crawled through mud, surrounded by live charges that exploded yards from us. We were subjected to live fire as we ran the obstacle courses. And every time we thought we'd run the last leg of a five-mile or eight-mile or ten-mile run, we'd be told to pick up the IBL and go at it again. Nobody died, and nobody went to the hospital, although there were lots of sprains and banged-up knees, elbows, necks, and shoulders.

The worst day was the final day, Friday. So-Solly Day, as in "So solly, sailor." More Round-the-World Cruises, runs, an obstacle course enlivened by the biggest live charges yet, a hard swim, then a final turn around the beach in full fatigues, steel pot, and wet kapok life jacket. I've got a photo taken on So-Solly Day—I must've learned the lesson well because I'm right in front of the group, running alongside the instructor.

Saturday, the Commander, Amphibious Force Command, John S. McCain, came to give the roughly three dozen of us who'd survived Hell Week some encouragement. We took his words to heart. (He must have been inspirational at home, too. His son, John, now a U.S. senator from Arizona, was a POW in Hanoi from 1967 to 1973, where he proved his toughness and mettle under conditions tougher than any of those we ever suffered.)

We were an interesting group, those who made it through. We'd been tempered by hardship; we were confident there was virtually no physical demand we couldn't accomplish. The hot pain of our wounds became a warm glow of pride for not having quit. We had watched seven out of ten quit—and we had not. It was as if I'd suddenly been admitted to some exclusive club with its own secret handshake and decoder ring. Because now, having passed the hazing and the initiation rites, I was going to Puerto Rico and St. Thomas, where I'd learn the secrets of the temple: the deepwater diving skills and demolition techniques that would make me a real Frogman.

As I looked around at those of us who'd survived, I realized something I'd carry with me for life. It was a simple truth, but a good one: never stereotype anyone. Never assume just by looking that someone is suited for anything. For example, there's no physical prototype for a Frogman—or for a SEAL for that matter—although the stereotype is probably a big, heavily muscled guy in the Arnold Schwarzenegger mold.

I was built like a football player. But my swim buddy, Ken MacDonald, looked like a toothpick. What was true for UDT was true two decades later for the Navy's most elite unit as well. SEAL Team Six's Gold Dust Twins, Frank and Larry, stood only about five seven, Snake was about five ten, Indian Jew was about six feet, while Aussie Mick and Horseface were the size of large armoires. If they had anything in common at Six, it was huge chests and big arms developed after long sessions on the weight pile to achieve the immense upper-body strength we needed to climb ropes for clandestine sea-borne assaults. But overall, non-Six SEALs come in all configurations. Under combat conditions, however, they are all equally deadly.

In UDT training class 26, we were all shapes and sizes, too. And our personalities were as different as our physical types. Some of us, like *moi*, were loud—some might even say obnoxiously so—from time to time. If there was a bar open, you could find me there after-hours, partying until last call. Others were quiet, introspective brooders who spent their off-hours with books.

If I had to categorize those of us who made it through UDT training, I'd say the one thing that bound us all together was that we were outsiders as opposed to ticket punchers. Some might call us social misfits, but that would be stretching the point. Sure, we were hell-raisers. We were aggressive and we liked to show it. God help the Marine or sailor who decided he'd show what a tough guy he was by taking on a Frogman, because we'd be killed before we'd let ourselves get beaten. But beyond the aggressiveness, the showboating, the macho bullshit, we were all driven by something that pushed us further than others dared to go. We were mission oriented and would do what we had to do to achieve it. The instructors had managed to convince us—or maybe we did it to ourselves—that there was nothing we couldn't do. The principles I learned during Hell Week I'd use again and again over the next two and a half decades, to show the men I led there was nothing they couldn't do. My men didn't have to *like* everything they did—but they had to *do* it all.

We were a real wild bunch, those three dozen who made it through Hell Week. Lean and mean and confident as five-hundred-dollar hookers; precisely the sort of playful young tadpoles the U.S. taxpayers should spend hundreds of thousands of dollars to teach how to blow up almost anything. Which is exactly what happened next.

Imagine a place where there are unlimited women, a never-ending supply of aged booze and fresh lobsters, and all the deadly toys you could ever want to play with.

Heaven, right? No. This place exists: it is called St. Thomas, and it is where we Hell Week survivors were sent for ten glorious weeks of training.

We actually did train. We were taught how to navigate underwater, using only a compass, a plumb line, and a depth gauge. It takes concentration because below the surface it's easy to get disoriented. Once, Mac and I got good and lost —we're lucky we didn't drown ourselves. We took an incredible amount of grief from the training officers for our little escapade, but we also learned a valuable lesson: if you screw around, you can die. That thought really hadn't occurred to me before.

We were sent on swims from Roosevelt Roads, Puerto Rico, to Vieques Island, seven miles to the east. (We called Roosevelt Roads "Roosy Roads." The "Roads" stood for "Retired On Active-Duty Sailors," in honor of those who were lucky enough to pull permanent duty there.) The phrase *Did the earth move for you?* took on a whole new meaning during our stay in St. Thomas and Puerto Rico. We explored the fine art of placing bangalore torpedoes so they'd blow gaping holes in concertina-wire defense perimeters. We practiced destroying concrete pillboxes with satchel charges. We developed the knack of blasting a landing-craft channel through a reef. I discovered the joys of dynamite, nitro, and plastique and managed to keep all ten fingers attached to my hands while I did. We were instructed in the basics of Aqua-Lung diving, and we used the German-made Draeger bubbleless, self-contained apparatus for the first time.

And we swam. Oh, did we swim. One of our jovial instructors, a good-natured, wise-ass LT (jg) from New England named Aliotti, gave us extra swims on Saturdays to keep us away from the bad influences of demon rum and wanton women. Worse, he'd make us tow a bladderlike sea anchor while he and a date lounged on a raft and watched us struggle. The better to make us strong and virile Frogmen, he'd say when we complained.

It didn't take long for us to become totally comfortable in the water; we learned to deal with the unexpected (it's a mess, for example, when you get a bloody nose fifteen fathoms down from popped sinuses. The inside of your mask fills up, and you wonder whether or not to purge the blood because there are barracudas and moray eels and sharks in the water close by. You purge anyway. And you survive). So we blew things up and we swam, and we shot .45-caliber grease guns and .38-caliber pistols—the weapons of choice for the UDT in those days—and we got tan from the sun.

But mostly we partied. We showed off our bodies by sporting water-buffalo sandals, shorts, and tight polo shirts whenever we meandered into Charlotte Amalie, the capital of St. Thomas—which was virtually every night. Mac met a lady from New York who designed jewelry; I reconnoitered a schoolteacher from New Jersey. The four of us would hit the clubs at about nine and dance and drink rum and Coke until about one, then move on to the beach or the girls' houses for a unique form of heterosexual PT, which could, I guess, be called "concentrated horizontal hip thrusts," done in rapid succession. At about five we'd wake up and jog back to the sub base at the edge of Charlotte Amalie, grab a few quick breaths of pure oxygen for energy, and then go straight to calisthenics. We had to: if we missed the morning exercise, we wouldn't get liberty at night. And God forbid that we'd miss a single nocturnal foray.

After our first taste of tropical bliss, it was back to the real world—Little Creek—where we participated in what were called Zulu 5 Oscar exercises. That was the E&E stuff—evade and escape—where we learned how to swim up to ships, attach limpet mines to their hulls, and get away undetected. I also got adept at swimming under ferryboats during E&E. The sailors' role in the Z/5/O exercise was to catch us doing the dirty deed. They hardly ever did.

In October 1961, I was assigned to UDT-21, based out of Little Creek; finally a full-fledged Frogman. To be honest I was only a junior Frogman, with no real Frogman specialties. I hadn't qualified as a diver yet or received jump training. But none of that mattered to me. It was like living a dream. The Navy fed me, clothed me, gave me wonderful toys to play with, and when I wasn't swimming or blowing things up, I could go out drinking with my buddies and beat the crap out of people in bars. Not that we'd start anything, but somehow, the biggest Marines and sailors would always pick fights with us. Maybe it was our tapered uniforms with the illegal detailing sewn on the insides of the blouse cuffs. Maybe it was our attitude. We had a very aggressive attitude. That's an understatement. Whatever the case, we seemed always to be getting into fights. Better, we always seemed to be getting into fights—and winning. It's a great confidence builder.

Dive qualifications came first. I went back to St. Thomas for six weeks of langostino, warm water, hot women, and rum. At the end of the session I was tanned, fit, well rested, and sporting the "Big Watch/Little Pecker" stainless-steel Tudor diving watch that they gave you after you qualified.

Next came parachuting. I was detailed to Ft. Benning, Georgia, for airborne training. I went as a member of the Zoo Platoon. Zoo because it included a Rabbit (as in John Francis), a Byrd, and a Fox, and we were all party animals engaged on a constant hunt for beaver and pussy.

Once I was qualified I discovered I liked jumping so much I began to skydive on weekends, experimenting with the then-new "flat" parachutes. At UDT, we did only static-line jumps—wearing old-fashioned, regulation 35-foot parabolic parachutes. In the trade, it is called rope jumping. I have always thought of it as the monkey-on-a-string technique.

I was fascinated by the newer, 28-foot flat chutes. At that time, they were used mainly as pilots' emergency chutes, but I believed they had real possibilities in combat situations. Their design made them more controllable than the 35-foot rope jumpers. They became even more maneuverable after we'd cut a new design of holes in the chute and added extra toggle lines so we could actually steer ourselves in the air.

I also liked the idea of pulling my own rip cord instead of jumping from a static line that did all the work. That meant I could free-fall. The thought of free-falling was wonderful. Doing it was even better. The freedom of flying through the sky, soundless, wind whistling past your body, was like nothing I'd ever done before. It was the same sense of freedom I felt underwater, but floating five or ten thousand feet in the air was even better: here I could breathe and see everything for miles. I'd go up as many times as I could, jumping from higher and higher altitudes, and allowing myself to fall closer and closer to the ground before I "pulled," or opened, my chute. I took grief from the instructors, but I figured that in combat you're less of a target free-falling than you are drifting lazily. So why open at five thousand feet and let some enemy platoon turn you into a bull's-eye, when you can open at five hundred and stay alive?

I learned how to pack and rig chutes. I got myself a sport "flat," which I modified to make more maneuverable. I bought whatever books on skydiving I could find and studied the intricacies of plotting a jump so that you land exactly where you want to, despite thermals, downdrafts, wind shear, and the thousands of other little variables that can cause cracked bones or broken skulls.

Despite the fact that we had to become jump-qualified, there was no intensive parachuting program at any of the UDT teams in the fifties and sixties: all the jump training was run by the Army. In fact, traveling back and forth for one lousy practice jump could take all day. There were no facilities near Little Creek, so we'd have to convince one of the pilots from Langley Air Force Base—across Norfolk Bay—to fly us up to Fort Lee, one hundred miles west in Petersburg, Virginia, or about the same distance northeast to Fort A.P. Hill, where there were approved drop zones. Finding pilots wasn't difficult, as all the USAF "bus drivers"—transport pilots—had to qualify regularly in CARP, which stands for Computerized Airborne Release Point flying.

CARP, if pilots do it right, drops the 82nd Airborne right onto its predetermined target. If pilots do it wrong, you get Grenada, where drop zones were missed, timing went awry, and paratroopers were put in jeopardy. Most of the time, pilots do it wrong.

Anyway, we'd fly up to Ft. Lee or Ft. A.P. Hill, do a single jump, then like ET, we'd call home and wait for a bus from Little Creek to come pick us up. Much of the time we did our waiting in one establishment or another that served liquid refreshments. Sometimes we'd receive visitors, gentleman callers in Army khaki, who—after the proper pleasantries had been exchanged—we would mash into paste.

During my first year or so as a Frogman I had a pair of unique experiences. One was that I got married. The lucky lady was Kathy Black, who I'd tried so hard to toss into the Livingston Avenue pool back in New Brunswick the summer of 1958. We'd dated since then. I'd seen her whenever I went home on a visit, and it seemed like a good idea at the time. In the early sixties you didn't shack up—not if you were from a good Catholic family (or even, like me, from a bad Catholic family). So we made our relationship formal.

She said she'd be willing to put up with the long periods I'd be away from home; I really liked her, and we made a nice-looking couple. We didn't have a lavish ceremony, but a nice one. Then we went on a brief honeymoon, Kathy got pregnant, and I left for a six-month Mediterranean cruise. Typical Navy marriage.

The second thing that happened to me was that I became a lab animal. It was poetic justice. What do you find in science labs? Rats, monkeys, and frogs, right? So what more perfect animal to test a new airborne retrieval system than a Frogman.

It was called the Fulton Skyhook Recovery System, and I volunteered as a guinea frog on a TAD, or Temporary Additional Duty (I've always thought of it as Traveling Around Drunk), that took me from St. Thomas to Panama City, Florida. Skyhook was designed to recover special-forces operators or CIA agents from behind enemy lines, snatch VIPs effectively and covertly, or retrieve (tranquilized) hostile prisoners captured by our forces.

The principle was simple. The snatchee climbs into a bunny suit, which is a reinforced, one-piece, hooded jumpsuit, into which is constructed a heavy nylon harness, radio cable, and a microphone in the hood. The harness snaps onto a bungee-cord rope about eight hundred feet long, which is in turn attached to a helium balloon floated from a tether.

Then a low-flying aircraft equipped with outriggers and sweeper bars comes in at about 130 knots or so and snags the line below the balloon. The line is locked automatically onto a winch through the use of explosive charges. Then—depending on the kind of plane that's doing the snatch—the snatchee gets reeled in, either through a hatch in the belly or up a tail ramp, and it's aloha, *bon voyage*, and sayonara.

The system had been tested mostly on sandbags, although twenty-two human lab-rats—company reps and Army special forces operators—had also participated. I was the Navy's first volunteer, and the first pickup to be attempted without any emergency-parachute backup system.

I showed up at an airfield near Panama City, changed into the bunny suit, strapped in, hunkered down, held my knees, and watched as the plane, a Navy Grumman S-2 Tracker, banked in and came straight toward me at about five hundred feet.

It passed overhead and caught the line tethered to the balloon. I felt the line go, took about a step and a half, and then—shiiiit, talk about your standing starts!

I felt as if I were riding at the end of a huge rubber band at 130 knots. I must have absorbed six g's—snapped into the air like a cartoon character whose hundred-yard arms can't hold on to a window ledge or tree limb.

The ground went bye-bye. The line pulled me higher than the aircraft—I went way above horizontal—and then I started to fall.

It occurred to me at that instant that maybe I should have worn a chute. I mean, what goes through the monkey's brain is something like, "Okay, I've been twanged. So here I am on my back, and I'm moving forward at 120 knots or so. But am I moving because I'm being *pulled*, or did the line break and I'm moving on my own—and about to go splat?"

The only way to find out was to see for myself. So I did a scissors kick and body-rolled onto my stomach.

Terrific. Now, by craning my neck into the wind, I could see the plane—and the line—and I knew I was okay. I tried to call the crew, but my roll had broken the radio cable and the microphone was useless. So I decided to have some fun.

I threw a hump—rolling my shoulders forward and dragging my hands, which is what you do in a parachute free-fall to move yourself laterally—and brought my body level with the top of the fuselage. Then, by finning my hands at my sides, I discovered I could break left and right.

I began to water-ski behind the Tracker, cutting through

the prop wash to port and starboard. I tried waving at the pilots, but discovered, as I later put in my report, that activating any of my extremities too dramatically led to turbulent repercussions—in plain English, if I moved too much, I'd start to corkscrew. It was not a pleasant sensation.

So I spent the next fifteen minutes banking lazily left and right, while the air crew reeled me in, wondering what the hell was going on out there.

When I got close, I rolled over on my back again, reached down, grabbed my ankles, and tucked tight into a ball. That action brought me down so I swung like a pendulum and allowed them to winch me up into the Tracker's belly more easily.

My head came level with the deck. I reached up and hoisted myself through the hatch, grinning at the visibly uptight crew chief who ran the winch. "Morning, Chief."

"What the hell's been going on out there, sailor? Goddamn cable's been seesawing all the hell over the place. We thought you were unconscious, hurt—broken up."

"Just water-skiing, Chief."

"Don't you b.s. me, you shit-for-brains, numb-nutted asshole."

"Okay, you got me dead to rights, Chief. I wasn't water-skiing."

He smiled triumphantly.

"Screw you—I was bodysurfing."

When we landed, I briefed a bunch of officers and company reps about what had happened, and what I thought of the system. I didn't tell them about the aerial waterskiing, although I did suggest that if the snatchee was to be non-parachute-qualified, it would be better if his arms were pinioned, so he couldn't suffer turbulent repercussions.

One of the officers, a full captain, took me aside afterward and told me he thought I'd done a professional brief. He complimented me on my speaking ability and added that I obviously had initiative.

"Why don't you apply to Officer Candidate School, Marcinko?" he asked. He explained that the Navy annually took fifty enlisted-men candidates in something called the OIP, or Officer Integration Program, and I appeared to be exactly the sort they were looking for. "I'd be glad to write a letter of recommendation for you."

"Well, sir," I told him, "fact is, I'm not sure that OCS is for me. Right now, I'd rather be a chief in the teams than CNO of the whole goddamn Navy."

"How come?"

"You know chiefs, sir—they can get things done. They control the real power in the Navy. Nothing moves unless a chief says so—including admirals."

"You could get things done as an officer."

"I'm not so sure, sir."

"Why, Marcinko?"

"Hell, sir, first of all I'm a high-school dropout, and there are all these Academy-grad officers I'd have to contend with, so I'm at a disadvantage from the beginning, you know. So what would I have to look forward to? Probably a junior officer on some ship somewhere. And frankly, to be a junior-grade fleet puke—begging your pardon, sir—overseeing some raggedy-ass sailors, well, it's just better for me in the teams. We swim. We dive. We jump—we stay active."

He chewed on his pipe some and nodded the way officers nod when they've just switched off all systems. "Well, you be sure to let me know if you ever change your mind."

Chapter
5

ULTIMATELY, I DID CHANGE MY MIND ABOUT APPLYING TO Officer's Candidate School. But it had less to do with some captain writing me a recommendation than with a salty chief petty officer named Everett E. Barrett. Barrett was an EOD—Explosives Ordnance Disposal specialist—and a GM/G (Gunner's Mate/Guns) who'd just made chief when I was assigned to the Second Platoon of UDT-21. The Second-to-None Platoon, we used to call it.

If ever I had a sea daddy, it was Ev Barrett. Talk about typecasting. Barrett was the perfect movie version of a chief petty officer—he would have been played by somebody like Ward Bond, if William Holden didn't grab the part first.

I thought of him as an older guy, although he was probably only in his late thirties when I met him: a wiry, gray-eyed, sharp-featured man about five feet ten, with white-wall haircut—*very* short—and missing the ring finger on his left hand from playing with one too many explosive devices. He had a gravelly, bullfrog voice that preceded him by about fifteen seconds (you always heard Ev Barrett before you saw him), and he growled undeleted expletives in nonending strings and ingenious combinations—all in a New Englander's flat-voweled accent. The term *curses like a sailor* had probably been coined about Everett E. Barrett.

He wasn't an educated man—not formally educated, at least. He read exactingly and spelled phonetically. That's as in F-O-N-E-T-I-K-L-E-E. And more than once I caught him reading us a new regulation with the paper upside down. But upside down or no, he'd look it over and then go nose to nose with some poor LT (jg) and recite a bunch of official-sounding paragraphs. Confronted by Barrett's performance, most officers would habitually buckle slightly at the knees, say, "Yeah, sure, Chief, anything you say," and that would be that. Barrett knew how to scare the bejesus out of officers.

Oh, but he was good. He scared the bejesus out of not just officers but all of us—me included. During my first Caribbean cruise in UDT-21, the radio on one of our boats went out just before we started amphibious maneuvers. I may have been a radioman, but I was no electronics technician. That didn't matter to Barrett.

"Marcinko, you bleeping motherblanker, get your blankety-blanking scrawny blanking ass over here," he growled at me.

I got my blankety-blanking scrawny blanking ass in gear. One did when Barrett summoned.

"You will blankety-blank have that blankety-blank blanking radio blankety-blankety-blank bleeping blanking *fixed* by the time we bleeping climb into the blanking boat tomorrow, or I will bleeping kick your blankety-blank-blank-bleeping blanking ass into blanking next blanking week."

"Aye blanking aye, Chief." Now, I didn't know a transistor from a resistor, or a filter from a tube. But I broke out the schematics and worked all night, and the next morning, somehow—I still don't know what I did—I got the damn radio fixed and working.

Not that I was worried about Barrett's kicking my ass into next week—although the chief was perfectly capable of punting it straight ahead about forty-eight hours. It was just that he had this uncanny ability to challenge people successfully to do more than they thought they could do.

Whenever someone said to Ev Barrett, "But Chief, that's impossible," Barrett would look him up and look him down and say, "Just bleeping do it and shut the bleep up."

Barrett took hold of me like a groin-trained watchdog grabs a burglar by the nuts—and he just wouldn't let go. It was always, "Marcinko, you bleeper-blanker, do this," and, "Marcinko, you worthless blankety-blanking blanker-blanker, get your bleeping butt in bleeping gear." When we were detailed to Vieques Island for maneuvers and slept in tents on the beach, he'd make us police the area and rake the sand twice a day. Vieques had always been considered vacation time for UDT platoons. You dove for conch and langostino and drank beer and rum and lazed on the beach and worked on your tan.

Not under Ev Barrett you didn't. He made me take the platoon's empty beer cans, fill them with sand, and build little patio walls in front of the tents. He designed (and we built) palm-frond patio roofs and beer-bottle wind chimes. At one point he sat the platoon down and taught us how to make palm-frond hats because he thought we weren't being kept busy enough.

Frogmen making palm-frond hats? Ah, but to Barrett, making blanking palm-frond hats meant we had to climb the tallest blanker-blanking palm trees to get the tenderest, greenest, most lush blanking palm fronds on the whole blanking island. No detrital fronds for Ev Barrett. And in case you've never done it, climbing a 45-foot palm tree is *work*.

Thing about it was, I didn't mind the hazing and the yelling and the constant attention at all. I learned early on that the more Barrett ragged you, the more he thought of you. So he kicked my butt until I passed my high-school equivalency exam. And he made sure I went through advanced jump training. And he honed my administrative skills by making me type all his blanking platoon reports. And he finally coaxed and cajoled and bullied and domineered and strong-armed me until I took the Officer's Candidate School qualification test—and passed.

When we were back at Little Creek, he'd bring me home for dinner, and I'd sit around all night with Barrett and his wife, Della, drinking beer and listening to his stories about the old Navy. Why he adopted me—because that's exactly what he did—I still don't know. I wasn't the first sailor he'd taken under his wing and I wasn't the last. But I'm glad he did, because he probably spent more time with me between

1961 and 1965, in both UDT-21 and then UDT-22 (a new unit formed in 1963, where Barrett's Second-to-None Platoon was transferred en masse), than my father had all my life. And frankly, if you were a rowdy youngster in your early twenties (and I was), and you were looking for a positive male role-model (and I probably was), you could do a hell of a lot worse than Everett E. Barrett, UDT, CPO, EOD, GM/G.

And rowdy I was. When Second Platoon deployed on cruises, for example, it fell to me and a friend to clear the enlisted men's mess deck.

A little explanation is in order here. On board a ship, there is a rigid caste system. Officers live in Officer Country, where enlisted pukes don't blanking go without a good reason. Chiefs normally have their own goat locker—their own galley and mess—and the rest of the ship's company ate on the mess decks. That left us, and the Marines, at the bottom of the bilge. We were classified as troops, not as a part of the ship's company, and therefore were subject to trickle-down amenities. We ate last. We showered last. We shit last. And in time of emergency we'd die first.

But UDT platoons are tight little cliques. We bunked together, shared duties together, swam in pairs, and we wanted to eat as a group, not have to walk into the mess deck and squeeze ourselves in singly among strange sailors or (worse) Marines.

I was known as The Geek back then. Geek because I was geeky enough to spit shine the soles of my boots as well as the uppers. My buddy Dan Zmuda, real name Zmudadelinski, alias Mud, and I devised a method by which to clear out enough sailors from the mess deck so Second Platoon could eat together at the same table.

The technique we developed was simple and effective. First, we'd walk into the mess and fill our trays to overflowing with food. Everything from soup to nuts on the same tray. Then I'd sit down in the midst of a group of clean, neat, well-mannered sailors and bid them hello.

"Good day, gentlemen," I would say, nodding politely.

Then Mud would drop onto an adjacent chair with a thud. "Hi, tablemates," he'd add, genteel as a yeoman.

The cordial greeting would be offset by Mud's physical appearance. He was built like a fireplug, and just as solid, and he kind of permanently tilted into the wind. His round, bulldog jaw jutted defiantly, his big Slavic nose (broken in any number of fights) was slightly askew. The rest of his Polack face looked as if it'd been sandblasted. Even when he smiled, his eyes could develop this wonderful wild look—the sort of "watch carefully, folks, here it comes" grin favored by Hulk Hogan just before he trashes Andre the Giant.

The mascot of the Underwater Demolition Teams is a malevolent frog named Freddie. He wears a Dixie-cup sailor's cap at a rakish angle. The stub of a stogie is chomped firmly in the corner of his mouth. He carries a lit stick of dynamite in his right hand and a mad glint in his eyes. Mud developed the same look, and most sailors found it downright unsettling. He was perfectly cast to play Huntz Hall to my Leo Gorcey.

Then Mud, who habitually ate dessert before he ate his entrée, would take a knife from someone else's tray, smear a thick layer of ice cream—flavor unimportant—on top of his Salisbury steak, add half a bottle of A.1. sauce, and begin to eat. Mud ate very quickly—and without benefit of utensils. It was a replay of the Hell Week mess hall—except Mud and I were the only ones at the table who had been through Hell Week.

I would always begin my meal with peas. I ate them by sucking them through my nose. After the first couple of snorts, I'd look around and smack my lips. "Mmmmmm. Great!"

If there were no peas that day, there was usually spaghetti. I sucked spaghetti through my nose, too, although I found if the marinara sauce was too spicy my eyes would water.

If subtlety didn't work, we'd get gross.

"Coffee, Mr. Mud?" I'd ask.

"By all means, Mr. Geek."

"Cream?"

"No thank you, Mr. Geek."

"Sugar?"

"I don't believe so."

"Honker?" I'd clear my nose into his cup.

"Delightful." And he'd drink it down in a gulp.

We discovered that after about three days of these performances, word would spread. By the end of the first week at sea, all Mud and I would have to do would be to walk into the mess hall, load our trays, and head for a table. It would clear before we even sat down.

When Barrett heard what Mud and I were doing, he went bonkers. "Goddammit, Marcinko," he growled, "I can't leave you blanking alone for five blanking minutes before you blankety-blank get your blankety-blank blanking butt in blanking trouble a-blanking-gain." In addition to the sore ears, Mud and I also received extra duty. That was Barrett's unique way of saying thank-you for the performances that allowed the platoon to eat together. Mud and I suffered in silence. We knew why he'd done it: if he hadn't, he would have taken grief in the chiefs' goat locker, so to keep the peace he reamed us out.

I got word I'd been accepted to OCS just after I left on a six-monther to the Mediterranean aboard the USS *Rushmore*, a WWII-vintage LSD, or Landing Ship/Dock, that had originally been built for the Royal Navy. It was quite a farewell cruise. I had all the normal platoon work to do: reconning the beaches prior to amphibious exercises, practicing EOD demolition, and taking part in the Z/5/O evade and escape drills that were a part of UDT-22's ongoing training. Then there was the scut work: typing Barrett's reports and memos, servicing the equipment, and maintaining my UDT diving and parachute qualifications.

On top of everything else I began spending more and more time in Officer Country, watching how they acted, how they did their work, how they lived in their wardroom. From time to time I'd get up to the bridge, where the captain of our LSD, Captain B. B. Witham, even allowed me to drive once or twice after Barrett passed on the word I'd been accepted to Organized Chicken Shit, which is how OCS is known in the fleet. A chain-smoking New Englander, Skipper Witham made sure I was instructed in the rudiments of officerdom. He even knew enough about me to address me correctly—as Seaman Geek.

Of course, now that I was about to become an officer and a gentleman, Mr. Mud and I gave up our regular mess-deck performances entirely. It had been a great act, but even great acts have to close sometime. Besides, who wants to be called Ensign Geek?

Not that I assumed the cloak of total respectability either. Whenever we landed at Naples for supplies, for example, I'd take the wheel of the truck we were assigned. My logic was simple: I was going to become a ship driver; driving is driving; why not get all the practice I could? Naples is a hilly city, and there are long tunnels with pedestrian sidewalks running next to the traffic lanes (only fools walked those narrow tunnel sidewalks, as Neapolitans compare with the wild men of Beirut when it comes to driving).

Now, since we had wheels, we could take the time to make one or two stops for social beverages on the way to the supply depot, which would normally put us behind schedule. I often took it upon myself to make up the lost time by putting two wheels of the two-ton stake-bed truck up on the sidewalk and grazing the tunnel walls to pass slow-moving traffic. This technique made neither the chief, nor the eight Frogmen riding in the back nor the fleet motor pool, very happy.

Barrett tried to correct my driving style in his characteristically amiable manner, explaining to me pedantically that bleeping motherblanker trucks weren't bleeping made for driving on side-blanking-walks.

I nodded and kept driving. "Roger, Chief, gotcha."

Gotcha, indeed.

I "got" Barrett one last time the week before I left for OCS. We were scheduled for a parachute jump. I'd already attracted Captain Witham's unhappy attention by pulling low—waiting until I was under a thousand feet to pull the rip cord. Witham felt more secure when he could watch us open our chutes through binoculars. The thought of a HALO (High Altitude, Low Opening) jump made him sweat. I was determined to make him lose eight pounds of water weight.

My last jump was a water jump just off the starboard side of the LSD. The masthead on an LSD is 138 feet above the deck. I told the platoon I was going to pull so low I'd be level with the masthead when the chute deployed. In fact, I told everybody I could find that I was going to come in at 138 feet—with two notable exceptions: Skipper Witham, and Ev Barrett. I even had a guy named Bob Clark standing by on deck with a 16mm sound movie camera.

We went up, climbed to altitude, reached the zone, and jumped. When I saw the film later, it was wonderful. There are all these chutes opening, way high. And then there's me. Falling. Falling. Falling.

As the camera follows me closer to the water, you can hear Barrett's voice unmistakably clear on the sound track: "You asshole. You fucking asshole. You fucking dipshit asshole. Pull the fucking goddamn cord. Marcinko, you motherfucking cocksucking cuntbreath shit-eating turd-faced dipshit pencil-dicked pus-nuts shit-for-brains asshole geek, *pull the fucking cord!*"

I know when to take a hint, so I pulled the cord. I'd rigged the chute for a low deployment. It flared instantly. I had time for one oscillation of opening shock, at which point I came even with the masthead, and then—splash—I hit the water.

I went under, wriggled out of my harness, and came up laughing.

Barrett and B. B. Witham did not find the stunt amusing.

The skipper didn't wait until I came aboard. "Marcinko— read my lips. You're fucking grounded," he called on the bullhorn.

Barrett decided I needed a new asshole, so he reamed me one on the spot.

About a week later I left for the States.

The day before I left, Chief Barrett called me up to the goat locker and sat me down. He found a couple of cans of beer, opened them both, and passed one to me. "Dick," he said, "I think you're gonna do all right. You're gonna make a good officer—*if* you don't screw around too much, and *if* you take things serious."

"Thanks, Chief. I will."

He nodded. "I know. You're a good boy. Hard worker. Tough. That's good, too. You're gonna need all that when you go up against all them fuckin' Academy pukes." He pulled at the beer. "Course, the Academy pukes don't know much about fuckin' pulling level with the fuckin' masthead, do they?"

We both laughed.

"But there's something . . ."

"You name it, Chief."

"Look," he said, "you've learned a lot of stuff now. And you're gonna learn a lot more."

I nodded. "Yeah?"

"So I want you to promise me something. I want your word that what you learn, you'll pass on."

"Sure." I wasn't certain what he was getting at.

"You're wondering what the fuck I'm saying, right?"

"Uh-huh."

"Dick, it shouldn't matter whether you work with a guy once or whether you serve with him for years—you gotta treat him the same. You gotta help him do his job. Like I helped you—now it's gonna be your turn to pass it on."

He drained his beer. "I want your word."

I looked at him. The man was absolutely serious.

"You got it, Chief."

He nodded and cracked a half-smile. "Think of it as Barrett's First Law of the Sea—because what it is, is the Navy way, Dick."

I was naive in those days; I believed him. No—that's not quite true. Back then, Ev Barrett's Law *was* the Navy way.

I BREEZED THROUGH OCS AT NEWPORT, RHODE ISLAND, graduating in December 1965 as an ensign. I didn't do well because I was smarter than the others with whom I entered, but because I'd been in the Navy for over seven years, more than three of them with the fleet, and I knew how the system worked. When the instructors—chiefs, mostly—would say, during their lectures, "You'll see this again," I wrote what they were saying down because I knew it would reappear on tests. I knew to do it because that's how chiefs worked. When we had inspections, I made sure my bunk was so tight a quarter would jump a foot off the top sheet and the room was as spit polished as the soles of my shoes (I hadn't been The Geek for nothing). When we drilled, I marched as if I were a member of the drill team. When we shot, I'd score an unending series of tens.

I realized very early on that none of the officers or chiefs who taught us, drilled us, harassed us, and inspected us could come close to giving me the kind of intimidation I'd survived during UDT Hell Week. So I did my job, took whatever they gave me to do, completed it without complaining, and cruised through OCS as if it were summer camp. The guys at fleet had been right: OCS *did* stand for Organized Chicken Shit.

Fact is, if the character played by Richard Gere in the movie *An Officer and a Gentleman* had been a Frogman, he'd have ended up cleaning Lou Gossett's clock before the end of the first day. Frogmen eat drill sergeants for hors d'oeuvres. They also know how to take harassment and still do the job without complaining.

When I was selected a section leader, then battalion commander of my OCS training class, I took Ev Barrett's Law to heart. I helped the class runts through the physical segments of training; I showed the bookworms how weapons worked; and I taught those whose grades were low to listen for the key words *you'll see this material again* before they wrote anything down. One hundred percent of my section graduated OCS. Others suffered a fair number of dropouts—one even had a suicide. At graduation, former Seaman Geek received the class leadership award along with his ensign's bars. My wife, Kathy, pregnant with our second child, looked on proudly.

After OCS I was assigned to a small destroyer, the *Joseph K. Taussig*, as a snipe, or engineering officer, whose domain was the fireroom, where the ship's boilers are located. I was certainly the first fireroom officer aboard the *Taussig* who ever conducted his own hull inspections—I did my own diving—and who wore green fatigues while crawling over, under, around, and through the whole boiler and propulsion system before I signed off that any specific work had been done.

The six months aboard the *Taussig* were an essential transition period for me. Now, I lived in Officer Country and ate in the wardroom—but the only things really different about me were the single-bar tabs on my collar, my tan uniform, and the fact that many of the enlisted men called me Mr. Rick—which I thought preferable to being referred to as Mr. Dick.

Ensign or no, I still thought like an enlisted man. And that helped when it came to doing my job. I'd heard all the enlisted men's excuses before because I'd used 'em myself. I knew how to tell good chiefs from bad ones. I knew from the day I was commissioned I couldn't adopt the Academy-grad leadership style, which is often detached, cool, and aloof, toward my men because I'm not a detached, cool, or aloof kind of guy. On the other hand, I wasn't an enlisted man anymore, either, and I had to learn to lead—even if leading meant making tough choices.

So the *Taussig* became my laboratory. I tried to see how I could use the Navy's system to my benefit, and where I could adapt it. Somewhat to my surprise I discovered that leading is not easy. It takes the same sort of confidence you need to jump out of a plane to order a man to do something that may prove fatal to him—and have him carry out the order instantaneously and without question.

On a more mundane level, leadership is learning how to make a decision, and then sticking by it even though you are heckled, nagged, pleaded with, and cajoled to change your mind. The first time I canceled my crew's shore leave because there was work still to be done on the boilers was one of the toughest decisions I'd had to make to that point in my life. Why? Because I had been a sailor, and I knew how much a night out meant to them.

My background gave me several advantages. I came to my job with a Frogman's physical confidence—I knew, for example, that I could fight, swim, or parachute better than any man aboard the *Taussig*. Not to mention the fact that I could also turn anyone who tried to take me on into a pile of chopped liver. That made my life with the crew much easier.

The fact that I came from UDT also helped me establish a good working relationship with my fellow officers. Most knew what Frogmen could do and respected me for it, even if they had no desire to follow in my fin-prints. I also got along well with Earl Numbers, the *Taussig*'s skipper, and my ratings were well above average.

But there was no real future for me as a ship driver and I knew it. There were far too many Academy grads ahead of me in line. In the Navy of the sixties, the Academy fraternity was very strong. A class ring was a talisman for success—and I was bare-knuckled. There was no aircraft carrier or guided-missile frigate on my horizon—no USS *Taussig*, even.

Still, when I received my ensign's bars, I'd made a commitment to the Navy. It would, I decided, become my career. What I would do, however, was another question. Actually, that's not quite accurate. I knew what I wanted—the question was how to achieve it.

What I wanted was to become a SEAL. I'd known about SEALs since the teams were first formed in 1962. I saw my first SEALs at Little Creek as soon as I got back from one of my first Caribbean cruises because Two's headquarters was right across the soccer field from UDT-21. They certainly had a different look to them. First of all, they dressed sharp. They wore shiny, black Cochran jump boots, with their trousers bloused over the tops, while we Frogmen wore regular boondockers with untucked trousers. Some of the equipment Frogmen used dated back to World War II. SEALs got all the best war toys. And everything was new: new, deadly weapons; new, experimental equipment; even new, special-warfare operation techniques and strategies.

Best of all, they were always going off somewhere or other to train. Maybe it would be a month of parachuting or six weeks of jungle warfare or a session at arctic survival school—they were always on the move. Weapons schools, language schools, they were doing it all. And while I loved being a Frogman, I'd peer through the chain-link fence like a stagestruck kid on his first visit to Broadway, watching as the SEALs came and the SEALs went and vowing that somehow I, too, would someday become a SEAL. The opportunity arose because of Vietnam, when both SEAL teams underwent expansion, roughly doubling in size.

The first American combat units arrived in Vietnam on March 8, 1965. On that day, elements of the Third Marine Regiment of the Third Marine Division landed on the beach near Da Nang. The leathernecks were greeted by a sign that read, "Welcome U.S. Marines—UDT-12." Frogmen were among the first American military personnel to go to Vietnam. SEALs came later. I was on the *Taussig* in February 1966 when I learned that the first detachment, from SEAL Team One in San Diego, had left for Vietnam. I felt strongly that with the West Coast in play, SEAL Team Two wouldn't be far behind. So I pulled every string I could to get myself reassigned there.

What worked in my favor was that I was young—twenty-five at the time—gung ho, and an experienced Frogman. There weren't a whole lot of officers back then who met those qualifications. It took me three months of long-distance wangling, cajoling, coaxing, and threatening, but by May I'd gotten myself detailed back to Little Creek and assigned to SEAL Team Two as a squad leader.

Driving through Gate Five in June 1966, I returned the guard's salute and thought about the first time I'd come to Little Creek, walking through the gate with Ken MacDonald. "Mate, you ain't never gonna make it" is what he'd said five years before. Well, we'd both made it. He was still with UDT-22, out on a cruise somewhere in the Med.

I drove past UDT headquarters and parked in the visitors' lot, slipped into a dress blouse and a pressed pair of khakis, locked the car, and walked into SEAL Team Two's quarterdeck area.

Bill and Jake, two Frogmen I'd known in the teams, were reading the bulletin board. They turned as I walked in and saluted without looking at my face. I was just another asshole wearing a bar. Then they saw who it was.

"Goddamn—Geek!"

I reached out and grabbed them. "Hey, you sons of bitches."

Bill looked me over. "So you defected to Officer Country."

"Food's better. And the women're more genteel." We all laughed. "What's up?" I asked.

"We just got back from language school," Jake said. "Two weeks of Spanish, just in case the Vietcong take over Honduras. Hey, Dick, you comin' over here with us or you going back to 22?"

"Here. I told 'em I wanted to kick ass and take names and they scuttled my desk and sent me where I belong." I pointed toward the door marked XO. "Joe D in?"

"Yup."

"I better go get squared away. See you guys later for a beer or something."

Bill tossed me a sharp salute. "Aye-aye, Ensign Rick." He cracked a smile, then broke into full-faced grin. "I don't frigging believe it. You—an officer. Finally we've got someone who understands us."

I turned and headed for the executive officer's office. In a way they were right: I did understand them, and they knew I'd be around for a while; I wasn't one of the usual SEAL officers who had a reserve commission, did one tour, and then quit. On the other hand I could see the pitfalls of coming back to Little Creek only ten months after I'd left.

In the minds of many with whom I'd be serving I'd still be The Geek, the guy who ate peas and spaghetti through his nose. I was still the uncontrollable E-5 Frogman who had the reputation of being an animal. I was let's-drive-the-truck-on-the-sidewalk-through-the-tunnel-in-Naples Marcinko.

I knew I'd have to change their minds. I took a deep breath and walked through the XO's door. Joe DiMartino rose to greet me.

"Dick—welcome aboard."

"Thanks, Joe. Good to be here."

He gave me a firm handshake and a pat on the back. He was easily ten years older than I, and a full lieutenant. Joe had seen action in Korea, and he'd been around during the Bay of Pigs, when the CIA had used Frogmen to help train some of the Cuban maritime assets before the abortive invasion. He was one of SEAL Team Two's "plank owners" —those sixty officers and men who had been selected to form the initial unit back in January 1962.

DiMartino looked like his name. The boot of Italy was written all over his craggy face, from olive skin and dark eyes to an aquiline nose and uneven white teeth that showed when he smiled.

His uniform was anything but formal: khaki shorts and the blue-and-gold T-shirt in which SEALs did their morning PT. "Is that the uniform of the day?"

Joe D nodded affirmatively. "Roger that. You're overdressed, Marcinko."

"I'll remember tomorrow."

"Coffee?"

"Sure."

"Help yourself."

I took a paper cup, filled it from an urn that sat atop a two-drawer, olive-green file cabinet, and raised it in a steaming, silent toast in Joe's direction. "What's up?"

"The usual bullshit. We're halfway through a training cycle, and you're gonna have to play some catch-up. I'm planning to send you over to Bravo Squad at Second Platoon as soon as you finish your quals."

"Roger that. How's the CO?"

"TNT? He's okay, but he's overworked. He'd like to jump and shoot, but the son of a bitch is buried under a ton of paperwork. Makes him prickly, but don't take it personal. In fact we should get moving right now—see him before it gets too busy. He's got some things to say to you."

"Let's go."

We walked out into the corridor. The battleship-gray walls of the low building hadn't been painted in some time, and the floors were scuffed and dirty. But there was a good, lived-in feeling about the place. Moreover, it was both informal and low-key when it came to dress regs and spit and polish, which suited me just fine.

Joe D rapped on the CO's door. From inside came a distinct growl. "Come."

We stepped inside and saluted. Lieutenant Commander Tom N. Tarbox lifted his short, bulky frame from behind his desk and returned the salutes. His nickname was TNT because he often became too hot to handle. He brooked no bullshit.

TNT sat me down and read me the gospel. He asked how my wife was doing. I told him she was due to have our second child within the month. He nodded and ordered me to get Kathy squared away as soon as possible because families were a drain on an officer's time if they weren't settled down and comfortable. I'd be assigned to work in submersible operations—diving—until I satisfied all my SEAL qualifications. I'd have to go to fire-support school, where I'd learn how to call in artillery strikes from offshore vessels. I'd be required to take language training—Spanish—and requalify in HALO—High Altitude, Low Opening—parachute work, and was that all a roger, Ensign Marcinko?

I'd have to become familiar quickly with SEAL weapons and tactics, and if I was out of shape, God help me because Tarbox demanded that his officers lead from the front, not from behind, and did I get each and every word of that, mister?

"Aye-aye, sir."

He shook my hand, told me he was glad to have me aboard, and kicked us out. "I've got too much goddamn paperwork to deal with to play nursemaid. See you later at the Officers' Club for a beer, Ensign. Now haul ass."

* * *

There's a world of difference between UDT and SEALs. As a Frogman I was a conventional warrior whose operational boundary was the high-water mark of whatever beach I was sent to reconnoiter. As a SEAL, my real work only *began* at the high-water mark—and then it continued inland for as far as I felt comfortable. I was no longer just a Frogman, but an amphibious commando who could harass the enemy, carry out intricate ambushes that would confuse and terrorize adversaries, disrupt supply routes, snatch prisoners for interrogation, and help to train guerrillas.

In SpecWar parlance, when I became a SEAL, I became a force multiplier. The principle is simple: send me in with 6 SEALs and we will train 12 guerrillas, who will train 72 guerrillas, who will train 432, who will train 2,592—and soon you have a full-tilt resistance movement on your hands.

Another way of looking at it is that SpecWar operators like me can help a government out, or they can help a government *out*. It all depends on what kind of national policy you want to pursue. SEALs can't make policy. That's for the politicians to do. But if there is a policy that allows us to act, then we can throw ourselves into our deadly work with surprising ingenuity, passionate enthusiasm, and considerable diligence.

That's what happened in September of 1966, when the Navy ordered a contingent from SEAL Team Two to be ready to leave for Vietnam shortly before Christmas.

I was coming back from a training session in Puerto Rico with my squad—Bravo Squad of the Second Platoon—and we'd just flown into Norfolk Naval Air Station when I saw Two's new CO, Lieutenant Commander Bill Earley, on the tarmac.

As we came down the ladder, he waved us over. Earley, a West Coast SEAL who'd already been nicknamed Squirrelly because of his habit of constantly fidgeting his six-foot-two frame whenever he sat down, gathered six of us officers in a tight circle around him and gave us the good news.

"We're authorized for Vietnam. Two reduced platoons—twenty-five men in all," he shouted over the 100-decibel screams of unmuffled jet engines. "Twenty enlisteds—and five of you guys."

I have never been the shy type. I didn't wait for Squirrelly to finish another sentence. I grabbed him by his elbow and walked him down the ramp so I could pitch my case. He was taller than me, but I was stronger, and I had his arm and wasn't going to let it go until he gave me the answer I wanted to hear.

To his credit, Earley didn't laugh at me until he'd heard me out. Then he swung out of my grasp, told me I was an obnoxious son of a bitch, that I shouldn't shit a shitter, and that the con job hadn't worked.

When he'd finished taking all the air out of my sails, he added, "Marcinko, the reason I'm going to send you to Vietnam has nothing to do with logic, or with the pitiful excuse for begging you just performed. I want to inflict you on those poor Vietnamese bastards for two reasons. First, it'll deprive you of pussy. That'll make you especially mean, which will result in a high number of VC casualties, and I'll look good as a result. Second, you're the most junior guy here—so you're expendable—cannon fodder—if *you* step on a mine or get sniped, we don't lose much experience, and I'll still look good. So pack your bags."

Until that moment, I had never seriously considered kissing another man.

The weeks between September and Christmas are still a blur. The platoon leader, who also ran Alfa Squad, was an LT named Fred Kochey. He and I had about eight weeks in which to take twelve individual SEALs and make us all into a tough, effective, deadly combat unit.

My squad, Bravo, had real potential. Ron Rodger was part Indian, a strong young kid with a hell of a punch—when he hit you, it *snapped*. He carried the machine gun. When he hit you with that, *you* snapped. The utility man, Jim Finley, was the kind of guy who could go anywhere, walk into any foreign country and talk to people even though he didn't speak a word of the language. We called him the Mayor because wherever we went, he'd be out pressing the flesh within minutes, just like a goddamn politician.

The radioman was Joe Camp, a real hustler, who doubled his salary playing poker. Bob Gallagher, the dark Irishman we called Eagle (because he was a bald, beady-eyed, competitive s.o.b.), loved to bar brawl, shoot, and generally raise hell. My kind of guy. I made him assistant squad leader and assigned him to cover our rear. Jim Watson—Patches, because he liked to sew so many school patches on his uniform he looked like a walking Navy recruiting ad—was point man. Jim was one of Seal Two's plank owners—an original SEAL. It was right that he'd be the tip of the Bravo Squad spear. We had no medic in Bravo Squad. I told the guys that was because junior men didn't die—only old guys, like Kochey's antiques in Alfa, would need to be patched up.

Beneath the black humor lay reality. Indeed, my job would be to get Bravo Squad back in one piece. The key to staying alive would be team integrity. We practiced constantly, first at Camp Pickett, in Blackstone, Virginia, then at Camp Lejeune, North Carolina. The problems seemed endless. All the mundane tradecraft things I'd never thought much about now became huge tactical obstacles. How do five-and-one or ten-and-two walk a trail? How do you look for booby traps? How do you use a point man—and what about rear security? Where in the squad does the radioman go? Or the machine gunner? If there's an ambush, who'll break right and who'll break left?

We constantly practiced our fields of fire because there are no safety regs when you're walking with weapons locked and loaded on jungle trails. The asshole who stumbles and shoots his buddy in the back can cause a lot of damage. The solution is for everybody to know how everybody else is carrying his gun, and what portion of the clock his weapon is responsible for. Point man, for example, can deal with a wider field of fire than fourth man, who can only shoot from two to four-thirty on the right, and from eight to ten o'clock on the left.

There were so many questions—and so little time to find the answers. What about the problem of right-handed shooters? Everybody in my squad was right-handed. That meant we all carried our weapons slung over the right shoulder pointed toward the left—so we were unprotected on one side. I decided that half of us were going to carry weapons southpaw-style.

On the plus side was our squad spirit. My guys were absolute renegades—all they wanted was to take on bad odds. I could put them on a ridge and feed them ammo and they'd melt their barrels before they'd give an inch. In fact, one of the toughest problems I had to face at first was keeping them from chasing the enemy and running into an ambush. Because if these Bravo Squad sons of bitches got fired on, they wanted *revenge*.

(Their aggressiveness would carry on to Vietnam, where all five of my men, Rodger, Finley, Watson, Camp, and Gallagher, would win the Bronze Star or Navy Commendation Medal on our first tour. Bob Gallagher went on to complete *four* Vietnam tours. On his third, although he was wounded so seriously he could hardly walk, he saved his squad—brought them all, including the squad leader, whom Gallagher carried, out to safety under heavy fire. For that escapade, "Eagle" won the Navy Cross, the nation's second-highest military decoration.)

But spirit alone doesn't keep anybody alive. We'd have to be able to kill the enemy before he killed us. This is more difficult than it sounds. I first realized how tough it was going to be at Camp Pickett—in the dead of a fall night. I was running a night-ambush, live-fire exercise. I'd strung us out into pairs along a ridgeline of dunes, forty yards above a simulated canal. The situation was supposed to resemble the Mekong Delta, where we would be assigned. But instead of a sampan filled with VC and supplies, we'd be shooting at a six-by-eight-foot piece of plywood towed behind a jeep.

We'd set up nice and quiet—we'd learned by now how to move without upsetting leaves and branches, and we'd moved quietly into our places and dug firing positions. Our weapons were locked and loaded. We lay in pairs, waiting for the "sampan" to come by. The woods returned to normal: the only sounds we heard were the birds and the bugs.

We were in full combat gear. Green uniforms, load-bearing vests full of 30-round magazines for the M16s we carried, double canteens—everything. All I could see were problems. The green uniforms had to go. They provided no camouflage; we were always visible against the foliage. The vests had to be redesigned because they made too much noise—jingle-jingle is not a good sound in the jungle-jungle. Our boots left gringo-sized footprints on the trails. Easy to follow if you were a VC looking for a Yankee to hurt. We did not want the VC walking a mile in our shoes.

I gave hand signals. "Enemy coming. Get ready." The squad went down in their holes.

Now the jeep started to move. "Ready."

I waited. "Now—"

The ridgeline erupted as six 30-round magazines were expended in unison. I was blinded by the muzzle flashes and lost my target picture but kept shooting anyway. I ejected, thrust another 30-round mag in my M16, and blasted away. So did everybody else.

"Shit—goddamn it, son of a bitch!" Gallagher's voice came down the line, followed by Gallagher, who exploded out of his hole six feet straight into the air. He landed on top of his partner, Watson, and started throwing punches. "You asshole scumbag—"

I ran up the line and pulled them apart. "What the—"

"It's his fault, Mr. Rick." Gallagher ripped his fatigue shirt off. His back was covered with ugly red blisters. "It's Patches' friggin' shell casings. The son of a bitch ejected them down my neck."

"I didn't do it on purpose."

"You dipshit—"

I shook them by the scruffs of their necks. "Oh, this is just peachy. We are supposedly in the middle of a fucking ambush, and you shit-for-brains assholes are arguing about where your hot brass is going, while the fucking enemy is cutting your throats."

I stomped off toward the jeep path to check the targets. "This is no way to run a fucking war."

What I discovered made me even more unhappy. There were six of us. We had each emptied two 30-round magazines at the six-by-eight target, which had been moving at a speed of five miles per hour, at a distance of 120 feet. We had fired 360 shots. There were precisely two bullet holes in the target.

The squad was summoned. I poked a ballpoint through each hole.

"So, this is what a highly trained, well-fucking-motivated squad of killers can do when it tries, right?" I growled in a passable Ev Barrett parody.

I let their perfidy sink in. I looked at the crestfallen faces.

"Didn't you go to marksman's school?" I put an index finger over Patches Watson's heart. "Don't you hang a fucking Expert Marksman's Badge on that walking billboard you call a jumpsuit?"

He hung his head in shame. "Yes, sir, Ensign Rick."

The Barrett in me took over. "Well, it is not fucking good e-fucking-nuff for you to wear a motherfucking cocksucking dingle-fucking-dangle *medal* and shoot only two fucking holes in this motherfucking piece of plywood. Or do I have it all wrong, gentlemen?"

No answers.

"Boys," I said softly, "those probs and stats don't fuckin' excite me at all."

Silence.

"Now, I'll tell you something—we're all at fault here. I mean, how many times did I hit the target? Okay, so we've got a prob to solve. Let's solve it. Are we leading the target too much? Are we not leading it enough? I mean, what gives?"

We did what was necessary: we drilled again and again and again until we could shred the plywood target whether it was towed at five miles an hour or fifteen. We practiced shooting in teams of two—remember swim buddies, and how I said you would see that material again?—from a confined space, like a camouflaged hole, or from behind trees. Each of us learned how to fire from close quarters without showering his neighbor with hot brass.

Our training continued from fall into early winter. For Halloween we visited the Vietcong village at Camp Lejeune, where Marines in black pajamas and cartoonish Asian accents carried AK-47s and tried to play trick or treat with us. Marines should never attempt war games with SEALs. We gave the bogus VC our own brand of So-Solly U.S. Maleen, booby-trapping their booby traps, playing hide-and-seek during their ambush exercises, and staging our own sneak attacks on their "secured" VC hamlet. It was all fun and games and playacting. We hiked. We camped. We shot the hell out of targets. When we had time, we'd waltz into Virginia Beach for some full-contact bar-brawling.

A word or two here about that. I have always believed that being a SEAL, like being an NFL linebacker, requires a certain amount of aggressive, close physical contact with your fellow human beings. Some may disagree with me. But I find that there is something truly rewarding about putting your back up against the back of someone you trust with your life, and taking on all comers. Sure, you take a certain number of dings in the pursuit of these unruly activities. But in the long run, I believe the rewards outweigh the liabilities. And when, as an officer, my most important job is to build unit integrity, there are few better ways in which to build it than late at night, in a bar, when it's you and your five guys against the rest of the world.

Thus endeth the sermon.

Early in December, we trooped over to the infirmary and upgraded our inoculations. We were still nursing sore arms and butts when the base legal officer sat us down and drew up last wills and testaments for those of us going overseas. Then the yeomen from BUPERS—the Bureau of Personnel—came and told us about supplemental insurance and death benefits we could sign up for, and we arranged to have our paychecks direct-deposited in our checking accounts.

This was a no-shitter. This was the real thing. My kids, Richie, who was three, and little Kathy—I called her Kat—who'd been born July 5, less than six months before, were too young to realize what was happening. But my wife, Kathy-Ann, knew, and she—like the other SEAL wives—was apprehensive. She got nervous whenever I jumped out of a plane or went out on a dive. She hadn't cared for the fact that, as a SEAL, I'd been away for five of the preceding six months on training exercises. Now, the thought of my spending six months in Vietnam with angry, small, yellow people shooting at me did not make her happy at all. While I could comprehend her concerns, I couldn't understand them. War was what I'd trained for since I'd joined the teams, and nothing would keep me away from combat.

There were tears and sniffles and lots of kissing and hugging, and then just before Christmas, we SEALs climbed onto a C-130 Hercules loaded to the gills with equipment. Instead of seats there were long, greasy web canvas slings strung along the sides of the fuselage. In the wide center aisle were pallets swathed in cargo netting, piled high with all the deadly goodies SEALs need for six months of fun and games. This was a true no-frills flight. No seats. No seat belts. No tray-tables. No food. No stewardesses to plump pillows behind our heads. In fact, there were no heads, only a tube by the tail ramp where we could take a leak.

Over the next seven days, we meandered west so we could reach the East, while we tried to find somewhere to stretch out and grab some sleep. That is harder than it sounds. The C-130 is a loud aircraft—it helps if you wear earplugs—and it is an uncomfortable aircraft because there is nothing soft on which to lie down. We also, I remember thinking at the time, landed on every bloody rock in the Pacific to refuel. Midway, Wake, Saipan, Guam, Philippines—we did 'em all. Then over the South China Sea, south of Saigon, and a long, lazy approach that finally took us over Vietnam itself.

I climbed up the ladder to the cockpit and looked through the windshield. I'd expected an endless panoply of lush, tropical jungle. Instead, it was dull green and mottled brown, with square-mile sections of moonlike craters pitting earth the color of dried blood.

"Where the hell's the jungle?"

"Gone," the pilot explained. "B-52 strikes. Defoliants. Napalm."

I pondered that. "Where are we landing?"

"Binh Thuy."

"Big airfield?"

"Not so big. We always take rounds, too, so we're gonna make a fast approach. Once we're on the ground we like to move quick—so if you could get you and your stuff clear in a hurry, it'd be appreciated."

"That's a roger." I scurried down the ladder and found Kochey. "Pilot says we're dropping into a hot zone. What about locking and loading now?"

Kochey screwed his chin up and pondered. "The regs say we can't do that. It bothers the Air Force."

"I wonder if Charlie's read the regs."

Kochey pondered that for about half a second. Then he slammed me on the arm. "You're right. Tell 'em that anybody who wants to can lock and load."

I gathered my squad and we pulled M16s and magazines out of our canvas hang-up bags. We slammed home 30-round mags. Then, when the Air Force crew wasn't looking, we pulled the charging handles back—*raaatchet-click!*—and chambered rounds. Then we thumbed the M16 safeties to their horizontal ON position.

The Hercules was circling now, dipping its port wing as it

dropped lower and lower. We could hear the hydraulic whine of flaps extending, then the rumble of landing gear, and then, *ba-bump-ba-bump*, we were on the tarmac and taxiing, and the rear ramp was whining as it slowly lowered toward the ground. All thoughts of home vanished. My heart was pounding a steady *kaboom-kaboom* at a rate of about 120. Oh, this was going to be fun.

Chapter

7

IT SMELLED WARM AND HUMID AND NICE AND FRESH AND rustically pastoral, like pig dung. You know how when you climb off a plane there's that first whiff of strange, new air that tells you everything at once about where you are? The first whiff that came through the lowered ramp made me think of Puerto Rico, and I knew instantly that I was going to like Vietnam a whole lot.

I looked around. There were sandbags, and there were revetments for aircraft. There were Hueys *whomp-whomp-whomping* just above the tarmac. But there were also palm trees and rice paddies, and beyond the barbed wire and the minefields I could see farm hootches with chickens running in the yards and pigs rolling in the mud behind crude wood fences.

I stretched, raising my M16 over my head like a barbell, and sucked my lungs full of the beautifully humid, tropical, petroleum-laced air. Yeah. Puerto Rico. Panama. The aroma was definitely Third World. Strangely, for someone—me—who had never spent much time in the Third World, it was eerily like coming home.

Within a couple of hours we had settled in at Tre Noc,

about a mile away from the Binh Thuy air base. Tre Noc sits on the Bassac River, one of five major waterways that run through the Mekong Delta region. (From south to north they are the Mekong, Bassac, Co Chien, Ham Luong, and My Tho rivers. Each one follows a generally west-to-east course running from Cambodia into the South China Sea.) The Navy had a PBR—Patrol Boat/River—headquarters on the river at Tre Noc: Task Force 116.

We'd been assigned to 116 to support riverine operations in the region, which had been given the appropriate-sounding code name Game Warden. Our assignment was to help the PBRs interdict VC supplies that were shuttled on sampans or portaged through the shallows by bearers. We would also intercept VC couriers, kill or capture them, and pass whatever information they were carrying to Navy Intelligence.

We drove the couple of kilometers from Binh Thuy to Tre Noc half expecting to see tents and slit latrines when we arrived. From the scuttlebutt we'd heard before we left, living conditions at riverine HQ were primitive.

No way. As we drove up, I could see concrete buildings, air conditioners sticking out of a few windows, a good-sized mess hall, a large dock and mechanical emplacement, and an HQ complex that, while it wasn't Little Creek, was far better than anyone expected.

As soon as we pulled up, the four lieutenants—Jake Rhinebolt, Larry Bailey, Bob Gormly, and Fred Kochey—and I left the two platoons outside and wandered into the steamy HQ of Task Force 116, which was commanded by a senior officer who bore the title of commodore. We checked our paperwork in, then walked down the hall and rapped on the door of the commodore's office.

"Come."

We walked into a room hazy from cigarette smoke. The commodore, a captain in a grimy tan shirt, sleeves rolled to the biceps, waved us in without looking.

We snapped offhanded salutes in his direction.

The commodore looked up. His eyes wandered in our direction, then they focused on me. "Holy shit. You still pulling low, Marcinko, you geek?"

B. B. Witham, the former captain of LSD-114, the USS *Rushmore*, where I'd done my final cruise as an enlisted Frogman, mashed his omnipresent cigarette into the sawed-off shell casing he used as an ashtray, jumped up, slammed me on the shoulder, and pumped my right arm vigorously. "Son of a bitch."

Witham scrutinized the single-bar tabs on my collar. He reached out and touched them to make sure they were real. The crow's-feet around his eyes wrinkled into what I remembered as the New Englander's weather-beaten smile. "I never would've believed you made it through OCS."

Finally he took notice of the other four guys in the room, told them to stand at ease, and then slammed me on the chest good-naturedly. "This son of a bitch almost gave me a heart attack when he was an enlisted man and I commanded an LSD," he explained, joyfully punching me in the arm.

"Shit, sir," Rhinebolt, who was the senior SEAL, said earnestly, "he still does that. In training, he'd—"

"Good for Marcinko," the commodore interrupted. "Read my lips. If there's anything I like in an officer, it's consistency." He looked at me like a prodigal son. "Right, you geek asshole?"

What could I say. The man was a prince.

Then Witham sat us down and gave us the skinny about the quality of our lives in the foreseeable future. We'd live in one of the half dozen flat-roofed, one-story concrete buildings that were divvied up into four-man bunkrooms. We'd have a mess hall, showers—all the conveniences, even a hootch maid to keep our clothes clean. And she'd have her hands full, because Witham wanted to keep us busy. "You're gonna be spending a lot of time in the mud, so I hope you don't mind getting dirty." Finally, he kicked us out, told us to get squared away in a couple of hours, and then he'd see us for a beer later.

B. B. Witham was given to understatement. It took almost a week to square everything away. The ammo had to be stored, the equipment sorted and laid out, and our weapons cleaned. I quickly became a fanatic on clean weapons because I realized the climate would start ruining 'em within a few hours. Moisture, rust, mud, dust—we were constantly battling against them.

By the end of the third day I was getting restless. The quartet of lieutenants—Rhinebolt, Kochey, Bailey, and

Gormly—had choppered north to the Rung Sat Special Zone, a killer, 600-square-mile mangrove swamp that ran from just southeast of Saigon to the South China Sea, to visit SEAL Team One and eyeball the way the war was being fought. Their thought was to copy SEAL One's technique—set up a static ambush and wait for the enemy to show up.

Meanwhile, Boy Ensign and his merry band of junior idiots were left behind. We were too young to tag along, said the grown-ups.

"Get some rest," Jake Rhinebolt told me. "Go play with your toys."

So I sat and pouted and got some sun for about half a day. That was a loser. I hadn't come to sunbathe. I visited the intel shop, where I asked the pigeon-entrails readers how the VC in the area operated, and where they were most likely to be found. That evening, the six SEAL pups of Bravo shared a case of beer and plotted. When adults go off and leave the children unattended, all sorts of unforeseen adventures can occur.

The next morning, Eagle and I sauntered down to the dock and sweet-talked ourselves aboard a PBR for the morning patrol. The PBR is a wonderful craft. It's thirty-one feet long and runs on a Jacuzzi propulsion system, which means it has a shallow draft and it's fast—like about twenty-eight or twenty-nine knots—and very maneuverable. They were armed with twin .50-caliber machine guns in the bow, rifle-fired 81mm mortars astern, and Honeywell 40mm Gatling guns over the engine covers. The four- or five-man crews carried an assortment of M16s, M60 machine guns, as well as .45 automatics and an occasional .38. So—in addition to fast—the PBRs were deadly.

The crew cast off and we edged out into the opaque green-brown water. It wasn't eight o'clock yet and it was already more than ninety degrees. The humidity was fierce—you could almost see the air move if you chopped it with the edge of your hand. Over the engine growl I asked one of the deck crew if it was okay to stand by the conn, and receiving an affirmative nod, I clambered into the cockpit and sidled up next to the chief who had the wheel.

He was archetypal. He looked somewhere in his late thirties, with thinning, light-brown hair trimmed flattop above and white-wall on the sides. His ears stuck out like jug handles. A series of tattoos ran up his muscular forearms and disappeared under the smartly rolled sleeves of a weathered chambray work shirt. Most of the sailors who ran PBRs wore green or tan. Not this guy. He was an old-fashioned mother, and he wanted you to know it.

"Morning, Chief."

He spun the wheel out and the boat moved into the current. He applied a little more throttle now, moving us against the river. He kept his silence until we were well off the twin fingers of the dock. Then he ordered the gunners to clear their weapons. Finally he turned to me. "Morning . . . sir." There was a *thousand-one, thousand-two, thousand-three* pause between the first and second words.

I looked at the green underbrush that overlapped the riverbank, now fifty yards away. "Nice day for a cruise, Chief."

"If you say so . . . sir." He turned away and shouted a blankety-blank command to one of his aft-deck blankety-blanking crewmen.

I knew what he was thinking. Here was yet another gung ho, dipshit, puke ensign looking to punch his ticket, play a war game or two, and go home.

I waited until he turned back to the conn and ignored me for another ninety seconds. "Hey, fuck you, Chief."

That got his attention. "Say what?"

"I said, 'Hey, fuck you, Chief.' I'm here to learn—so break me in. Gimme a dump. Gimme a real no-fucking-shitter. What the motherfucking hell's goin' on out here?"

He spun the wheel again, shifting us more into the middle of the channel. He cut the throttle so we were moving steadily but very slowly. He reached under his flak jacket, pulled a Lucky out of his chambray shirt pocket, tamped it on the back of his watch, lit it, sucked deeply, then exhaled through his nose.

"You're a pus-nuts fucking smart-ass—sir."

"That's what they used to tell me in the teams."

A quizzical wrinkle of eyebrow. "You from the teams?"

"UDT-21 and 22. Five years."

"Where'd you do your cruises?"

I stuck my thumb back toward Tre Noc. "Last two were

with ol' B. B. Witham himself in the Med—aboard the *Rushmore*."

"The 114? No shit."

"No shit."

He turned his attention to the river, throttling down so that the boat barely moved against the current. Like hovering a chopper, it is a piloting move that takes training and experience. He pointed starboard. "There's a sandbar there. You'll want to watch it when you take your boats out."

"Roger, Chief."

"Cigarette?"

I shook my head.

"You ever do time in Naples?"

"Shit, Chief, every friggin' cruise. And before that I did a year there—worked as a radioman 1960–61."

"What was your rating?"

"In Naples? E-3, Chief—a 'designated striker.'"

He took a drag and exhaled a perfect smoke ring that hung in the humid air for what seemed an eternity. "I always liked fuckin' Naples. I did five years in Naples—'55 to '60. I got fat eating pasta and I got fuckin' laid a lot—I lived with a fuckin' *bella ragazza*—and I messed with the fuckin' officers. It was a great fuckin' tour."

"The ugliest fucking female officer I ever knew ran the motherfucking commo center in blanking Naples in 1960 and '61."

"I heard about her. Two-hundred-fuckin'-pounder."

"I used to call her Big FUC—Big Female Ugly Commander."

He half-cracked a smile but restrained himself from going any farther. "No shit." He looked me over, up and down, just like Ev Barrett used to. He took another drag on his cigarette, exhaled, then flicked it—a perfect parabolic arc into the Bassac. He watched it hiss then disappear in the brown water. "What the fuck you say your name was, son?"

I smiled the smile of the newly blessed. "Marcinko, Chief. Marcinko. But call me Rick."

Officers seldom listen to enlisted men enough. I do. I've made a habit of it. And I've learned a lot. From my newfound sea-daddy chief on the PBR, for example, I learned that Charlie had the habit of keying his ops to our PBR patrols. The officers at 116 had formatted the war. Operations were done by the book: constant and consistent. The result, the chief said, was that Charlie knew exactly how we operated.

What Charlie'd do is wait for a PBR to come by. Then he'd send a decoy—maybe a civilian, maybe a volunteer—across the river in a sampan or a raft. If the poor schnook got shot or captured, well, too bad. But Charlie had also surmised that, according to our official U.S. Navy method of operations, once an action was initiated, accomplished, and terminated, it was over—and the PBR would move on. After it chugged out of sight, the VC would mobilize their main supply convoys or troops or whatever and move across the river.

Decoy ruses work best if you can set your clocks by the enemy's operations, and the VC had been able to set theirs by the U.S. Navy. I was determined to change all that.

First, I had to see what kind of firepower I could assemble. About thirteen kilometers west of Tre Noc was a place called Juliet Crossing, which was a hotbed of VC activity. Just downriver from Juliet was a small island—maybe three hundred meters by one hundred meters. It was a free-fire zone: there were no friendlies anywhere on it.

The night after I'd taken the PBR cruise I took Bravo Squad and loaded up a pair of STABs—Seal Tactical Assault Boats. STABs are fiberglass jobs with dual 110-horsepower Mercury outboard engines. That's fast. Amidships, there's a .50-caliber machine gun mounted on a tripod. The forward gunwales have pintles for port and starboard M60 machine guns. We also carried shoulder-fired 57mm and 90mm recoilless rifles that fired both high-explosive and "beehive" rounds, which were filled with pellets and caused a lot of trauma if they hit someone.

We stowed enough ammo to sink the STABs by half a foot, then at about 1830 we went on a little pleasure cruise to Juliet Crossing. Patches Watson took the wheel of STAB One, and Bob Gallagher ran STAB Two about one hundred yards to my port flank.

We'd almost reached Juliet when Gallagher called me on the radio. "Mr. Rick?"

"Roger, Eagle."

"Look at the fish jumping behind us."

I looked behind me. Sure enough, there was a school of small, phosphorescent fish breaking the calm, dark surface of the river. I looked again. "Shit, Eagle, those aren't fish—it's fucking automatic weapons fire."

I slapped Patches on the shoulder. "Bring her around." I watched as the bullets followed us, *plink-plink-plink*. We couldn't hear anything because of the noise generated by our Mercs. But Charlie was sure as shit shooting at us, and the firing had to be coming from the free-fire island.

We watched, transfixed, as bullets hit the water. Next to me stood a SEAL named Harry Mattingly, who'd come along for the ride. All of a sudden he screamed, "Oh, shit—I've been hit."

I knocked him to the deck and looked. A ricochet had spun off the water and got him right between the eyes. He was bleeding like hell. But he was also okay—the wound was only superficial. His face had been less than a foot from mine— this shit was for real.

"You're one lucky son of a bitch," I said. "Get up and shoot back at 'em."

Patches spun the wheel, Gallagher followed, and both STABs headed for the far side of the river. I grabbed the radio mike. "I'll follow you in. When he starts firing at you, I'll spot the muzzle flashes and hit him with the recoilless. Then it'll be your turn."

For two hours we raked the island with everything we had, alternating Eagle's STAB and mine as we charged in, expended ammo, and veered away. From the pitiful amount of fire being returned, I guessed there were no more than one or two VC out there. But numbers didn't matter. What was important was that they'd shot at us, and we were returning fire.

At about twenty hundred I decided to call in aerial support. I got on the radio and requested Spooky, the call sign for a Puff the Magic Dragon—a C-47 equipped with four Vulcan Gatling guns that can each fire 6,300 rounds a minute.

"No can do without PROCOM—Vietnamese Provincial Commander—authorization, Silver Bullet," said the Air Force voice on the radio.

Silver Bullet was me—it was the most grandiose radio "handle" I could come up with on the spur of the moment. Authorization? No prob. I simply got the PROCOM out of bed and asked for fire support. "I got a hot one here, sir."

"Who are you?"

I told him.

He groaned audibly. "You American assholes are always making trouble." But he authorized my Spooky.

We watched as the plane floated one hundred meters above the island at about ninety knots. Even in the darkness we could see trees, bushes, and earth flying as the Vulcans raked the ground. Spooky made five slow, lethal passes and then wagged his wings, banked, and flew northward. I got him on the radio. "Thanks, guys. Silver Bullet over and out."

I called Gallagher. "Not bad, huh?"

"Right on—Ensign Silver Bullet." I could hear Eagle guffaw over the speaker. "Why didn't you just call yourself Hot Cock?"

"I would have if I'd thought of it." I swung my STAB to port. "Let's go home."

We'd had four hours of fun, and it was 2230 by now, high time for a few cold ones. "It's Miller time," I radioed Gallagher. We wheelied the STABs and hauled ass downriver like a goddamn twentieth-century armada. I couldn't stop smiling. We'd shot off every frigging bullet we'd carried with us, and we stunk of cordite and sweat. We smelled like the warriors we'd always wanted to be. War was great!

The natural high lasted until we reached dockside. I saw him from the river, some yahoo asshole jumping up and down like a monkey on a leash, his mouth working in four-quarter time.

As we got closer, I picked him out. It was the OPS boss, a lieutenant commander named Hank Mustin. Now, I didn't really know Mustin except by reputation. He was an Academy grad whose daddy and granddaddy were both admirals, all of which just impressed the shit out of little old arrogant me, right?

By the time we were within twenty yards I could hear him shouting over the throaty rumble of our twin Mercs. "Who the fuck are you calling in an air op without my authorization? Who gave you the goddamn authority to get the goddamn PROCOM out of his frigging bed? Who gave you permission to use this friggin' unit's call sign?"

To be honest, I'd never given any of those questions any consideration at all. You waged war, and that was that. You didn't put your hat in your hand and say, "May I?"

So I answered him back in kind. "Hey, you asshole, I came here to kick some fucking VC ass and take some fucking VC names—and that's what I fucking did tonight. And if you don't fucking like it, then fuck you and all your fucking kind, you sorry shit-for-brains cockbreath pencil-dick numb-nuts asshole."

He got absolutely white-faced, screamed, "You are in trouble, mister," and stomped off. I never gave the incident another thought, until the next afternoon.

Every day just after noon, Captain B. B. Witham used to lie in a hammock he'd strung alongside his commodore's hootch, to read, smoke, sip coffee, and work on his tan. The day after our escapade he called me over as I passed by on my way to chow.

He plucked off the blue baseball cap that covered his thick, closely cropped, gray-blond hair, thumbed his sunglasses onto his forehead, and squinted at me. "Dick, you're starting." He reached for a cigarette, lit it, and blew smoke in my direction. "You're in trouble already."

"Moi?"

"Oui, toi, mon petit phoc."

What the hell was he babbling? "What did I do?" I really didn't know.

Witham traded the cigarette for a mug of coffee, sipped, returned the cup to an ammo-crate table, and picked up his Marlboro again. "Do the words Hank and Mustin mean anything to you?"

"Ah, so—"

Witham rubbed his coarse blond mustache in irritation. "Don't 'ah so' me. He could bloody well get you court-martialed. He's a senior officer. He's got juice in Washington. He's an Academy grad. And he's not a bad guy—in fact, Ensign Geek, if you got to know him without his wanting to cut your balls off and fly 'em from the frigging flagpole, he could become a real help to you."

"Aye-aye, sir."

"Don't give me any of your 'aye-aye' horse-puckey either,

Dick. I'm serious when I say he can help you. Hank writes the ops plans."

"So? Big deal."

"You are the most arrogant s.o.b. ensign I have ever met." Witham took a drag of Marlboro. "Read my lips, Dick. He's the one who's designed the SEAL deployment out here."

"But he ain't a SEAL, sir. He's some Academy twit who tells me, 'When you run into the enemy, you have to ask me, "May I?" before you can fire one goddamn round.' "

"That's not what he's saying."

"That's how I read it."

"You go and shoot up a free-fire zone without telling anyone. You get the PROCOM out of bed to give you fire support and authorize it using the 116 Task Force—of which I am the goddamn commodore—call sign. And you're telling me that Hank Mustin is an asshole because he's upset? Screw him, Dick—*I'm* upset."

"Well—maybe I got a little steamed last night."

"Read my lips. Desist, desist, desist. You go around telling too many lieutenant commanders to go fuck themselves the way you did last night and they're gonna fly you out of here in shackles."

"Okay, I got it. Wilco."

Witham shook his head. "Good." He paused and sipped his coffee. "Fact is, there has to be some sort of order to things around here, Dick."

"I agree. But the way it looks to me, Skipper, everyone around here thinks very conventionally. You ride the boats, you listen to the chiefs. From what I hear, Charlie knows what we're gonna do because we run everything by the book."

"So?"

"So it's time for a new book—something he hasn't read yet."

Witham shook his head. "We've got a new book. And Hank Mustin wrote it—SEALs will support riverine operations, and—"

"Skipper, *we're* the ones who should have written our own plan. He sees SEALs as support units. Screw it, Skipper— Hank Mustin may be a terrific guy, but what he's designed is conventional, Academy Navy pus-nuts thinking. For chrissakes, Skipper, SEALs're supposed to be unconventional.

That means *not* by the book." I waited while he sipped his coffee. "I didn't come here to sit and wait for Charlie to find me, Skipper. I want to kick Charlie's ass on his own turf. *That's* unconventional."

"Like you did last night?"

"Hey—last night was just a rehearsal. I wanted to give my guys some practice before we went out for real."

Witham sighed. "I'll tell you something, Dick. There's no practice out here—no rehearsal. Every bloody day is for real. You want to expend four hours' worth of my ammo, then bring me back a VC prisoner or some intel or something else I can use."

He was right. Dammit—he was right.

His tone softened. "Did you at least *get* anything out there?"

"If there was anything on that island, Skipper, it wasn't moving after we got done. We came home bone-dry. Not a round left—even in the M16s."

"Boy, you do like living dangerously." He shook his head. "Look—stay out of Hank Mustin's way for a couple of weeks. I'll smooth things over, and you'll end up friends. But Jesus —what a way to start."

He slid his sunglasses down, replaced the long-visored cap, and picked up his paperback. "Dismissed, Ensign Geek."

Chapter

8

BRAVO SQUAD DIDN'T SEE ANY ACTION FOR ABOUT A WEEK after my little escapade. I was the junior man, and it was decided by the lieutenants that combat patrols would be assigned in order of seniority. Bravo had to wait until last. Finally, after what we considered an interminable lull, we got to go.

I'd obtained some intel about VC activity at Juliet Crossing, close to the free-fire island where we'd tested our firepower. Now, Bravo would try its luck there again, this time in what I hoped would be a face-to-face confrontation with Mr. Charlie.

We planned a textbook riverine operation. "Consider this a KISS mission—Keep It Simple, Stupid," I told my guys. And indeed, the plan was so elementary it could have been designed by Hank Mustin. We'd insert onto the westernmost tip of the free-fire island, which overlooked Juliet Crossing, a major north-south VC transverse point on the Bassac River. There, we'd wait for a VC courier to show himself. We would ambush and kill him, recover whatever intelligence we could, bring it back to Skipper Witham, receive a pat on the head and an "attaboy," then go find some cold beer and party.

The killing was an important element for a couple of reasons. First, that's what we were in Vietnam for. Second, you never know whether you can kill someone until you do it. I wanted to make sure that each member of Bravo was up to the task. It could prove deadly to the squad if even one man was reticent. We left Tre Noc just after sundown, all of us in a single STAB. We'd blacked out our faces and hands and wore camouflage greens, jungle boots, soft caps, and web gear, and we carried one canteen, our assault knives, and lots and lots of bullets and grenades.

We were part of a miniflotilla. One of the SEAL Two lieutenants, Larry Bailey, took command of one Mike boat —an armored Landing Craft, Medium, or LCM—which held an 81-mike-mike (81mm mortar), plus pairs of M60 and .50-caliber machine guns. A second Mike boat was commanded by a SEAL One officer on TAD from Rung Sat Zone. He was a pretty-boy bleach-blond California surfer I'll call Lt. Adam Henry. I didn't like him. We were also joined by one of 116's PBRs, with its machine guns and 40mm Gatling. If we got into trouble, Adam would play John Wayne—he'd shoot the hell out of Charlie, while the STAB would hit the shoreline and extract us in a hurry. Larry's mission was to sniff and snuff out any VC crossing the river upstream.

As I think about it now, Larry would have been a better choice for the John Wayne role. A dark, lanky Texas boy with eyes like a cobra's, he'd been the most aggressive of the lieutenants during our predeployment training. It was a foregone conclusion that Larry would be SEAL Team Two's tiger in Vietnam.

The boats drew abreast of our target area. The STAB moved toward the island at six knots while the PBR and both Mike boats continued on a course upriver. Adam should not have gone along. The growls from their heavy engines and the STAB's Mercs would cover any noise made by our insertion, while the larger boats would also prevent any VC at Juliet Crossing, or serving as lookouts on the riverbank, from seeing us drop off the STAB. We were sixty yards south of the island, and just east of the tip. I tapped Patches Watson. He rolled over the far gunwale and dropped into the warm water. Now Ron Rodger went. Then me, Joe Camp, Jim Finley, and last, Eagle Gallagher.

The STAB continued upriver, disappearing into the darkness. Faces half out of the water, we dog-paddled slowly toward the island, moving as quietly as we could. Eight yards off the southern bank I dropped my feet down and was immediately sucked into ooze that covered my boots. I kicked free and dog-paddled again until my knees touched the muddy bottom.

I moved cautiously onto the bank, which was overgrown with vegetation, slid my M16 over my head, and flipped off the safety.

I waited. The lap of the water was interrupted by the sound of the other SEALs as they arrived one by one. I peered. We were all present and accounted for. I gave hand signals: move up the bank; spread into preassigned positions; set up the perimeter.

The drone of the boats was now quite distant. I shivered in the cool evening air. I would never have thought I'd shiver in Vietnam, but I was cold.

We crawled up the bank, moving mere inches at a time along the fifty-yard-wide tip of the island, until we'd set ourselves up in ambush position behind the stump of a downed tree. Four of us—Patches Watson, Camp the radioman, Ron Rodger with his Stoner machine gun, and I—separated into two pairs eight yards apart and scrutinized the southern shore of the river, a spit of sand and mud a hundred and fifty yards away, for any hint of movement. Jim Finley and Eagle Gallagher took rear guard, fifteen yards inland, and covered our butts.

By now I couldn't hear the support boats at all, and I was suddenly overcome by an incredible sensation of aloneness. Simultaneously, I was struck by a degree of paranoia I'd never known before. Shit—we were actually out in the jungle with live weapons and people who wanted to kill us. If this was a trap, if Charlie was laying for us—Jesus. I shook myself out of it. I blinked, squeezing my eyes tight and then releasing, to control the hyper stage into which I was rocketing. I tried breathing-control exercises. They worked. I relaxed.

The dial on my watch read 2140. It'd taken us about twenty minutes to crawl through twenty-five yards of jungle scrub and river grass into our ambush position. So far, we'd been on station half an hour. The island had accepted our arrival

ROGUE WARRIOR

and was alive again with the sounds of unknown critters that chirped and whistled and buzzed all around us. I found the ambient noise to be loud and decided it was accentuated by my alert condition.

We hadn't spoken a word since we'd left the STAB. We didn't have to.

I looked up. The sky was as clear as I'd ever seen it. The stars—millions of them—shone as brightly as if it were a crisp fall night in New England. The air had turned quite cool, and my teeth started to chatter. I forced my jaws together to stop. How goddamn incongruous. To be cold in the tropical jungle. I thought about Ev Barrett, and Mud, and pulling low on my last Med cruise. I thought about St. Thomas—rum and Coke and humping that wonderful, big-titted schoolteacher from New Jersey. I thought that maybe tomorrow I'd write a postcard to each of my kids. Souvenirs for them when they learned to read. I remembered how terrified I was the first time the freight train pinned me against the wall in the tunnel to Hauto when I was seven.

Then I heard it. *Creak-creak*.

The hair on the back of my neck stood up. I got goose bumps.

Creak-creak. Wood on wood. An oar in an oarlock. *Creak-creak*.

From the sandspit opposite where we lay, the nose of a small sampan poked into the slow-moving river.

I raised my finger slowly. Wait. He's 150 yards away. He'll come closer. Don't spoil it by going too soon. I held my breath. Not a hair on any of my guys moved, even though four weapons were following the sampan.

He came across slowly, slowly, agonizingly slowly. One Vietnamese in black pajamas, no hat, no visible gun; an Asian gondolier, his single oar stirring a creaky, steady "J" stroke against the Bassac's sluggish current. He came right at us.

I let the first shot go when he was less than twenty feet away. The others fired so quickly after my round that the poor guy must have thought he was looking down one big 16-inch barrel. Whatever he was thinking, it was the last thought he ever had. All of us hit him simultaneously with full 30-round mags. But it was Ron Rodger's Stoner that really did

99

the damage—a hundred and fifty rounds of .223, every twentieth round a tracer.

"Let's go." I was up on my feet, scrambling for the bank. I charged down to grab the VC's body and empty what I could from the shredded sampan before it sank.

Patches was hot on my tail. Ron Rodger wasn't far behind.

I sloshed through the water, my feet sticking in the mud. The sampan began to slip into the water. It became a footrace. I was swimming now.

"Come on."

Patches and I reached the sampan first. I pulled myself over the gunwales. The inside of the boat was covered with blood, bone fragments, and shreds of black pajama. But it was empty except for a small cloth pouch, which I grabbed.

"Find him," I shouted.

Patches dove. I followed. We came up empty. He'd probably been blown backward into the water by the Stoner. Shit.

We were dragging at the sampan when the water around my head started kicking up. From the bank, Joe Camp pointed. "Automatic fire—eleven o'clock." He dropped to the ground and let a full mag of covering fire go over our heads. "Get your asses back to shore."

Patches and I swam like hell, dragging the sampan, and made it to the bank. We scrambled up and over, back into our firing positions, and I dove for the radio. The M16s and the Stoner didn't have the range we needed. It was time to call in the cavalry—the PBR and Mike boat, which had .50-caliber, the .57 recoilless, and mortars.

I grabbed the receiver from Joe Camp. I gave our call sign and coordinates. No answer. Only static. I tried again and again without success.

Eagle Gallagher's urgent voice cut through the firefight. "They're coming from the back side, Mr. Rick."

Were there VC on the island? I wasn't about to take chances with my men. "Use grenades. Frags and WPs." WPs were the white phosphorus kind that burned brightly. And God help anyone hit by one.

We took fire for maybe eight or ten minutes—an eternity —while I called and called for the PBR or Mike boat. Finally, one of the STABs showed up. We moved down the bank, shouting for covering fire as we slithered, ducked, and rolled our way through the jungle underbrush, as VC bullets sliced the leaves just over our heads or dug divots too close for comfort as we scrambled toward the STAB. I jumped for the boat only to discover that there were already three PBR sailors in it, as well as the two-man crew. STABs are only supposed to hold nine. This one now held eleven, and it was heavy.

I waved my squad aboard. The STAB reversed its twin Mercs and backed off the island—onto a sandbar. As the sailors fired over our heads, Patches, Finley, and I went over the side, floated the boat clear, reboarded, and hauled ass.

I was furious. That is an understatement. I wanted to *kill* somebody. "Where's Henry's Mike boat? Where's the PBR? What are these crewmen doing here?"

A sailor said, "Lieutenant Henry saw a sampan and gave chase. He didn't think you'd have any problems so he took the two other boats and sent us back for you."

Christ, he was supposed to be backing my mission up, not chasing VC sampans. If Charlie'd fielded a sizable contingent, Bravo Squad would be hamburger by now, thanks to Adam Henry. Goddamn it to hell. I checked my guys over to make sure we had all our fingers and toes, then looked up to notice we were heading away from Tre Noc, moving farther upriver.

I grabbed a sailor by the flak jacket. "What the hell's going on?"

"Lieutenant Henry wants you."

"Hey, my guys are cold and wet. Let's turn this thing around."

"No can do, sir."

I considered the possibilities. Maybe Adam was in trouble and needed us to save *his* ass. It was unlikely, but not totally impossible. We sat hunkered on the deck and I steamed for fifteen minutes until we reached Henry's Mike boat and tied up to its onshore side as it chugged steadily up the river. I clambered up and found Henry. "What the hell's up, Adam? You in trouble?"

He shook his head. "Nah—there's an outpost under attack about two clicks from here. I want to go support it."

"Screw that. I'm gonna take my guys and go home."

He put a restraining hand on my web-gear suspenders. "No,

Dick, I may need you. It's better if you ride the Mike boat with me. The STAB is too small, and besides, it's unarmored."

I removed his hand delicately. "Look, schmuck, it is now almost twenty-three hundred. My guys made their bones tonight—we got ourselves a VC courier, and we got him good. Why not let us take our toys and go home. We don't want to play with you right now."

"Play?" His baby blues seemed to darken. "What the hell do you think this is, Marcinko—a game?"

"Hey, asshole, the only games that are being played right now are the ones you're trying to run on me."

"What the hell you mean by that?"

"I mean that you fuckin' left me hanging out there to dry. You were supposed to be supporting me—not looking for your own goddamn VC to shoot at."

"If things had really been bad enough, I'd have been there."

"Really?"

"That's a roger, Dick, and you know it."

"I don't know what you would or wouldn't do." I grabbed two handfuls of Henry's shirt and brought us nose to nose. "Listen, you dipshit pus-nuts pencil-dicked asshole scumbag, we took automatic weapons fire from two directions. Is *that* bad enough for you? The STAB you finally sent to snatch us was filled with frigging sight-seeing sailors—and we got stuck on a goddamn sandbar while Charlie made bang-bang at us. Is *that* bad enough for you? I pleaded for covering fire and you were so goddamn far upriver you were out of goddamn radio range. Is *that* bad enough for you, you pussy?"

I shoved him up against the cockpit bulkhead, popping his back against the gray metal with every other syllable. "I *mean*, old *pal* of *mine*, just *how* the *fuck* do you define 'bad enough'?" He sagged into a sitting position and just stayed there, his eyes unfocused. I felt like breaking the son of a bitch's neck. Instead, I retreated to the portion of the deck where my squad now was. (Asked about this incident today, Larry says it never happened.)

We watched, sodden, cold, and miserable, as Adam ordered the Mike boat into firing position. The incredible high we'd experienced only a few minutes before had totally evaporated. We'd been transformed from warriors into spectators by this insensitive, unproven asshole. He was trying to get himself a kill, but he was doing it at the expense of my men, and I didn't like that one bit.

To add injury to insult, when he commenced firing, I saw that his red-hot .50-caliber machine gun casings were raining down on my STAB, with its open cockpit and exposed gas tanks. Worse, since the STAB had been moored to the on-shore side of the Mike boat, it was being shot at by the bad guys. Mike boats are armored. STABs are fiberglass.

After about five minutes of Henry's screwups, I'd had enough. "Come on, guys, we're going home."

We rolled over the side, unmindful of incoming fire, the Mike boat's hot .50-caliber casings, and the water plumes made by VC mortar rounds. We jumped into the STAB. Gallagher hit the starter, Jim Finley and Patches Watson cut the tether lines, while Joe Camp and Ron Rodger laid down some covering fire.

I grabbed the wheel, peeled away, and put the pedal to the metal. The twin Mercs slalomed us easily through the water-spouts of enemy fire. I veered sharply, cut the STAB's sleek hull around the back of the Mike boat, and headed downriver at top speed. I could see Adam Henry's face as we sped away. He was shouting something at me, but it was impossible to hear anything over the roar of the Mercs. I saluted him with my middle finger.

The following week, Bravo Squad and I bid a not-so-fond farewell to Tre Noc. Skipper Witham, no fool, realized I was going to kill Henry, or that Hank Mustin was going to have me carted off in chains to Leavenworth.

So it was decided that Marcinko's Merry Band of Murdering Marauders would move forty kilometers northeast to My Tho. There, the Navy kept a PBR flotilla on the river. And there, Commodore Witham decreed, safely out of Hank Mustin's way, I could broaden the horizons of SEAL deployment on the Delta without the temptation to kill any of my fellow American officers with my bare hands in the process.

The senior man at My Tho turned out to be a terrific officer named Toole, a commander, who had never worked with SEALs before but had the good sense to leave me alone, just as long as I gave him results. Toole was an uncommon Navy boss, a lean, mean, caustic, wry curmudgeon whose aggressiveness was a big bolster for Bravo's morale at My Tho. He wore olive-drab jungle fatigues instead of an officer's tan blouse and slacks. He trusted his chiefs. He'd prowl the PBRs and tinker with the .50-caliber guns. He'd actually go out to see what action was like.

Best of all, he didn't second-guess me or set up parameters that confined us. He realized instinctively that SEALs are unconventional warriors and encouraged me to be as unconventional as I thought prudent and effective. Bravo was responsible for covering a 60-mile section of river, along with its innumerable canals, tributaries, bayous, brooks, streams, creeks, and ditches.

My Tho was more rustic than Tre Noc. The PBR dock was jerry-built—wood planks atop floating 50-gallon oil drums, attached to a pair of flimsy pilings. The offices, shops, and supply lockers were right alongside the river in Butler buildings—Tinkertoy structures of concrete slab and aluminum siding—or Quonset huts. Decidedly unfancy. We did, however, live well. Two blocks from the river was an old European-style hotel—it could have been transplanted from Hemingway's Paris—where all the Americans slept. There were creaky fans suspended from high ceilings, louvered windows, and French furniture.

By now we'd grown accustomed to Vietnamese cooking, and although there was Western-style food both at the hotel and the Navy installation, we'd visit the innumerable vendors on our way to and from the river each day, tasting and experimenting. In fact, Jim Finley—the "Mayor"—somehow managed within hours of our arrival to slip away and discover the best dozen food hootches. By the time the rest of us found the time to get out and about, he guided us from stall to stall and we were greeted like long-lost family.

We started our patrols slowly, riding the river with the PBRs, talking to the chiefs, learning what Charlie's routes were, when he crossed the river, where he staged his crossings, and why he was moving. Then came short patrols—night insertions like the one we did out of Tre Noc—and static ambushes. I called those patrols "Mustins" because that's how Hank had envisaged SEAL deployment—as support for the full spectrum of riverine operations. But I wanted to go beyond Mustins, to "Mar-chinkos."

"Mar-chinkos" entailed longer patrols—twelve, eighteen, even twenty hours in the Delta—and different tactics. Aggressive tactics. It made sense to me that the closer to the Delta Charlie got, the more alert he became. And why? Because that's where the PBRs and Mike boats and SEALs were. But when Charlie was still staging his convoys, three hundred, five hundred, seven hundred meters away from the river, he was relaxed—because he was on his own turf.

I knew instinctively that the earlier I could hit Charlie the more damage I'd cause. But I knew we couldn't go balls to the wall quite yet. We were still green; still learning the ways of the jungle. So, like the first days of UDT training, I did nothing outrageous. Instead, I built the squad's confidence with soft hits, patrols that were guaranteed to include VC kills without endangering Bravo. But each time we patrolled, I'd take us farther and farther up the canals. When Bravo was comfortable with the canals, we extended onto the dikes. We began yards at a time, until we were comfortable moving a kilometer or two. We snatched our first prisoner—Patches Watson and Eagle Gallagher came up out of a bunch of reeds and almost gave the poor asshole a heart attack—and interrogated him before turning him over to the ARVN, the Army of the Republic of Vietnam, which I normally referred to as Marvin the ARVN.

After about a month I started pushing the guys more. We'd insert at night, roll off a STAB, swim up a canal, clamber onto a dike or footpath, and set up an ambush three hundred or four hundred yards farther inland than Charlie ever expected us to be. As we became more confident, we moved farther and farther up-country from the river, running the dike trails over which VC couriers carried intelligence, and ambushing sampan convoys as they loaded the goods that had been carried down through Cambodia from Hanoi along the Ho Chi Minh Trail.

We learned about intelligence, and what to look for. At first we left some of the VC's personal stuff behind. Now I realized it was important source material, and we took everything we could get our hands on. Forget all those TV-movie scenes of the grunt who finds the picture of the dead VC's kids and wife and goes to sentimental pieces as he realizes he's just killed a fellow human being. Scenes like that are probably written by people who've never had shots fired at them in anger.

Fact is, Comrade Victor Charlie wanted us dead, deader, deadest. And if taking a cute snapshot or a letter from a VC corpse somehow helped us in the effort to get him first, then too bad for Mr. Charlie, Mrs. Charlie, and all the little Charlies.

I also used to booby-trap our VC kills. The enemy often booby-trapped their own dead, so we did it to them, too. It made me feel good to hear an explosion after we'd left the area. One less Charlie to shoot at us—maybe more.

This probably sounds as if I were a cold, unfeeling, chilled-out dude in Vietnam. Fact is, there's very little time for introspection on the battlefield. We saw the enemy up close and personal on a daily basis, and we sometimes had to look him in the eyes as we killed him. It gives you a different perspective.

What you learn very quickly is that your men—your unit —are everything. Like a mafioso, you take an oath of blood with your men. You cherish them, nurture them, protect them. You keep their foibles to yourself. You must be completely loyal to them—and they will be the same to you.

I regard my first Vietnam tour as a sort of SpecWar Genesis, in which I was re-created out of the primal mud of the Delta and the purifying heat of our gunfire. In the beginning, I was a green ensign who'd spent his whole life talking about kicking ass and taking names, but had never done it.

Then came the evening and the morning of my First Day —the free-fire island, where I went to create noise and play with my toys.

The evening and the morning of my Second Day was the courier ambush, where I learned how to use the water and the land to my advantage, and how to kill my enemy.

The evening and the morning of my Third Day I learned to treasure the fruits of intelligence, and I began to harvest every scrap of paper so we could learn where Charlie's head was at.

The evening and the morning of my Fourth Day I learned not to set patterns, and so I began to work both day and night patrols, selecting targets of opportunity instead of coming back to the same places again and again.

The evening and the morning of my Fifth Day I began to encourage our support systems to "Be fruitful and multiply." And verily, there were choppers and Spookies as well as Mike boats and PBRs, and they were good and they were deadly and they helped me kill my enemies.

The evening and the morning of my Sixth Day I began creating operations in my own image—expanding their range and their ferocity and their potency by weaving scores of disparate strands together. I began listening to Marvin the ARVN's intelligence as well as our own; I began taking *chu-hoi*—VC defectors—on patrols, watching how they moved on the trails and paying close attention to the way they talked to the locals, or looked for booby traps and hidden bunkers, so I could teach my SEALs how to copy their techniques.

In fact, the VC changed the way I looked at waging war. Charlie was pretty good at war—I had to be better. So I stole what worked and discarded what didn't. I revamped things as basic as the way we patrolled: from Charlie, for example, I learned to travel light. By the early spring of 1967 we were carrying one canteen instead of the regulation two, substituting bullets and grenades for the water weight. We took no food—there was no reason to leave garbage behind, and in any case we were never in the field long enough to require rations. We modified our field gear, leaving packs behind in favor of load-bearing vests, into which we punched holes so the pockets would drain both mud and water immediately. We took no changes of clothing, or ponchos. We slept in the open, camouflaging ourselves with whatever we had around us. Like the VC, we became guerrillas—living off the land instead of acting like invaders.

The techniques worked. Bravo was undinged, except for a few scrapes, bruises, and minor wounds. No serious casualties; no KIAs. As we became more familiar with the region, our deadly efficiency increased. That made me happy. It made Skipper Toole ecstatic.

And after I had learned all of these things and was proficient in the art of stalking and killing, it was the evening and the morning of my Seventh Day.

According to the Bible, on the Seventh Day, God rested. But for SEALs, the evening and the morning of the Seventh Day is the time to go out and annihilate the enemy. The God of SEALs, after all, is Yahweh—the Old Testament God—the tough, harsh, severe, vengeful, eye-for-an-eye desert deity; the God who said, "Go and smite Amalek, and utterly destroy all that they have, and spare them not. . . ."

Let me put it another way: we each have our own personal vision of the Supreme Being. In *my* mind, God is a UDT master chief petty officer. He sounds just like Ev Barrett. And he doesn't give time off for good behavior.

The evening and the morning of my Seventh Day fell on May 18, 1967, at the mouth of the Mekong Delta, on a thickly jungled piece of real estate called Ilo-Ilo Island.

Chapter
9

BY MID-APRIL, FRED KOCHEY AND HIS ALFA SQUAD HAD LEFT Tre Noc and joined me at My Tho. There was enough action for two squads, and Fred, like me, preferred an aggressive style of patrolling. By May we were within a couple of weeks of ending our tour, which meant no more patrols. Instead, our time would be spent packing equipment, some of which would be shipped back with us to Little Creek, while the rest would remain behind in containers for the next SEAL Team Two contingent.

I had mixed emotions about leaving. I considered my tour a success. Bravo had done roughly fifty patrols over our five and a half months in-country. We'd learned how to use the jungle to our advantage. We'd refined our techniques—the unit-integrity theme I'd preached during training had really taken root. Now we could move, think, and fight as one man. But we hadn't had a single operation that put everything we'd learned to the test. We'd harass Charlie; we'd take prisoners, shoot up sampans, burn his supplies. Sometimes we'd kill him—Bravo Squad had eighteen confirmed VC kills and five probables on the books by the time we left—and I believed the "probable" figure was at the very low end of the scale.

Yet we hadn't run what I thought of as a major operation—something that really hurt Mr. Charlie bad. That was where Ilo-Ilo Island came in.

I'd been hearing about Ilo-Ilo for months. There was nothing on it from the NILO—Naval Intelligence Liaison Officer—at My Tho, but then Naval Intelligence, which some people believe is an oxymoron, was usually about ninety days old when they finally got around to disseminating it at the squad level. It was always my sense that the Navy never felt intel could be as useful to field units as it was to admirals. So, while the intel squirrels were great at collecting their factoid nuts, and analyzing what they had, and wrote briefing papers and memos by the ream, they hardly ever sent anything back our way. Which says something about the way the Navy fought wars, even then.

The problem with intelligence-gathering in those days (and to a great extent today as well) is that virtually all military intelligence collection is geared toward supporting—and therefore reporting about—large units. And yet for a SEAL, even a 100-man company is a major overload if you run into one on a narrow jungle trail.

Despite the fact that the Navy didn't know about Ilo-Ilo, its name kept cropping up elsewhere. Village chiefs from up and down the river mentioned it. VC prisoners talked about it. *Chu-hoi* gossiped about it. Marvin the ARVN's intelligence gophers would chatter about it. Marvin believed it to be a big VC R&R center, where Charlie would send his guys after they'd been harassing us. The *chu-hoi* thought it was a staging area for VC strikes north into the Rung Sat Zone, or the northeastern portion of the Mekong Delta. Whatever it was, I felt it was worth a trip to find out.

Ilo-Ilo sat in the mouth of the Delta, where the My Tho River ran into the South China Sea. A nutmeg-shaped island, it lay three-eighths of a mile from either shore. It wasn't all that large—perhaps half a mile long and a thousand feet wide. At its western tip was a big canal that ran eastward in a series of S-curves, cutting through some incredibly thick underbrush, until it finally seemed to peter out. On the opposite —easternmost—side, another series of smaller canals ran into the ocean. From the air, they looked like spiderwebs as they snaked north and south in random geometric patterns.

It seemed to me Ilo-Ilo was ideal real estate for a major VC encampment. It had the same trio of prerequisites as a good investment property anywhere in the world: location, location, and location. And best, it was virgin territory: there had never been an American operation there. I took my idea to Commander Toole. He approved a daytime operation. I told Fred Kochey about it, too.

"Sounds like fun, Rick. Mind if I come along for the ride?"

That was fine with me. I liked Kochey. Like me, he was a Pennsylvania boy. Unlike me, he was one of those perpetually calm, unflappable types. If the two of us ran three miles, I'd be sweating buckets when we finished; Kochey, a slightly built guy about six feet tall, would look as cool as when he'd started. He was a methodical, thorough planner. Best of all, he was dependable in combat—in fact, combat was the only time Fred would actually get excited. "Sure—it'll be fun to have you come play with us if you want. But you gotta bring your own toys."

Ilo-Ilo was forty miles downriver from My Tho, too long a run for STABs. So early on the morning of May 18, we tied a STAB alongside our Mike boat, piled on as much ammo as we could carry without drowning, and chugged down the river at a steady eight knots.

The day was typical Vietnamese Mekong Delta spring weather: ninety degrees, 100 percent humidity. In our tigerstripe camouflage and blackened faces we sweltered. The trip down the river took four, seemingly endless, hours. We arrived just before noon to a nasty surprise—huge quantities of Delta mud. As we neared Ilo-Ilo, the Mike boat almost ran aground on a series of sandbars clogging the channel. The problem was silt that had probably traveled all the way from Cambodia. But wherever it had come from, it was a definite bummer. It was impossible to make the head-on approach that had, from the map, appeared to be the most effective way of inserting onto the island.

When in doubt, improvise. So Bravo, Kochey, and I dropped into the STAB, and with the Mike boat *chunka-chunking* offshore, we went round the back to see if there was another way in from the ocean side.

We rounded the southwest tip of the island, feinted a couple of times to confuse anybody who might have been watching, then rolled off the STAB on the offshore side and swam into the biggest of the canals. Even swimming, mud was a factor because the water was loaded with silt. It got worse as we moved forward, chest deep in the canal. The bottom was sticky as hot tar, making our progress slow—and worse, noisy.

The mud went everywhere: pockets, boots, guns, magazines. After an eighth of a mile in the canal we dragged ourselves up onto the bank, set up a defensive perimeter, and spent half an hour cleaning weapons. The silt was so bad we had to disassemble our M16 30-round magazines and rinse the springs and followers clean. There was almost an inch of silt at the bottom of each mag—more than enough to make them totally unusable.

The temperature had risen to about one hundred. The men were already bitching. I could hear Eagle Gallagher muttering to Fred Kochey about crazy Mr. Rick, his screwed-up notions about patrols, and the quality of the mud in the canal. Patches Watson looked skyward and asked the Lord what he'd done to deserve this unhappy fate.

Ron Rodger played the God role: "Because you piss me off, my son," he said in a booming basso profundo.

I've always believed a bitching sailor is a happy sailor, so I decided to make the men ecstatic by leaving the smaller canals. Instead, we'd blaze a trail through the thick, thornbush underbrush toward the center of the island. There, I hoped to find the major canal and follow its meandering S-curves westward. If there were any VC on Ilo-Ilo—and I was convinced there were—they'd be adjacent to that main canal.

We moved out to the sounds of rumbling clouds and grumbling SEALs. Patches Watson took the point. After him, Ron Rodger and the Stoner machine gun. Then me, followed by Camp, Finley, Kochey, and Eagle Gallagher. We found a few trails, although they obviously hadn't been used in some time. Still, we stayed away—no sense running into hostile strangers—and hacked a new path, spacing ourselves at five-yard intervals, watching carefully for any sign of Mr. Charlie.

It was tough work, and we measured out progress in feet, not yards. The brunt was born by Patches Watson, who had the point. It was he who did the most cutting, chopping with his machete while simultaneously staying alert for trip wires, booby traps, and pungi pits.

Ilo-Ilo was different from any place I'd seen in Vietnam. The vegetation was more like one of the Virginia or North Carolina coastal islands than Southeast Asian jungle. At the shoreline there were no palm trees; instead we found dense, tough saplings, thorn bushes, and heavy vines that had to be cut with machetes. As we progressed inland, it grew more tropical, with palms, big-leafed jungle plants, and the tall marsh grasses we were accustomed to in the Delta. Just before two P.M., it rained. The coolness was welcome—there was steam coming off us as the water cascaded down for about fifteen minutes, then eased to a drizzle. Finally, it stopped. We didn't.

Patches Watson held up his hand. I signaled for a break. He slid his machete back into its sheath, made his way back up the line to where I hunkered, and sat down heavily, leaning on his CAR-15. His uniform had tripled in weight from the Delta water, rain, and perspiration.

"Mr. Rick?"

"Yo."

"Screw this shit. I've had it."

"You tired?"

"Tired? I'm bleeping ragged. There's nothing here."

"Says you?"

"Says the damn jungle, Mr. Rick—loud and clear. This op is an Adam Henry goatfuck—we're gonna come up dry. I can't see six feet in front of me. Let's go back to the boat."

I shook my head. "I love you Patches, but you're outta here. If you don't think we're gonna find anything, you ain't gonna keep a sharp eye. We need a fresh man on point because there's VC—somewhere. I can smell it."

I waved at Camp. "Joe—take another minute, then relieve Patches."

Camp nodded. We'd just gotten to our feet, and Camp hadn't gone three meters, when his hand went up, signaling me forward.

I halted the column, then moved ahead to Camp's position. Camp pointed. I looked. It was a canal, perhaps ten feet wide. On the far side was a good-sized bamboo hootch, built on stilts five or six feet off the ground to protect it from the tidal surges. Eureka. We'd hit pay dirt. I waved Patches Watson forward and pointed.

"Holy shit. Well, mud-suck me, Mr. Rick."

"You said it, I didn't."

I gave hand signals. Two men flanked right, three of us took the center, and two flanked left. Moving silently, we slid through the low vegetation, over the bank, and down into the canal, submerged ourselves up to our necks, and dog-paddled across. We lay on our backs on the far side, protected by the natural roll of the four-foot berm. Our weapons were balanced on our chests.

I signaled to Gallagher and Patches. They went up the bank and scrambled toward the hootch. Seconds later they rolled back over the top and dropped into the canal, all excited.

Gallagher was absolutely ebullient: "It's empty, Mr. Rick —but Charlie was there. He was there. Only a couple hours ago, too. There's a cooking fire and it's still warm."

"Great." I drew a circle in the air with my index finger. We pulled ourselves up the bank, put out perimeter guards, and searched the hootch. There were big tins of medical equipment, some paperwork, and a few odds and ends. We took what we could carry and set fire to the rest. I got on the radio to the Mike boat.

"Bravo to Docksider."

"This is Docksider."

"We're hitting pay dirt, so don't you guys be sunbathing out there."

"Roger Bravo. What's your location?"

"We're moving up the big canal toward the main exit."

"Roger-roger, Bravo. We'll be waiting."

We divvied up the VC booty, stuffing it into the pockets of our fatigues. Then we started moving westward in the canal, taking it slow and easy. Moving in water was certainly easier than hacking our way through vegetation, but nowhere was it written that Charlie wouldn't booby-trap canals the way he did jungle paths, so we kept our eyes open. We moved in a crouch, protecting ourselves from being seen by using the water and the berm, which rose three to four feet, to mask our movements.

We hadn't gone three hundred yards when we came around a sharp, leftward curve and the strong smell of smoke hit us.

It's amazing how often in the Delta that would happen: we wouldn't hear, see, or smell anything until we were right on top of it. It was as if the jungle were divided into rooms separated by invisible walls.

Patches signaled. "Enemy ahead."

We moved inch by inch until we heard voices, then we crept even slower, keeping the canal bank between us and the sound of Vietnamese.

I slid my nose above the berm line. Not twenty yards away was a large clearing—maybe twenty by twenty-five meters—with three hootches on stilts and a good-sized cooking shed. In front of the hootches, five VC in shorts and loose, black pajama tops were squatting in front of a fire, chattering like Boy Scouts, while they watched a pot of something boiling away. Their AK-47s were leaning against the hootches, their sandals were off. Three of them were smoking.

In the distance, I could hear the growl of the Mike boat's diesels. Charlie could hear it, too. But the sound did not concern him.

There had probably been hundreds of boats chugging past Ilo-Ilo, and never any unwelcome visitors. So Charlie was not worried. He hadn't set out any recon. It wasn't necessary: Charlie knew he could read the Americans like a book.

I dropped back down, hardly able to keep myself from smiling. We were about to write them a new chapter—with a surprise ending, so far as I was concerned.

Using hand signals I sent the squad on its way, and we spread out into firing positions. The canal took a horseshoe curve around the hootches, which meant two wonderful things for us tactically. First, it kept us out of sight while we took our time flanking the unsuspecting VC. Second, it gave us a natural killing zone because our expanded field of fire would catch the hootch area from three sides instead of straight on.

On my signal, we rolled our M16s and Stoner over the top of the berm and hit them with full automatic fire. It was going nicely when somebody—no one ever owned up to it later—decided to help things along by tossing a frag grenade.

The grenade bounced against a tree trunk and—almost in slow motion—caromed back toward us, bouncing and rolling inexorably closer and closer to our firing positions.

"Oh, shiiiiit—" Fred Kochey's voice was loud and clear over the gunfire. "Grenaaaade—down!"

Seven men rolled back and dove underwater as one, chased by the concussion and deadly metal fragments.

I surfaced, coughing, spouting the brackish canal water like a statue. "Everybody okay?"

Nobody had been dinged. We held our fire. Jim Finley peeked over the top of the canal. "They're history."

Patches and Eagle charged up the bank, followed by Kochey, me, and the rest. Patches rolled the bodies, both to see how we'd done and to make sure no one was playing possum. We'd hit them well, with lots of head shots and upper-torso wounds. We grabbed the weapons. I gave them a quick once-over. They were Chicom AK-47s. I grabbed one and slung it over my shoulder and passed one each to Patches, Gallagher, and Kochey. AKs were rare. Then we searched the area thoroughly, grabbing everything we could find. I was euphoric. What we'd come upon was exactly what I'd hoped we'd find: a major VC waystation; a pit stop for couriers as they made their way north and south, moving to and from Saigon, or west toward the Cambodian border. It was as big a VC camp as I'd ever seen.

Behind the hootches were a pair of camouflaged bunkers. We blew them up with grenades. We took the cloth pouches the VC carried instead of wallets, and all the papers we could grab. We found a can of kerosene, splashed it over all the medical supplies and food, then set everything on fire.

We laid the VC in a neat row, so their pals would find them easily. Then we booby-trapped the corpses. April fool, Mr. Charlie.

We also made a discovery. Outside the hootches were three pairs of what looked like rubber snowshoes, made of old tires and canvas. Ron Rodger found them and brought one of them over to me.

"What the hell's this?"

I scratched my head. "You got me."

Kochey fingered the goods. "Looks like a snowshoe."

Eagle Gallagher nodded. "Mud shoes," he said. He pointed at the VC corpses. "They don't generally weigh but seventy-five pounds soaking wet. They wear these and walk on water—keep themselves out of the mud. Us big gringos in our goddamn boots sink like stones. Charlie glides"—he imitated someone ice-skating—"and leaves no tracks."

Kochey nodded. "Sounds good to me." He looked around. "Dick?"

"Sneaky little bastards, aren't they?" I looked at my watch: 1655. Almost five hours on the ground. "I think we should check out."

"I don't think we can carry any more souvenirs."

"So let's haul ass." We formed up and went back into the canal, loaded with booty. We staggered the men—two shooters, then a souvenir carrier. It was time to be extra careful, too, because there was no way Charlie didn't know he had visitors now.

I looked back at the five corpses. The sorry mothers never knew what the hell had hit them. Good—that's the way it should be.

A point should be made here about the way Americans tend to regard the act of killing. Like most of my generation, I grew up on Western movies where the hero—Hopalong or Roy or Gene—chivalrously tosses his gun aside after the black-hatted villain runs out of bullets and subdues the bad guy with his bare fists.

That may work on celluloid, but not in real life. In real life you shoot the motherfucker and you kill him dead—whether or not he is armed; whether or not he is going for his gun; whether he looks dangerous or appears benign. That way, you stay alive and your men stay alive. Many of our senior officers do not believe this. They would rather that *we* got killed than our enemies did. That attitude is stupid and it is wrong.

In Vietnam, I witnessed large numbers of senior officers who spent most of their time sitting behind desks, putting each other in for medals—and we're talking Bronze Stars and Silver Stars here—because they rode a PBR or Mike boat once or twice. These were the same men who jumped all over me because my interrogation techniques could get a little rough—I wasn't above manhandling VC or slapping them around to get information. Or got upset with me because I'd allow my merry marauders to make sausage out of two or three young, innocent-looking, unsuspecting VC. Well, I wasn't about to worry about whether or not I was killing the

VC properly (I wonder what improper killing is) because at least my guys and I were out in the boondocks *killing* 'em, not sitting behind some desk back in a cozy bunker stroking our mules.

During the U.S. invasion of Panama, a U.S. Army sergeant waxed some Panamanian civilians—"civilians" who attacked U.S. soldiers at a roadblock with hand grenades. His officers rewarded him for probably saving his comrades' lives by court-martialing him. Not only did they destroy morale, but they did the sergeant a huge injustice. Fortunately, he was found innocent. But the chilling effect such actions have on combat troops cannot be underestimated.

Conversely, during the summer of 1990, an Israeli Navy lieutenant in charge of a patrol craft killed four Palestinian terrorists by machine-gunning them in the water after he'd sunk the rubber boat in which they were trying to infiltrate the Israeli coast. He justified his act by explaining that he didn't know whether or not the Palestinians were concealing hand grenades that might have been used against his craft and his men. The lieutenant was promoted to captain on the spot by the commander of the Israeli Navy. The message sent loud and clear to young Israeli officers was the right one: you will be rewarded for putting the lives of your men above the lives of your enemies.

To me, a Purple Heart is not a badge of honor. To be blunt about it, I've always considered them enemy marksmanship medals and I'm happy not to have ever "won" one.

So, my philosophy in battle has always been to kill my enemy before he has a chance to kill me and to use whatever it takes. Never did I give Charlie an even break. I shot from ambush. I used superior firepower. I never engaged in hand-to-hand combat unless there was absolutely no alternative—to me, the combat knife should be a tool, not a weapon. All the whiz-bang, knife-fighting, karate/judo/kung-fu b.s. you see in the Rambo-Jambo shoot-'em-up movies is just that: bullshit.

The real-life rules of war are simple and effective: stay at arm's length whenever possible and shoot the shit out of the enemy before he sees you. So the fact that seven of us had just made bloody hamburger out of five undernourished, un-suspecting, unarmed Vietnamese didn't strike me as ruthless, immoral, or unfair. All my SEALs were still alive; and there were five fewer of the enemy.

We made our way west, using the canal as cover. About five hundred yards from the VC hootches, we hit another score: sampans. There must have been half a dozen of them, rafted together and moored to the bank. There was no sign of life, but we advanced cautiously, three SEALs approaching underwater to flank the VC boats, then coming up close and slipping over the gunwales only after we'd done a thorough check for booby traps.

The sampans were empty. We sank them and moved out as quickly as we could. Not fifty yards down the canal Patches Watson held his hand high. He waved me forward.

"Mr. Rick—"

I saw it. "Jesus." Across the five-yard width of the canal a trip wire lay suspended, almost as invisible as a single strand of spiderweb. We backed off. "Let's track it."

Patches and I headed toward opposite banks. I followed the strand as it led up the berm, through a hedge of thorn bushes, and up to a thick tree trunk, where it was attached to a shaped charge.

The bastards—they were good. I whistled for Eagle Gallagher, Bravo's EOD expert. Slowly, Eagle disarmed the charge, then we all moved forward again. Ten yards up the canal we discovered another series of booby traps. This time, the VC had laid charges in the canal itself and run both trip wires and hand detonators through the heavy overgrowth that ran right down to the water. Goddamn—if we'd come in through the front door, we'd have been chopped to bits. No wonder the VC at the way station weren't worried.

I was sweating profusely, so I sank back into the canal to cool myself off, taking hold of an overhanging limb to steady myself. Another lesson learned. We'd taken the back door by default. Maybe in the future we should spend more time looking for back doors when we came calling on Mr. Charlie.

Absently, I glanced up at the branch I was grasping so I could shift my hand and pull myself forward. Three inches from my right knuckle, a viper's head rested on the limb, its distinctive fleur-de-lis pattern visible against the dark tree bark.

Oh, shit. Dickie'd had a rough day in the jungle. There'd been a lot of mud. A grenade bounced back at me. I'd almost blown myself up on booby traps. Now, here was a snake that could kill in less than ten seconds.

The viper's hooded eyes and mine made contact. Mine said, "You son of a bitch, if you don't screw with me, I won't screw with you."

Slowly, slowly, slowly, I slid deeper into the water, and . . . just . . . let . . . my . . . fingers . . . slip . . . away. Two feet downstream, safely out of range, I pointed at the branch. "Viper—there."

A chop from Jim Finley's machete cut the foot-long snake in half. He smilingly offered me the still-moving tenderloin portion. "Hungry, Mr. Rick?"

It took us another two hours to work our way to the mouth of the canal. We could have moved faster, but I was nervous about booby traps—not to mention vipers. Moreover, we were also slowed by the weight of the VC bounty—AKs, medical supplies, documents, notebooks, diaries, and other records.

It was almost evening by the time I radioed the STAB to extract us. We rendezvoused with the Mike boat, climbed aboard, and headed back upriver, exhausted and exhilarated. We had good cause to be both. We'd spent the entire day on this operation and gone where no Americans had ever gone before.

Bravo's excursion to Ilo-Ilo Island would be called "the most successful SEAL operation in the Delta" by the U.S. Navy. For leading it, I won the first of my four Bronze Stars, as well as a Vietnamese Cross of Gallantry with Silver Star, from the ARVN.

It had been a long evening and morning of my Seventh Day. We dozed on the way back to My Tho. The wrathful God of SEALs finally allowed his lethal children to rest. I dreamt of warm women and cold beer.

Chapter
10

I ARRIVED BACK IN THE STATES FROM MY FIRST VIETNAM tour with mixed emotions. I felt positive about the way my squad had performed. We'd become a totally integrated unit—thinking and acting as one—protecting each other against both the Vietnamese enemy and the American bureaucracy. I was happy that although I'd brought them home with dents and scratches, no one had been seriously wounded. I was elated that each member of Bravo Squad would receive decorations for what he'd done in Vietnam. I was also happy with my own progress. I'd proved myself in battle—and was promoted to lieutenant, junior grade, shortly after my return stateside.

The medals and commendation reports were the outward evidence of something more seminal. I now believed in myself as a leader. My instincts about combat had turned out to be solid and largely reliable. Moreover, I'd been able to discover ways to beat the system we'd been saddled with, or at least make it work in our favor.

On the down side, I was turned off by the high level of mismanagement and addle-brained thinking that seemed to pervade our effort in Vietnam. All too often, we SEALs were

121

sent out to war by small-minded naval officers who hadn't a clue about our capabilities, or any idea how to use them. So they employed us the same way they employed their regular troops. That may work if you've got a battalion of unmotivated grunts. It doesn't when you're fielding small, deadly units of highly trained men who can think for themselves and who take pride in showing initiative.

I saw both the best and the worst of my fellow officers in Vietnam. On the plus side, there were guys like Fred Kochey, who'd lead his men to hell and back if there was a chance of intercepting a VC convoy or sinking a bunch of sampans. Then there were the others—the cowards, who sent their men to do the things they wouldn't, or couldn't, do themselves. And the bureaucrats, who busied themselves in paperwork instead of leading their men into the field, then put themselves in for Silver Stars because they heard the sound of gunfire one day. And the thieves—officers who just plain stole their commendations.

I remember one pus-nuts captain (he called himself Eagle, but he was a real turkey) who stole an enlisted man's Silver Star—he actually commandeered the bloody medal itself— because Lyndon Johnson was coming to Cam Ranh Bay and he wanted the president to pin it on him.

Had the captain been in combat? Let's put it this way: he rode in a PBR every six or seven days. The rest of the time he shuffled paper. Had he been shot at? Maybe—once or twice. Not like the enlisted man, a chief who commanded a PBR and who had been in the thick of it for months. But it was the chief who got screwed. Sure, he eventually got his medal, but the president should have pinned it on him, not on the tunic of some self-important turd.

That kind of behavior when it came to medals was typical. I'd almost been court-martialed by Hank Mustin because of Bravo Squad's first night out on the river—the night I called in a Spooky, we shot up the free-fire island, and came home without a single round of ammo left in our weapons. Well, a funny thing happened on the way to the brig: it turned out that by dumb luck, Bravo had interrupted what Navy Intelligence later described as a major North Vietnamese crossing. We'd blundered into the middle of it, and by sheer chance we'd given the enemy a royal screwing.

Guess who got himself put in for a Bronze Star, for what now was called the first successful SEAL operation in the Delta?

Lieutenant Commander Hank Mustin did. Never mind that his contribution to the evening's festivities had been less than zero. So, when I got back to the States early in June, I took myself over to the Awards Section at the main Navy building in Washington, D.C., and complained about it.

I don't know whether or not they ever pulled Mustin's Bronze Star—all I wanted was to go on record with my personal objection. But one thing was sure: from the looks I got, no ensign had ever come in to object about a lieutenant commander's medal before.

In Vietnam, I'd developed a reputation as a renegade, a maverick, a loner. Some of it was deserved—I've always had a hard time taking orders from people I don't respect, and I let them know it. My fitreps—fitness reports—from 1967 reflect my iconoclast's attitude. I was judged "Outstanding—One out of 100" in such areas as Imagination, Industry, Initiative, Force ("the positive and enthusiastic manner in which he fulfills his responsibilities"), and Professional Knowledge. But I was rated only "Exceptional" in the areas of Reliability, Personal Behavior, and Cooperation.

Now, "Exceptional" may sound good, but—as I was told at the time—it doesn't help smooth the old career track very much. And the areas in which I was graded lowest were those areas that rankled my superiors the most. My personal behavior was aggressive and abrasive. I swore like a sailor. I wasn't above using my hands on people if they pissed me off. I was cooperative when I believed it would do my men some good, but I wasn't shy about telling people to screw off, no matter how many stripes they wore on their sleeves. And I was reliable in the following order: to my squad, to my platoon, and to SEAL Team Two. Those were my priorities. Outsiders were on their own, so far as I was concerned.

So those fitreps were an honest reflection of who I was in those days. As an enlisted man, I'd hated the bureaucracy but wasn't able to do much about it. That's why I'd always wanted to become a chief. So far as I was concerned, chiefs, not officers, ran the Navy. That's why I told the captain who'd wanted me to go to OCS I'd rather be a chief in the Teams than an admiral. Still, as an ensign, I'd hoped I could change the system—move it just an iota. I discovered differently.

Indeed, as an ensign I was subject to even more bean counters and paper pushers than I had been faced with as an enlisted man. As a UDT sailor, I had Chief Barrett to protect me from officers' stupidity. As an officer, I had to deal with my colleagues' chronic assholia on a daily—even hourly—basis.

In the field, for example, we'd be out for two, even three days at a time on patrol, and no one in Bravo would complain. But it seemed whenever we had to make a trip to the local personnel command center for something or other, the four-eyed, smarmy apparatchiks who manned the desks would shunt me or my men off to the side while they took their scheduled coffee break, and God help you if you asked for ten extra seconds of their time.

Now, Bravo was a combat unit—and we looked the part. I grew to resent the smirks and sneering that greeted us when we walked into some office without pressed fatigues, or flaw-lessly rolled shirtsleeves. And more than once I got into trouble for pulling some officious son of a bitch over the counter by his lapels and ordering him to answer my sailor's damn question, or to help us fill out the goddamn forms—right now this minute—or suffer broken bones or worse.

Then there was the caste system. At one point early in 1967, Patches Watson and I were up in Saigon chasing down some gear, and we decided it would be nice to grab ourselves a real American steak and a cold brew or two. So up we marched to the closest eating facility—it turned out to be an Officers' Club—and walked in the door.

There was an MP on duty. He looked at my ensign's tabs and nodded. But he put a hand on Patches' chest. That was a dangerous thing to do.

"Sorry, sir," he said to me, "officers only."

I grabbed Patches before he did bodily harm. Then we went out the door and around the corner. We were wearing green fatigues and Marine Corps cover, so I took my ensign's bars, put one vertically in the center of my cap and one on Patches' cap, just like Marine lieutenants wear their bars. Then we walked back inside, threw the MP a salute, and had our steaks.

Screw the regulations: I've always felt if a man's good enough to die with, then he should be good enough to eat with. Many of my fellow officers, however, feel differently. That's their prerogative. Just don't ask me to serve with them.

I may not have been able to deal with the bureaucracy, but it certainly dealt with me. Late in June 1967, just two weeks after I got home, I was assigned to go on a public relations tour. SEALs always had been a top-secret unit. In Vietnam, we didn't even wear name patches. Instead, we were given numbers—mine was 635. Now, all of a sudden, the Navy decided it wanted to publicize its own Special Forces troops. We were given no reason for the abrupt about-face, although scuttlebutt had it that the CNO was sick and tired of reading about the Army's Green Berets. Whatever the cause, I was detailed to a PR tour, explaining what SEALs were, how we operated, and what we'd done in Vietnam. The high point was a trip to New York City, where I gave newspaper interviews and demonstrated SEAL weapons aboard a ship in New York harbor and the next morning found my name and my picture in the New York *Daily News*. The writer, columnist Sidney Fields, said I had "Hollywood good looks." (I always thought Fields should have won a Pulitzer for that column.)

One bit of fallout to my fifteen minutes of stardom was—five months later—finding my name on the cover of *Male* magazine. I couldn't believe what I read when I opened it up. It was an atrociously written piece of fiction that had me jumping out of a plane at twenty-five thousand feet above the Mekong Delta carrying a 57mm recoilless rifle! The headline read: "Lt. 'Demo Dick' Marcinko—the Navy's Deadliest Viet Nam Shark-Man." The article's author had never interviewed me. He purloined some of his material from the New York *Daily News* profile—and must have made up the rest.

The ripples from my publicity tour, incidentally, lasted longer than I expected. First, after the *Male* piece came out, no one called me Mr. Rick anymore. I was either Demo or Dick or Demo Dick. The second afterlife I only discovered much later. It turned out that the Vietcong and North Vietnamese read *Male* magazine, too.

When I returned to Little Creek, I convinced SEAL Team Two's commander, Squirrelly Earley, to assign me a second stint in Vietnam. As a lieutenant, junior grade, I was eligible to command my own platoon. I'd been a junior-junior ensign the first time around, and although Fred Kochey had given me free rein most of the time, I hadn't been able to get as down and dirty as I'd wanted. Moreover, I believed that if I was given a full platoon, I could use the larger, 14-man unit to push the parameters of Navy SpecWar further than they'd ever been pushed before—although I certainly didn't say that to anyone in the command structure.

It took me about two weeks of constant lobbying, but after some requisite squirreling, Skipper Earley finally gave me the Eighth Platoon. I thought of it as an early Christmas present—sort of like electric trains for adults.

My desire for a second combat tour did not go over well on the home front. Between SEAL training, my six-month stint in Vietnam, plus a three-week extension at Binh Thuy to help indoctrinate the new SEALs and my public-relations tour, I'd been gone almost a full year. Now I was about to go out again and who knew when I'd be back. I was a stranger to my kids, and to my wife. But the fact was, I wanted to go, I was used to getting what I wanted, and for better or worse, Kathy had signed on as a Navy wife.

I'm sure it was tough on her, but she was no different from thousands of other Navy wives who lived within the one hundred square miles or so that made up Virginia Beach and Norfolk. Every family sending someone overseas had to put up with separation and inconvenience.

Besides, our male-female roles were much more well-defined in the late sixties than they are today. Back then, Kathy's job was taking care of the kids; mine was taking care of the guys. I'd discovered in the field that when you're crawling through a rice paddy in the middle of the night surrounded by people who want to kill you, you don't spend a lot of time thinking about home and hearth. In fact, you don't spend any time at all thinking about those things—because if you don't concentrate on killing the enemy, he *will* kill you first. So far as I was concerned back then, my home life was less important than my job. Period. I realize that to say those things today may sound unfeeling, callous, and unenlightened. Well, maybe I *was* unfeeling, callous, and unenlightened. But that's the way most of us SEALs behaved. And in truth, I felt closer to the men with whom I served than I did to my wife and kids. We'd been through more together than most husbands and wives go through in a lifetime.

I set about training Eighth Platoon with a vengeance. I was determined to hit the ground running when we got to Vietnam, and I wanted to prepare the men for what they'd find. I pushed them to the limit. I took them to Panama so they'd get used to working in a tropical climate, letting the Army's Latin American Special Forces trainers do their "De hungle ees your frien' " number. Then I volunteered my platoon as the aggressor force during some Green Beret training sessions. I was gratified to see that we knocked the crap out of the Army. We played all kinds of head games on them: snuck up at night and tied them up in their hammocks. Stole their food and weapons. Took their wallets out of their fatigues and wrote nasty letters to their wives and sweethearts. A couple of Special Forces officers accused us of not playing fair.

"Tell that to the VC when you're sitting on the Cambodian border," I answered. "Just walk into the jungle with your fingers crossed and shout 'finnsies.' They'll pay attention. They just love to play fair. Every VC I've ever killed carried a leather-bound copy of the Marquis of Queensbery rules right next to his picture of Ho Chi Minh."

Rules? I broke a lot of them during training. But I was more concerned about making the situation realistic for the men than I was about not bruising some officer's ego. Despite regulations, for example, I emphasized live-fire sessions that simulated the sorts of situations I'd encountered in Vietnam, not the safe, easy exercises that don't prepare you to get shot at. When we walked the trails at Camp Pickett or Fort A.P. Hill, we did so with our weapons locked and loaded—just like walking the trails in Vietnam. I remembered how badly Second Platoon had done firing at towed targets, so we spent weeks practicing, until we could hit what we aimed at—day or night. We worked on infiltration and extraction techniques over and over, until we could move quickly and quietly into an ambush, because I'd discovered under fire that those were the times a unit was most vulnerable.

I taught the men of Eighth Platoon to hone their instincts,

and to react instantly. "Never assume anything," I kept saying. "Not even when you feel most safe and secure."

I preached unit integrity endlessly. And we practiced what I preached. We ate and drank and partied as a group. We'd bust up bars in the Virginia Beach area, and when we'd finished taking on all comers, we'd set about demolishing each other. It was an unconventional rite of initiation for these fourteen men, who'd trained as warriors but—with a couple of exceptions—hadn't been bloodied yet in battle. And the way I went about preparing them would stay with me: I'd use it again when I commanded SEAL Team Two, and I'd use it to fuse SEAL Team Six as well.

What I did back in 1967 I did by the seat of my pants. But my instincts were good. The endless contact got the platoon thinking as a unit. Each man became comfortable with the others, while the rough edges and annoying habits were worn away by the day-in, day-out rubbing of bodies and personalities. We began to think like a family; to put the group's needs above our own personal desires.

Drinking was an important element of the fusion process. It was more than just aimless, macho-bullshit partying, or frat-house chugalugging. I've always been a believer in the phrase *in vino veritas*. Five or six hours of hard partying after a 12-hour day of rough training allowed me to see how my guys would act when they were wrecked, almost out of control and weird—and how well they'd do the next morning, when they were nursing throbbing heads and bloodshot eyes—but still had to swim six or seven miles, run ten, or shoot to qualify. Fact is, you can tell a lot about a man by the way he handles his alcohol.

The bar time was a social accelerator, too. The more they drank together, the more they had their backs up against each other and took on the world, the closer they bonded. I've never believed a man should have to drink alcohol to prove himself, but I do believe that a unit as small and as tightly knit as a SEAL platoon should party together on a regular —even a nightly—basis, to achieve the kind of fusion only after-hours camaraderie can develop. This unique form of unit-integrity development worked. By late November, I had fourteen tough motherfuckers; men who would—and did—

drink each other's piss, who I was certain would hunt and kill with the best of them.

It was a first-class group that set out in early December 1967 for a two-week odyssey that would end at Binh Thuy, Republic of Vietnam. We stopped in California for a few days of R&R, and I knew that the platoon's training was complete when we rode down to Tijuana for two solid days of partying, and most of the men chose to infiltrate their way back to the States instead of coming through the normal border crossings.

My number two was Lieutenant (j.g.) Frank G. Boyce, aka Gordy, a little fireplug of a guy. Gordy was a real pocket rocket: arrogant, intense, cantankerous, mouthy—everything I liked in a man. He was a reserve officer, younger than I, who came from old New England money—his father was a pal of Ellsworth Bunker's, the tall, white-haired, patrician American ambassador to Vietnam. But Gordy never let the wealth or the background bother him. In fact, Gordy was so crazy he was freaky. He didn't drink, for example. But he could get as absolutely shit-faced on tap water or Coca-Cola as if he'd had a case of beer. He was an incontrovertible walking, one-man frat party.

Then there was Harry Humphries. Harry was a fellow Jersey boy, a big, strapping, dark-haired mick lad of six feet and two hundred pounds. Best of all, he was a real renegade. He came from a wealthy Irish family in Jersey City and had gone to Rutgers. But college life hadn't provided enough excitement, so he'd enlisted in the Navy and gone through UDT training. When I first knew him, he was in the Fourth Platoon of UDT Team 22. By the time I'd done my first tour in Vietnam and come home, Harry's hitch had expired. He was back in Jersey City, dragooned into the family fat-processing business by his mother. To me, rendering lard seemed like a waste of his real talents.

Still, the conditions under which he was wasting away were plush. He'd traded enlisted-man's housing for the Humphries family compound, a square block of Jersey City surrounded by a ten-foot wall. Inside, behind wrought-iron gates—kind of like the estate in *The Godfather*—were seven almost identical red-brick houses. Harry'd been given one, where he lived with his wife, Pat, a former model whom he'd met on St. Thomas, and one young child. Cushy.

Jersey City wasn't too far from New Brunswick, so on a trip to see my own in-laws I dropped in on the Humphries household. Harry and I went out for a couple of cold ones and got caught up.

After a few beers, Harry let me know he was bored processing lard and suet. "I wish I'd stayed in the Teams, Dick. By now I'd have been deployed to Vietnam like you."

I played it cool. I told Harry how much fun I'd had on my first tour. I told him what Bravo had done and what games we'd been able to play. "I'm gonna go back, too. Take my own platoon."

"No shit. That's great, Dick."

"Great? Hell, Har, it's gonna be a vacation. Excitement, fun. Life in the mud. Get shot at. Shoot Japs. Good shit."

Humphries held his glass in front of his nose and looked through the beer into the bar mirror. I knew what he was thinking. I set the hook. "You're right—too bad you left. We could have had some real fun together."

He nodded. "That's a roger." He sipped his beer. "Y'know, I haven't been gone that long—I could make up my quals easily, if you could get me into SEALs."

"Why the hell would you want to trade what you got for an enlisted-man's billet?"

"Cause I'm in the goddamn fat-processing business, Dick, and I don't wanna be."

I put my beer on the bar. "Tell you what—you want to reenlist, I can probably get you into SEALs. You're parachute and dive qualified. The rest of it we can do in a couple of months."

He thought about that for a few minutes. A self-satisfied smile crept across his face. "You know Pat's gonna kill me," he said.

"Nah."

"Wanna bet? She loves the fact I'm in business. She loves the compound—especially now that she's pregnant with our second baby. We've got everything we want—and what's she gonna get in Virginia Beach—a tract house? A mobile home?"

"She'll get used to it."

"Wrong. She may do it, but she'll never get used to it." He sipped at his beer. "And my family's gonna shit when they learn I wanna quit."

I hit him on the shoulder. Hard. "Quit?"

"The business."

I hit him again. "Screw the business. When you're forty, you can do *business*. You're what? Twenty-six, twenty-seven years old? Have some fun. Hop and pop. Shoot and loot. Then—*then* you come back, and you wear gray flannel suits for the rest of your life, and nobody argues with you."

I drained my beer, called for another round, and offered him the rim of my glass. "Come on, Harry—here's to the reason you joined the Teams in the first place: to be a hunter."

I didn't have to do much convincing because Harry'd made up his own mind long before we went out for those beers. But you couldn't have convinced his wife or mother that his reenlistment wasn't completely and totally my fault. It was the elder Mrs. Humphries who was most upset. By the time Harry and Pat moved south to Virginia Beach, Pat'd had the new baby. Harry's mom came with them to take care of the infant while they found a place to live (and yes, they ended up in tract housing).

The last time I saw her, she shook a dirty diaper in my face and screamed like a wrinkled Irish banshee. "Damn you, damn you to hell, Richard Marcinko. You got my boy to reenlist, and now you're taking him to Vietnam, where he could get killed, and you're leaving us holding these!" I looked at Harry, and the relieved smile in his eyes told me, "Better her than us."

My corpsman was Doc Nixon. He was a SEAL Two plank owner—one of the original East Coast SEALs. His first name was Guy and his middle name was Richard, but I can't remember anyone ever calling him anything but Doc. He was a brooding, blue-eyed warrior. A real slave to his dick, too—a dangerous man with the women.

Number one Stoner man was Ron Rodger, who knew what to expect from me because he'd been part of Bravo Squad on my previous tour. Eagle Gallagher and Patches Watson were also going back to Vietnam, but they'd been assigned to Seventh Platoon this time. Rodger, however, got to come with me. That made me happy. The son of a bitch was a good fighter. His punches still snapped when he hit you—and there wasn't anything he wouldn't do if asked.

Then there was Louis Kucinski—another SEAL Two plank owner. I called him Hoss, or Ski. He was an archetypal, big, jug-eared Polack bosun's mate: strong, and silent. His face was as rough and pockmarked as if it had just been sand-blasted. And smart—Hoss never had to be told anything twice. Seldom, in fact, did Hoss have to be told anything even once.

Kucinski was married to a beautiful, long-haired tiny mos-quito of a woman named Tiger, who loved him so utterly and completely she would try to beat the crap out of him regularly when they'd had a few beers. She'd flail away, and he'd just laugh and laugh and pick her up and kiss the hell out of her.

Frank Scollise was a short, asthmatically thin chain-smoker from Blacksburg, Virginia, a hardscrabble two-horse town in the Appalachian foothills about twenty-five miles due west of Roanoke. He was our mountain man—the hunter who made sure we had squirrel or venison to eat every time we went on maneuvers at Camp Pickett or Fort A.P. Hill, and he brewed our morning coffee with both eggshell and a dirty sock in the pot. He was a tiny guy—no more than 140 pounds or so soaking wet—with a heavy beard that needed shaving two or three times a day. In fact, he looked like a miner because no matter how many times we'd throw him in the shower or whatever body of water we happened to be around, he'd still have a gray, sooty pall to his skin. You could leave him in the sun for weeks and he'd still be sickly looking.

I called him Slow Frank because that's the way he moved —lackadaisical. Never so fast that he'd cause any breeze in his wake. He was an old-fashioned sailor. He usually kept bourbon in his canteen, and an unfiltered cigarette always hung from the corner of his mouth. Scollise was subject to a constant, jarring smoker's cough that he somehow managed to muffle whenever we were out on patrol. He hated swim-ming, but I couldn't have wanted a better man with a blow-torch—or a rifle.

Freddie Toothman was a Panamanian, a dark-skinned, easygoing, Spanish-speaking giant of a guy who turned out to be gifted at working with the Vietnamese. Maybe it was the similarity of temperament, maybe it was the fun of staging anti-VC hits. Whatever the case, he found true happiness leading raids staged by the PRU, the Provincial Reconnaissance Units made up of VC defectors, as part of the Phoenix program.

Number two Stoner man Clarence Risher was the platoon's James Dean. A lanky, curly-haired young rebel with a kind of sloe-eyed charm, he'd grown up on a series of military bases where his father, a Marine lieutenant colonel, had served. Risher was the youngest man in the platoon—not chronologically, but in the way he behaved. He was quiet and moody and given to petulance when he didn't get what he wanted. He was mischievous, but not in the roughhouse way most of the old guys from the UDT teams were. Frank Scollise or Ron Rodger, for example, would throw you up against a wall and pound the shit out of you when they wanted to have some fun. Risher was more into verbal stuff—the adolescent give-and-take of the schoolyard that always seemed to degenerate into "I dare you" and "I double-dare you."

I always felt that SEALs shouldn't be into that sort of juvenile game, and it concerned me. What worried me about Risher came through most clearly when he drank. He was a happy drunk. But after a few beers he'd always seem to drift into a monologue about Colonel Daddy. After a while it got like a soap opera. He'd joined the Navy because Daddy was a Marine. He was an enlisted man because Daddy'd somehow convinced him he wasn't good enough to become an officer. He'd become a SEAL because it was the best way he could show Daddy that he was a man, too.

Just before we left for Vietnam, Risher got himself married. Not because he was desperately in love, or because he was afraid of losing the girl. He did it because somehow he felt it was the thing to do. But juvenile or not, Risher was also talented with the Stoner machine gun. He was big—over six feet—and strong—190 pounds or so—and he could carry almost half his weight in ammo. The kid may have been an immature pain in the butt, but he always pulled his share.

Dennis Drady was another old-time dirtbag. He was the platoon's resident yenta—the mother-hen pain in the ass—who habitually nagged us until we'd beat the crap out of him. "Did you bring enough ammo?" he'd ask Hoss. "Did you remember to clean the machine guns this morning?" he'd badger Ron Rodger or Clarence Risher. "Did you get fresh intel?" he'd query me.

Drady was a little guy whose long nose, small, dark eyes, big, ratlike front teeth, and squished face gave him the ferretlike look of a malevolent rodent. The similarity was reinforced by mousy-brown straight hair, and his quick, almost jumpy movements.

I kept repressing the urge to strangle him because he really was a nudge. On the other hand, without Dennis, we'd probably have forgotten our heads. He had a good brain for details. He was a gifted and talented point man. And as for being a yenta, when we found ourselves thirty or forty clicks from friendly forces and discovered that we'd forgotten extra firing pins for the AK-47s, or we'd lost our roll of trip wire, it was most often Drady who'd reach into his pocket with a self-satisfied smirk, come up with the missing item, and tell me, "You mean you didn't bring one of these, too, *sir?*" He may have pronounced it "sir," but he was spelling it "cur." I loved it when he did that.

There were fourteen of us in all—each man better than the next—and the platoon's stats showed it. We arrived at Binh Thuy on December 17, 1967; we left on June 20, 1968. In the six months between, we conducted 107 combat patrols. We killed 165 VC that we could confirm, plus another 60 or so probables. We captured just under 100 Viet Cong, destroyed five tons of their rice and eleven tons of their medicine, grabbed bunches of weapons, grenades, explosives, and other lethal goodies, sank scores of sampans, and blew up more hootches, bunkers, and canal blockades than I care to remember.

We didn't do it by sitting on our butts in static ambushes either. That was the passive tactic Hank Mustin had devised on my first tour. And the surfer-cool West Coast SEALs from Team One sitting up in the Rung Sat Zone were still dutifully going out every night and hunkering down in the jungle, waiting for the VC to come along—and regularly getting themselves killed in large numbers as they did so.

That was the crux of the problem: the SEAL role in Vietnam had been formulated, designed, and was under the direction of non-SEALs. That was wrong. Vietnam was the first war in which SEALs fought. All the things we'd been trained to do, we were not being allowed to do. Why? The simple answer was because we were being commanded by officers who'd trained as ship drivers, aviators, or nuclear submariners, not as mean, lean, bad-ass jungle fighters. What we needed was brass-balled warriors. What we got was pus-nuts bureaucrats.

They thought of war in the conventional way, as a static affair in which the lines don't shift very much. They thought of Vietnam as if it were Korea, or Europe in World War II —a war in which one side attacks the other, territory is taken, and the war is won. They had no concept of guerrilla operations; of wars being won or lost on the squad level. Worst of all, they wanted SEALs to be passive.

Not me. I wanted to go fucking hunting.

Part Two

UNODIR

Chapter

11

REACHING BINH THUY WAS LIKE COMING HOME AGAIN—
except that during the six months I'd been gone, improvements had been made. The whole Navy complex had been
moved a couple of clicks down the road, and enlarged to more
than double its original size. By the time Eighth Platoon
landed on December 17, the new compound had lost the gold-
rush, mud-in-the-streets, boomtown atmosphere. It was almost like coming back to Little Creek.

Gone were the ramshackle docks with their rickety pilings
and floating oil-drums. There were new piers of concrete and
wood. The barracks buildings, built of wood, had air conditioners in the windows and American-style toilets and showers
along with American-style water pressure. The Quonset-hut
offices had disappeared. A new complex of warehouses and
repair facilities was built around steel A-frames that sat on
massive poured-concrete slabs. Even a small airfield had been
put in.

There was an O Club, enlisted-men's clubs, a gym, equipment sheds for our gear, and scores of air-conditioned admin
offices where the intel squirrels lived, typing reports that dis-

appeared into a void and probably ended up in some admiral's round file in Hawaii or back at the Pentagon.

I got my troops settled, reported in to Hank Mustin, who was still on scene as ops boss (although he would rotate back home within a few weeks). I'd brought Hank a couple of packages from home and he looked happy to see me. His friendly expression told me nothing had surfaced on my complaint about his Bronze Star.

Mustin reminded me I was in-country to be a part of a team, not to play Lone Ranger. He told me I'd be expected to file operational plans so HQ would know what Eighth Platoon was up to, and to spend the majority of my time supporting riverine operations. "Things have changed here, Dick. Take a couple of weeks to familiarize yourself with the current procedures, then get to work."

I shook his hand, pumped my biceps, saluted smartly, and said, "Whatever you say, sir."

That's what I *said*. Within six days of our arrival, however, Eighth Platoon was already slip-sliding away. Unencumbered by such niceties as chain of command, or "By your leave, sir," Marcinko's Muscle-bound Merry Murderous Marauders designed our own unique form of riverine support.

We left on our first patrol December 26, with lethal tidings of discomfort, and no joy whatsoever, for the VC. My elves did a nighttime insertion onto Tan Dinh Island on the Mekong River in Vin Long Province, went hunting, and killed five of Mr. Charlie. Melly fucking Clistmas.

When HQ discovered I wasn't supporting anybody that night, they tried to get me on the radio to call us back. Somehow, as I earnestly explained later, the signals from Binh Thuy to the PBR were just too faint to read. And after we'd inserted, well, we were on radio silence so we had our receivers turned off. Besides, I'd told them what I was doing. I'd filed my ops plan, just like I'd been ordered to.

"UNODIR—Unless Otherwise Directed," I wrote, "Eighth Platoon will insert covertly on Tan Dinh Island to recon the area and probe for enemy troop concentrations, courier networks, communications facilities, and general VC infrastructure." It didn't matter that Hank Mustin or the 116's commander, a dipshit captain, hadn't got a riverine operation going within fifteen miles of Tan Dinh. I wrote out the plan, left it at the communications center, and ordered the radioman to wait two hours before he delivered it to Mustin. No one directed me otherwise, so we did exactly what we wanted to do. By the time we got back, Hank was furious. But what could he do? We'd gotten five confirmed kills and three more probables—a good night's work for a seasoned platoon, much less a green bunch of newcomers. He just shook his head, halfheartedly reamed me out, and then left us alone.

That set the pattern. The next night, UNODIR, we hunted south and east to Dung Island almost to the China Sea and killed a trio of VC.

Six days later we celebrated United Nations Day, January 2, 1968, by hunting VC in Ke Sach, in Ba Xuyen Province southeast of Binh Thuy. We bagged half a dozen that night. A happy Frank Scollise told me we'd probably gone over the legal limit. "We wuz poachin' for sure by the end of the night, boss," he said, laughing, after the boats had come to extract us and we sat scrunched on the PBR's deck sipping a couple of cold ones.

Forty-eight hours later we disappeared UNODIR into Phong Dinh Province near Can Tho and snatched five VC out of their hootches in the middle of the night. There were probably a dozen of the enemy sleeping nearby, but no one heard us coming or going.

On January 9 we disappeared on a two-day patrol back into Phong Dinh Province. The VC had set out lots of pickets in the area because we'd made them lose a lot of face by kidnapping five soldiers. We got 'em again—wounded two and snatched six more right out of the hootches. This was getting to be fun.

By the end of our first twenty-five days we'd run just under a dozen patrols, killed about two dozen VC, captured a dozen more, destroyed forty-nine huts, sixty-four bunkers, three thousand pounds of rice, burned two fishing stations, and sunk a bunch of sampans. I heard some grumbling about our methods, but no one from Hank Mustin on down could complain because we were just too goddamn effective. Mr. Charlie definitely knew somebody *baaad* had just moved into the neighborhood. He just didn't know precisely who we were— and we weren't about to let on.

One reason for the VC's confusion was we'd already begun

to go native. I'd stopped wearing U.S.-issue combat boots on my first Vietnam tour in favor of the sneakerlike beta boots worn by South Vietnamese troops. No sense leaving lug-soled, size 11, U.S.-government-inspected, gringo-sized footprints for Mr. Charlie to follow. Within our first month in-country we began trading our Marvin the ARVN beta boots for the tire-soled sandals favored by the VC. We didn't wear them on every patrol, only the ones that took us way up the tiny canals and tributaries, where we'd walk the dikes for miles and recon a VC village before we snuck in and snatched bodies. As we moved farther and farther up the dikes and into the jungle, I even began to go barefoot on the trails. It was easier to sense booby traps without shoes on—and the prints I left really made the VC scratch their heads.

Some of the guys began leaving their M16s behind and bringing captured AK-47s instead. AK ammo was always plentiful because we'd take it from VC corpses—there were more VC than round-eyes in the neighborhood—and the rifles had their own distinctive sound, quite different from the *craaaack* of the M16's high-velocity .223 ammo.

It was more than just switching shoes and weapons. We began to think like guerrillas, getting spookier and spookier and dirtier and dirtier. Hoss Kucinski would always carry two or three LAWS, the disposable, single-shot light antitank weapons, with us. They were useful in blowing up hootches or collapsing tunnels. We'd leave the LAWS cases behind—booby-trapped. We'd also doctor the VC's ammo. If we found a big cache of it, we'd bring a couple of cases back with us, then have it fixed so it would explode when it was fired. The next time we'd go out, we'd take the cases with us, then leave 'em behind. Doom on you, Charlie.

I discovered new and wonderful ways in which to screw with Mr. Charlie's head. Sometimes we'd wear our gringo boots long enough to leave a noticeable trail—footprints so wide and deep they radiated like neon. But then we'd switch to beta boots or sandals or go barefoot, backtrack carefully, and—just where the gringo footprints became most obvious —we'd conceal pressure mats on the trail. The mats were detonators, which we'd attach to Claymore mines—deadly, shaped explosive charges. It was Eighth Platoon's personable way of telling the VC, "Hi, guys, we're heeeere."

The first week in January, I ran into a SEAL buddy of mine named Jose Taylor, who was attached to Mike Force, the CIA's elite special reaction units. Mike Force teams worked with groups of Montagnard tribesmen staging quick, effective raids on large VC and NVA positions, or coming to the rescue of Special Forces teams that were in danger of being overrun. Some of the Mike Force people had begun wearing VC-like black pajamas on their raids, and the idea seemed like a good one to me. I asked if he could grab me a couple of dozen blacks, sized large. They arrived the next day. From another source I dug up some old French camouflage fatigues and we stockpiled them, too.

What I wanted was to cause the VC to wonder just who these masked men really are. Are they black-pajama ghosts or are they leftovers from the French Foreign Legion or what? Were we 14 men—or were we 114? The more unsettled the VC became, the better off my SEALs would be.

We should also, I believed strongly, expand our area of operations. Despite the fact that some of the senior officers thought my UNODIR sorties were outrageous, because they weren't staged in direct support of a bigger operation, I was convinced that what I was doing fell under the rubric of conventional SEAL ops: infiltrations, ambushes, and snatches. And they all revolved around water, whether it was rivers, canals, or rice paddies.

On my first tour, I'd begun hitting the VC while they were off guard. I'd done it by moving out of the river and up the smaller canals and tributaries, traveling along the dikes so we could hit the enemy before he got into an alert, defensive mode.

Now, I wanted to get closer to the main supply routes, to cut off Mr. Charlie's head before he even began the staging process. So far as I could tell, the best place to do that would be up on the Cambodian border, where hundreds—even thousands—of North Vietnamese were regularly infiltrating, with their supply convoys, along the series of Ho Chi Minh trails that led from the north.

The provincial capital closest to Cambodia was a city called Chau Doc, which sat not five clicks from the border. Problem was, even though Chau Doc sat right on the Bassac River, which ran all the way northwest to Phnom Penh, it was about seventy-five miles from Binh Thuy, and the Navy had no riverine operations anywhere close. Nor, when I checked, were there plans for any. Worse, the Army's Special Forces considered Chau Doc their personal domain, and the Navy brass wasn't about to ruffle the Army's feathers.

It was time for another UNODIR. Gordy and I were sitting in the O Club having a few cold ones when I broached the subject of Cambodia with him. He was ready for anything, as he'd just finished a command performance of his pièce de résistance, the Dance of the Flaming Asshole, which always brought the house down.

D.O.T.F.A.? It was an interpretative maneuver in which Gordy would first get himself smashed on bottled water, or perhaps even something as strong as ginger ale. Then he'd jump up on a table, drop his trousers and skivvies, stick toilet paper up into the crack of his ass, unroll about six feet, then have someone light it. The object was to see how close he could let the flame come to his asshole, before pinching the fire out. It was a great, classic SEAL-type act.

He was smarting because he'd waited too long until pinching this particular evening. "Listen, shit-for-brains, I've got the perfect cure for your sore sphincter," I told him.

"What's that, boss?"

"A couple of days of sight-seeing over the holidays." It was coming up on the Vietnamese Lunar New Year—Tet—when things generally slowed down.

"Anyplace special?"

"I was thinking about Chau Doc."

"Chau Doc for the Tet holiday." Gordy thought about that for a few seconds.

"We see the sights up there, then just before the cease-fire we go out in the woods and set up a listening post."

A beatific look spread across his face. Gordy knew what was coming. The technique was one I'd devised on my first tour. When I was instructed to not make contact with the enemy, I'd simply set up a listening post so far behind VC lines that they'd stumble across me and start shooting. I was allowed to shoot back. "That should really piss everybody off," he said.

"I thought so."

"How do we do it?"

"We just go."

"UNODIR?"

"Whatever. Screw 'em. If anybody asks, we're taking the platoon on R and R."

So the second week in January, I commandeered a couple of Navy Seawolf helicopters, took the whole platoon along for the ride, and choppered upriver singing "I Can't Get No Satisfaction" as we went. The pilots got into the mood of things, too, buzzing villages and swooping down to wet their skids on the river surface as we careened up the Bassac, northwest to Chau Doc. We dropped into a dusty Special Forces compound at the edge of the city, an old French hotel that had been buttressed with sandbags, Quonset commo shacks, reinforced ammo bunkers, concertina wire, and guard towers.

We'd dressed ourselves like good tourists should: the full camouflage number on our faces, our heads wrapped in bandannas, sporting our new black pajamas and beta boots. There were bandoliers of ammo draped Pancho Villa style around our necks, and we carried a good assortment of special weapons to assist us in any show-and-tell we might be asked to perform. I affected a silenced 9mm pistol in a shoulder holster and slung a Swedish K submachine gun over my arm. Gordy Boyce brought his stainless-steel, short-barreled, 12-gauge, pump-action shotgun with its duckbill attachment. It sprayed a deadly horizontal pattern of buckshot and was effective in the paddies. Hoss Kucinski humped four LAWS on his back. Ron Rodger and Clarence Risher carried their Stoners and wrapped their upper bodies with ammo belts. Doc Nixon and a few of the others had AK-47s. No one wore dog tags, or any sign of rank or unit.

Six of us dropped out of the first chopper, waved it off, and then brought the second one in. It disgorged the rest of the platoon, heaved itself skyward, rotated, and flew south.

A wide-eyed Special Forces sergeant major came prancing out of the HQ, looking like the Queen of the Morning. He eyeballed us through the dust, and his expression told me he didn't like what he saw. "Who the hell are you?"

"Marcinko," I said with a grin. "Lieutenant JG Marcinko, SEAL Team Two, Sergeant."

I saluted. So did he—eventually. "We're from the riverine force at Binh Thuy."

He looked at me dumbly. I spoke slowly. "SEALs—you've heard about us? Navy SpecWar units attached to Task Force 116?" I was drawing a blank. "We're interested in looking at the vulnerabilities here in Chau Phu district, and expanding our maritime activities into your theater of operations."

"We don't have any vulnerabilities, sir."

I winked through my camouflage. "Glad to hear it, Sergeant." And fuck you very much, too.

Upon request, Gordy and I were ushered in to visit a commander, a colonel, whose spotless office boasted a huge American flag on a six-foot staff that sat behind his gunmetal-gray metal desk. He looked like a recruiting poster: starched uniform, web pistol belt and fancy stainless-steel Colt .45 pistol, sitting at attention, his painstakingly rolled shirtsleeves exposing tanned biceps, his steel-gray hair precisely and severely crew-cut. His creases were ironed to perfection. His salute was drill-team flawless.

But it was all a facade. Sitting behind his handcrafted SECTOR CHIEF ADVISER desk sign, Colonel Spit and Polish reeked of stale whiskey. Behind his radiant, gold-rimmed aviator glasses, his eyes were betrayed by a red-veined alcoholic tinge. Behind them lay the frightened soul of a gun-shy mannequin who'd lost all hunger for combat. I could read him like a book—and I didn't particularly like a single sentence.

He greeted Gordy and me with the sort of arched-eyebrow distaste and repugnance Park Avenue matrons reserve for drooling street people who invade their space. He asked why I carried no sign of rank or wore no dog tags, and why my weapons were nonregulation. Most of all, he wanted to know who the hell had sent me onto his sacred turf without written permission.

I held my tongue and explained myself. I told his exaltedness what SEALs were, and how we could help him by providing skills his Special Forces guys didn't have. He looked right through me as I spoke, but nodded in all the appropriate places.

Then I asked for a field brief. "Fieldwise, we've got the situation in hand, Lieutenant. I deploy regular patrols, and they keep track of all untoward enemy movements. The VC and North Vietnamese cadres are numerous, but they're kept in check through consistent forward patrol activity. Further, I'm pleased to say we get good cooperation from our valiant RVN counterparts."

It was boilerplate chickenshit, of course. But the colonel's subtext was clear. He wanted no part of me or what I offered. He emphasized the fact that he had U.S. troops—12-man units—blanketed all over the region, working with Marvin the ARVN nice and close, and coordinating with RFPF—Regional Force/Provincial Force units, known as ruff-puffs—which were supposed to ferret out VC or NVA cadre activities on the village level.

"It's all going smoothly so far as I'm concerned . . . Lieutenant. I'm not sure we need your unique capabilities up here. Seems like it's an awful long supply route from Binh Thuy in any case."

"Just a half-hour chopper jump, sir. Really—nothing more than a hop and pop."

He nodded. "Good to know, son. If anything comes up, I'll give you a call." He saluted, then swiveled his well-lubricated chair back toward his paperwork. We were dismissed.

Gordy and I walked outside. "To hell with him. He doesn't want anybody upsetting his goddamn applecart. Too sweet and quiet up here."

I formed the platoon up. "Let's go for a walk."

Being SEALs, we headed toward liquid. We wandered along the riverfront, stopping for a couple of beers and a few spring rolls as we traipsed through the old French colonial city. A quarter of a mile down the quay, we came upon a big white house that backed up right onto the Bassac. It was a no-shit residence: concertina wire was rolled outside; heavily armed guards in black pajamas similar to ours lounged, eyeing us suspiciously as we sauntered down the road.

I looked at the guards. These were no Vietnamese, but Chinese Nungs—mean, mercenary mothers. They ate the hottest food I'd ever tasted. They'd just as soon kill you as look at you—and they liked to kill you slow. My kind of people. They worked for my brothers-in-arms from the organization we fondly called Christians In Action—the CIA.

We walked up onto the porch and I rang the doorbell.

It was answered by a tanned, reedy, sandy-haired man in his mid-twenties wearing a wrinkled pair of tropical-weight trousers, sandals, a light blue barong—the Filipino shirt that looked like a guayabera and was favored by many Americans in Vietnam—and a .45-caliber automatic.

"Hi," he said without so much as a flicker. "My name's Drew Dix and I'm the regional CORDS adviser. Who the hell are you?"

"Hi, Drew," I said. "My name is Dick Marcinko, I'm a SEAL, and I do dumb things. I'd like some wine for my men, some hay for my horses, and some mud for my turtle."

He roared, "Well, fuck me," and opened the door wide. "How about two out of three? Welcome to the White House. Come on in, have a few cold ones, and we'll talk about the dumb things a man can do up here."

I smiled through my camouflage. "Louie—this could be the start of a beautiful friendship."

As PSA, or Province Senior Adviser, for CORDS—the acronym for the Civil Operations and Revolutionary Development Support pacification program, which had been created in 1967—Drew Dix coordinated civilian pacification programs with both U.S. and Vietnamese military operations. It was a tough job. Drew was a Special Forces sergeant on loan to CORDS. He had done his best to develop an intel network in the area, and to work closely with the Vietnamese. But he was continually frustrated, he told us, because of both the structure of Vietnamese society, and the pigheaded stupidity down the street at the Army compound where Colonel Spit and Polish ruled the roost.

As with any civil war, Drew said, families had been split over both geographic and ideological grounds. So it was altogether possible to have an ARVN officer fighting against a VC cadre who happened to be his cousin or uncle or even his brother. It was often the case that opposing forces had grown up with each other, and word was passed across the lines when ops were run by both sides.

"What happens," he said, "is that Charlie stages an op, and Marvin goes out to hit him, and a lot of shots get fired, but no one is hit, and then they both withdraw and go home for the night. Frankly, Marcinko, that sucks."

"What about Colonel Spit and Polish?"

"What about him?"

"Doesn't he—"

"Shit, Marcinko, he hasn't left his goddamn compound in weeks. We collect intelligence and we give it to him, and he sits on it until it's too late to do anything, then he sends out a token force—he's worse than the goddamn Vietnamese."

Dix's opinion was confirmed by his friend Westy. "That sorry muthafucker hasn't lifted a finger to help out since we set up shop," Westy said in his broad Louisiana drawl.

The CIA man mopped his red moon face with a blue bandanna that he kept in his back pocket. "No account assholes," he growled, pointing his nose in the direction of the colonel's compound. I liked Westy. He was a slow-moving, Jack Daniel's–drinking Special Forces officer in his mid-forties—probably a major—on loan to Langley. He'd given up crawling around the jungle and now spent his time sitting in a rocking chair in the White House, perfectly content to let Drew have all the action.

Over a Nung dinner that made us sweat like pigs, Drew and Westy gave us the skinny about what it was like on the Cambodian border. "Just remember that once you've left the city," he told us, "the VC own everything. They've got a big training center in Cambodia. There's a supply route that moves through Seven Mountains, which is to the southwest of Chau Doc, and then due south to the Delta."

"You keep pretty good tabs on Charlie," Gordy said.

Drew nodded. "We got great intelligence. Problem is, we can't do anything with it." He drained his beer, opened another, and took a long pull from the can. "Nungs can't go out every day—and the colonel's a chickenshit."

I raised my beer toward the CIA agent. "We sure'd like to get a piece of your action. Hell, Westy, you got your intel, I got my animals. Seems like we could do good business."

Westy chopsticked a sliver of red Thai pepper, chewed at it, wiped his forehead with the big blue bandanna he used as a handkerchief, and pulled at his beer. "Shit, Marcinko, you wanna go shoot Japs, just go to it, boy. There's nobody bothering them right now."

Next morning I got on the radio, called in my Seawolves, and we rode back to Binh Thuy. As soon as I arrived, I arranged for two PBRs to be sent up the Bassac to Chau Doc. After a chat with the chiefs, I made sure they'd be loaded with good Navy steaks, good Navy ammo, and great civilian beer. Then I paid a social call at the neighborhood Seawolf chopper squadron and told them that we'd discovered it was open season on Charlie up at Chau Doc. That made the pilots very happy and assured us air support whenever we needed it.

We put a couple of more patrols under our belts out of Binh Thuy while the paperwork for detailing the PBRs was shuffled, cut, and dealt. Then, on the twenty-eighth of January, I filed an UNODIR with Hank Mustin, and off we went to go hunting.

We left Chau Doc on the evening of the thirty-first—Tet eve. The idea was to set up a listening post above the Vinh Te canal, about fifteen hundred yards north of the city. The canal was only two hundred yards south of the Cambodian border and ran parallel to it for miles. Sitting there, we'd present a tempting target for the VC—and if they made a move to overrun us, we'd kick the shit out of them.

Colonel Spit and Polish—I'd begun calling him Colonel Shit and Polish—had ordered me to file a fire plan, which I'd never done in my life, before we went out. Basically, a fire plan would give him the map coordinates of my position so he could call in artillery support should I need it. A fire plan may work if you have a division stumbling around in the jungle. But SEALs don't want or need massive ground artillery support from a firebase twenty miles away. SEALs carry their own firepower—and if they need more, they can call in the mortars on Mike boats, or the recoilless rifles and machine guns on PBRs.

Moreover, fire plans are restrictive. First, they give you fewer choices. We could operate only in three small areas because the artillery dip-dunks were either unwilling or unable to plot more than a trio of coordinates on their maps. So if we weren't dead center on first base, second base, or third base, we didn't get artillery support. That didn't bother me. What really made me mad was that my men and I were vulnerable to friendly fire if we strayed off the areas we'd committed to. Another problem with fire plans was op-sec—operational security. The more people who knew where I'd be, the more chance there was that someone would let Mr. Charlie know. Colonel Shit and Polish maintained close contact with Marvin the ARVN. And there were a lot of Marvins who had relatives in VC cadres.

I considered telling Colonel Shithead to screw himself, but Drew and Westy warned me not to get playful. So I filed the paperwork, giving myself the discreet, dainty, self-effacing radio call-sign Sharkman One. Then we took our PBR and started upriver.

Eleven of us left at dusk, loaded down with as many lethal goodies as we could carry. Hoss Kucinski, the rear guard, brought half a dozen LAWS. I carried a 9mm pistol with a hush-puppy—silencer—and my M16, with lots of extra ammo. Risher had his Stoner; Dennis Drady and Frank Scollise carried extra mags. Doc Nixon carried the radio and stuffed his medical bags full of frag grenades. We might be out for two to three days—who knew how long the cease-fire would last—and we wanted to be prepared.

Drew Dix, Westy, and the Nungs watched as we cleared the pier behind the White House, moving slowly because our PBR crews didn't know the river. We left Chau Doc behind and steamed north. I stood in the cockpit with the lead PBR captain, a seasoned chief named Jack.

He adjusted the power and scanned the river, carefully watching for sandbars. "Gonna have some fun, Mr. Dick?"

"Hope so, Chief."

"How long you gonna stay out?"

"Two days if we're lucky."

He nodded. He reached into his pocket, took a cigarette, and lighted it. "Sounds good." He took a deep drag on the butt and exhaled smoke through his nose. "We'll stick around tonight," he said. "Not much sense cruising during the day tomorrow, but we'll be back on site tomorrow night."

"Sounds good to me, Chief." I paused. "This part of the river is new to you."

He shook his head. "New to everybody. We gotta be real careful up here."

I knew what he was talking about—and it wasn't just sandbars. The river got narrow and took a lot of ninety-degree turns north of Chau Doc. Many of those turns took you across the Red Line—the invisible border separating Vietnam and Cambodia. Tonight's mission, in fact, would start in Vietnam, although where it would end was anybody's guess. The idea was to come in from north of the Vinh Te canal—the direction Americans would be least expected to come from—and set up an ambush that looked like a listening post. If I was right, we'd catch Mr. Charlie trying to break the Tet holiday truce, and we'd kick his ass. If I was wrong, we'd have two lovely, quiet days in the countryside and come home none the worse for wear.

About eight kilometers from the city, just below the Red Line, Jack began a series of sweeps that brought the PBRs close to the shoreline. After three or four of these feints, we inserted covertly, leaving Jack and his crews to continue the pattern. If Charlie was watching, he had no idea what was going on, as no PBR had ever come this far up the Bassac before.

The brown water was warm as we went over the side, and we swam quickly onto the bank, crawled into the underbrush, popped the plugs from our rifle barrels, and moved onto the shore. The landscape was more like Virginia than Vietnam, filled with tall reeds and thick, green bushes that scraped like holly plants as we slithered under them.

By the time we'd moved twenty yards from the river, the ground turned hard and flat and the vegetation got brambly. We could make out a mountain eight or ten kilometers ahead. I knew from my map it was in Cambodia. On the other hand, so were we. Big deal.

We took bearings and began to move southwest, along a pattern of dikes that ran through a series of drained rice fields separated by small ditches. Beyond the flat fields, a tree line beckoned. Somewhere to the south, just behind the tree line, lay the Vinh Te canal. I wanted to move across the plain, through the tree line, toward the canal, and set up an ambush. The VC would be coming from Cambodia, from their trails and supply caches. We'd be waiting for them, and *gong-hay-fat-choy*—happy New Year!

By now it was about 2230. We were moving very slowly because we'd had reports about VC minefields from the

Nungs, although we hadn't come across any so far. The platoon was strung out over about twenty-five yards. My rabbits, Denny the Yenta Drady, Jack Saunders, and John Engraff, were up front, nosing a path through the rice fields for the rest of us to follow. Then came Risher, with the Stoner. I walked behind Risher, followed by Doc Nixon, who carried the radio. Dewayne Schwalenberg followed in Doc's footprints. Frank Scollise, Gordy Boyce, Harry Humphries, and Hoss Kucinski brought up the rear. I wanted the old guys—they hated it when I used to say that—behind me. Their instincts were perfect—and they could drop and shoot without my having to say a word to 'em.

We turned east. I'd hoped for a dark night, and I got my wish. We'd brought starlight scopes, low-intensity-light devices that allowed us to see in the dark. I carried one. So did Gordy Boyce, and so did Denny Drady. If VC were hiding out there, we'd see them before they saw us—or so we hoped.

Ahead of us, the sky was black. However, back at Chau Doc, Colonel Shit and Polish had evidently decided he'd put out flares. So to our south, the sky was bright, almost like when, coming up the Jersey Turnpike at night, you first see the lights of New York just below exit 13. We'd be hooking south soon, and our starlight scopes wouldn't be much help once we did. Maybe, I thought, the colonel would make enough noise so that nobody would pay any attention to eleven SEALs. Fat chance.

I could barely make out Denny Drady, a hundred feet or so ahead of us, inching forward. He held up his hand. We all froze. We hadn't advanced twenty yards yet. Drady waved for me to come forward—slowly. I made my way to his shoulder.

The fidgety little guy was pointing like a hound on scent. I followed his shaking finger.

It was barely visible in the chaff of the field, but Denny's keen eyes had picked it out—the button detonator of a VC antipersonnel mine.

"Shit." Were we at the beginning, middle, or end of a minefield? I had no idea.

I signaled the platoon not to move. "Minefield," I hissed. The warning was carried back down the line.

My senses were so sharp I could feel it as a single rivulet

of sweat made its way down the inside of my shirt. The tension was electric. Together, Denny and I dug around the perimeter of the mine, lifted it slowly out of its hole, and placed it gingerly on the ground.

I cracked a smile and tapped Denny on the back. "Good work, Yenta. Now, make me a path," I said.

He nodded, his beady, little round eyes bright with excitement. "Aye-aye, boss. Presto-chango—you're a path."

"Screw you, Yenta."

He blew me a kiss. "Not unless you shave first." Drady dropped to his knees, his knife out, probing the ground as he moved forward inch by inch, sweeping a path eighteen inches wide for the rest of us to move along. We followed behind, creeping slowly as he scrutinized every lump and bump.

It took us almost an hour to move less than two hundred feet. We didn't feel safe until we'd crossed a small drainage ditch and cut eastward, away from where Denny thought the pattern of the minefield lay.

He dropped into the ditch exhausted. "Shit, boss, I've had it."

He had good reason. He was soaked through with sweat; his mousy hair had matted under the black kerchief tied around his brow. His eyes had gone red with fatigue and stress. But he'd brought us through. Halfway through the field he'd pulled another mine out of the ground and guided us safely, leaving discreet markers so we could find our way back if we had to.

I hit him on the arm. "Take a break. I'll grab the point for a while."

"Thanks, boss."

We moved out toward the distant tree line. I took a slow pace, still moving carefully—more mines were a possibility. It was strange being on point, a role I usually did not take in the platoon. I wanted to be in the middle of the men, where I could control both front and rear. But tonight, with Denny exhausted, I somehow felt it was my turn.

On my first tour I'd watched Patches Watson lose five, six, even seven pounds of body weight every time Bravo Squad went out on a patrol, from the sheer physical and mental strain of taking the point. And Patches was a big, robust, strapping lad. Denny Drady was skinny to start with—now, the strain of getting us through the minefield had begun to take its toll and he looked like the proverbial drowned rat.

No question, point drains you. There has never been any war movie or book that has adequately described the overwhelming sensations that run through your mind, or the effects on your body, when you walk the point in a combat situation.

You can't let up, even for a microsecond. Every molecule in your body becomes an antenna, absorbing the endless succession of outside stimuli that bombard your senses, evaluating every infinitesimal change that takes place around you. Sight, sound, touch, smell, taste—each of these senses is being used to its utmost. And if you screw up, you get dead.

I was ten, perhaps fifteen yards ahead of Denny as we approached the tree line. I was moving one foot slowly in front of the other, inching along the dry drainage ditch.

My eyes swept the brush beyond the ditch's berm, then fell, searching for any telltale signs of footprints, not to mention trip wires. My fingers probed the ground for pressure pads or land-mine detonators. My ears listened for any foreign sounds—easy-to-detect ones like the metal on metal *raaatchet* of an AK-47's bolt sliding back, or the harder ones, like the sound of human breathing. My nose twitched like a bloodhound's, searching for the VC's distinctive body odor, accentuated by the *nuc mam* they poured on everything they ate.

I stopped. I held my breath. There was something out there. I could sense it. I could almost taste it. The hair on the back of my neck stood straight up.

Behind me the platoon waited.

To this day I don't know why I did what I did next. Instinct? Maybe. Luck? Probably.

I threw myself onto the ground.

As I dropped, the muzzle blast of an AK-47 came at me from no more than ten feet away.

I rolled, spraying at the flashes with my M16 as I did so, and screamed at the platoon to return fire. They were already hosing the tree line above my head, shrieking at me to get back.

I careened on hands, knees, and elbows toward my platoon, firing blindly over my shoulder while a firefight raged six inches above my head.

"What the—" I shouted to Gordy Boyce.

He calmly dropped a mag, inserted a fresh one, and sprayed the tree line. "Lots of muzzle blast," he bellowed at me. "Maybe thirty, forty of the bastards."

I peered at the incoming fire. "Shit—maybe more than that. Let's get the hell outta here." I rolled further down the ditch. "Hoss—"

"Boss?"

I pointed toward the VC. "LAWS, Ski. Hit the muthas."

The big Polack primed one of his antitank weapons, aimed it toward the tree line, and let it go at the biggest concentration of muzzle flashes. There was an explosion and a blast, followed by screams.

I waved my right hand in a circle. "Let's move it."

Firing as we went, we scrambled back the way we'd come. We hadn't reached our ambush objective—third base—but we'd rounded first and second, so I grabbed Doc Nixon's radio and called Colonel Shit and Polish for some of his much-vaunted artillery support.

The voice at the other end came back like a bad parody of a war movie. "No can do, Sharkman One, over."

"Why not, Command?"

"Because there's a tight situation here at command center—a VC attack and no assets can be spared in your direction. You're on your own."

Typical. Thank you very much for your care and your concern, Colonel, I thought. I will remind myself to come and visit you when all of this is over, and then I will break both of your fucking arms off, beat you senseless with them, then take what's left of the stumps and stick them up your ass.

I punched up a new frequency into the radio keypad and called the PBR.

"Jungle Gym, this is Sharkman One. We're coming out—pursued by one humongous group of unfriendlies and low on ammo. I need fire support at extraction point Alfa."

Jack's voice came through loud and clear. "Roger-roger, Sharkman One. I wilco. We'll be waiting. Kick some ass on the way home, too."

I had to laugh. God bless all Navy chiefs.

Okay—we'd called our taxis. But first we had to get to the bloody river. I could see the VC moving in the shadows, not fifty yards from us. There were lots more of them than there were of us, and they knew it. They came in hot pursuit—something that had never happened to me before.

I saw one distinctly and hosed him with my M16. He went down, only to be replaced by three more. I hosed them, too, ducked away from the returning fire, and kept moving.

Hoss dropped to one knee and loosed one of his LAWS. That left two. Risher called out for another Stoner belt. There wasn't another Stoner belt. Harry Humphries shouted that he was down to his last three AK magazines.

He wasn't the only one. We were all running low on ammo. If the PBR missed the pickup, we'd be hamburger.

Denny Drady led the way through the minefield—trotting. We followed in his footsteps, praying. It must've worked because we didn't set anything off. Maybe a few of the VC sons of bitches would blow themselves up coming after us.

We bolted through the drained paddies, staying low in the ditches. Branches we'd managed to evade earlier now became sharp-edged weapons that slashed at us as we passed. Vines became trip wires. Chuckholes waited to snap our ankles.

This was not going the way I'd planned at all. We were at a dead run by the time we hit the riverbank, scores of VC in hot pursuit.

The PBRs were there—bows beached—right where they should have been. Their twin .50s and mortars gave us covering fire as we scrambled over the gunwales, pushed out into the current, reversed engines, did what amounted to wheelies, and spun into the middle of the river.

I counted heads, then collapsed in the cockpit, the wonderful lethal odor of cordite wafting over me as the crew raked the shoreline with fire. Jack turned up the speed and the boat raced into the night, moving south. I could see tracers walking toward us from the shoreline, but we moved quickly out of range.

I pulled myself to my feet and slammed the chief on the shoulder. "Thanks for saving our ass, Jack."

"Forget it. But we ain't finished yet, Mr. Dick."

"What's up?"

"Chau Doc—they're being overrun. The VC launched a big attack against the city, figurin' everybody'd stood down because of the Tet truce."

"No shit?"

"No shit, sir. And y'know what else? That dipshit pencil-dicked scumbag pus-nuts asshole colonel's keeping all his guys inside the compound. Westy and Drew got some real bad problems. They need us."

"So? Home, James—and don't wait for the stoplights either."

Chapter

12

WE GOT TO CHAU DOC AT OH DARK HUNDRED BUT DIDN'T
land until first light. I wasn't real familiar with the town's
layout, and besides, we couldn't tell the good guys from the
bad ones without a scorecard. So we hunkered down, chilled
to the bone, and listened to the gunfire. Just before six, Jack
put his bow into shore, nosed the boat onto a wide set of
stone steps, and we went over the gunwales directly below
the main town square, about a quarter mile north of the White
House.

There was a lot of shooting going on. We dodged rico-
cheting bullets and mortar blasts and ran, tumbling ass over
teakettle into the Special Forces compound, where I caromed
into the TOC—the Tactical Operations Center—to find out
what the hell was going on.

A frazzled Special Forces major in impeccable fatigues gave
me a quick intel dump. The situation was bad, he said. The
VC—how many there were he didn't know—had overrun
much of the city. Civilians were trapped somewhere—he
didn't know how many or where.

The man was a fount of useful information. Then he actually
gave me some good news: Colonel Shit and Polish, he whis-

pered conspiratorially, was over the edge. He'd locked himself in the radio room, where he currently sat, listening to the chatter. But colonel sir was still technically in command, major told me. Moreover, he'd ordered that no U.S. troops could take any action outside the compound, a command the major was obeying with relish.

I got on the radio to Westy. "This is a goatfuck over here."

"I know. How many you got with you?"

"Eleven."

"Great. I put my three dozen Nungs out on the south end of town. You and your guys take the north side. Flush the VC back the way they came."

"Gotcha. You got ammo at your place?"

"All you need."

"What about medevac?"

"I can get it if you need it."

"What about Colonel Shitface?"

Westy snorted. "Screw him. I'll kill the son of a bitch myself after this is all over."

"I got first dibs."

He laughed. It sounded tinny through the radio. "There's another problem."

"What?"

"Three American civilians—a nurse and two school-teachers—pinned down a few blocks away from you."

"I got no transportation, Westy, and I don't know the city. Hold on a second." I turned to the major. "Westy says we got civilian women pinned down, Major. Can we go get 'em?"

He shrugged. "Nothing I can do, Lieutenant."

"Come on . . ."

"Hey, Lieutenant, the colonel's orders say no one goes out. That includes you and your men now that you're here." He picked up a mug of coffee and started to sip.

I grabbed the asshole by the pressed lapels of his fatigues. The cup went into the air and coffee splattered all over him. I lifted his feet six inches off the ground. "Say what, Major?"

"Okay, okay. You can leave. But our guys stay."

"You queer cockbreath pussies can bugger yourselves day and night for all I care." I tossed him across the room and watched him crumple against the wall.

160

I picked up the radio again. "Can you send anybody to pick us up?"

"We got a jeep with a fifty-cal on it. I'll send Drew—he knows where the civilians are."

"We'll be ready."

I commandeered ten hand radios, made sure the batteries were fresh, and tuned them to Westy's channel. Then we all went out into the sunshine. Drew showed up in the jeep about six minutes later, doing a nice wheelie as he careened into the compound, chased by automatic weapons fire. I waved Harry and Doc Nixon into the vehicle. "Go play cavalry. Maybe you'll get laid."

Harry flashed a thumbs-up. "I hope so." He straddled the backseat, took the machine gun's grips in his hands, and fired a short burst. "Works nice."

"See you." Drew spun away. We laid down covering fire as they sped off.

Risher, Drady, Hoss Kucinski, Johnny Engraff, and I made up one blocking force. Frank Scollise, Dewayne Schwalenberg, Gordy Boyce, and Jack Saunders broke into another, and we all set off toward the White House.

It was like the TV series "Combat." Chau Doc was a French-designed city, and we fought street to street, alley to alley, house to house, in an Asian version of WWII.

We'd see fire coming from a window. I'd whistle for Hoss. "There—"

He'd set up with a LAWS, fire through the frame, then Drady and I would kick in the door and rush the place, firing, to finish the VC off. If any came out, Risher would kill them with the Stoner, and we'd go on to the next house.

"Fire from the rooftop," Drady called out to me.

"I see it. Risher—"

Risher swung the machine gun up. The bullets cut through the edge of the roof line like a buzz saw. A VC tumbled two stories into the street.

We moved another few yards and cleared two more houses. We were still taking fire from above. The VC had a good idea. I pointed up. "Let's take 'em from the top."

We kicked a door in and clambered up two flights of stairs, climbed through a trapdoor and onto the roof. The houses were side by side, close enough so that we could jump from roof to roof. Twenty yards away was a VC holding a hand grenade with no pin. I brought my M16 up and stitched him across the chest. He went down on top of the grenade. It blew him off the roof in three pieces.

We worked our way along one street, around the corner, and up the next, firing down into clusters of VC. It was grueling work. By midmorning we'd cleared only three streets.

Meanwhile, Harry and Doc were having their own kind of fun, as I found out later. They'd pulled up in front of one house, where a nurse named Maggie lived. VC fire came from the second story. Mindless of the bullets, Drew kicked the door in while Harry returned fire with the .50, and Doc Nixon washed the windows with his M16.

As Drew went in the front door, a trio of VC were coming in the back. He hit them with a burst from his M16 and they went down. Another pair shot down the stairwell at him. He killed them, too.

"Maggie, Maggie, it's Drew—where the hell are you?"

"Here," a quivering voice from a cupboard in the living room answered. Drew ran and pulled the frightened nurse out from where she'd been hiding. He threw his arm around her. "Come on."

As they ran, more VC came through the back door. Drew spun, pushed Maggie out the door, and shot them. He slammed the front door shut, tossed the nurse into the jeep where she landed on Doc Nixon, and they sped back toward the White House. In all, Harry, Doc, and Drew made six round-trips—and they got all the civilians out without a scratch. But Doc Nixon insisted the best was when Maggie'd landed on top of him.

"What a great pair of knockers," he told me. "My kind of woman."

Shortly after noon, the VC started pulling back. There weren't a lot of them—not more than a couple of hundred. But there were fewer than fifty of us, including the Nungs, to confront them. Still, we'd overrun many of their positions by midmorning, and they disappeared, melting into Chau Doc's warren of streets and alleys, or changing clothes and once again becoming the loyal, docile, friendly local population.

The good news was that Westy's Nungs had been successful in ejecting the enemy from the south side of town, pushing them east into the countryside. The bad news was that, during the fighting, the fuel farm had blown, and a lot of civilians had been cooked. The pungent smell of burning flesh was evident from half a mile away. (The next day, we scheduled medevac choppers for as many of the burned Vietnamese as we could. Jack took a bunch more on the PBR, sailing down-river to the hospital at Sa Dec, over on the Mekong River. Maggie went with him. When she got back, her clothes smelled as if she'd just spent eight hours working at a barbecue.)

In the early hours of the attack, the VC set up firing positions in Chau Doc's church and hospital. It's a guerrilla tactic still used today that forces anyone attacking them to destroy the civilian target, which gives the guerrillas a propaganda victory even if they lose the actual battle.

That's what happened at Chau Doc—we pushed the VC out, but both the church and the hospital were left in ruins. And within days, VC cadres started circulating word through the countryside that the round-eyed bandits (that was us) had destroyed civilian targets without cause.

It also wasn't until after twelve o'clock that we first saw any Marvin the ARVNs poke their noses out of their defensive perimeter, which was near the army compound. That was par for the course. The Marvins generally liked to keep their heads down during times of hostile activity—they'd been trained by Colonel Shit and Polish, after all, and he was still locked inside his radio room. But afterward, they always came around for mopping up—I always thought it was because that's when they could find lots of VC souvenirs to sell on the black market. But the Marvins weren't alone in their cowardice. Once we cleared out all the VC, Colonel Shitface would probably throw on a flak jacket, perform an inspection—and put himself in for a medal. (I don't know what happened to the colonel, but Drew Dix did win the Medal of Honor for his actions during the battle of Chau Doc. The one thing I don't understand about that was that Harry and Doc Nixon were with Drew the whole time—and all they ever got was Bronze Stars. That made me wonder whether the criteria were higher for SEALs than they were for Green Berets.)

With the VC in retreat, we decided to clear as much of the city as we could, working block by block. We split up into pairs and much like cops on the beat, strolled the sidewalks. Hoss Kucinski and I took one side of a street; Scollise and Risher were opposite us. The enemy fire was intermittent—almost none one minute, thick the next. We worked in a choreographed plan. I'd slide up to a doorway, kick it in, roll a grenade, and wait to see if anything happened. If it was all clear, Hoss would leapfrog me and do the next door. If I heard anything, I'd wait until after the grenade exploded, then go through the door and spray the room with my M16. The SEALs on the opposite side of the street did the same. It was the perfect way to spend a lovely, sunny Tet holiday afternoon in greater metropolitan Chau Doc.

Then we started taking fire from down the street. Hoss and I dove into a doorway. So did Scollise. Risher didn't. The kid took his Stoner and walked out into the middle of the street, screaming and firing. It was Dodge City, Vietnam. The machine gun was cradled in his arms; this crazy smile was on his face.

He was screaming, "Come on, you assholes—come on, you assholes." They'd shoot at him—you could see the puffs at the ground around his feet as the shots hit. He paid them no mind.

Hoss and I were screaming at him.

"You asshole—get the fuck off the street."

"You dipshit, get down."

He was laughing. The crazy motherfucker was actually laughing.

Then—there was this incredible instant of silence in the middle of all the noise and confusion.

I knew what was gonna happen. I yelled at Risher, "Noooooo—"

It was too late. I heard it. One shot. One sniper's shot.

It caught him in the center of the forehead.

He dropped the Stoner and sagged to the ground. I was there quick enough to catch him. Hoss let a LAWS go in the direction the shot had come from. I don't know if it hit anything. I was otherwise occupied.

I dragged Risher out of the street. My hand, which was holding the back of his head, was wet. The shot had gone through. His brains were spilling into my hand. I tried to push them back inside the skull, but it was impossible.

I shot the kid full of painkillers, but he didn't feel anything anyway. Hoss called for medevac. We got on the radio to Drew, Doc Nixon, and Harry, who drove over under fire in the jeep to pick us up and take us to the chopper pad at Westy's, which was about six blocks away.

They arrived in minutes, Drew at the wheel. Harry jumped out and took Risher's legs. Doc had him under the arms. I held his head.

"Shit." Harry eased the kid's body into the back of the jeep. He held one of Risher's hands, his face grim. Doc Nixon had the other hand. "You dumb fuck," Harry said to Risher. "There's a couple of cases of cold beer at Westy's. At least you could have waited—"

Doc covered Risher with a blanket. Somehow, we all clambered into the jeep and Drew took off.

He was going. I'd morphined him right away, and he wasn't in any pain. But he was going. It was in his eyes. His eyes were already dead.

He knew it, too. He looked up at me like a fucking puppy.

I was mad at the son of a bitch. He'd asked for it. "You stupid cockbreath pus-nuts asshole," I kept saying, holding his head in my hands, trying to push his goddamn brains back inside his shattered skull with my thumb.

My black pajamas were sopping wet with his blood. My hands were sticky. I could feel skull fragments on my fingertips.

"You stupid dumb fuck," is all I could say as he lay dying in my lap.

There was incredible rage in me right then. Some of it was directed at Risher himself. If he hadn't been dying, I would probably have killed him myself. He was dying because he'd been stupid: he'd walked down the middle of the street. You don't do that, and he knew it, and he did it anyway, and therefore he was a stupid asshole cuntbreath and he deserved what he'd gotten.

Except he didn't deserve it, and as he lay there, his head in my lap and his brains in my hand, I knew he didn't deserve it at all.

There was incredible rage in me right then because I felt

Risher shouldn't have been there in the first place. We were SEALs. We were jungle warriors, not dipshit urban policemen. The goddamn colonel and the Special Forces should have been out in the street taking the point instead of sitting behind six rolls of concertina razor wire and ten-foot-high concrete walls in his fucking neat-as-a-fucking-West-Point-parade-ground compound.

There was incredible rage in me right then because my man had been killed by some goddamn, stinking, seventy-pounds-soaking-wet, VC Mr. Charlie pus-nuts sniper. Right then I hated all Vietnamese, a useless class of *nuc mam*–swilling subhumans who needed two sticks to pick up one grain of rice but used only one to carry two buckets of shit.

And there was incredible rage in me right then because, when Risher was sniped, my own immortality got nicked as well. First night out in Vietnam the AK round came skipping across the river and popped the guy next to me between the eyes. Why him and not me? I was running the trails on Dung Island barefoot one day, and the man behind me stepped right into my footprint, and—blam—a small land mine went off. It blew the beta boot right off his foot. Why him and not me? Guys on either side of me had been hit. Why them and not me?

Why? Because I was fucking immortal, that's why.

That's what I'd felt. That's why I'd do anything, go anywhere—against any odds—and tell my men that with me, they were always gonna be okay. Dings, yeah. Scratches, yeah—even an occasional pop now and then. But nobody dies with Marcinko.

Unit fucking integrity. Nobody dies. You will be all right with Lieutenant (j.g.) Rick Marcinko, Demo Dick, Sharkman of the Delta. Now hear this: nobody dies.

In the last twelve hours I'd ducked an AK round shot straight into my face at ten paces—and survived. I'd run my platoon through a minefield at night—and we'd made it without a scratch. We'd been chased by a company of VC—and no one had anything more serious than a sprained ankle. Eleven of us had taken on two hundred VC, and we'd driven them out of the north side of Chau Doc, block by goddamn block, and no one was any the worse for wear.

Until now.

I don't know who I hated more: the VC scumbag who'd shot Risher, or Colonel Shit and Polish, who was too much of a pussy to do his own fighting, or the goddamn Vietnamese who had been doing this crap to each other for generations. Fact is, any of the above wouldn't have wanted to be alone with me right then. It would have been dangerous.

I caressed Risher's dying face with my hand. "You stupid dumb fuck."

I learned some bitter lessons from Risher's death. The most important one affected the way in which I waged war from then on. My primary mission, as I now saw it, was to bring my men back home alive. How I did that was of no consequence to me. If it meant that during interrogation sessions I became tougher, even brutal, to VC suspects, so be it. If it meant that we had to become more ruthless in battle, then that's what we did. Indeed, if keeping us all alive was my first priority, killing VC was my second. And third was the development of SEAL tactics—using the war to find the most effective way to employ SEALs in a hostile environment. Those lessons stayed with me for the rest of my career. There are those who think I'm bloodthirsty—too "dirty"—when it comes to tactics. Fact is, I'll do what has to be done to keep my men alive, and kill as many of the enemy as I can.

Further, I realized after Chau Doc that we Americans meant nothing to the Vietnamese. Not to our alleged allies in the South, and not to our adversaries from the North. It was their war. They'd been fighting it for centuries. We were simply another impediment to them, another ephemeral invasion of round-eyed, white-skinned ghosts. So they'd mess with us—both our allies and our adversaries. For example, ever since *Male* magazine had put me on its cover—"Lt. 'Demo Dick' Marcinko—The Navy's Deadliest Viet Nam Shark-Man" was how it read—I'd become the target of dozens of jokes and pranks from my fellow SEALs. I didn't mind them—I got even with each and every one of the pranksters. And I can take a joke as well as anyone.

I wasn't too keen, however, about the VC Wanted Posters tacked to trees and hootches all over the Delta about three months after the *Male* article was published. The first of them read, "*Award of 50,000 piasters to anyone who could kill First*

Lieutenant Demo Dick Marcinko, a gray-faced killer who had brought death and trouble to the Chau Doc Province during the Lunar New Year."

That was me, all right. And I didn't much care for the fact that they not only knew my name but knew that I'd been at Chau Doc for Tet. So much for operational security.

I took down another one during a raid we staged in Ke Sach in mid-May. "*Award of 10,000 piasters to anyone who could kill the leader of the secret blue-eye killer's party that massacred many families [here] during the United Nation Day of 2 January, 1968.*" That was me, too. We'd been the only ones operating in Ke Sach January second. We'd killed six— maybe even seven—VC.

Such tactics from the VC were to be expected—although to be honest I found it ironic that they read *Male*. It took me longer to learn to how to "read" the friendlies. They had their own ways of playing head games with you.

When the platoon would go through a village, we'd often stop to have a meal. Gordy and I carried Vietnamese piasters, and we always paid for the rice and fish we ate. It served two purposes. One, we didn't have to carry food, which allowed us to make up the weight in bullets. Second, it brought us, I'd always thought, closer to the people. I thought so because it made sense to me, round-eyes that I am, that by eating with them and spending time with them, they would come to trust us.

And in fact, the villagers we spent time with were friendly. They would often come up to us and touch us as we hunkered down with our rice bowls.

In the beginning, I thought it was because we were strangers and they wanted to feel our uniforms, made from unfamiliar material, and see the weapons up close and see if our hairy, white skin felt the same as their smooth, yellow skin.

Then I learned what they were really doing when they touched us.

They were passing on their demons to us.

They were protecting themselves and their villages; passing on their evil spirits to the round-eyes by touching them. In Vietnam, evil spirits are passed that way.

So I began passing them back.

When kids touched me, holding me around the knees, I'd

take them in my arms and wipe some of my camouflage grease on their faces or their hair. When the elders rubbed my arms to feel the hair, I'd rub them right back. I'd smile and grab them and say, "*Chao hom-nay-dep-troi*," which was the equivalent of "Have a nice day."

Fuck me, Charlie? *Du-ma-nhieu*—Fuck *you!* Doom on you, Charlie.

Chapter

13

I FLEW BACK TO VIRGINIA BEACH EARLY IN JULY OF 1968 to take on an assignment that turned out to be tougher than fighting VC—becoming a full-time husband and father. My son, Richie, was five; my daughter, Kathy, was three. Neither had seen much of me before. (Little Kathy screamed and screamed when I picked her up during the first couple of weeks I was home.) Nor, for that matter, had I seen much of Kathy-Ann. Between training sessions and my two Vietnam tours, I'd been away from home more than twenty of the previous twenty-four months—and the visits home had been in one- or two-week spurts.

So there was a fair amount of settling in to be done, not to mention a two-page, single-spaced list of "honeydews"— house and yard maintenance chores—that had gone awaiting because I was overseas. I was proud of our home, a tiny brick ranch house around the corner from the Princess Anne Shopping Mall. The place was small, and it was modestly furnished. But it was ours—we'd bought it between my first and second Vietnam tours. That act alone made me different from my parents, who'd never owned any of the houses in which we'd lived.

Over the summer of '68, I spent my days with the Teams, working as a training officer for the kids who were about to ship over to Vietnam. Most of the time was spent at a place we called Dismal Swamp, which was located near the North Carolina border. I took Richie with me on one trip. He had a blast. He shared my sleeping bag and got to plink beer cans with the BB gun I bought for him. He met some of the SEALs from Eighth Platoon and watched, amazed, as Freddie Toothman caught water moccasins with his bare hands and wrung their necks.

He also tasted his first venison. One night, a deer made the mistake of swimming across the river just below our campsite. The guys saw it, and I jumped off the pier with a short machete, cut its throat, and dragged it underwater to drown it. Then I pulled it out onto the shore and Richie watched as I gutted it—I even showed him how we'd learned to crawl inside the carcass to stay warm during survival training—and he ate grilled Bambi chops for the first time. He loved 'em.

I played SEAL trainer until November. Then I volunteered to go back to Vietnam.

My argument was that I couldn't really be an effective trainer unless I knew what was happening in-country. The games that had worked for me during the first six months of 1968 might not work for SEALs during the first six months of 1969.

The Navy, however, had other plans. In its infinite wisdom, the Bureau of Naval Personnel—BUPERS—assigned me to a vacant slot as the special operations adviser at COMPHIBTRALANT. For the uninitiated, that's Navyspeak for COMmander, AmPHIBious TRAining Command AtLANTic. I'd still be working at the Little Creek Naval Base—in fact, COMPHIBTRALANT was only two blocks from SEAL Team Two's HQ. But those two blocks of sidewalk were separated by a vast gulf of tradition and behavior. As the SpecWar/COMPHIBTRALANT, I'd hold a staff position.

At the Teams, everything revolved around the physical. You trained endlessly. You drank with the boys nightly. The world was rough-and-tumble macho, full of fuck-you-very-much tough talk and I Am the Baddest Motherfucker on the Block attitude. T-shirts and shorts were the uniform of the day, and if your hair wasn't quite perfectly combed, well, tough titty, dickhead.

Now, all of a sudden I was going to become the kind of officer I'd always ridiculed—a staff puke. The prospect of turning into a bureaucratic, dip-dunk, whining, drag-ass paper pusher did not excite me in the least. And I wasn't shy about expressing my sentiments to anyone who'd listen.

"What the hell do I need this staff crap for?" I asked Kathy-Ann one night. We were sitting in our living room. The kids had been put down for the night and we had a couple of beers in our hands.

"I don't know. What *do* you need it for?"

It was a valid question. I thought about it. "Career track I guess."

"So . . . ?"

"There's so much bullshit involved," I said evasively. I sipped at my beer, peering over the can at my wife. In fact, I wasn't worried about bureaucratic bullshit at all. I knew I could handle that. What made me apprehensive was much more fundamental and deep-rooted. At COMPHIBTRA-LANT I knew I would have to prove myself on a battlefield that was not, so far as I was concerned, tilted in my favor.

In Vietnam, I'd gone nose to nose with Naval Academy grads or ROTC reserve officers and won. I was a tougher, more resourceful warrior than any of them, and they knew it. Because I'd been an enlisted man, I could talk trash with the boat crews or curse out sailors with a two-minute stream of profanity as articulate as any master chief's. Because I'd spent my time pushing the limits of SpecWar, there was nothing I wouldn't do on the battlefield—with or without the permission of my superiors. That was fine so long as I remained overseas. But the rowdy renegade's reputation I'd won in Vietnam was not, I knew, something that would ultimately boost my Navy career.

Regular Navy officers—ship drivers, aviators, or nuclear submariners—mistrust SpecWarriors. That is a fact of life. Even when I was a full commander, wet-behind-the-ears ensigns straight out of the Academy would look at the Budweiser crest—the eagle, anchor, and trident emblem all SEALs wear—on my uniform blouse and sneer. They knew that in the Navy caste system I was an untouchable; that my kind were seen as unpredictable knuckle-draggers. They knew they'd make admiral, while we SEALs would not.

Moreover, success at COMPHIBTRALANT would be based on the way I expressed and conducted myself, and— to be frank—I had no idea whether or not I could carry it off. Despite the fact that I'd just been promoted to full lieutenant, I was still a high-school dropout. My GED certificate had been won during a Med cruise at the behest of Ev Barrett, whose spelling skills stopped somewhere short of words with three syllables. Sure, I'd handled Barrett's paperwork during my time at UDT-21 and UDT-22 and written "barn-dance cards" (after-action reports), fitreps, and commendation citations for my squads and platoon in Vietnam. But I had no experience in report writing; no training in the Machiavellian craft of memo-drafting. As a COMPHIBTRALANT staff officer, I'd be as vulnerable and exposed to bureaucratic flak as any NILO roach would have been to the real thing at Chau Doc during Tet.

There was a secondary element to my unease, too: Kathy-Ann. She'd never taken on any of the ticket-punching volunteer work that officers' wives are expected to do. How could she? She was stuck with two young kids and a house to maintain, and a husband who hadn't been around for the better part of two years. Still, if I planned to make the Navy my life—and I did—we'd both have a bunch of rough edges to smooth off in a big hurry. I'd need a college education, and Kathy would need to begin acting like a junior officer's wife, if we wanted to whirl ourselves up the old career cone. I had more butterflies in my gut over my new assignment than I'd ever had in Vietnam.

Things took a definite turn for the better the day I met the admiral for the first time. I was summoned to a "meet and greet" command performance in his office one morning. The admiral was a two-star named Ray Peet, a bushy-eyebrowed, impeccably turned out officer who looked as if he'd been sent over to play the part by Central Casting. I'd seen him climbing in or out of his car on the base. To little old snake-eater me, he was impressive. He never had a hair out of place. His shoes were mirror polished, his nails smartly buffed, his tie perfectly tied, and the creases in his trousers razor-sharp. It was downright disheartening. I must have spent two hours getting myself ready to meet him. I don't think I'd ever worked so hard at spit and polish—not even in my Geeky days, when I polished both the tops and soles of my boots.

A beribboned aide ushered me into a huge, plush office. Admiral Peet swiveled his high-backed judge's chair to face me across a desk the size of a small aircraft carrier. I saluted. He returned it, glowering. Then a smile as warm as a Vietnam sunrise spread across his face. He rose, came out from behind the desk, and shook my hand.

"Glad to have you aboard, son."

"Thank you, sir."

"Sit." He indicated a wing chair at one end of a long cherry coffee table. I sat at attention. He took the end seat on the Queen Anne sofa, next to an inlaid corner table on which sat an ornate brass lamp made out of an antique fire extinguisher, a big, multiline phone console, and a foot-high stack of reports, the color on each cover sheet denoting the level of security classification contained within. The pile looked like a rainbow.

"So, Lieutenant, what brings you to COMPHIBTRA-LANT?"

I'd thought about what I'd say if I was asked that question. The Geek in me would have answered, "Because it was time for a dip-dunk puke staff assignment and the asshole cock-breath shit-eating goatfuckers at BUPERS won't let me go back to Vietnam."

However, I looked Admiral Peet right in the eye and said, "Well, sir, I've just spent the last year and a half in Vietnam, and I thought it was time to give the younger guys a chance to do some fighting, while I took the opportunity to develop some staff expertise." I said it with a straight face, too.

"You did pretty well over there—Silver Star, four Bronze Stars, two Navy Commendation Medals."

"Yes, sir. But—"

"But?"

"Admiral, I'm a damn good SEAL, and I love to fight. But to make the Navy a real career, I have to understand how the Navy works—and that you can learn only as a staff officer. Besides, sir, working here would also allow me the time to attend night school. You've seen my jacket, sir. I don't have a college degree. I think it's important to go to night school so I can compete for a slot in the Navy's BA/BS program at Monterey."

Peet nodded. "I think you're looking at things realistically, son," he said.

We talked for another twenty minutes or so. He asked me about my family, and why I'd become a SEAL, and what Vietnam had been like. He told me what he expected of me, which was to begin coordinating SEAL activities within the amphibious training command, and to represent unconventional warfare's point of view on his staff. Then it was time to go. An aide slipped into the room and coughed discreetly. "Your next appointment is waiting outside, sir."

I stood and saluted smartly. "Thank you for your time, sir." At the doorway, I turned back toward Peet. "By the way, Admiral," I said, "if you should ever want to go shooting or jumping, or try your hand at demolition work, I'm sure I can arrange it."

The admiral's eyebrows jolted a full inch, as if he'd received an electric shock. Then he laughed out loud. "I'll be sure to keep that in mind, Lieutenant. Dismissed."

It took a couple of months of adjustment, but I actually began to enjoy staff work by early 1969. Part of it was the challenge of getting the SEAL viewpoint included in amphibious warfare doctrine, something that had not happened at COMPHIBTRALANT before I arrived.

Any success I enjoyed was largely because of Admiral Peet, who was an understanding and encouraging boss for whom to work, and a lanky captain named Bob Stanton, who showed up a few weeks after I'd started. Bob was being parked at COMPHIBTRALANT while the Navy decided whether or not he'd get his first star. He drove down from Washington in a Fiat 600, which looks like one of those tiny circus cars. I watched as he pulled himself out of it. It was like Jack and the Beanstalk: he just kept coming and coming. I'd never met anyone that tall before—he must have been almost seven feet.

Stanton was a former UDT officer, which meant that he and I spoke the same language. He was also the kind of old-style Navy officer who operated under Barrett's First Law of the Sea, which meant he took me under his wing. He taught me the intricacies of getting a superior's "chop," or approval, on a draft memo that the superior might in fact not like at all. He gave me research assignments that forced me to become intimately familiar with the base library. He blue-penciled my memos and reports, making me rewrite them again and again until they read like English instead of bureaucratese. He protected me from the backstabbing that is routine on all staffs. By the time Captain Bob left, I was sailing along under my own power. The work may have been tough, but it was gratifying to me that I could do it as well as any of my diploma-toting colleagues.

Workdays were tolerable, if long. I'd report before eight and finish about four, then drive thirty miles to the College of William and Mary, or up to Old Dominion University, for five hours of night classes. After school I'd head home, arrive just before midnight, and grab a late supper. I'd get a few minutes with Kathy-Ann, hit the books until two, then sleep until six.

My weekends were my own. I'd play with the kids, catch up on housework—I even managed to plant a prize-winning flower garden one summer. Once a month I'd have to requalify in demolition work, and I'd take my jumping quals once a quarter, and diving quals every six months. But aside from that, I had virtually no contact with SEAL Team Two or any of my old friends from UDT. If I had a specific question about operations, I'd call with it. But the nights of beer drinking at local bars and the brawling went out the window. I was, for the first time since I'd been married, a full-time husband and father. It wasn't as bad as I'd thought.

About a year after I arrived, Admiral Peet was replaced by an old sea dog named Ted Snyder, a salty ex-submariner who kept a sub's Klaxon diving horn in his rec room. When he'd get a little frisky from his whiskey, you could hear him hit it half a mile away—*awhoooga, awhoooga, DIVE! DIVE!*

Snyder and Peet were opposites in almost every way. Peet was a professional bureaucrat, a paper warrior; Snyder was a deepwater sailor and professional ship driver. Peet was bank-president impeccable in his demeanor; Snyder was more informal—even sailorly profane from time to time. But I was glad to have the opportunity to serve them both. From Peet I learned to appreciate the planning that goes into good staff work. You cannot control large units by making seat-of-the-pants decisions, and Peet's methodical, do-it-by-the-numbers style of command taught me both tactics and execution. From Snyder, I learned something just as valuable: the care and feeding of flag officers.

The old man took a shine to me. He brought me along to meetings and let me sit in. He took me to cocktail parties, slipping me a wink and a nod—"Buy that guy a drink" or "Take this guy's phone number." He'd talk to me about the politics of officerdom, teaching me about the sorts of ticket-punching activities, such as becoming a scoutmaster or making speeches to the local Rotary Club, that promotion boards weigh heavily when making their decisions.

To help me move along the old career track, he put me on the board of directors of the Planetarium, Little Creek's quarters for visiting flag officers. Why "Planetarium"? Because that's where the "stars" slept. Talk about scaling the salt off. You don't talk to stewards in the Ev Barrett mode. Nor do you carry on with the blankety-blank-blanking language when you're negotiating with admirals' wives over decor. Perfectly coiffed Mrs. Three-Star Admiral Jones does not like to hear young Lieutenant Dick say the word *fuck*.

I learned a new word: *subtlety*. I discovered, for example, that such little details as fresh flowers nicely arranged can make a friend for life of a three-star's wife—which, Admiral Snyder reminded me, was often just as important as making friends with the three-star himself.

To sharpen my pea-snorting, spaghetti-sucking social graces, he ordered me to take charge of arranging his own cocktail parties. So I learned to deal with the base commissary. My entire previous experience with food had consisted of slinging hash at Gussy's, and working in a bakery during my Team days. Now I was becoming a maven on the subject of hors d'oeuvres hot and cold, exotic liquors and imported wines—even discovering through a process of elimination which knives and forks were proper for what dishes.

The same energy I used when training Bravo Squad or Eighth Platoon was now channeled into the new and uncharted area of catering. I was as demanding as a meticulous maître d'—making sure that everything was delivered and set up on time. But more significantly, as those flag-rank parties unfolded in front of me, a curtain was lifted on a style of life I knew nothing about.

As a Team member, even as a SEAL officer, I had ridiculed everything about "pinky in the air" behavior. It was something I mimicked before throwing someone through a plate-glass window. Now, I realized, the highfalutin stuff, as I'd called it, was part of a complicated social ritual. It was a code—a code that I was beginning to break. And as Admiral Snyder was quick to point out, once I'd broken the code successfully, there was no height my career could not reach.

So—how doth the child learn? The child learneth through imitation. My regular contacts with the mess stewards allowed Kathy-Ann and me to begin giving our own parties, albeit on a lieutenant's budget. I'd wander over to the Planetarium and tell the chief, "Chief, I'm planning to have thirty people over Saturday night. The budget is sixty dollars."

For that sixty dollars, we would receive finger food and all the booze we needed, as well as two stewards in starched white jackets to serve it all up nice and proper. The surroundings may not have been as elegant as the Snyders' quarters, but we were definitely a couple of steps above the beer-and-pretzels backyard barbecues I'd held at the Teams. And we became consistent entertainers, making a point of throwing a cocktail party every couple of months for the last year and a half I was on Snyder's staff. The guest list was varied—a mix of officers from COMPHIBTRALANT, as well as my old colleagues from SEAL Team Two such as Fred Kochey and Jake Rhinebolt. Gordy Boyce came, too. But he was no longer encouraged to perform the Dance of the Flaming Asshole.

Admiral Snyder also prodded me to write a paper on the use of remote sensors in riverine warfare, a paper that he ran through channels until it was accepted as Navy tactical doctrine and gained me a letter of commendation. At his urging I also made an oral presentation to the Amphibious Warfare Board about improved ways in which UDT or SEAL teams could be delivered on-site, including one recommendation (it was later actually implemented) to reconfigure nuclear subs as underwater SEAL delivery vehicles, with launch capabilities for SDVs—Submersible Delivery Vehicles—and other SEAL transportation.

The hard work paid off, too. Snyder wrote me a terrific set of fitreps *("Lt. Marcinko is one of the most dedicated, hardest working and professionally knowledgeable officers this reporting senior has observed, an officer who eats, sleeps and thinks Special Warfare, especially SEAL activities.")*. But better, he called the Navy program in Monterey, California, and virtually ordered them to accept me for the 1971–72 academic year. They did.

I went out and bought a VW camper—one of those vans with a fabric pop-top roof. Then I rigged a tow bar for our beat-up Renault; we packed up the house, said our farewells, stowed the kids in the van, and took off for California in May 1971, looking all the world like a family of Gypsies.

We spent sixteen glorious months in Monterey, where I finally received my college degree, a BA in international affairs. When I wasn't going to school, or bowling or sport jumping or camping in the California mountains or riding the quarter horse I bought the kids, I was ticket-punching. I joined the Jaycees. I became a Cub Scout packmaster. (My Cubs were probably the only ones ever to hunt, kill, and skin frogs and eat fresh frog's legs during overnight hikes. Some of the daddies got queasy, but the kids were all right.)

I performed regularly on the public-speaking circuit, talking about Navy Special Warfare at civic organizations, churches, and schools. I was selected for inclusion in the 1972 edition of *Outstanding Young Men in America*. And I can personally testify that ticket-punching works. I was promoted to lieutenant commander in 1972—two years early.

During my last six months of college, I spent three days a week monitoring Vietnamese language courses over at the Army foreign-language school. Rumor had it I was going to be sent back to Vietnam as the chief round-eyed adviser for all South Vietnamese Navy SEALs. But at the last minute the job was withdrawn, part of the Vietnamization of the war. Instead, I got a call from an admiral's office in Washington.

"Lieutenant Commander Marcinko?"

"Speaking."

"Please report back at your earliest possible convenience for training."

"Training?"

"At the Defense Intelligence School. You have been selected to become the ALUSNA—chief naval attaché in Cambodia—as soon as you complete the requisite intelligence and language qualifications."

Chapter

14

I MOVED KATHY-ANN AND THE KIDS BACK TO VIRGINIA Beach, bought a new house, got them settled in and enrolled at school, then drove north to start eight months of spy school in Washington. All attachés—whether they're posted with allies or adversaries—are trained as spies. The difference is that we are more subtle about spying on our allies than we are about spying on our adversaries. And unlike the CIA intelligence officers who work covertly under diplomatic cover, it is a common understanding among nations that military attachés are all primarily intelligence gatherers, reporting everything they see back to their headquarters.

And so my colleagues and I studied the gentle art of espionage. We were taught such rudiments as how to take a properly exposed picture and then develop the film ourselves. We learned how to become walking dichotomies—smiles on one side, knives on the other—while maintaining cordial relationships with everyone. Indeed, the instructors spent a lot of time teaching us how to survive social situations. We were drilled in ways to get others drunk while keeping ourselves sober. We were coached in the making of discreet notes (it's done by writing with the stub of a pencil on a small piece of paper concealed in your trouser pocket. I always thought it looked silly, as if you were scratching your balls). We were instructed in the niceties of wheedling and coaxing information out of our fellow attachés. We were indoctrinated in the covert joys of spreading disinformation.

I was given a crash course in ELINT—ELectronic INTelligence gathering—so I'd know what sorts of antennas to look for in the field. I studied photo interpretation and learned how to tell what ships were carrying by analyzing the containers on their decks.

And of course, we were schooled in the arts and crafts of memcon writing. Memcons are the stock-in-trade of the diplomatic set. The word is an acronym for MEMorandum of CONversation. And if you've ever spoken with a diplomat or a spy in an official situation, your remarks have probably been committed to paper and sit somewhere in a reference file.

To hone our newfound talents we engaged in an endless series of exercises, trying to elicit information from each other, throwing parties at the Anacostia Navy Yard O Club bar to see who could stay the soberest, driving out into the Virginia countryside to take covert pictures of country estates.

After spy school, I crammed six months of French-language study into seventeen weeks; put my household affairs in order; commandeered a pallet-load of SEAL goodies from SEAL Team Two to be shipped to Phnom Penh; and flew off to the glorious Orient.

I had no qualms about leaving Kathy-Ann and the kids behind. First of all, it was going to be a dangerous assignment. Phnom Penh was a combat zone, so the Navy wasn't keen on allowing dependents to accompany anyone posted there. Second, I had played daddy and husband at home for the last four years—pretty successfully, too. Now it was Kathy-Ann's turn to take over single-handedly and let me go do my job. We'd always had a traditional home, in which I worked as a full-time Navy officer, and Kathy-Ann worked as a full-time mother and housewife. That arrangement suited her—in fact, she insisted on it—and it suited me as well.

We took one long weekend before I left—a camping trip to West Virginia. It was a perfect weekend: clear skies, cool evenings, and the kind of sunsets you see in Kodak ads. I cooked hamburgers and hot dogs, we ate baked beans and coleslaw, and we sat outside our tent as the fire died and scanned the skies for shooting stars. Later, the kids crawled into their sleeping bags and slept. Kathy and I sat outside and had a couple of nightcap beers.

I poked my thumb toward the sleeping kids. "I'm gonna miss them."

"They'll miss you, too. They've only gotten to know you, and now you're going again."

"Hey—missing kids is part of what being a SEAL is all about."

"There are times, Dick, when your being a SEAL begins to grate on us all."

"It's what I am, Kathy—it's what I do."

I had only one concern about going to Cambodia: the posting would displace me for one or two years from the bureaucratic chain that leads to a command opportunity. Before I'd left the COMPHIBTRALANT staff, an admiral named Moore, who commanded LANTFLT's (AtLANTic FLeeT) Amphibious Operations Support Command in Norfolk, the step up the paper trail to which COMPHIBTRALANT reported, gave me an outstanding fitrep. *Lt. Marcinko is one of the most promising young Officers I have known, with great potential for a naval career,*" he wrote. *"In order to continue his development it is recommended he be detailed to command a SEAL team upon completion of his postgraduate studies at Monterey. He is recommended for accelerated promotion."*

Command a SEAL team? That sounded good to me. Frankly, I'd never really considered becoming a commander of a SEAL team—or any other team for that matter. CO was a job for the Academy grads or the Naval Reserve officers who thrived on paperwork. It was a job for old guys, not young warriors like me. Besides, deep in my soul, I was still very much the Geek, the guy who'd voluntarily disenrolled from high school and enlisted in the Navy because it was one way of getting out from under my dead-end existence in New Brunswick.

But after Vietnam, as my salt was scaled away by such admirals as Peet and Snyder, I began to explore options I'd never really thought about before. It was a given fact that the Navy was going to be my life. But now, with a staff assignment under my belt and a college degree hanging on my wall, my career track could indeed take an unexpected turn toward the old command cone. That pleased the shit out of me.

Trouble was, the men I'd be competing against had spent more time ticket-punching than I had. I was still a very junior lieutenant commander. I hadn't spent time in Special Warfare Group One or Special Warfare Group Two, or been tasked with staging the SEAL regatta in Coronado or organizing the Navy Olympic bobsled team. More significantly, the Phnom Penh posting would make it impossible for me to get an all-important executive officer assignment.

Executive officers—XOs in Navyspeak—are a unit's expediters, personnel managers, and chief schedulers. Want three boats in the water at 1425 hours? Talk to the XO. Need eight volunteers for some pissant duty? Talk to the XO. Commander ream you a new asshole and you want to get him off your back? Talk to the XO. XOs learn how the CO thinks, then anticipate what he's going to need and get the job done before the CO even asks. They are also the sounding boards for COs—the one man the commander can talk to and—hopefully—get a no-shit, honest opinion from. Great XOs can make a unit. Not so great ones can hurt.

I, however, would get a chance to be neither. I arrived in Phnom Penh in September 1973, happy to smell the pungent Asian air that filled my nostrils. The city was an incredible mélange of Third World and French colonial. I rolled down the windows of the embassy car that picked me up at the airport and breathed deep.

The Cambodian driver craned his neck to give me a once-over. *"Vous êtes officier de marine?*—You're a Navy officer?"

"D'accord," I said, "right on." I pointed to the Budweiser on my chest. *"Je suis un phoque*—I'm a SEAL." I looked out the window. I could see the river, with its ferryboats and floating restaurants. In the distance was the Silver Palace. The dusty streets were thronged with people, beautiful, brown-skinned, friendly people. *"Oui, je suis un officier phoque,"* I said again. I laughed out loud. "And I can't wait to meet the phoquees!"

Life turned out to be better than I expected. Instead of a barracks room or BOQ suite, I was given a two-story house

184

with a quarter-acre garden filled with tropical flowers and hundreds of orchid plants. The house had big rooms with whitewashed walls—perfect for entertaining. There was a live-in houseboy—Sothan—and a driver—Pak Ban—and within a month after I got settled in, a crew of nieces and nephews and other assorted in-laws showed up, which brought my staff to more than half a dozen. What the hell—numbers didn't matter. I gave Sothan a wad of money and had him outfit everybody. I put the girls in black sarongs, and the boys in black slacks and white shirts. As a *coup de maître*, I added Navy white waistcoats on which I had the SEAL Budweiser (the eagle, pistol, anchor, and trident crest that had just been approved as the official SEAL emblem) embroidered in gold.

I was in business. Or so I thought.

I went to pay a courtesy call on Commodore Vong Sarendy, the Cambodian chief of naval operations, and got smacked by reality. First of all, my carefully studied French was virtually useless. The Cambodians spoke their own style of French, much the same way Haitians speak theirs. So I stuttered along as best I could, but basically I had to speak English. Second, the CNO was very distant, even cold, to me. At the embassy, later in the day, I found out why. The officer I'd replaced was a full commander—a *capitaine de frégate*. I was only a *capitaine de corvette*—a lieutenant commander. So far as the CNO was concerned, the U.S. hadn't cared enough to send him the very best, and he took it as a diplomatic slight. Screw him—he'd never met any SEALs before.

The embassy was a large white building one block from the river. It was surrounded by a wrought-iron fence topped by barbed wire—an easy hit for the Khmer Rouge, I thought, as we drove through the gate.

There was no ambassador in residence, so I checked in with the deputy chief of mission, or DCM, Tom Enders. Enders, a protégé of Henry Kissinger's, cut an imposing figure. He stood about six feet eight inches tall, with longish silver-gray hair combed back over his ears and Coke-bottle-thick eyeglasses. The product of an upper-class Connecticut family and a Yale education, the man looked as if he'd been born to wear pin-striped suits.

He gave me a perfunctory glance and explained the situation in a rolling, aristocratic basso profundo. One: the communist Khmer Rouge forces basically controlled the countryside, so whatever supplies the government got, from bullets to rice to soap, they got by way of the river. Two: the guy I was replacing was okay but hadn't done very much to improve the situation. Three: the situation was simple—the Khmer Navy was largely ineffective in stopping Khmer Rouge attacks on the supply convoys that came up the river from the South China Sea. Four: terror-bombing attacks inside Phnom Penh had increased twofold in the past six months, which didn't do much to help morale or public confidence.

"Anything else?"

"Sure, Commander—fix it."

Aye fucking aye, sir. That's what I thought. I bit my tongue. "We'll give it a shot, sir."

Actually, I liked Enders. He wasn't your everyday temporizing, memo-writing, weak-kneed State Department diplodink who caved in at the merest hint of a threat. Enders never backed away from a fight. He understood the necessity for covert operations and unconventional warfare. He was continually pushing the Cambodians, trying to get them geared up to strike decisively at the Khmer Rouge.

Fix it? Okay. I developed a pattern early. I'd get up before 0500, drive to Cambodian Navy headquarters, and get an intel dump on the previous day's operations and the look-ahead for the current ops. Then, at 0730 I'd go over to the embassy, grab some coffee, and brief Enders. Then I'd go home, work out for an hour, clean up, and go back to Navy HQ. I'd stay there all day, watching and listening, or hit the river for a patrol. Early in the evening I'd go back to my villa for dinner, catch an hour's nap, then return to HQ at about 2200 to watch how they dealt with night operations. If the Cambodians were running an operation—which was most nights—I'd tag along with the crews to see how they did. From 0300 to 0400 I'd catnap at home, then I'd get up, change, and be back at Khmer HQ at 0500 again. I spent a total of 396 days in Phnom Penh. During 291 of them, I was in combat.

Despite my rocky start with the CNO, I got along well with the ops boss, an energetic Khmer officer named Kim Simanh, who spoke good English and gave me free run of his HQ. Even CNO—that's all anybody ever called Commodore Vong Sarendy—after watching me come and go for about three weeks, suddenly decided that, well, yes, he could speak English after all. He came up to me one day and put his arms around me, and from that time on, there was nothing I asked for that I didn't get from the Cambodians.

I became a Kooperating Khmer: I started riding the PBRs that protected the convoys, showing the junior Khmer officers—I called them MiNKs, for Marine Nationale Khmer—how to take the offensive against enemy ambushes.

I sent two PBRs downriver one night to clear out a Khmer Rouge ambush site twenty-five miles or so south of Phnom Penh and went along for the ride. They'd hit a small landing craft near the center of the narrow Mekong River channel. The LCM had been hit in the engine compartment at the stern. It had only partially sunk, though, as its interior compartments, which were called cofferdams, were still filled with air. So the bow protruded four or five feet above the surface of the river, and as marine traffic slowed to avoid it, the bad guys would open up from the riverbanks, less than one hundred yards away. Obviously, we had to blow the boat.

I explained how I'd do it to Kim Simanh. I'd run a line along the keel, to which I'd rig a pair of satchel charges. When I exploded both satchels at the same instant, they'd create what Frogmen called a bubble charge, which would lift the whole LCM a few feet off the river bottom. The craft's own weight would cause the hull to crack as it dropped back onto the silt. The cracked hull would, in turn, release all the air trapped in the cofferdams, and the craft would settle nicely onto the bottom in two or three pieces. It was, I told him, a textbook example of a UDT operation—a perfect teaching opportunity for the young Mink officers and men.

I spent a couple of hours back at Villa Marcinko getting my gear in shape. I cut fuses to the proper length, tied detonating cords together, and rigged blasting caps. Then I prepared two fuse igniters, rolling condoms over them and tying off the ends to keep them waterproof. It was an old Frogman trick. I'd only need one igniter to set off both satchel charges, but Ev Barrett had taught me always to rig them in pairs. "You stupid blankety-blank blanker-blanker," he'd growl lovingly. "And what the blank are you gonna blanking do when you're blanking sitting fifty blanking feet underwater and the only blanking fuse igniter you blanking brought

187

doesn't blanking work? Answer that, you pencil-dicked shit-for-brains numb-nuts sphincter-lipped asshole geek, Marcinko."

The only correct answer was, of course, "Aye-aye, Chief, I rig two fuse igniters, just like you so kindly suggest I do."

Number one houseboy Sothan watched critically as I unrolled the rubbers over the igniters. "You go fuckee-fuckee tonight Mr. Dick?" he asked.

"*Bien sûr*—you bet. I'm gonna screw the Khmer Rouge," I said, examining my handiwork. "Give 'em a good screw."

Sothan wrinkled up his face. "Seem to me like a waste of good rubbers."

It was just at the end of the monsoon season—November —and the nights were so humid that you became wet just walking outside. The river was high. We left the docks, and the PBRs' Jacuzzi engines growled as the Khmer chiefs steered them carefully into the middle of the current.

I had one Khmer lieutenant commander with me, two lieutenants, and twelve enlisted men. It was important to me to teach Khmer officers how to lead from the front. That was a problem in Cambodia—officers tended to stay behind and let their men do the down-and-dirty fighting. It's no way to win a war. I chose to coax them somewhat lightheartedly: "Why," I kept asking, "are you letting your enlisted men have all the fun?"

We weren't five miles south of the capital when we started taking fire. The officers' first reaction was to order the boats swung around back toward the city. I countermanded the orders, launched a flare in the direction of the firing, grabbed the PBR's .50-caliber machine gun, and raked the shoreline.

"See?" I motioned to the senior Mink. "Now—you do it."

The lieutenant commander nodded at me, took the grips, and let go a long burst.

The hostile firing stopped. I slammed him on the back. *"Voilà!"*

We pulled up just north of the ambush site about an hour later. The jungle was quiet—no Khmer Rouge tonight. At least not yet. The PBR coxswain pointed at something in the water about one hundred yards to our south. I hit it with the spotlight—the blunt, gray bow of a landing craft poked out of the water.

"Let's get closer."

We pulled alongside. I slipped out of my green fatigues and pulled an inflatable vest, tank and regulator, mask, flippers, weights, and a waterproof flashlight on a long lanyard out of a nylon bag.

"You guys wait here." I shrugged into my gear, slung the flashlight and a pair of Mk-135 satchel charges around my neck, went over the side backward, and dropped into the water. The current was stronger than I'd expected, and the forty or so pounds of explosives I was schlepping didn't help much, either. I swam to the sunken boat, attached a rope to the bow, submerged, and felt my way down the craft's port side. It occurred to me as I held on with one hand and reached for the light with the other that the Khmer Rouge might have set booby traps inside the wreck. Doom on you, Demo.

The water was opaque—full of monsoon silt—and I had real trouble seeing anything. I pulled myself along the gunwale until I reached the muddy river bottom, then worked myself around the landing craft. Where the broad stern had buried itself in the mud, I attached the rope, then tied off the satchel charges ten feet apart. Then I surfaced, waving at the PBRs fifty feet away. I pulled out my mouthpiece. "Toss me a line."

I pulled myself back aboard the patrol boat and explained what I'd done. "Now we blow the sucker."

It was simple: I'd swim back down, attach a waterproof timer, set it, swim back to the boat, and watch as the LCM disintegrated. Basic Frogman stuff.

Except: on my second trip down, Mr. Murphy was waiting for me. First, I cut my arm as I pulled myself down the LCM's keel. Nothing terminal, but it would take stitches to fix. Then, I discovered that one of the satchel charges had come loose, and it took me five minutes of groping to find it. Then, I cut myself again on the hull reattaching it. This was becoming more complicated than I wanted. Finally, everything was in place. I double-checked the explosives. I double-checked the detonators. I double-checked everything. Then I pulled the initiator on my fuse igniter. Nothing happened. I reached for the second igniter and yanked it. It worked perfectly. Thank you, Ev Barrett.

Finally, I resurfaced, my mask poking cautiously out of the

water by the LCM's bow, the flashlight a beacon so the PBRs could see me. I'd preset the timer fuses for ten minutes.

A bullet caromed off the metal six inches from my head. The goddamn Khmer Rouge had shown up. I swam around the other side of the wreck and looked for my boats. They were nowhere in sight—they'd pulled an Adam Henry on me and I swore I'd kill the Mink lieutenant commander if I ever got my hands on him. Then there was a flurry of pings and dings, and rounds slapped at the water, and I dove again into the blackness.

This was jolly. Twenty-five feet below me were forty pounds of C-3 explosive, rigged to explode in, oh, seven minutes. Khmer Rouge gunners were shooting at me from both shores. And my goddamn PBRs had gone bye-bye.

After what seemed like an eternity, I heard the Jacuzzis growling on the surface. I popped up like a cork, waved the light at them, and heedless of the firing surface-swam like a bat out of hell.

I grabbed a trailing rope, pulled myself alongside, up, and rolled across the gunwale. "Get outta here—she's gonna blow!"

I don't think we were two hundred yards away when the charges exploded—the water geyser drenched the PBRs and the shock wave lifted my boat into the air.

Kim Simanh was at Khmer HQ when I got back. He looked at my bloody, bedraggled fatigues and dour countenance.

He gave me a wry look. "Bad day at the office, Lieutenant Commander?"

I stayed off the boats for two days. Enough was enough.

My biggest contribution to CNO was the creation of a force of Cambodian Marines—although the Cambodians called them Naval Infantry—a 2,000-man unit that used 105mm howitzers based along the Mekong River to protect the convoys and hit the Khmer Rouge offensively. I told Kim Simanh and CNO about my two tours in the Mekong Delta; explained how I'd hit the VC up the dikes before they were prepared, and how the tactic could work for them as well.

Kim Simanh ran with the idea. And the Naval Infantry did, just as I hoped it would, cut down on the frequency and intensity of Khmer Rouge ambushes. Tom Enders was happy. And I felt that I was earning my pay.

Life, I should add, wasn't all drudgery. I had fun as well. I led some ambushes, which got the juices flowing again. And I took up bodysurfing. The Mekong River is wide, warm, and calm just south of Phnom Penh, and I used to jump into the water with a towline and bodysurf behind the patrol boats. If I'd thought of it, I would have had someone at SEAL Team Two ship me a pair of water skis. But I made do with what I had: my two feet. During one of my outings about fifteen miles south of the city, my PBR took some fire, and it slowed down to pick me up.

I waved them off and screamed for the pilot to put the pedal to the metal: *"Imbéciles—foutez le camp d'ici!"*—Get the hell outta here!" Then I dropped onto my belly and let them drag me upriver. Shit, it was safer to bodysurf through an ambush than give the enemy a slow-moving target to plink at.

My social life was as busy as my professional schedule. Women were plentiful. There were the local LBFMs—Little Brown Fucking Machines—brought in an endless supply by my houseboy Sothan. There was a British nurse who hung out at my place for days on end, and a young secretary at the French embassy who thought that I was a pretty good *phoque* for an *Américain*.

I lunched two or three times a week with CNO and his deputy, whose name—I swear—was Sous Chef. Our conversation moved easily now, from French to English to pidgin Khmer, as we ate lemon-grass chicken and drank Hennessy VSOP cognac. I threw cocktail parties at least once a week, dinner parties twice a month, mixing and mingling in the best spy-school tradition with attachés from the other embassies. My favorite adversary was the Soviet naval attaché, Vassily. We'd drink shot for shot—me with my gin, him with his vodka—and tell each other lies.

"How many children you have, Marcinko?"

"Seven. All boys. And you?"

"None. I am bachelor!"

Fat chance. He had a wife at home in Moscow and three kids, so the gossip went, and he probably knew my whole story, too. But we sat and we drank and we lied and everyone had a good time, and the taxpayers were footing the bill.

The biggest downside to my posting was that I went to a lot of Khmer funerals. Fact was, the Cambodians were losing a lot of people. The casualties caused an ethical dilemma for me, as a duly constituted representative of the American government. The reason was, I knew CNO was skimming goods from the U.S. military aid packages, as well as taking a cut from all the civilian convoys he protected. If I'd been a strictly by-the-book attaché, I would have reported his actions. But the truth of the matter was that he did it to take care of his people. Unlike the U.S. military, the Cambodians provided no death benefits, so if a sailor got waxed, his family got axed from the payroll. CNO and Sous Chef provided for the families of KIAs from their graft. I thought what they were doing was terrific for morale, so I kept my mouth shut.

About six months after I arrived, Sous Chef and Kim Simanh decided they'd really mess with me. I'd already been through a bunch of subtle Khmer tricks with them and had paid them back in spades. I was a veteran of mind-fucking the Vietnamese, after all. But they still played their games. Like eating turtle, for example. Cambodian tradition says that if it's passed to you headfirst, it means you have a limp dick. Well, after I learned that, I'd serve myself, then turn the dish around, smile demurely, and pass it back the way it came—headfirst, right to Kim Simanh. Phoc *me*? Nah, fellas—*Do-mah-nhieu*. Phoc *you*.

CNO would roar with laughter when I did that. "See," he'd tell his aides, "*tu as complètement oublié que nos ami le capitaine de corvette petit Richard, le grand phoque américain, a barbouille le camouflage sur les visages des enfants vietnamiens*—you're forgetting our old pal little Richard the SEAL used to smear Vietnamese kids' faces with camouflage."

Now it was about to get serious. We piled into the old black Ford Falcon staff car Sous Chef used and drove to Kim Simanh's apartment. Gathered there were three dozen or so senior-level navy officers. "*Bienvenu*, Richard," Kim Simanh said. He pointed to the table and indicated where I should sit. "Welcome to the cobra feast."

I smiled at him. "You are a devious little brown-skinned son of a bitch."

"Thank you so much, you crotch-sucking monkey-furred

heathen." I roared—the man was actually learning to talk like a SEAL.

The pleasantries over with, we began lunch with green salad. The salad was somewhat chewy because it contained small morsels of cobra skin. I finished and put down my chopsticks. "Good."

"I'm glad you liked it," Kim Simanh said, ringing for the servants.

Next came a kabob of cobra meat, which wasn't so different from rattlesnake. I ate two helpings.

"You must like cobra," Kim Simanh said.

"That's why they call SEALs snake-eaters," I said.

He smiled inscrutably and called for the next course.

The cobra eggs arrived. They were somewhat gamy, but no worse than Chinese thousand-year-old eggs, or Korean pickled eggs.

What could be next?

Two trays of shot glasses arrived. One held cognac. The other held an opaque, dark liquid.

"And this is?" I asked my gentle host.

"Ah," Kim Simanh said. "*Le sang du cobra*—cobra's blood." He lifted his glass. "Your health."

I lifted mine. "And yours." We drank. Blood first, then cognac. Cognac never tasted so good.

Sous Chef couldn't restrain himself. "And now, dessert." He was virtually jumping up and down in his chair.

Dessert? I liked the sound of that. At my quarters, when I ordered "dessert," number one houseboy Sothan would produce a LBFM, and I'd eat my "dessert" in bed.

The room quieted down. I realized there would be no LBFMs today. Instead, five servants brought in trays of what looked like huge Old-fashioned glasses. In each was cognac, and something else. It looked like a marinating baby octopus.

"*Qu'est-ce que c'est que ça?*—What the hell's that?"

Kim Simanh's eyes narrowed evilly. "That, my friend, is *le venin*—the venom of the cobra. The poison sac."

This was truly nefarious, genuinely diabolical. The sacs rested on the bottom of the glasses, opaque, oozy, and loathsome. These were no mountain oysters. I am no fan of mountain oysters, but I would have sucked down five dozen instead of one of these little treasures.

Kim Simanh grinned and picked up his glass. "Your health."

"And yours."

I wolfed down the sac and cognac, neither chewing nor tasting. Incredibly, I managed to swallow it whole. But I could feel it when it hit. Not three seconds later, my forearms broke out in huge beads of sweat. Then my whole body—chest, legs, back—began to perspire profusely, quickly soaking through my uniform. The room lost color and started to turn black and white. I saw dots. It was like going through a nine-g turn in a fighter. I fought for consciousness for what I thought was minutes, but what was in reality no more than thirty seconds.

Then as suddenly as it had come on, it was over. The sweat stopped; my body felt strangely cool and relaxed. My vision returned to normal.

I wiped my eyes, clasped my hands in front of me, and performed the traditional Cambodian gestures for grateful humility to Kim Simanh. "Please, sir, could I have some more?"

The Cambodian Navy is a small organization, so it didn't take long for the word to get out about my little cobra feast. My performance got me respect wherever I went. But it also began a nasty tradition among Khmer COs, who would each try to fix me a bizarre little snack that I wouldn't eat.

Moi turn down a meal? It never happened. Braised chicken beaks? Ate 'em. Crocodile tail? Ate it roasted, baked, steamed, and salted. Fish eyes? Ate 'em by the bowlful. Dog? By the time I left Phnom Penh I could have written a Cambodian cookbook called *50 Ways to Wok Your Dog*. I liked my roaches panfried, my grubs sautéed, and my maggots in chili and garlic sauce. One enterprising young Naval Infantry officer fed me raw monkey brains plucked from a still-live monkey. I ate those, too. In truth, however, there were times over the next six months when I'd think of the cobra feast— venom and all—with fond nostalgia.

It was in Cambodia that I first learned about visiting legislators. It was an eye-opener, too. We received a fair number of codels in Phnom Penh during my posting. *Codel* is bureaucratese for COngressional DELegation. Allegedly, these trips—which are sponsored by various House and Senate committees, subcommittees, and working groups—are fact-finding missions that help our duly elected public servants make educated decisions when they vote on the nation's future. Most of the codels I spent time with, however, were made up of congressmen and senators who wanted only to shop or get laid, or both.

At first I was insulted—outraged that they didn't want to discover anything about Cambodia or learn about whether or not the Cambodian military was up to its tasks. But the embassy staffers brought me up to speed. There were legions of horror stories about the shameful ways in which codels had acted abroad. Embassy secretaries told stories of congressmen fondling them, or worse, raping them—without any recourse. The political officers and consuls each had their stories, too, about pulling this congressman or that senator out of jail in Hong Kong or Caracas or Warsaw.

So, as I got wise to the fact that these trips were really boondoggles—vacations taken at the taxpayers' expense—I asked not what I could do for my country's legislators, or what they could do for me. I simply wrote out a three-page briefing paper on the state of the Cambodian military, slipped it to each exalted representative and senator, and told them to read it on the plane going home.

That gave them lots of free time to accomplish their real mission: visit the best gold stores, buy some incredible and cheap temple rubbings, and smuggle stone carvings or antique Buddhas home on their Air Force jet. The question most asked by codels was, where can a congressman get an absolutely perfect blow job, or some incredible fuckee-fuckee. My diplomatic answer was always the same: "Wherever you'd like it best, Congressman."

I'd give them the use of my car, and Pak Ban would take them around to get themselves bejeweled and be-blown. I'd go be-back to work.

Henry Kissinger, who was the national security adviser back then, used to call the embassy a lot. Tom Enders would sometimes invite me into the bubble—the ultrasecure room within a room we used to receive the most secret calls and hold the most secret conversations—to listen in on Kissinger's rumbling Teutonic musings about the ebb and flow of events in

Southeast Asia, and his plans for bringing the Khmer Rouge to the negotiating table. I'd listen to Henry as he tried to play Metternich, but in truth he sounded less like the great nineteenth-century statesman than he sounded like my grandfather Joe Pavlik, ruminating on the sorry state of the world while sitting at a miner's bar in Lansford, Pennsylvania. On the one hand Kissinger's head games ultimately meant nothing. The Khmer Rouge won Cambodia because they were fiercer on the battlefield—and screw the negotiations.

On the other hand, I gleaned a lot from listening in. I was able to see firsthand how the State Department thought; I discovered about the various tongs back in Foggy Bottom, each of which wanted its own hegemony on Cambodian policy. I learned how a country-desk works, and how the information an ambassador sends back flows through the diplomatic capillary system. I also found out that there were too many Foreign Service officers who believed that any negotiation was better than no negotiation—and in believing so, would sell the Cambodians down the drain rather than face the possibility of taking a hard stand.

Then, having been inculcated in the labyrinthine ways of diplomacy, it was time to move on. Not that I particularly wanted to return to the States. Indeed, despite the fact that I knew I'd been wired to become commander of SEAL Team Two, I didn't want to leave Cambodia. I liked the Khmer people. They were basically lovers, not fighters, but they could fight well if they were given the right training and motivation.

I'd achieved all the goals Tom Enders had given me when I'd arrived. I'd been able to triple CNO's manpower during my fourteen months in Phnom Penh, as well as design and launch a naval infantry force that had proved potent and effective in battle. And I'd gotten CNO new boats—armored gunboats we called Monitors—and three howitzer batteries. The infusion of manpower and weaponry and the new, offensive tactics worked. The number of convoys lost to the Khmer Rouge dropped to next to nothing. The bombings in Phnom Penh had been brought under control.

I extended my tour by almost three months, so that I could stay through the dry season, when the boats are most vulnerable. Then my replacement arrived. George Worthington was a SEAL of a different stripe. He was a tall, lean, aristocratic Naval Academy graduate whose talent lay more in establishing himself as *le grand phoque* at the poolside cocktail bar at the *cercle sportif* than playing full-contact mud-sucking with the Khmer Rouge. A lanky bachelor who could make polite conversation with the best of them, he'd earn a reputation in Phnom Penh as *le nageur d'amour*, the love swimmer, even as I'd earned mine as *le nageur de combat*, the combat swimmer. It was unlikely he'd ever bodysurf on the Mekong River, much less be invited to a cobra feast. I hung on, but was finally ordered out—told in no uncertain terms that I would lose my promotion to commander, as well as any chance at a field command, if I remained in Phnom Penh. So I set a departure date, and on it, regretfully, I left.

In the month before I did, however, CNO and I ate a lot of cobra together. We had a lot of dessert, too. Yum, yum.

Chapter

15

THE CHANGE-OF-COMMAND CEREMONY IS A RITUAL AS OLD as the Navy itself. The regulation reads: "A commanding officer about to be relieved of his command shall, at the time of turning over his command, call all hands to muster. The officer about to be relieved shall read his orders of detachment and turn over the command to his successor, who shall read his orders and assume command."

The uniqueness lies in the fact that, during the formalized passing of the command, the total assumption of responsibility, authority, and accountability—for a ship, or a unit—is transferred directly from one naval officer to another. This happens nowhere else in the military.

My incoming change of command took place in the huge Little Creek Amphibious Naval Base gym, as it was October and too cold to have it out of doors. At the north end of the block-long, tile-walled facility, a podium had been erected. Behind it, a twenty-by-thirty-foot American flag provided a moving, patriotic backdrop. From the side door to the podium a red carpet lay on the polished wood basketball court. Along the carpet's edges stood chromed five-inch-shell cases draped with bleached, starched white hawser. A chief boatswain's mate and five boatswains stood at attention, ready to pipe the official party on board.

Perhaps two hundred seats had been set up for visitors and friends. Kathy-Ann and the kids had front-row center seats. My mother, Emilie, showed up, along with two of my uncles. That gave me no small satisfaction. My Navy career had generally been treated with indifference by my family. They couldn't have cared less that I survived Hell Week and became a Frogman. When I graduated from OCS, they grudgingly noted what I'd done. No one had shown up to see me receive my four Bronze Stars or my Silver Star. But now that I was about to become the commanding officer of an elite unit, they couldn't have been nicer. There were presents for the kids, offers of support, and compliments galore. Still, I took the kudos with the requisite grain of salt because—in truth—as I sat on the podium and looked out on my mother and my uncles, I also saw the faces of officers and enlisted men to whom I felt much closer than I could ever feel to my own flesh and blood.

The men of SEAL Team Two, deployed by platoons, stood at attention, resplendent in their dark blue uniforms. On their chests were displayed rows of battle ribbons and commendations. Every Team member active between 1966 and 1972 had spent at least two tours in Vietnam; many had spent three or four tours there; a few had spent six. You could tell the new men aboard—their chests were bare. Next to the SEAL Two ranks stood representatives from the Underwater Demolition Teams and other naval units.

Change of command, like all Navy ceremonies, does not recognize dry land. The symbolism and terminology are nautical. SEAL Two's HQ, from which the official party was just leaving, is known as the quarterdeck. And as we arrived at the gym, a ship's bell would be sounded—*clang-clang, clang-clang, clang-clang, clang-clang*—and we would be piped aboard, saluting the chief boatswain's mate, as our ranks were called out just as if we were climbing from a barge onto a battleship.

Clang-clang, clang-clang. "Lieutenant commander, U.S. Navy, arriving."

That was me. I strode down the red carpet ramrod straight, returned salute, climbed the podium, and waited for the fun to begin. It didn't take too long. The chaplain read the invocation. The guest speaker was introduced and made a few short remarks. Bob Gormly, Two's outgoing commander, read his orders. Then I read mine: "To Lieutenant Commander Richard No Middle Initial Marcinko, from Bureau of Personnel: You will assume command SEAL Team Two effective 10 October, 1974."

Bob looked at me. "I am ready to be relieved," he said.

I looked at him. "I relieve you, sir," I said. It was 1038 hours, according to the big clock on the side wall of the gym. Twenty-nine minutes before, I'd been piped aboard as just another thirty-three-year-old lieutenant commander. Now as I left the podium, the chief boatswain's mate called out, "SEAL Team Two, departing." The words were like music to my ears.

Although the ceremony was virtually flawless, my journey to command had not been an especially easy one. One reason was my rapid rise within the SpecWar community. I was relieving Bob Gormly, who had been a full lieutenant when I was an ensign. Now we were both lieutenant commanders. That meant in the ensuing eight years he'd been promoted only one rank. I had been promoted three. Moreover, I'd jumped over a whole generation of SpecWar officers in order to be able to take command of SEAL Team Two. That made certain people very unhappy, especially those who had been passed by.

On the other hand, I'd taken risks many SEAL officers chose not to take. Most of those I'd been jumped over had stayed in Little Creek, where they'd built up their real estate portfolios, played volleyball and football on weekends, joined the parachute team, and drunk beer at the O Club. Perhaps more significantly, they'd formed cliques and tongs to help each other out, both personally and professionally. I came back from Phnom Penh owing no one anything. I was the outsider who'd taken a three-year staff job with no demolition or jump pay, gone to college, and then overseas to Cambodia as an attaché. Some in the SpecWar community saw these assignments as desertions, not as a way of expanding capabilities.

That was their problem, not mine. I felt that my three years at COMPHIBTRALANT staff and the subsequent attaché tour had given me the ability to move in circles SEALs hadn't traveled before—which could only be good for SpecWar in general, and SEAL Two in particular. For example, I'd come home on a short leave in May of '74, in order to brief the chairman of the Joint Chiefs of Staff and the chief of naval operations on the situation in Cambodia. While I was in Washington, I had the opportunity to visit Little Creek for a change of command ceremony at Navy Special Warfare Group Two. There, I met Rear Admiral Greene, the man for whom I'd be working when I returned to take over SEAL Team Two. Greene gave me the once-over during the ceremony. Afterward, he asked who I was, and why I was wearing a four-strand epaulet (which signified that I represented a four-star officer).

I explained I was naval attaché, Phnom Penh, and that I represented the president of the United States. Admiral Greene and I chatted for a while. He asked for a situationer, and I gave him a two-minute brief on Cambodia, saluted, and let him get back to his guests. I went on to mix and mingle. I saw him eyeballing me from time to time, noting that I could talk to three-stars as easily as I could to chiefs, watching me hold a cocktail without dribbling it down my chin, nodding approvingly as I made the admirals' wives laugh.

Now, as commander of SEAL Two, I was going to work for this guy—and his staff. It was in my favor that I'd already met him in a social situation, and he knew I was capable of briefing the chairman of the JCS and the CNO. On the other hand, Bob Gormly, who'd worked for Admiral Greene for almost six months, hadn't gotten to know him at all. Bob's attitude was, "If Staff doesn't specifically call, don't bother 'em." It was typical for a SEAL commander—I'd had a similar attitude when I was in Vietnam (remember all those UNODIRs?).

But in Vietnam, I'd had only fourteen men to worry about, and others to take the heat if I screwed up. Now I had 150, and the buck stopped with me. Furthermore, as a unit commander, like it or not, I had to exist—and succeed—within a command structure. SEAL Two fit within the parameters of a strategic framework. As much as I'd have preferred it to be otherwise, SEAL Team Two was not autonomous. So, if I wanted bigger budgets, better equipment, more exotic training, and top-of-the-line weapons, I'd have to go through Admiral Greene and his staff to get them. That was the political reality. For me, however, there was a much more gut-level issue. Command—whether it is of a ship, a submarine, a naval air wing, or a SEAL team—is a once-in-a-lifetime experience. Most officers get a single shot at it. I made up my mind I wasn't going to squander my tenure at Two.

Indeed, exactly *how* I'd lead Two was a matter of some concern—both to me, and to the troops. I'd returned from Cambodia in early September and spent a lot of time—some people thought too much time—hanging around SEAL Two. I drank with the men and listened to their complaints over beer. They told me how happy they were that I, an old Team guy, was about to take over. The men were open and unguarded with me. After all, I was one of them—I was Rick the Geek from UDT-22, the guy who sucked peas through his nose. Or I was Mr. Rick, the ensign of Bravo Squad, whose merry marauders had wreaked havoc on the VC and driven Hank Mustin crazy. Or I was Demo Dick, Sharkman of the Delta, the guy who ran barefoot in the jungle and told Special Forces colonels, "Kiss my ass."

In truth, I was all those things—and I was none of them anymore. Yes, I liked a good brawl. Yes, I liked to drink beer with the guys. Yes, I had no problem telling officers of any rank to go screw themselves. But this was 1974. I'd been away from the Teams for six years, and I'd changed—changed radically. The raw energy was still there. But most of my rough edges had been smoothed away, either through schooling or by watching how the most sophisticated operators got away with things others didn't. So when the troops spoke longingly of returning to the good old days, when Roy Boehm, Two's first CO, would lead the men through two hours of PT—Physical Training—in the mornings, followed by a four-mile run to the Oysterman's Club, where they'd drink beer the rest of the day, I listened. But I made no one any promises.

I went up to Fort A.P. Hill, where Two did its field exercises, and watched as the platoons trained. I wandered in and out of offices, looking at how the paperwork was handled and the assignments made. I didn't like much of what I saw, either. In Team-puke parlance, everything sucked. The budget sucked. Grooming standards sucked. The condition of the buildings sucked. The equipment sucked. I was not a happy camper as I wandered around, peering into nooks and crannies.

During my reconnaissance period I asked Two's operations officer, Rich Kuhn, to be my XO. Kuhn was a rock-hard, six-foot-tall lieutenant who'd served two tours in Vietnam as an ensign. The dark-haired 27-year-old—who sported a Buddy Holly spit curl—had subsequently done an exchange tour with the famed British Special Boat Squadron. This was the sea-going version of SAS, and their exercises were tougher than anything we'd ever done at SEALs. The overseas duty had widened Rich's horizons just as my attaché tour had expanded my own. He'd gotten more than a taste for port from the Brits—he'd been forged on their unique anvil. He came back even more solid, dependable, and imaginative than when he had left. The Brits also passed on to him their penchant for organization. Indeed, Rich was now a superb manager, an absolute requirement for a good XO. Best of all, he could do all of the above things in a passable cockney accent.

Although I'd never worked with Rich, he struck me as the sort of man I wanted as my number two: he was honest, reliable, and battle tested. He had a terrific sense of humor —the man was a larger, more sophisticated version of Gordy Boyce. Moreover, his instincts were good: he could predict how I'd react and be right much of the time. And he had the sort of understated, tough personality I wanted my officers to project. I invited him out for a beer and put the question to him. Kuhn, the fool, gave me a thumbs-up.

Change of command was on a Friday morning. I gave everybody the weekend off and ordered Rich to have the officers assembled in my cabin at 0900 on Monday morning. Early Monday, I jumped in the SEAL Two CO's jeep, drove the six blocks to COMNAVSPECWARGRU TWO—Navyspeak for COMmander, NAVy SPECial WARfare GRoUp TWO —and paid a courtesy call on Admiral Greene. I showed up in full uniform, fresh crew-cut with the close-cropped sides we called white walls, and muscles bulging from my hour-long workout.

I gave the admiral my respects, then told him that while I'd signed for the command, I hadn't signed for the equipment because it wasn't up to my standards. Therefore, I reported, I was about to conduct a full-scale inventory of SEAL Two. As long as I was doing one, I continued, what about the SpecWar chief of staff, Captain Cravener, performing a full administrative inspection at the same time.

Admiral Greene cracked a wry smile. "That's going to mean a lot of work—for SEAL Two and for my staff."

"Yes, sir." A complete inventory meant that every nut and bolt, every bullet and firing pin, every Aqua-Lung and Emerson breathing apparatus was going to be enumerated, along with every index card, paper clip, and notepad. By the time we finished, we'd know how many goddamn staples SEAL Team Two owned.

The administrative inspection would force us to defend our training methods, our war plans, and our budgets. Every facet of SEAL Two's operational and organizational procedures would be gone over with the proverbial fine-tooth comb.

"I gather you think it's justified to spend the time and effort, Dick."

"Sir, there hasn't been an admin inspection in more than six years. Our mission has changed since Vietnam. It's time we looked at how we do business."

He nodded. "And you say you haven't signed for the equipment?"

"Admiral, my guess is that a lot of what we have was brought back from Vietnam in bad shape. The inventory may say we've got our full complement—but I'd give five to one odds that most of it doesn't work very well. Thing is, if I sign for it, it's mine, whether it works or not."

The admiral looked intently at me. "Gotcha," he finally said. He rapped on the desk as a sign I was dismissed. "Keep me posted, Dick. And tell the chief of staff I concur about the admin inspection."

"Thank you, sir."

I walked out of NAVSPECWARGRU TWO HQ half an hour later leaving the chief of staff and most of the staff openmouthed. Who was that spit-and-polish, bull-necked, white-walled asshole anyway? Marcinko? *Impossible*.

Rich Kuhn had the SEAL Two officers waiting in my cabin, sprawled on the floor because there were only four chairs. Most wore the blue-and-gold T-shirts and tan shorts that were uniform of the day for SEALs. That was about to change. Rich, who'd had a premonition, had worn his uniform. Lucky for him.

I walked in. Rich called out, "Tenn-hutt!" They straggled to their feet. Somebody said, "Hey, Sharkman—" but I cut him off with a cold stare.

"Gentlemen," I said, "I have just briefed the admiral, and I have volunteered us for an administrative inspection and a full inventory."

"What the—?"

"Furthermore, this place is a shithouse," I said. "I've spent the past month poking around, and I can tell you gentlemen that there is very little that I like around here." I put both hands on my desk. "I don't like the fucking equipment. I don't like the fucking staffing. I don't like the fucking training. I don't like the fucking war plans." I swept the room with my eyes. "I don't like fucking *any*thing."

My voice got louder, deeper, and more insistent—the Barrett in me taking over. "From now on you're going to do something else besides jock it with the troops. You are going to fucking learn to lead. You are going to learn how to write fucking papers. You are going to learn how to write fucking messages. You're going to learn how to write fucking plans."

I turned to Rich. "XO?"

He snapped to attention in the best British style. "Sir?"

"You will call the Officers' Club and have them reserve a table for sixteen five days a week for lunch. Twelve-thirty to fourteen hundred. All officers will be expected to join the CO for lunch daily. There will be unit fucking integrity."

"Yes, sir."

Silence. Their faces were like stone. Two of the ensigns had their mouths open a full two inches.

I cut them all dead. "And from now on you can clean up your own offices—and I mean *clean*. I want the windows washed inside and out. I want the floors scrubbed—by you, gentlemen, not by some E-2 flunkie."

They became invisible. I turned to Rich again. "XO—"

"Yes, sir?"

"You will pass the word. There will be no beards. There will be no mustaches. Haircuts are back in style. Starch is back in style."

"Yes, sir."

"XO—"

"Sir?"

"You will pass the word. Call the post exchange and tell them there's going to be a run on calling cards and ceremonial swords. All officers will have fucking calling cards. All officers will have fucking swords."

I turned to my officers again. Their ashen faces looked as if they'd been mud-sucked. "Gentlemen," I said. "You will learn common fucking courtesy and protocol." I paused for effect. "Because as of today, gentlemen, you are all fucking back in the fucking Navy."

I swung back to Rich. "I think that's enough for right now, XO," I said sweetly. "I'll want all hands assembled at thirteen hundred. You may dismiss."

I walked out of the room and never looked back. This was fun.

Of course they tested me. Facial hair was first. The guy with the best-looking beard came to visit me in my office and refused to shave it. It was Eddie Mugs. He was no stranger. We'd had three Med cruises together in UDT-22 aboard the USS *Rushmore*. Like me, he was one of Everett E. Barrett's boys. He'd watched me suck peas through my nose as part of the Mr. Mud and Mr. Geek mess-deck vaudeville act. We'd been through scrapes in Barcelona. We'd chased whores in Rome. We'd gotten drunk in Athens. The night I'd driven the truck through the tunnels in Naples scraping the walls as I passed other cars, he'd been in the back, screaming and yelling like an Indian as Chief Barrett blankety-blank-blank-blanked at me at one hundred decibels.

He was Mugs, a big-fisted, round-faced son of a bitch, and I was Geek, a hands-on bar-brawler, and we'd been asshole buddies since Christ was a mess cook.

Rich Kuhn showed him in. He saluted. I returned it.

I sat behind my desk, a mug of steaming coffee in front of me, just like a real naval officer. "At ease."

He clasped his hands behind his back and spread his feet. There was an awkward moment of silence.

I sipped at my coffee and looked evenly at him, remembering a lot of good times. I guess he was doing the same. "Mugs?"

"Mr. Rick."

"You wanted to see me."

He nodded. "Sir—about my beard. I want to keep it. It's—"

I cut him off. "Look, Mugs, I have nothing against beards. The Navy says a sailor can have one. But on SEALs they're a safety hazard. If you have a full beard and wear a face mask, there's a good chance it won't hold a seal. That's dangerous. Maybe other COs didn't give a rat's ass about that, but I do. And as long as you're taking hair off, you might as well take all of it off—so the mustache goes, too." I cracked a slight smile. "That way I can see if you're giving me any lip."

"Yes, sir, I understand how you feel. But it's still Navy rules that we can have 'em. Until the rule changes, sir, I'm keeping the beard."

"You can keep it, Mugs. But not in SEAL Team Two." I sipped my coffee. "You're out of here."

He looked at me, as stunned as if I'd shot him.

"You have made your choice, Mugs, and I have made mine. Your peers set you up. They—and you—thought there was no way in hell I'd screw with you."

My voice turned hard. "Problem is, there's no way in hell that anybody's screwing with me."

Tears began to well in the corner of his eyes. "Sir—"

"That's final, Mugs. You're history. Take two days. Figure out where you want to go, and I'll do all I can to make sure you get what you want."

His jaw hung open but he couldn't say a word. My own face had turned to impassive stone. "I'm sorry—we could have used you around here," I told him. "But now you can go and tell the boys out there—'Don't mess with the CO because he'll mud-suck you like you've never been mud-sucked before.'

"Dismissed." I saluted, then swiveled my chair toward the pile of paperwork that sat on the credenza behind my desk as Mugs wheeled and left. I didn't want him looking back to see that the decision had been as hard on me as it was on him.

There were SEALs who thought I was too tough on the

men during my tenure. But they weren't from SEAL Two. The SEALs at Two liked being challenged—I know so because I had an extraordinarily high retention rate during the time I served as CO—more than 80 percent of the enlisted men stayed with me.

One basic problem I saw with SEAL Two was that too many junior officers were detailed to administrative work instead of being sent into the field. You don't lead warriors from behind a desk. I needed to find Two a talented admin puke—a young officer to hold the fort while we warriors went out to play.

It wouldn't be especially easy. SEALs had a hard time getting along with non-SpecWar types, and admin pukes came and went with the speed of office temporaries. But I had an idea. The SEAL officer detailer, Dick Lyons, was an old friend of mine. We'd gone through OCS together. He'd become a ship driver while I threw myself out of planes and sucked mud in the Delta. Now he was in Washington driving a desk. Being the able administrator he was, he'd know where I could find fresh bodies. I gave him a call.

"Yeah, I got a warm one for ya, Dick."

"I'll bet you do, you malevolent mick. Who is he?"

"Name's Tom Williams, a JG."

"Stats?"

"He's a reserve officer—completed flight training but he didn't have the stats to get an assigned seat in a squadron, so they bumped him. He was sent to a SOSUS unit in Bermuda—one of those tracking stations for the underwater sensors we deploy against Soviet subs. He was diddled there, too, because he was junior-junior to three ambitious schmucks who didn't want competition and decided to give him a screwing on his fitrep to get rid of him. Now—although he doesn't know it yet—the Navy's about to throw him out on his ass."

"Jesus."

"It's a tough deal. He ain't a bad kid. Lots of potential, but no one to take advantage of it."

"Wanna bet?"

Lyons laughed. It was a big, warm, boisterous Irishman's laugh that got people's attention in saloons and brought the women around. "You'd be doing me a favor. I need to stash him someplace for six months so the system forgets about him and he stays in service."

"Send him to me, Lyons. Send him to Father Marcinko's Home for Recalcitrant Boys. I promise I will educate the child."

"You'll give him a goddamn postgrad degree," Lyons roared. "Just keep him in one piece, okay?"

Lieutenant (j.g.) Thomas R. Williams arrived a few days later. He was a short, slightly built officer whose shy demeanor gave him the appearance of a Central Casting accountant. He checked in, got himself a room at BOQ—Bachelor Officers' Quarters—and showed up for work, looking more than a little insecure.

I watched him get buffeted around the quarterdeck by the SEAL officers. We tend to be confident sons of bitches, and the sight of this poor schlemiel trying to make headway in the face of blatant hazing made me cringe. But Williams had guts—instinctively he stood his ground. The kid also had heart. What he needed was to learn some assertiveness. And he had to start working out. The role of the 97-pound weakling is not a fun part to play when you're assigned to a SEAL team.

Although Tom was married at the time, he was taking this assignment as a single because it was only temporary (or so he thought). So Kathy-Ann and I invited him to dinner one night about a week after he'd arrived. She fed him a fair amount of beer, pasta, a big green salad, and ice cream, and then withdrew as I grabbed two more brews from the fridge and motioned Tom to follow me into the den.

I dropped onto the couch. He took the beer and sat, can balanced on his knee, in an armchair.

I raised the can in his direction. "Welcome to Little Creek."

"Thanks." He took a swallow. "It's a nice change from Bermuda."

"Dick Lyons thought you'd like it here for a while."

He nodded. "I do—so far."

"Guys giving you a tough time?"

He shrugged. "Not so bad."

"Then they're not trying very hard." I drained my beer and put the can on a *Time* magazine that sat on the coffee table. "Tom, I'm about to give you a no-shitter."

He looked at me with the eyes of a puppy about to be put to sleep. He'd been through this before—when he'd been cut from flight school, and when he'd been screwed at SOSUS. His face told me he thought I was going to can him. He swallowed hard. "Whatever you say, sir."

"The Navy's about to survey you out."

He flushed bright red. "What?"

"You're dead meat, kid. They think you can't cut it."

"That's—" He slammed his beer, inadvertently knocking it onto the rug. "Oh, shit, sir—I'm real sorry—"

I grabbed a dish towel from the kitchen, snatched two more beers, went back, and wiped the rug down. "Don't worry about it. Here."

He took the beer out of my hand and chugged it. "Goddammit." He slammed the empty can on the table. I got him another cold one, and he started working on it. Now his face had gone livid. "Goddammit to hell."

"What?"

"God damn the Navy. Screw the Navy anyway."

"Listen to me, Tom, you're a reserve officer. Take yes for an answer. Go home, make money. Get out of this bullshit rat race."

He shook his head. "No way."

Interesting: the kid's jaw had a firm line when he set it. He had grit. "Okay, so what do you want to do?"

"I want to stay in the goddamn Navy." He paused. "Assholes." He looked at me and laughed in spite of himself. "Fuck me—*I'm* the asshole."

"Okay, young Tom Williams, fuck you very much." I swallowed the rest of my beer, grabbed two more, opened them, gave him one, then sat down nose to nose. "Dick Lyons says you're a good kid. I like what I see. What do you say we screw the Navy a little bit?"

His eyes lit up. "Sounds good to me."

"Here's the drill. I need a kick-ass admin officer, and you've been recruited. You do the job and I'll protect you. The Team will protect you."

"You got it."

"Not so fast. There's more. You take PT with the Team. You get yourself in shape. You go to BUD/S."

"Jesus—"

It's a long way from my spit-and-polish days as Commanding Officer of SEAL Team Two. (OFFICIAL PHOTOGRAPH U.S. NAVY)

July 1991, Annual UDT/SEAL reunion—RADM George Worthington and me. He replaced me as naval attaché in Phnom Penh, Cambodia. (JOHN WEISMAN PHOTOGRAPH)

Ted Lyon, my nemesis, and me, the "Geek"—"I knew he always loved me." (JOHN WEISMAN PHOTOGRAPH)

My "rogue terrorist" look? I had to don long hair and beard for covert operations. (PHOTOGRAPH BY ROGER FOLEY, © 1991)

Practicing clandestine shipboard infiltrations in Egypt, 1982. (DICK MARCINKO PHOTOGRAPH)

Calm-water boarding exercise for SEAL Team Six. (DICK MARCINKO PHOTOGRAPH)

Not-so-calm-water boarding exercise for SEAL Team Six in the Atlantic. This is why my guys could bench-press 500 pounds. They had to—to pull themselves up these blankety-blank-blanking ladders. (DICK MARCINKO PHOTOGRAPH)

Gotcha! The bad guys are down—except, which one's the bad guy and which one's the hostage? (DICK MARCINKO PHOTOGRAPH)

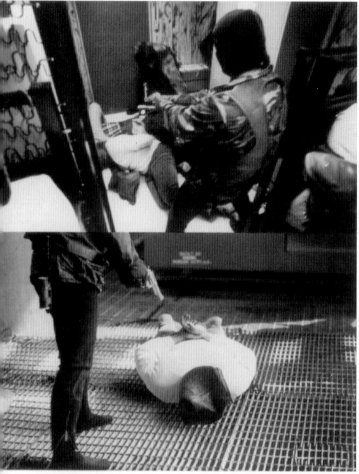

Trailer in his famous "Make my day" pose. He's done it more than once. (DICK MARCINKO PHOTOGRAPH)

Taking down an oil rig in the Gulf of Mexico on a SEAL Team Six exercise. The climb is bad enough . . . (DICK MARCINKO PHOTOGRAPH)

Knock-knock. Who's there? Ensign Trailer Court and a few of his friends come a-calling. (DICK MARCINKO PHOTOGRAPH)

(*four corner photos, top*) Heavily armed choppers and other major assets were very useful during our river and ground assaults, and helpful in getting my Bronze Stars. "Doom on you, Charlie!" (OFFICIAL PHOTOGRAPH U.S. NAVY)

left: Awards ceremony on the Little Creek Amphibious Base parade ground, 1968. I've just been presented my first (of four) Bronze Star. (OFFICIAL PHOTOGRAPH U.S. NAVY)

Cambodia, 1974. Ready for combat body-surfing on the Mekong River, with my PBR and crew of MNKs (Maritime Nationale Khmer). I'm probably one of the only naval attachés ever to have spent more days doing combat than diplomacy. (OFFICIAL PHOTOGRAPH U.S. NAVY)

►

Desert target practice during SEAL Team Six training. Those Smith & Wesson Model 66's got real hot, too—my ammo budget for 90 men was more than the entire U.S. Marine Corps got for training ammo. (DICK MARCINKO PHOTOGRAPH)

SEAL squad deployed in STAB (SEALs Tactical Assault Boat), Vietnam, 1967–68. (OFFICIAL PHOTOGRAPH U.S. NAVY)

Harry Humphries *(right)* and me, on the eve of TET, 1968, as our PBR (Patrol Boat/ River) pulled upriver for Chau Doc. Were we ever in for a surprise. (PHOTOGRAPH COURTESY OF HARRY HUMPHRIES)

VC weapons cache captured by the Eighth Platoon in January 1968. (OFFICIAL PHOTOGRAPH U.S. NAVY)

Me and some of my toys during my SEAL publicity tour in 1967. This picture and the interview that went with it formed the basis for the *Male* magazine article that nicknamed me Shark Man of the Delta and gave the VC fresh material for their wanted posters. (*NEW YORK DAILY NEWS* PHOTO)

Vietnam, 1967, a souvenir of our nighttime "snatches"—a VC suspect with a member of my first combat unit, Bravo Squad. (OFFICIAL PHOTOGRAPH U.S. NAVY)

Reconnaissance of hootches during a patrol by Eighth Platoon in the Three Sisters mountain region near the South China Sea, 1968. (OFFICIAL PHOTOGRAPH U.S. NAVY)

THƯỞNG 10.000ⁿ NẾU GIẾT ĐƯỢC THỦ LÃNH
ĐẢNG GIẾT NGƯỜI BÍ MẬT MẶT XANH ĐÃ
TÀN SÁT NHIỀU GIA ĐÌNH NHÂN NGÀY
LỄ HIỆP CHỦNG QUỐC. 2/1/68

VIETNAMESE TRANSLATIONS

3 March 1969

SUBJECT: Viet Cong "Wanted Posters"

A. Award of 50,000 piasters to any one who could kill First Lieutenant
Demo Dick Marcinko, a gray-faced killer who had brought death and trouble
to the Chau Phu Province during the Lunar New Year.

B. Award of 10,000 piasters to any one who could kill the leader of the
secret blue-eye killer's party which had massacred many families during
the United Nation day of 2 January 1968.

I certify this to be a true translation.

NGOAN VAN DAO
Copy) Asian Dept
Comd) Lang Sch, G3
USAJFKCENSFWAR

Wheezing round the final bend during Hell Week, I am in the lead. I didn't have to like it—I just had to do it. (DICK MARCINKO PHOTOGRAPH)

October 1961, graduation picture of UDT/R Class 26: middle row—"Mr. Geek" (that's me), second from right; and "Mr. Mud," first on left. (OFFICIAL PHOTOGRAPH U.S. NAVY)

Dressed in a sailor suit, 1942. Did my mother, Emilie, know something I didn't? (DICK MARCINKO PHOTOGRAPH)

Panama City, Florida, 1964. No, I am not imitating Peter f---ing Pan. I've just been yanked off the ground at 130 knots by a Grumman S-2 Tracker while testing equipment for the Fulton Skyhook Recovery System. (OFFICIAL PHOTOGRAPH U.S. NAVY)

Lt. Joe DiMartino *(rear)* and a couple of unidentified SEALs man an experimental SDV (Swimmer Delivery Vehicle). Joe helped get me into SEAL Team Two in 1966. (OFFICIAL PHOTOGRAPH U.S. NAVY)

"You get qualified as a SEAL officer."

"But—"

"I don't want to hear *but*, Tom. SEAL Two is a family, and I want you to be part of it, not some distant fucking relative. That means you gotta pass the initiation—meaning BUD/S. So get yourself lean and mean. Work with me, and I'll work with you. And then we'll go back and we find those sorry motherfucking cocksucking pencil-dicked shit-for-brains pus-nuts goatfucker assholes who screwed with you, and we ream them new sphincters."

The kid laughed my kind of laugh. He stuck his hand out, spit on it, and offered it to me. "Deal, Skipper."

I did the same.

He took me seriously—and we took him seriously, too. The "qualified" wardroom hazed him unmercifully. But at my order they practiced Barrett's First Law of the Sea. They showed him the tricks of the trade and brought him along one step at a time through diving and demolition basics, parachuting, and unconventional warfare tactics. Tom worked out with the troops every morning, pushing his body farther than he ever thought it could be pushed. He did it all—the runs, the swims, the rope climbs, the target practice.

After six months, he was ready, and we sent him off to BUD/S. He made it through easily, and we welcomed him home in October 1975, pinning the Budweiser on his tunic just about a year after he came aboard.

There is a postscript to this story. On November 30, 1990, the ship's bell was rung and a chief boatswain's mate called out, "Commander, United States Navy, arriving," as Tom Williams marched down a red carpet onto a podium inside the Meeting House at the Little Creek Amphibious Naval Base.

Forty minutes later, as he left, the bell sounded once again: *clang-clang, clang-clang*. But this time the chief announced, "SEAL Team Two, departing," as Tom Williams proudly returned the salute and marched down the red carpet as SEAL Two's sixteenth commanding officer.

It didn't take too long after I'd assumed command to realize that very little had changed about the way the Navy viewed SpecWar in general and SEAL teams in particular. Our mis-

RICHARD MARCINKO

sions were designed by idiots in Washington who were either
ship drivers or nuclear dip-dunks; officers who had no idea
about the capabilities of SEALs, or the limitations of such
elements as terrain, weather, or what the nineteenth-century
strategist and philosopher Von Clausewitz referred to as
"friction"—the fog of battle that is a fancy way of restating
Murphy's Law: "What can go wrong will go wrong."

The result of this sort of fuzzy thinking at the Pentagon
was that, during exercises, we'd be given a task like "neutralize the enemy by moving ten kilometers through Camp
Swampy in five hours."

You can't move through a swamp at two clicks an hour in
a boat, much less do it on foot through hostile territory.
Hadn't any of these people ever wrestled their way through
the Mekong Delta with the booby traps and the pungi pits
and the trip wires? The Navy unit I was leading wasn't pointed
on one end, painted gray, and named after a state. And "neutralize the enemy"?

*"Does that mean I can kill the motherfuckers, Admiral, Your
Grace, sir?"*

*"No—we're concerned about the media image you might
generate if you cause large numbers of casualties. Just neutralize them."*

*"Do you have any suggestions about how I do that, Admiral,
Your Panjandrumcy? Perhaps I could hire a company of hookers to keep them busy while I sneak in and hog-tie 'em."*

*"That's your problem, Commander. Just file your plan in
triplicate, sign each copy, attesting to the fact that if there are
any screwups they were your fault not ours, then burn them
all so we don't leave a paper trail for the media and the
Congress."*

"Aye-aye, Your Worship."

There had to be a better way of doing business. The chain
of command was so cumbersome as to impede the sorts of
things that SEALs do best. So, one of my first goals was to
change the way requests went up the ladder and orders came
back down.

That was made easier when a new commodore arrived at
SpecWar Group Two. He was a captain named Dick Coogan,
a ship driver, but one who'd once worked on the Mekong
River. So he knew about SEALs, and he knew about riverine

212

environments, and he was open to new ideas. More significantly, as it turned out, he'd left his wife and kids back in Newport, Rhode Island. He was a *célibataire géographique* who lived at the BOQ, which happened to sit right across the street from SEAL Two's HQ.

At one time Coogan had a chief of staff, Scott Sullivan, a West Coast SEAL. That was significant, too. First of all, East Coast SEALs don't think much of West Coast SEALs. In Vietnam, the SEAL One groups were much more passive than we were, sitting up in the Rung Sat Special Zone on their butts rather than getting out into the villages and up-country.

In the U.S., the West Coasters tended to be more system oriented than those of us from Little Creek. In rock-and-roll terms, if we from SEAL Two were the Rolling Stones, the SEALs from California were the Monkees.

So Scott Sullivan set up shop. He didn't like the East Coast. He didn't like SEAL Team Two, and he didn't like me. I said *fuck* too often for his taste. I was too wet and wild. I didn't like to go home at four-thirty and sit across the Formica dinette from my wife and ask her how her day had gone. I didn't say "May I" every time I broke wind. And I had the nasty habit of going straight to the commodore when I needed to get an urgent question answered. That really upset Scott's sense of order and decorum.

I'd come in at three-thirty with something I needed from the commodore and try to see him. Most often, Scott would say, "He's busy, Dick. I'll handle it for you tomorrow."

"But I need to know this now, Scott."

"Well, that's impossible. He's tied up."

After one too many "It's impossible," I set up an alternative system.

Remember, Commodore Coogan lived at BOQ, right across from our HQ. When he finished work every afternoon, Dick Coogan used to drive up, park, drop his briefcase off, then head to the BOQ bar for a beer before he went back to his room to do whatever homework he'd brought with him. He wasn't the sort to screw around, so all he ever did was work.

I called a meeting of all my junior officers in my cabin.

"There will be," I told them, "a commodore watch from

now on. You will assign yourselves a schedule. You will watch for him to drive up. You will go to the BOQ bar. You will get the fucking stool next to the commodore's and you will keep him company. You will fucking keep him amused. You will fucking tell him stories about what we are doing, and how well we are doing it. And each commodore watch officer will see me before he goes off to work, just in case there is any little fucking tidbit I want dropped on Commodore Coogan that particular day."

I ran a regular public relations program. One night the commodore learned about my PT program. Another, he learned about the exercises at Fort A.P. Hill. Another, he learned about our new counterinsurgency tactics. The officers even invited him out to play war games with us—and he accepted. At one point, I had to take a run over to Ft. Bragg, 240 miles away. I was having a beer with Coogan and asked if he'd like to go.

"Sure, Dick."

So off we went. The next morning Scott Sullivan looked high and low for his boss—except he was with me, watching a Special Forces exercise and learning new things about SpecWar capabilities.

Now these sorts of stunts used to piss Scott Sullivan off something fierce. He hated it when I'd end-run him by talking to the commodore after business hours at the BOQ bar, then telling him the decisions we'd reached the next morning.

"You can't do that," he'd whine.

"Do it to thyself, Scott," I'd say. "Read my lips—I don't work for you. I work for the commodore."

It came to a head early on. I had two foreign-exchange officers with Two. One was a Brit from the SBS—the Special Boat Squadron with which Rich Kuhn had served a tour. The other was a German from the *Kampfschwimmerkompanie*, the German combat-swimmers.

I believed that SEALs should train with other NATO special forces, and I'd gotten Dick Coogan's chop on plans to go to Europe and do just that. Then Rudy, the German who was posted to us for a year, suggested that it might be fun to have a group of *Kampfschwimmers* visit us, and we'd go to Puerto Rico and play there.

So he drafted a message to his boss—who approved the idea and sent a detachment to train with us. But being a good, orderly German, he also cc'd the minister of defense's office in Bonn. The bureaucrats in Bonn went ballistic because things were being done out of sequence, and not enough people had said "May I?"

A nasty message went from the German minister of defense to the Pentagon. It got passed to the CNO. The CNO said, whoa, there, and sent a rocket to CINCLANTFLT, who mortared COMNAVSPECWARGRU TWO, where it was received gratefully by Scott Sullivan, who called me on the carpet and chewed my ass out but good.

"Who the hell are you to be asking exchange officers to send messages to their goddamn minister of defense, Marcinko? You may not work for me, but the goddamn chain of command still applies to you—and when it comes to message traffic, which is an administrative function, not a tactical function, I am fucking God, do you hear me fucking loud and fucking clear?"

He did, in fact, have me by the balls. "Aye-aye, sir."

"So from now on, Marcinko, any goddamn messages you want to send, you will clear through Staff—which means through me. Got it?"

"But—"

"No buts. You have run rampant over chain of command. You've tried to make me look the fool. You've rubbed my nose in it. Now it's payback time. Every damn message that goes out from now on will have to be cleared through Staff and chopped by me, or it doesn't move."

After work, Rich Kuhn and I found ourselves a booth at a friendly tavern and talked it over. I spoke of murder. He calmed me down. I described unique forms of torture. He, being the excellent XO that he was, channeled my energy in more realistic and constructive directions. We drank beer. We plotted. We schemed.

Scott had chewed my ass on Thursday. We sent no messages on Friday. Over the following weekend, I set up a typing pool to draft messages. By the time we were finished, I'd drafted somewhere close to 150 of them. At 0630 Monday morning, I signed them where it said "DRAFTEE," time-stamped each one, then carried them over to Staff.

"Morning, Scott."

He saw the fourteen-inch pile of papers. "What the hell—"

"I've got a couple of messages for you to sign."

"Leave them with my secretary. I'll get to them when I have time." He looked at me with a malevolent grin. "*If* I have time."

"Whatever you say, Scott. But they all have time stamps, and many of them are time sensitive, so if you are late getting them out, it'll be reflected on your watch, not mine." And I walked out.

By the time I got back to my cabin there was a message from him to get back to Staff immediately. "Screw him," I told the yeoman. "We don't work for him. Let him wait."

Half an hour later he called me back.

"I'm giving you a direct order—get the hell back here and pick up these goddamn messages."

"Say what?"

"You heard me loud and clear, Marcinko—get the hell back here, and that's an order."

"Excuse me, Scott, but I don't work for you, so you can't order me to do anything. Now, as to the matter of messages, I was only following your administrative guidance. You wanted all our messages—you got 'em. Now, asshole, the ball's in your court. You'll have to send them out. I can't, because you haven't signed off on any of them yet, and I'm the draftee, not the clearance officer. And besides, Scott, you're the Staff puke paper-pusher. So push your goddamn paper—I have a goddamn command to run."

"Marcinko—"

"Screw you, Commander. Uppa you ess, as we used to say."

He went screaming to the commodore, but it didn't do him any good. He had to sign off on every message anyway. And that afternoon, a piece of paper from Staff, with Scott's chop attached, was messengered to SEAL Two HQ, telling me I had the authority to release my own messages once more.

That evening, I took commodore watch myself. I sidled up next to Dick Coogan as he sat at the bar, ordered myself a Bombay on the rocks, and said, "So how's it going, sir?"

He looked at me kind of funny. "I hear you and Scott were really going at it today."

"Jeez, I don't know about that, Commodore. Y'know, he runs your staff, and I run my command, and I try to make it all work smoothly."

"Didn't sound so smooth today. Scott tells me you were really out of line."

"Commodore, sometimes I follow his guidance. But when I don't like his guidance, I get yours. I don't think he likes that very much."

Coogan laughed. "Probably doesn't like it at all." He ordered a fresh drink for himself and told the bartender to pour me a second Bombay on the rocks. "I'll tell ya one thing, Dick," he said, ticking the rim of my glass with his, "the son of a bitch was pounding up and down the quarterdeck, spitting bricks. You really had him talking to himself today."

I raised my gin and toasted him. "Just doing my job, sir."

Chapter

16

I NEVER SET OUT TO MAKE ENEMIES. BUT I HAVE ALWAYS been both an aggressive and a mission-oriented creature, so I will do whatever it takes to get the job done—and damn the consequences. That attitude never won me a lot of friends among the ranks of conventional Navy officers, many of whom I intimidated, coerced, strong-armed, threatened, and occasionally pummeled into the concrete. Still, I prospered within the system. One reason was that my adversaries habitually underrated me. They saw only the hard-drinking, bar-brawling, madman-under-fire Marcinko. They never knew that my fitreps as a staff aide and attaché were just as proficient as those from Vietnam. They thought because my shirtsleeve is 35 while my inseam is only 32 and I said "fuck" to admirals I was nothing but a coarse, knuckle-dragging snake-eater. Sure I said "fuck" to admirals, but not *all* admirals—just those who said "fuck" to me first. I've been known to use words with more than one syllable; I've been known to write coherent documents in simple, declarative sentences.

It has always served my purpose to keep people off-balance. I kept Charlie off-balance in Vietnam by hitting him hard where he least expected to be hit. I kept my officers and men at SEAL Two off-balance by continually challenging them to do 100 percent more than they thought they could do. And I kept staff assholes like Scott Sullivan off-balance through a combination of unpredictability, bureaucratic harassment, profanity, and the underlying threat of crude, rude physical intimidation. Much of the time it was an act—an act intended to bring political results—but Scott and those like him didn't realize it.

Indeed, my enemies traditionally overlook the fact that I have always been a political animal. I discovered early in my career, for example, that it was easier to drop something on people from a great height than it was to push it up through the chain of command. I broached the idea of going to college with Admiral Peet, rather than saying "May I?" to some commander; as an attaché, I briefed admirals who could help the Khmer Navy instead of wasting my time on junior officers who couldn't. And when I wanted to take SEAL Team Two on a full command deployment to Puerto Rico, for example, I didn't write a memo to Scott Sullivan and ask him, "Please, sir, pass it on."

I finagled a meeting with a vice admiral I knew and sold him the idea of moving SEAL Team Two to Roosy Roads, lock, stock, and barrel, for ten weeks of full-tilt exercises. My logic was irresistible: in a U.S./Soviet war scenario, we wouldn't deploy Two squad by squad. Instead, the entire command would be shifted to a forward position.

But the whole command had never been moved at once before, and didn't the admiral think it was about time we tried to see if it was feasible?

Absolutely, the admiral said. I'll see that this gets approved, the admiral said.

So I watched like an innocent bystander as he dropped my plan from three-star heaven downward, onto the heads of unsuspecting junior officers. When commodores and captains came to me and said, "What hath you done and why are you causing me all this shit?" I looked at them innocently and said, *"Moi?"*

That's what I said. We all knew better, of course. What I thought was, *"Parce que je suis un phoc et vous êtes les phocees*—I be the fucker and you be the fuckees."

But I had plausible denial—and I had my command deployment. It was a complete success, too: the first full-scale deployment ever of an entire SEAL team and its support mechanisms. Still, the officers I offended probably filed my name in the "what goes around comes around" bin.

I have been accused of arrogance—and I admit to it. I have been accused of rubbing people's noses in manure—and liking it too much. Guilty as charged. To be honest, there is a part of me that has always been self-destructive—a part that wants to "pull low" no matter what the consequences may be. Part of it is easy to explain: I like the feeling of living life on the edge, of pushing myself to the absolute limit, of feeling immortal.

During my enlisted days, my self-destructive urges could be attributed to the exuberance (or foolishness) of youth. As a junior officer in Vietnam, I could plead bloodlust and the ecstasy of battle—adrenaline addiction, if you will. But as a unit commander, I had no real excuse for playing the sorts of malevolent head-games on my superiors that would return to haunt me later. Yet that is what I did—and they did indeed come back and whack me. In most cases, I fought for my men—for their welfare, comfort, or to ensure that they had the best equipment and training. In others, I screwed with my brother officers because I just plain didn't like their attitude.

During my second Vietnam tour in 1968, for example, the CO of SEAL Two was a lieutenant commander named Ted Lyon, or, as he pedantically signed all his reports, E[dward] Lyon III. He was a prematurely gray, ascetically thin, ramrod-straight marathoner whose Spartan, punctilious, by-the-book perspective seemed—to me, at least—the sort of austere mentality that, all too often, is the sorry end product of ruler-wielding, guilt-inspiring parochial-school nuns.

Ted was an okay CO, in that he left me alone and wrote me good fitreps. (*"A dynamic, aggressive officer . . . of athletic build and fine appearance . . . unhesitatingly recommended for promotion when due,"* is representative of his prose.) But as a SEAL leader, a sea daddy, a man to look up to, I found him lacking those ineffable, deadly hunter's qualities that make great warriors great warriors. When I thought of Ted, which in truth wasn't very often, I always thought of him with a loaded clipboard in his hand, not an M16.

Segue eight years, to 1976. I was now a lieutenant commander and had Ted's old job commanding SEAL Team Two.
He, a full commander, was CO of UDT Team 21. Our outgoing change-of-command ceremonies were scheduled for the
same day. About two months before they were to take place,
Ted called me.

"Dick, could you change your change-of-command date?
I'd like to use the parade ground, but I see by the calendar
you've already got it booked for your ceremony. Seems to
me that, since I'm senior to you, you could move from Friday
back to Wednesday and let me have it."

He sounded so . . . prissy. That was it. Ted was a prissy,
clipboard-carrying asshole, and I couldn't stand him. So screw
him. "Fuck you," I told Ted. "I've had this planned for a
long time."

"So have I."

"Well, then, you should have planned better, shit for
brains, shouldn't you? I've got the goddamn parade ground
blocked off, and that's the way it's staying. Course, if you
want to share it, there's plenty of room."

His voice turned to ice. "No thank you, Dick. I shall make
other arrangements."

And so he did. He held his change of command behind the
Quonset-hut motor-pool buildings on a small, greasy maca-
dam parking lot. And I held mine on the immaculately manicured parade ground with its bleachers and the big Navy
marching band playing "Anchors Aweigh" as the guests
arrived.

I forgot the incident. Ted Lyon did not.

I spent ten months after I left Two batching it in Mont-
gomery, Alabama, while I attended the Air Command and
Staff course at Maxwell Air Force Base. Simultaneously, I
got a master's degree in political science at Auburn University. From Alabama, I moved straight to Washington. Kathy
and the kids arrived two months later. There was an action
officer's slot open at OP-06, Navyspeak for Office of the Deputy Chief of Naval Operations, Current Plans and Policy
Branch. My career was in a "hold" mode: I wasn't eligible
for a second command slot and hadn't had enough time as a
lieutenant commander to be promoted again. So I needed to

find a job where I could wait until I made commander, while putting together the network of sea daddies I'd need to make my leap to captain, and then vault on to flag rank.

Besides, I'd never done a tour at the Pentagon, and the thought of getting to know those 17.5 miles of corridors—not to mention a slew of friendly admirals—seemed like a good idea at the time. The reality of the situation was different from my preconceptions. Navy action officers, either commanders or lieutenant commanders, were the lowest rungs in the "chop chain"—the paper-trail staffing ladder descending from the chief of naval operations, the CNO, and the JCS, the Joint Chiefs of Staff. The Pentagon's bureaucracy is much like that in Congress. Up on Capitol Hill, it may be the members who vote on bills. But let there be no misunderstanding: it is the congressional staffs that do the work behind the scenes; it falls to legislative assistants to handle most of the internecine negotiations that make those bills possible; and it is the committee and subcommittee staffs who draft the legislation's precise language.

We faceless creatures did much the same for the CNO, just as other action officers from each branch of the armed services worked for their chiefs of staff. Each of us was a mixture of research staffer and lobbyist, negotiating with our counterparts, and trying to sell our particular service's point of view.

Once tasked, we'd write a memo for the planning officers, who were generally captains. They were the senior-level staffers, the ones who would venture into three- and four-star heaven to brief the Olympians. Sometimes, junior pukes like me would be invited along to carry someone's briefcase, run the slide projector, or handle the pointer. But the general rule was that action officers didn't get much—if any—face time with admirals. So much for networking.

If we didn't see them, our paperwork did: we provided virtually all the background memos for the chief of naval operations when he attended JCS meetings. We didn't brief the CNO, of course—he was spoon-fed his information by the vice CNO or one of the many deputies, assistants, or assistant deputy CNOs. They, in turn, were briefed by planning officers. We briefed the planning officers. It was sort of like the kid's game "telephone."

When the CNO asked a question, it would drop on us like

a depth charge. We would scramble to do the research and draft an answer. Our superiors would "chop," or approve, our work and pass it up the ladder. At each rung, the memo or report would receive a new chop. If it didn't get one, it would be sent back for more work, or a change of tone or content.

I enjoyed two incredible strokes of luck, however, which propelled me higher and faster than I had any reason to expect. The first was that I had the good fortune to work for a captain named Ace Lyons. Ace was an Academy grad, a small-waisted, barrel-chested ship driver in his late forties who'd done a three-year stint as the senior aide to the deputy chief of naval operations (Current Plans and Policy). He was one of the Navy's golden boys—on a fast track to admiral. But unlike most of those frocked to flag rank, Ace thought like a warrior and often swore like a sailor. I found it reassuring when he called me "asshole" and came to realize that I was making progress when that sobriquet changed to "shithead." It occurred to me more than once that Ace was somehow related to Ev Barrett.

The second break came after about five months on the job, when I was given an additional portfolio—intelligence. The intel officer was leaving; he knew I'd been an attaché, which meant I knew about intelligence work. Moreover, as a SpecWar operator, I understood how valuable "hot" intelligence could be. Ace had given me the freedom to expand SpecWar ops into JCS plans. I'd been able to meet most of the key players at the four-star level. The intel job gave me the real key to power at the Pentagon: close-hold information. I was now cleared to read material no one else except the CNO or the deputy CNO could see. That gave me large amounts of face time with them both.

Every morning I'd get to work two hours early and read the cable traffic, browse the CIA and DIA messages, and check the NSA intercepts. Then I'd highlight the most important sections, straighten my tie, slip on a sports coat, and go brief the deputy CNO for plans and policy, a straight-shooter three-star named William Crowe, who later went on to become the chairman of the Joint Chiefs of Staff.

I liked Crowe, a big, amiable bear of a man who had a reputation as a first-rate though somewhat bookish administrator. A 1946 Naval Academy grad, he'd gotten his MA at Stanford, his Ph.D. at Princeton, and his education as an adviser to the Vietnamese Navy. Despite his courtly manner with subordinates and soft Kentucky accent, he was one of those admirals I could say "fuck" to. His office on the fourth-floor E ring was huge, and the shelves behind his desk were filled with an immense collection of hats—everything from old fire hats and French berets to English bobbies' helmets and plaid golf caps.

It didn't take more than a few months before Crowe started calling on me every time he needed something from the intel shops. I became a pseudo crisis-control officer, dealing with action officers from the CIA, NSA, DIA, NSC—the whole alphabet soup of spookdom. My clearances were astronomical—code-word letter stuff—that allowed me to see everything from high-resolution satellite photos to underwater intercepts.

The late seventies were a time of flux in the intelligence community. President Jimmy Carter's director of central intelligence, Admiral Stansfield Turner, redirected the priorities away from human-based intelligence—"HUMINT" is what it's called in "intelbabble"—and more toward signals interception, technical information gathering, and electronic surveillance, which are known as SIGINT, TECHINT, and ELINT, respectively.

The impersonal nature of SIGINT, ELINT, and TECHINT probably appealed to the remote Turner, a nuclear-Navy dipdunk, who was one of those men in the Hyman Rickover mold who prefer statistical models to real life because they are neater and don't complain. But there's a problem with that: war doesn't follow any statistical pattern. War is totally unpredictable. It is a continual series of screwups, each one worse than the last.

Even the lowliest dogfaces of WWII knew that. "How's it going, soldier?" SNAFU, they'd say: Situation Normal, All Fucked Up. Or TARFU—Things Are *Really* Fucked Up. Or FUBAR—Fucked Up Beyond All Repair. But Turner's kids didn't know SNAFU, TARFU, or FUBAR because they'd never sweat their balls lying in ambush waiting for Charlie to show up and watching the situation turn to shit.

TECHINT's biggest flaw is that it relies on statistical

models. Let's say the U.S. has a Key-Hole spy satellite up in the air. And let's say that the object of its cameras is obscured by low clouds. Then what most often happens—because you need intelligence *now*—is that the whiz kids will take frames from previous passes and develop a simulation. "This is what happened before," they say, "so this must be happening now."

Except, whiz kids are mathematicians and analysts and professors, and they've never been shot at. They don't understand decoys and deception; they don't understand the enemy's will to win, or the genius of one particular commander. They can't tell you if the porosity of the sand you're looking at will support the weight of a C-130, or only an Arava STOL (Short Takeoff Or Landing) aircraft. Or whether the sandy patch two hundred miles below is really a quicksand pool that formed only two weeks ago.

So, as I relayed intel briefs to Crowe and his crowd, I'd often add my own insights—gathered from other sources—giving them a better idea of the alternatives available; adding how SpecWar operators could provide information no satellite system or high-flying SR-71 "Blackbird" could ever deliver. By late 1978, Bill Crowe and I were on a first-name basis: he called me Dick, and I called him Admiral.

On November 4, 1979, Iranian militants seized the U.S. Embassy in Tehran, and took all its diplomatic personnel hostage. Eight days later, Major General James Vaught was charged by the Joint Chiefs of Staff to form a task force—it was called a TAT, or Terrorist Action Team—that would plan a military hostage-rescue option. I was assigned to the TAT as one of two Navy reps.

I liked Vaught instinctively. He was a slow-speaking, cool-headed South Carolinian, a bony, white-walled airborne, ex-enlisted rifleman who'd seen service in World War II, Korea, and Vietnam. He never seemed comfortable in a suit or a Class-A uniform, but wore off-the-shelf fatigues as if they'd been custom-made for him. Vaught looked and talked like my old Eighth Platoon guys from Vietnam—Frank Scollise or Hoss Kucinski—men who always seemed to be in pain, but just kept going and going.

The man picked to lead the rescue, Colonel Charlie Beckwith, I'd first met in Vietnam. Chargin' Charlie, as he was often called, was one of the Army's best unconventional warriors. A profane, Georgia-drawling veteran of hundreds of Special Forces ops, Charlie had realized early on there was a need for an elite, mobile, highly trained unit to fight terrorism, conduct surgical behind-the-lines operations, gather intelligence, and provide nonconventional options to low-intensity-conflict scenarios. The unit he'd conceived and built to do the job was called SFOD-D—Special Forces Operational Detachment–Delta—or more commonly, Delta Force.

The chairman of the JCS, Air Force general David Jones, was precisely the wrong man to be in charge of any mission calling for SpecWar capabilities. He had the sort of personality that would have guaranteed him a successful career at a major corporation. He was tall, distinguished looking, bright—scholarly, even—and reportedly a gifted although cold manager. No one, however, ever referred to him as a charismatic leader of men.

General Jones loved to discuss options. Endlessly. At one point, he ordered us to write up and brief him on forty-two separate options for the rescue mission, each one more farfetched than the last. One of his whiz kids came up with a chopper-crash option, in which the hostages would be rescued by a force that would crash-land their choppers on the roof of the embassy. And how would they escape? Aha—you just found the one small flaw in the plan!

Like most military apparatchiks, Davey Jones was squeamish about the thought of casualties. I discovered this when we were planning a penetration operation to test the porosity of the sand at the landing site we called Desert One. The test was necessary to see if the ground would hold the weight of fully loaded C-130s.

Someone asked the obvious question "What happens if a couple of Iranians show up when you're running the test?"

Without thinking, I said, "You kill the cocksuckers."

The room went silent. Davey Jones's face turned to stone. He glared at me, and if looks alone could have court-martialed, I'd have already been in the stockade at Leavenworth doing hard labor.

"How could you even think that?"

How could I not? I tried to deflect him. "I'm sorry, General, but if somebody's out there, then he's violating the Iranian curfew, and so all I'd be doing is carrying out Allah's will."

The chairman did not find me amusing. But I saw Jim Vaught stifle a giggle.

Jones canceled a diversionary scheme of mine because he thought it would cause too many Iranian casualties. One potential problem Delta would face was the Iranian Air Force. The rescue plan called for the hostages to be choppered from Tehran to an unused Iranian airfield called Manzariyeh, about a half-hour's flight from Tehran. Delta and the hostages were vulnerable—during the on-load, the chopper flight, and the transfer—to IAF strikes. My idea was to bomb the runways at Tehran's airport—which was used for military flights—so Delta and the hostages could not be pursued. I designed a one-plane air strike that I called Attack of the Wooden Soldiers.

It was a real KISS (Keep It Simple, Stupid) operation: a C-130, from which I and two other SEALs would toss dozens of explosive-laden railroad ties that had been attached to parachutes with static cords. The wooden soldiers would be rigged to explode on impact. The ten-foot craters they would make in the runways would render the facility inoperable.

Other, smaller charges would also be dropped. These were tubes packed with plastic explosive and bomblets that would devastate any on-ground personnel. The tubes would be wrapped with chains, whose links would break apart and spread like grapeshot when the C-4 exploded, just like over-sized Claymore mines. The red-hot chainlinks would damage support equipment, puncture and ignite fuel tanks, and help cause general chaos. Another group of wooden soldiers would have explosive squibs attached, so as they descended, they'd go *brrrrp*, as if paratroopers with tommy guns were attacking.

Delivered properly, the whole package would take Tehran airport out of the picture. Equally important, it would provide a significant diversion while Charlie and his Delta guys were busting into the embassy compound in the middle of the city. And if the Iranians shot us down, well, then it was one C-130, five fliers, and three SEALs lost—nothing to write home about.

For security reasons—like the fact that the Soviets were constantly eavesdropping on the high volume of message traffic in the area—Charlie Beckwith moved Delta from its headquarters at Ft. Bragg, just outside Fayetteville, North Carolina, to a smaller and more secure training area. Delta referred to it as Camp Smokey, but the place was actually Camp Peary, the CIA's huge site for training spies, infiltrators, and covert operators. The Farm, as it's called in the spook world, is a 25-square-mile parcel of land just northeast of Williamsburg, Virginia, running between U.S. Route 64 and the James River. It was where the CIA built Charlie and his men a model of the Tehran embassy compound so they could rehearse their every move once they went over the wall.

Meanwhile, I perfected my wooden-soldier project. After work at the Pentagon, I'd drive or fly down, meet the SEALs I'd recruited to help me—a couple of enlisted men from SEAL Two named Larry and Bob—and we'd set to work, often going all night. At oh dark hundred I'd head north again—to arrive in time to read and précis the daily intelligence package for Admiral Crowe before the official workday began at 0800.

Charlie Beckwith liked the idea of wooden soldiers. David Jones did not. To scotch it—and anything like it—the chairman put out a ridiculous obiter dictum: Thou Shalt Not Kill, he told his soldiers.

A second—and more significant—failure was in the area of HUMINT. To put it succinctly, there was none. The CIA didn't have a single on-the-ground operative in Iran, so far as I could tell. We were able to obtain fragments of information through foreign embassies, and there was still a large contingent of foreign nationals in Iran—Turks, Germans, French, Irish, Canadians—but there was no organized network, and nobody supplying the "hot" information a team of special operators needs to mount a rescue operation.

One of the TAT's goals, therefore, was to infiltrate as many operators into Iran as we could, in order to have at least a few assets on the ground. Each service was instructed to search for Farsi speakers, and given the operation security requirements of the rescue mission, I was selected to be the Navy "cutout" for all potential infiltrators. Sailors who spoke Farsi were culled through a computer search. They'd be ordered to leave their units—without knowing the reason—and take a plane to Washington. More than a dozen sailors showed up at various airfields in the capital area. I'd meet them, bring them to my home, swear them—and sign them—to secrecy, then pass them along to the flesh handlers on Vaught's staff. Some were rejected, others chose not to volunteer. Among those who did choose to become part of the mission was a Navy captain from Annapolis who agreed to drive a truck loaded with Delta troopers into Tehran.

Two SEALs also ended up as infiltrators. Both had worked for me when I commanded SEAL Team Two. One—I'll call him Kline—was a first-generation American who had grown up speaking German at home. He was slipped into Iran as a German businessman, and his information about the embassy compound proved invaluable. (He was "thanked" by being left behind after the debacle at Desert One—with no hint of what had happened. Being a SEAL and therefore self-reliant, he walked the six hundred miles from Tehran to the Turkish border, got himself across to safety, and came looking for the whiz-kid assholes who'd left him high and dry with murder in his eyes. Incredibly, Kline, whose real-time intelligence was crucial to the mission, was never recognized for what he did. No medals, no commendations, no promotions, not even an "attaboy." I couldn't blame him for being bitter.) The second SEAL was a little guy named Joey, who got in masquerading as a monk. He should have been called Friar Dick, because he was a ladies' man. Joey wasn't on the ground very long—only a couple of days. But he did his job, and he got out clean.

The night of April 24, 1980, was probably the longest one of my life. There were roughly forty of us crammed into a SCIF—Special Classified Intelligence Facility—on the second floor of the Pentagon, just across the corridor from the big JCS situation room with its wall-sized screens, state-of-the-art communications, techno-bells, and electro-whistles. There, on the other side of the hallway, behind thick, padded doors, Chairman Jones and the rest of the Joint Chiefs sat in their upholstered swivel chairs doodling on their personalized notepaper or doing whatever four-stars do.

We, the junior action officers, planners, spooks, and SpecWarriors, sat on molded plastic and worked ourselves into Anacin headaches compounded by caffeine overload.

Our SCIF was actually a 16-by-30-foot room suspended within a larger room, so as to preclude any penetration by eavesdropping devices. We got into it only by passing through three SOD—Special Operations Division—checkpoints, each manned by armed guards. The SCIF had raised floors, low ceilings, and fluorescent lights that gave everything a greenish cast. There were two long meeting tables in the center. On the tables (along with a collection of moldy coffee cups, crumb-laden paper plates, and butt-filled ashtrays) were half a dozen small, square loudspeakers. The speakers were attached to cables that ran across the floor to wall jacks.

Two speakers were labeled NSA. Those would carry ELINT intercepts from the National Security Agency. The rest carried transmissions coming from Wadi Kena, Masirah, Desert One, and Tehran, where one of the American agents on the ground had his own PRC-101 radio transceiver tied into the satellite network. Everybody was on the same frequency, so we'd hear Delta's transmissions, the chopper pilots' chatter, and General Vaught's comments—all at one time.

Against one wall were the desks where we TAT action officers had camped out since being banded together the previous November. Another wall was covered with maps, charts, and photographs of the target areas. Just in front of the wall, on overhead tracks, were black drapes that could be pulled closed before anyone without the proper clearances came into the SCIF. There were a couple of easels for show-and-tell briefings, and under the tables, against the desks, and along the wall, piles of three-ring binders and notebooks provided us with a reference library about Iran, the militants, the Iranian military, the hostages, their families, as well as papers outlining scenarios for every conceivable way to get our people out.

I felt vulnerable and helpless sitting on the edge of a gray metal desk in my shirtsleeves, sipping cold coffee out of a paper cup. I felt I should have been with Delta, or have been infiltrated into Iran to help with the mission, instead of relegated to desk work. We had only one Navy officer with Charlie—the captain who volunteered as a truck driver—and no SEALs. Dammit, I should have been there, too. My eyes wandered around the room, hazy with cigarette smoke. I realized at that moment what the tension must have been like for the mission-control people in Houston as the moon lander left *Apollo 11* and started its drop onto the lunar surface. There was nothing they could have done if anything went wrong. There was nothing we could do if something happened to Delta, either. I finished the coffee, crumpled the cup, and launched a hook shot at an olive-drab wastebasket ten feet away. Swish. Two points. Maybe it was an omen.

We heard Delta's every move over the speakers. Our secure SATCOM—SATellite COMmunications—system relayed the American chatter. Iranian communications were monitored and passed in real time by the NSA's big ears out at Fort Meade. It was like a live international radio show, without benefit of announcers or script. We heard Charlie leave Egypt and arrive at Masirah; we heard as our eight RH-53D choppers cleared the deck of the USS *Nimitz* in the Gulf of Oman on the way to the rendezvous at Desert One, where they'd pick up the rescue team that was flying from Masirah in MC-130 transport planes. We heard the first chopper report "Feet dry" as he crossed the Iranian coastline just west of Chah Bahar.

Almost immediately, bells started ringing in Iran. Military outposts were reporting to Tehran about invaders. Militia units were moving. Jet fighters were scrambled. What the hell was going on? How did they learn about us so soon?

It was a long five minutes before we realized the Iranians weren't reacting to us—that the scramble was in the northwest, near the Iraqi border. Along the southern coastline, where we were operating, everything was copacetic.

Another chopper called feet dry, and then the rest of them made their landfall. Delta was already more than half the distance to Desert One aboard its MC-130s.

While they were still in the air, we got the first inkling of trouble. An NSA intercept told us one of the choppers was experiencing mechanical problems. We listened as the stricken aircraft autorotored onto the desert and its crew was picked up by another RH-53D. Two other choppers ran into sandstorms and got lost. Well, losing a chopper or two had been foreseen. We were still in a SNAFU mode: Situation Normal—All Fucked Up.

The first element of Delta's landing at Desert One went

smoothly. Then Mr. Murphy's law really went to work. An Iranian bus drove by the landing site. It was stopped and its forty-five or so passengers were detained under guard. Moments later, a gasoline tanker truck appeared from the opposite direction. It was stopped with a LAWS shot, but the driver jumped into another vehicle that was driving along the road and fled. Meanwhile, flames from the burning tanker were climbing more than a hundred feet into the desert sky. We'd progressed to the TARFU stage.

"What should we do with the Iranians from the bus?" somebody at Desert One asked General Vaught in Egypt.

I answered for him. "Kill the sons of bitches."

My colleagues looked at me incredulously. "Just kidding," I told them. I wasn't kidding at all.

Vaught radioed back an order to ship them out on a C-130 and return them after the operation.

There was now real confusion in the disembodied voices on our speakers. Nothing was going according to plan. There were too many elements. There were multiple aircraft. There were chopper pilots who, despite their training, were still uncomfortable flying long-range missions over desert terrain. There was a Rube Goldberg chain of command, in which an Air Force ground commander at Desert One answered to an Army two-star in Egypt, who was being second-guessed by hordes of three- and four-stars in Washington. It violated the most important rule I knew about special operations—keep 'em as KISS as you can, and they'll probably work.

I had real bad vibes about what was happening in Iran. And yet—it *had* to work. We'd been at it for five months. This was the Super Bowl and the World Series all wrapped up in one.

At the desk next to me, a CIA guy I'll call Jones shook his head in frustration. "You were right, you know," he said. Jones was an old-fashioned warrior who fought against the CIA's increasing bureaucracy and its technological predilections under Stansfield Turner. We spoke the same language. "This is gonna be a goatfuck," he said quietly.

I nodded in agreement, although there was nothing Jones or I wanted less to be true.

Only six of the eight choppers arrived at Desert One; only five were in flyable condition. The plan had always called for a minimum of six to carry Delta to the hide site, then come into Tehran and snatch the hostages and their rescuers. Charlie decided to abort. It was his call. General Vaught, in Egypt, wanted him to go on. So did others, including me. But you don't second-guess the man on the ground. It was Charlie's call, and he decided to scrub. He sounded like a man who'd just lost his best friend when he announced he was coming home.

Then shit really happened. One of the choppers, maneuvering to top off its fuel tanks for the long return flight to the *Nimitz*, hit an EC-130 refueling aircraft in which Delta's Blue element had just loaded. The chopper and the plane both exploded in a huge fireball. The mission had gone all the way to FUBAR.

Fists clenched, numbed into horrified silence, some of us swallowing back tears, we could hear screams and chaos—the sounds of brave men burning to death. Then, finally, after what seemed like an eternity of shouting, confusion, explosions, and devastation, we listened as the remaining C-130s got off the ground, and what was left of Delta flew back to Masirah.

To say that we all sat in that smoky, dead-air room stunned would be a gross understatement. This was the unthinkable. We'd just failed in an operation that had been almost half a year in the planning and billions in the funding. And there was no way of salvaging it. The black eye the United States was about to receive in world opinion would be a long, long time in healing.

The world's alleged dominant superpower had just blown a one-timer against a bunch of rag-head terrorists, and we'd done it to ourselves. Bye-bye, au revoir, ciao, aloha, adios, sayonara. There wasn't going to be any tomorrow.

To be honest, I don't remember much about the rest of that night. Yes, there was work to be done. Salvage work—like bringing back the human assets we'd left behind in Tehran. But I don't recall very much at all about what was said, or what I or anyone else did. I do recall I felt like putting somebody's head through a wall, except I couldn't figure out whose head I wanted to smash.

Not even Risher's death affected me as badly as the debacle at Desert One. Risher had been responsible for himself—it was his own recklessness that had killed him. And besides, it happened in battle. Men die in battle. At Desert One, we'd all had a hand in the deaths of men who died for no reason at all; brave men were killed before they'd been allowed to do what they'd been trained to do.

From the top down, it had been one humongous goatfuck. One big waste.

Chapter

17

AT THE MOVIES, THE SOUND TRACK WOULD SWELL INTO "The Impossible Dream" from *Man of La Mancha* and the gallant soldiers would rise from the ashes, go out, and win one. In real life it doesn't happen that way. In real life soldiers die. In real life the gods on Capitol Hill and in the White House demand human sacrifices. So Charlie Beckwith and Jim Vaught were offered up by Davey Jones and the rest of the brass, even though the buck hadn't stopped with them.

Charlie—no politician—didn't realize what was happening until it was too late. I met him wandering down an E-ring hallway about a week after Desert One. His eyes had a befuddled, thousand-yard stare. "Dick," he said, indicating the JCS's offices with his thumb, "them boys just *left* me out there."

The experience was a real big tic on the learning curve for me, too. I saw them eviscerate Charlie Beckwith, a good and tough man who had gone out and put his life on the line because he believed in his mission and he believed in his men, but he wasn't given a chance to do things his way. And then, having taken much of the command and the control away, the big bureaucratic machine blamed him for its mistakes.

"Aha," the voice inside my head that always sounded like Everett E. Barrett growled to me: "Marcinko, you shit-for-brains numb-nuts asshole geek, if they ever give you a similar opportunity, they'll mud-suck you just as bad as they mud-sucked Charlie Beckwith."

And although no one was singing "Impossible Dream" (or anything else, for that matter), work on Operations Snow Bird and Honey Badger, the second set of plans to rescue American hostages in Iran, began on April 26, 1980, just two days after Desert One.

Concurrently, a Joint Task Force, or JTF, was organized at the behest of the secretary of defense, Harold Brown. The mandate was to plan and conduct military operations that would counter terrorist acts directed at the United States, its interests, or its citizens. Although the JTF would include Army, Navy, and Air Force elements, each service would be outside its normal administrative chain of command, reporting instead to an Army general at Ft. Bragg, North Carolina.

The idea was pretty radical for the armed forces. It meant that instead of each service working separately and often in direct competition with one another, the forces assigned to the JTF would work together. Command and control would be unified. The left hand would know what the right hand was doing. Or, as I'd preached to my SEAL platoons in Vietnam, there would be unit integrity. Talk about a revolutionary concept!

I was assigned to the JTF as a Navy action officer and helped frame the initial language that defined its mission and organization. I worked out of a basement office in the bowels of the Pentagon, which—considering the mood of the building—suited me just fine.

Three floors above me, Charlie Beckwith was also helping draft the JTF papers. A unified special-operations command was something Charlie had dreamed about for years. Being the loyal Army Special Forces type that he was, Charlie designed his version of the JTF around Delta's unique capabilities. But since he was also a realist, Charlie soon saw the JTF would also need SEALs to target maritime objectives: tankers, cruise ships, and military assets like navy yards, aircraft carriers, and nuclear submarines.

I, too, believed SEALs must be included, but not as an

add-on element under someone else's thumb. I was convinced an entire SEAL team was essential to the JTF. So, when the first draft of the staffing papers floated across my desk in May of 1980, I changed Chargin' Charlie's prose slightly. As written, the staffing memo called for a SEAL *element*. I whited out the word *element* and replaced it with the word *Command*.

The different meaning of those two words was immense. A SEAL *element* was a small group—one or two platoons—that would become a maritime auxiliary of Delta Force, putting the Navy in the untenable position of being ancillary to the Army. Indeed, while the JTF was designed to diminish interservice rivalries, there was a certain amount of Navy institutional ego and pride at stake no matter what the secretary of defense or anyone else may have liked to believe.

A SEAL *Command* meant a self-contained SEAL unit, under its own CO. A SEAL Command would become an equal player in the JTF, along with Delta Force, and the Air Force's First Special Operations Wing.

I passed the memo along. The next time it came back across my desk, the words *SEAL Command* were still there. In mid-June, the final draft of the JTF memo was about to be voted up or down by the Joint Chiefs of Staff. If approved, which was a virtual certainty, it would be sent as doctrine to all the major theater commanders as well as the heads of the military intelligence agencies. The new SEAL Command would be written in stone.

Of course, in making my editorial change, I'd created one tiny, little problem: there *was* no existent SEAL Command that could become part of the JTF. Therefore, before the plan went into effect, I'd have to create one.

The question then became, which SEALs should become part of the JTF? The Navy had already established specialized counterterror—or CT—training for SEALs. On the West Coast, four of SEAL Team One's twelve platoons had received CT training. On the East Coast, SEAL Team Two had dedicated two of its ten platoons to CT activities. A young lieutenant commander I'll call Paul Henley, the officer who ran the CT program at Two, called his CT platoons MOB-6, or MOBility-6.

Despite the fact that the West Coast had trained more SEALs in CT than the East Coast, Paul Henley's CT operations were better planned and executed than anything on the West Coast. One reason was that, at SEAL One, operators got their training and then returned to their regular platoons. On the East Coast, MOB-6 worked as a unit all the time. I liked that. It indicated that MOB-6 had unit integrity.

Moreover, because SEAL Team Two operated primarily (though by no means exclusively) in NATO countries, MOB-6 had done joint exercises with Britain's Special Boat Section, the SBS; the German *Grenzschutzgruppe-9* (GSG-9); France's GIGN *(Groupement d'Intervention de la Gendarmerie Nationale)*; the Italians' *Groupe Interventional Speciale* (GIS); the Royal Danish Navy's *Fromanskorpset* combat swimmers; as well as CT units from such countries as Turkey, Spain, and Belgium. I liked that, too.

On the West Coast, CT training centered mainly around shooting skills. MOB-6's commander, Paul Henley, improved his men's shooting skills, too. But unlike the West Coast SEALs, his MOB-6 platoons had also boarded ships underway alongside SBS teams. They'd experimented climbing oil rigs in the North Sea. They had practiced rescuing hostages and neutralizing hostage-takers. Henley trained his men the way I would have done if I'd still been CO at Two. But no matter how good they might have been, there were still only two platoons in MOB-6. I'd need at least six platoons to form the nucleus of a new command. Meaning that four platoons would have to come from the West Coast or from non-MOB-6 SEAL Two personnel. The COs wouldn't like it at all. Still, that's what we needed: six platoons of *phoques*. *Phoque six*. Mean mother*phoquers*. And terrorists would become the *phoquees*.

I did some mental arithmetic, a lot of scheming, then worked my butt off writing a memo outlining the idea of a new SEAL unit specifically trained to fight terrorists in a maritime environment. I rewrote my prose for three days, until it glowed like the shine on my Geek-polished combat boots.

My nominal boss, a captain named Jim Baker, was so used to my forays into the world of black programs and SpecWar that he'd developed the running gag of taking an occasional glance at my work by covering his eyes then spreading his fingers apart half an inch.

"Omigod," he'd say. "Richard, what are you *doing* to me?

Let me take a look." As soon as he saw what I'd written, he'd cover his eyes again. "I don't want to *see*, I don't want to *know*."

"Then how do we deal with this unseen, unknown document that suggests murder and mayhem?" I would always ask politely.

"Forge my chop on it and send it up the line." Then we'd laugh like hell.

This memo, however, I kept to myself. Captain Baker would slip up behind my desk and try to peek, but I was having none of it. I'd flip the papers before he could see anything, climb out of my chair, and sit on them.

"You brute," he'd say, trying to move me aside. "I outrank you. Give us a break here."

I shrugged helplessly. "Do you have three stars?"

"Richard . . ."

"Have you ever eaten cobra?"

"*Rich*ard . . ."

"Jim, this memo can only be read by people who have A, three stars on their shoulders, or B, eaten cobra." I flashed the cover page in his direction. "See?"

Baker retreated to his desk. "You are going to give us a heart attack, Richard." He watched as I slipped my little missive into a code-word-secret folder with a vivid, inch-and-a-half stripe the color of violet grenade smoke running diagonally across both front and back. He was used to that. Much of the work I did was related to spookdom.

"Oh, I get it—it's *that* kind of memo."

I winked at him and waved the folder in his direction. "Right, Captain. I could tell you what's in here—but then I'd have to kill you."

He flushed red as a beet and giggled, "Omigod, omigod, okay, okay, okay, okay, okay. I don't want to know anything. I never saw you. I don't even know your name."

Folder tucked under my arm like a football, I sprinted up five flights of steps and marched down the fourth-floor E-ring corridor, my shoes beating out a tattoo on the marble floors.

Just outside Bill Crowe's suite, I paused to catch my breath. I was about to play some very high-stakes poker, and I wanted to appear calm. Crowe was then the deputy chief of naval operations for plans and policy. Despite the fact that he was subordinate to the vice chief of naval operations, Admiral James Watkins, Crowe had supplanted Watkins as CNO Thomas Hayward's closest and most trusted adviser. That was natural: Crowe handled operations; Watkins was chiefly an administrator. Thus, Bill Crowe's relationship to the CNO was more of an XO's relationship than an admin assistant's —less formal and more conversational. Whatever the reason, according to Pentagon scuttlebutt, Crowe had virtually replaced Watkins as the CNO's top gun. If I wanted to get the CNO's blessing on my plan, it would need Bill Crowe's chop first.

I opened the door to Crowe's suite. One of his aides, a captain, looked up from a desk across the room. I waved the folder at him so he could see its distinctive violet stripe.

"Gotta see the old man. Code-word stuff."

He waved me through. I slid into the admiral's cabin and closed the heavy door behind me.

Crowe looked up from his desk. "Come on in, Dick." He pointed me toward the chair in front of his desk. "Park it. What's on your mind today besides your falling hair?"

I slid the folder in front of him.

Admiral Crowe dropped his half-glasses onto the bridge of his nose, slid his feet onto his desk, pulled the memo onto his stomach, and read it slowly, scowling at the pages as he scanned them.

He looked up. "Does anybody know about this?"

"No, sir, I've been working it on my own."

He grunted and went back to reading. I spent my time examining the vast hat collection that sat on half a dozen shelves behind Crowe's desk.

Finally he finished. The half-glasses were slid up until they rested on his forehead just above his eyebrows. He scrutinized me closely, his face telling me nothing. Then he broke into a broad smile. "I love this. It'll give the Army a goddamn heart attack. I can guarantee the CNO's gonna love it, too."

He looked at me and slapped the desk for emphasis. "Do it, Dick—run with it."

What I had wrought was a new SEAL unit devoted exclusively to counterterror. It would become a coequal part of the JTF, alongside Delta and the Air Force's SOF, with worldwide maritime responsibilities. Not that I saw our job stopping at the high-water mark, either. So long as we carried water in our canteens, we'd be in a maritime environment—or close enough for me.

I called the unit SEAL Team Six. Six because there were already six platoons that had received CT training. And Six because the number would make the Soviets believe that there were five other SEAL teams somewhere, when there were in fact only two. Doom on you, Russkies.

SEAL Team Six would be lean and mean—seventy-five enlisted men and fifteen officers. They would look like civilians. Modified grooming standards—long hair, earrings, beards, and mustaches—would be maintained, so they'd pass as blue-collar workers anywhere in the world. Language skills would be encouraged. Unlike SEAL One or Two, whose activities were limited geographically, SEAL Team Six would be available on four-hour notice to deploy from its Virginia base to anywhere in the world.

The initial mission of Six was to join the second hostage-rescue operation, which was being planned, though not scheduled. Six's objective would be to insert covertly into Iran, where we would destroy a number of Iranian military targets just prior to Delta Force's second rescue attempt. But Six's ultimate CT mission would be much more wide-ranging. It was, as I wrote in my memo, imperative for the Team to train for virtually any maritime scenario.

My proposal stated confidently that SEAL Team Six would be operational six months after we got the go-ahead to start the selection process. Six months for ninety men to go from the equivalent of prone position to breaking the sound barrier. I believed it could be done. I even drew up a calendar for the first year of SEAL Team Six training. There were 12 months and 365 days boxed on the paper—and I spent a week trying to shoehorn 408 days of training to fit into those 365 boxes. I decided the men would sleep on planes.

The late spring and early summer of 1980 were spent smoothing out logistical details, dreaming up budget and equipment lists, and working out as much of the minutiae as I could. The SEAL Six project was close-hold—code-word secret—and I worked in a bureaucratic vacuum. Even so, there were probably rumors in the Navy SpecWar community that something was afoot. I began making the three-and-a-half-hour drive to Little Creek after I finished at the Pentagon. The visits were informal: I'd spend time with the senior chiefs of SEAL Team Two and over beers, ask questions. "How would you do this, Chief?" or "If you had to do such and such, what's the best way to get it done quietly?"

I spent night after night in the kitchen of an old friend, a master chief named Mac, whom I'd known since we'd gone through UDT training together. Working on coffee-stained legal-sized pads of yellow lined paper, Mac, a chief petty officer I called Fingers, and I drew up the logistics requirements for a new SEAL command. We also sketched out preliminary budgets and organizational charts and put together shopping lists of new and wonderful toys for the men to play with. We designed a training cycle that rotated two teams of three platoons each through a continuous schedule of shooting, jumping, diving, and CT hostage-rescue exercises. If Six got off the ground, I'd decided that Mac should become its command master chief. He was a tough, stringy little bird. His sardonic, often derisive management style would keep the troops on their toes; his long Team experience would keep the gears grinding. I wanted Fingers aboard, too. Both of them said they'd love to come and play, although Mac complained bitterly about the parachuting. He'd always hated throwing himself out of a perfectly good aircraft.

I also paid a lot of attention to what Paul Henley had done with MOB-6. Henley had just been promoted to lieutenant commander and was in the process of moving to the West Coast, where he'd been assigned as the XO of the BUD/S training unit at Coronado. He visited me in my basement hideout just before he and his wife, Marilyn, left for California. He had come north to see the personnel managers at BUPERS and bitch about his new assignment.

I'd never worked with Paul, yet I liked him. He would, I'd already decided, be the perfect XO for SEAL Team Six. Paul's was a real success story: he was a Naval Academy grad who'd fought his way up from a poor, tough Irish neighborhood in Philadelphia called Fishtown.

Paul was a smallish guy, dark haired and sharp featured, but a tough bantam rooster you wouldn't want to fool with. He made the mistake of telling his first-year advisers at Annapolis that he wanted to become a Frogman. No way. Academy grads, he was told, do not become snake-eaters. If you want to succeed, you will drive a ship. So, after he received his ensign's bars in 1970, Paul was sent to become a ship driver.

He got to BUD/S anyway, and even got there for the best of all reasons so far as I was concerned: brawling. He was at a junior officers' club called the Datum one night and stepped into a fight between a commander, who'd had a little too much sauce, and a couple of large, nasty linebacker-sized lieutenant JGs, who'd decided to tattoo a new set of stripes on the commander's face. Paul put both JGs on the floor and got the commander out of the club before the shore patrol showed up. Within three months, he was at BUD/S, the result of some friendly commander-to-commander phone calls.

Paul had made a lot of good moves for a guy who'd been a SEAL less than a decade. He was an accomplished parachutist—a member of the Navy's parachute team. He'd served twenty-six months with the *Kampfschwimmers*, the West German combat swimmer company based at Ekernforde, on the Baltic Sea, and was fluent in German. Softspoken, good with his men, and well respected, he'd probably be given a CO's slot as soon as he made commander. But Paul had a warrior's mentality, and he hated the thought of a two-year assignment that would keep him chained to a desk, writing reports about dumb-ass trainees who had just fallen off a log and sprained their ankles.

He sat in my basement office the last week of June and complained about his sorry fate. "What the hell am I going to do, Dick?"

I shrugged. I wasn't about to tell him anything about SEAL Six—yet. "You go out there and do the job."

"What about MOB-6?"

"What about it?"

"I was just getting it in shape. We were just beginning to get to some good scenarios. Did I tell you about the SBS boarding tactics? A ship under way. Well, I reworked 'em, and—"

I cut him off. "Listen, boychik, you've got a good junior officer to take over MOB-6. Think of this as ticket-punching."

He went to California, but he went kicking and screaming.

Little did he know what I'd have in store for him, if everything went according to plan.

According to plan also meant that I had to make some changes in my own timetable. I'd been selected to attend the National War College at Ft. Leslie McNair for the 1980–81 academic year. Selection to the War College is a virtual prerequisite for promotion to captain, commodore, and then up the ladder to flag rank. The courses are taught by a distinguished faculty. One's colleagues are the "command-select" elite of the armed forces, State Department, and CIA. More than just a low-pressure academic year and a full social schedule, the War College allows professional bonds to be formed, bonds that will pay hefty dividends later in a career, when who you know is just as important as what you know.

I was ready for a year of low-pressure fun and games. So was Kathy. Our kids were teenagers, and didn't need the constant mothering she'd provided for so long. I'd been in the Navy almost twenty-two years, and early in 1980, Kathy had started asking me to think about retirement. I could understand her concerns: it was as if she'd signed up for a 20-year hitch as a Navy wife—but she wasn't sure she could make it to thirty. That was to be expected—thirty years is a long time to live with the constant emotional and physical separations. But in her heart of hearts Kathy also knew I wasn't ready for retirement yet, so a year at the War College seemed like an excellent compromise. It would be a 12-month vacation. We could relax, take time for each other, and enjoy the cocktail parties, picnics, trips, and other perks at Ft. McNair.

But to be honest, I had conceived SEAL Team Six with me as its CO, and I wasn't going to be happy unless I got my way. The War College began its academic year in August. I said nothing to Kathy, but the last week of June, I requested an appointment with Bill Crowe.

"I got a problem, Admiral," I told him.

"Let's talk, Dick."

"I'm supposed to go to the War College next year."

"Which is where you should go," he interrupted. "Face it, Dick, you need a rest. A year at McNair will do you a lot of good."

"I'm sure it would, sir. But as you know, I've been working

for the past few weeks on this SEAL Six concept, and we still don't know who the commanding officer's going to be. Who you choose may affect my decision whether or not to attend."

"Well, I guess if we were looking around, you'd be on the short list. You're qualified to lead Six. But Dick, no one's given any thought to choosing a prospective commander yet."

"Well, Admiral, to be blunt about it, I'd like to be put on the list."

"I'm sure you would. On the other hand you've been going balls to the wall for almost two years now, Dick. Maybe it would be better if you took some time for yourself and your wife instead. Enjoy the War College. Teach them about snake-eaters over there."

"If you think that's the course I should follow, Admiral, then that's what I'll do. But sir, I've been with this counterterror thing for almost three years now, from the fall of the Shah to Desert One."

"I know that."

"Well, sir—frankly, Admiral, everything up to now has been a real goatfuck, so far as SpecWar's been concerned. Charlie Beckwith got screwed because the people around him didn't have any idea what SpecWar's about, or how to use the men. Goddammit, Admiral, that kind of dumb-shit thinking's been going on since Vietnam. My SEALs were always sent out by some numb-nuts who didn't know squat about what we did or how we did it. Maybe I'm wrong, maybe it's my goddamn ego, but I believe I can make a real difference when we go the second time. I know the people. I know the community—"

He flagged me to a halt. "I know, I know. But Dick, we really haven't given the matter any thought. Now that I know you're interested, I'll raise the issue. Remember, though: the final decision about a CO for SEAL Six rests with the chief of naval operations, not me."

"Do you think I should talk to Admiral Hayward, sir?"

He polished the lenses of his glasses, examined them closely, then replaced them. "It couldn't do you any harm to broach it." He squinted at me quizzically. "But Dick . . ."

"Sir?"

"A word to the wise. Don't use *goatfuck* as a noun around Admiral Hayward."

I laughed as I saluted. "Aye-aye, sir." But I knew Crowe was serious. If I wanted to command Six—and I wanted it worse than I'd ever wanted anything in my life—I knew I'd get only one shot to ask Admiral Hayward for the job.

I plotted my moves and my words with care, running a series of scenarios through my head until I was certain that whatever Hayward asked me, I'd react properly. Within a week, I was asked to carry an intelligence package into the CNO's cabin. That was the opportunity for which I'd been waiting.

I delivered the folder, then stood in front of his desk. The CNO was a tall, gaunt naval pilot who always looked as if he should be wearing oversized aviator-frame sunglasses. The large, avuncular, balding Bill Crowe exuded folksiness; Tom Hayward projected formality.

"Excuse me, sir."

He raised his eyes and looked at me. "Yes?"

"If you'll pardon the intrusion, sir, I was wondering if you'd do me a great personal favor and offer me some advice." I hoped that this opening would work with the CNO. Normally, admirals love to give advice. But Tom Hayward was no normal admiral. He was the only one of his kind in the Navy. You don't stand around and shoot the breeze with a CNO. My assignment was to deliver the papers to him, then depart quickly and silently.

"Sure, Dick." He kept his eyes on me as I stood at attention. He did not invite me to sit down.

"Sir," I said evenly, "I don't know if you're aware of it, but I have orders to report to the National War College in August." I hoped my pounding heart wasn't giving me away. I could feel the blood pulsing in my temples, my wrists, my chest.

"I didn't realize that. Congratulations."

"Thank you, sir. Well, you see, now there's this new command on line—the one at SEAL Team Six. And I was wondering, sir, if you'd be kind enough to advise me whether I'd be considered as a potential candidate. If I am being considered, which of the assignments would you recommend I take—the War College or SEAL Team Six?"

The CNO sat back in his high-backed chair and made a steeple out of his hands. "I know how hard you've been working, Dick," he said. "I know you've been under a lot of stress. And I know the hours you've been putting in." His eyes never left me. It was as if he were tracking a target. "How's your family doing?"

Good question. The subtext was clear: will your marriage stand two more years of constant separation or will it unravel? I pretty much knew it would probably unravel—Kathy and I already weren't on the best of terms domestically—but I was willing to take that chance to get this command. I decided to parry. "Well, sir, I'm married to a Navy wife, and I've got two Navy kids."

His eyebrows arched an eighth of an inch, then returned to normal. "Sounds fine," he said. He paused, then continued, "Well, Bill Crowe tells me you're his man because you've been carrying the CT load for a while. But it'll be a tough job. Question is, Dick, which assignment would you prefer?"

It was going to be mine, if I asked for it. An ineffable calm came over me—the same calm I had known in battle. Time slowed. I drank in each millisecond. My mind flashed to some of the men who had gotten me to this incredible position. Ev Barrett. B. B. Witham. Eagle Gallagher and Jim Finley and Patches Watson and Ron Rodger of Bravo Squad, my first combat command—Harry Humphries, Hoss Kucinski, Frank Scollise, and Gordy Boyce from my wonderful, crazy bunch of killers in Eighth Platoon. For an instant, I was back in Chau Doc holding Clarence Risher's body in my arms. Would there be others like him in this new unit? Probably. Could I face that challenge? Take that kind of pressure? Damn it, yes, I could. I knew my whole life had been spent in preparation for this one chance in a million to become a real warrior again, at the helm of a unit that I had created in my own image.

I looked the CNO in the eye. My voice was even and calm. I spoke formally because that is what CNOs like. "Sir, you know I'd be proud to be the first CO of Six. Command is the first thing in every sailor's mind, and this command would certainly be special to me because I've had so much to do with staffing it."

The CNO nodded. "I'd like that, Dick. I'd like you to be the first commander of SEAL Team Six."

Fireworks were going off in my brain, a real Fourth of July

celebration, but I didn't give a hint of the explosions. "Thank you very much, sir. Then I think the War College is no longer a point of discussion."

He extended his hand toward me. I shook it, stepped back, and saluted. "Thank you, sir."

Once outside the CNO's suite I let out a whoop that they probably heard at Little Creek. I galloped like a wide receiver down the corridor, skidded around the corner, and burst into Bill Crowe's suite. The secretaries and aides didn't even have a chance to react as I went through his door. I didn't say a word—just threw him a double thumbs-up.

Crowe looked back at me with a big, wide, warm grin that told me he'd greased the skids with ten yards of Vaseline. "I gather, SEAL Six, you didn't use *goatfuck* as a noun."

Chapter

18

THERE WAS A SPECWAR CONFERENCE AT LITTLE CREEK IN July of 1980. I went to it. I did a lot of listening, not a lot of talking. I badly wanted to be able to tell the commodores who ran NAVSPECWARGRU ONE and TWO—Dave Schaible at ONE and Ted Lyon at TWO—that I was forming a new command and I'd be coming to raid their turf for warm bodies after August 15. But the CNO had ordered me not to say a word about SEAL Team Six, and my compliance was a matter of common sense and basic mathematics. Ted and Dave were captains, and no matter how you add it up, four bars plus four bars does not equal four stars.

I began to realize the depth of the Navy's commitment to Six as I worked on the unit budget. The training-ammo allowance for SEAL Team Six's ninety men was larger than the training-ammo allotment for the entire U.S. Marine Corps. The overall first-year budget for SEAL Six was more than East Coast and West Coast SEAL budgets combined— about the same as two F-14 fighter planes.

But money doesn't mean much without the right men. On August 16, the day after the unit was officially "created" on paper, I drove down to Little Creek to begin interviewing prospective team members. I paid a courtesy call on the SpecWar commodore, Ted Lyon.

Ted was still as prissy as he'd been when we wrangled over the Little Creek parade ground. He didn't much care for the way I looked. I was letting my hair and beard grow out, so I was uncommonly shaggy. Instead of a starched uniform I dressed in jeans, an open-necked, button-down shirt, and a sport coat. Long gone were my Geek-polished boots. Instead, I wore ragged running shoes.

I dropped into a chair in his Spartan, meticulous office. "Morning, Ted."

He saluted formally. "Commander."

It was going to be one of those days. I rose and returned the salute. "Sir." I may have said "Sir," but I was thinking "cur."

I explained what I was doing at Little Creek, and that I'd be starting to talk to prospective team members immediately. Ted shook his head. "No, you won't. There's been no paperwork on this, Dick. And unlike some others I can think of, *I* do everything by the book." He rapped his knuckles on the desk to emphasize each syllable. *"By the book."*

I looked at him. "You're not serious."

"Oh, yes, I am. Just who the hell do you think you are to waltz in here and create havoc? This command will not respond to that sort of behavior. We actually observe a few of the formalities here. So, if you want something from now on, Dick—if you want *anything* from now on, Dick—put it in writing. Send it up through the chain of command. Send it to Staff, which will evaluate your proposal. If Staff approves, then your suggestion will be sent up the line for the appropriate action."

"Well, fuck you very much, Ted."

"And don't speak to me in that way. Unlike the days when each of us was a unit commanding officer, I am now your direct superior."

Actually, he wasn't. I wouldn't be reporting to Ted—he wasn't a part of Six's chain of command. Ted's view, however, was that any East Coast SEALs—including Six—came under his administrative purview. And he was determined to make me obey. This wasn't the time or the place to screw with him. So I gritted my teeth, rose, and saluted. "Aye-aye, Commodore. Now, what paperwork do you wish, sir, so that I may commence interviewing prospective personnel for my new command?"

Ted smirked. "A memo from the CNO routed through CINCLANTFLT and SURFLANT to COMNAVSPEC-WARGRU would suffice—*if* you can get it."

"Tell you what, Ted—it's Saturday. I'm going to go have a few beers with the boys. I'll be back next week and we'll talk."

At 0915 the following Wednesday, the exalted Commodore Edward Lyon III was shaking his head in disbelief as he read a rocket from Admiral Hayward, which I'd had sent directly to Ted's attention. It had been routed through CINCLANTFLT, SURFLANT, and COMNAVSPECWAR-GRU, just as Ted had ordered. The gist of the telex was simple: "You asshole, get out of Marcinko's way or I will squash you like a bug. Give him everything he wants. Strong message follows. Love and kisses, Admiral Thomas Hayward, Chief of Naval Operations."

The hate with which Ted looked at me was incredible. No wonder. His daughter, who worked as a bartender, had seen me drinking over the weekend with a number of SEALs and reported the fact to Daddy, who began our session by berating me for allegedly violating operational security guidelines. But despite the looks and the accusations, there was nothing Ted could do. Three hours later, I was interviewing candidates for SEAL Team Six.

I spent four days evaluating sailors at SEAL Team Two and the UDTs at Little Creek. For many of those who'd served under me six years before, it was a shock. They remembered the spit-and-polish CO who wore white-walls, demanded that Team members shave all facial hair, and ordered his officers to carry calling cards. Now they were being interviewed by a guy looking like Lobo the Wolf Man, who suggested strongly that they keep their hair unkempt and get their ears pierced.

What was I looking for? Shooters, of course. If you can't kill the bad guy, then everything else is FUBAR. Second question: what's the best way to get where the bad guys are? Ilo-Ilo Island taught me that: why knock politely on the front door and eat bullets when you can hop and pop through the back door—where you're least expected—and feed them some lead. And the option package includes all kinds of fun ways to arrive at the back door: you can swim or come by boat or chopper; you can climb up, or you can parachute down.

Third question: what sort of people can slide in the back door most easily? Dirtbags. Dirtbags with union skills—truck drivers, crane operators, bricklayers, electricians, longshoremen. But I wasn't looking for just any dirtbags. I wanted motivated dirtbags—AVISes—the guys who try harder. I went through each candidate's BUD/S records to see where they ranked in their classes. Whereas the number one man may have breezed through, the guy who was seventy-seventh probably had a bitch of a time in the water, didn't like crawling through mud, and hated demolition—but *he* never quit. Experience had taught me that warthogs who tough it out are better in combat than your natural gazelles.

I made my selection—just under half the unit. The rest of Six would come from California. I called Paul Henley at Coronado. "Paul—XO, what's happening? How's the job?"

"Not bad. It's a living."

I giggled. "Terrific. How about earning a living as my XO?"

"Wha—?"

"I mean it. I have a job for you."

"What is it?"

"Can't talk on the phone. I'm flying to San Diego tomorrow to do some interviewing." I gave him the flight number. "Meet me at the airport—I'll explain everything. And tell Marilyn to start packing. Your ass is coming East in less than two weeks."

September 1 was Labor Day. On September 2, I checked out of the Pentagon to assume my new command. I got a warm send-off from Admiral Crowe, paid my respects to a two-star admiral named Art Moreau, who had run yards of interference for me as I was putting SEAL Team Six together, and called Ace Lyons, who'd received his second star and was heading up the Mobile Logistic Support Force at the Seventh Fleet, out in the Pacific. My last stop was the CNO's cabin. Bill Crowe took me there.

Tom Hayward rose from his desk and came around in front of it.

"I'd like to thank you, sir, for the opportunity to command SEAL Six."

"You were the best man for the job, Commander," Hayward said.

"Do you have any final words of advice for me?"

The CNO took my hand and shook it solemnly, but warmly. "Yes, Dick," he said. "It comes down to this: you will not fail. That is an order."

A bunch of my prospective troops were waiting when I drove through the gate at Little Creek at about twenty hundred. It was like Papa Bear coming home—lots of "Daddy, Daddy, what did you bring me?"

We went to a private club, run by the Fraternal Order of UDT/SEALs near the base, and over several cases of beer I told them in general terms what I'd be asking of them, and not to be expecting much vacation time between the next morning and, oh, 1996. Faces fell.

"I said it was gonna be hard work, guys. I didn't say it wasn't gonna be fun." I took a bar napkin and a pen and drew a globe, framed by an old-fashioned "horseshoe" toilet seat. Above the drawing, I wrote PHOC-6; below it, the letters W.G.M.A.T.A.T.S. "That's the unit emblem," I said as the napkin got passed from man to man.

Somebody asked what it all stood for.

"*Phoc* is French for 'seal.' The globe means we have a worldwide mission, and the letters at the bottom stand for 'We Get More Ass Than A Toilet Seat.' "

We were a group of about thirty that night—the "close hold" core of SEAL Six, officers, chiefs, and enlisted men. That was one of the best things about Six—there would be no caste system in my unit. If a man was good enough to die with, he was good enough to eat, drink, and get laid with. SEAL Team Six would be run according to Barrett's First Law of the Sea, and Marcinko's First Law of Unit Integrity: screw everybody but us.

Paul Henley sat at my elbow, listening and not saying much. That was par for the course. He was yin to my yang. I was the archetypal LDO—Loud, Dumb, and Obnoxious; he was quiet and deep. Paul hadn't seen combat, but had everything else working for him: language skill, CT training, brains, and best of all, guts. And he was an Academy grad. If I was a bastard, at least I had a legitimate son as my XO.

Lieutenant Mugsy finished one beer and called for another. Mugsy was another Academy grad. A boxer, light heavyweight division, he'd been to EOD school so he could play with explosives. And he understood CT: he'd taken over Paul's old job commanding MOB-6. He was big, ugly, and aggressive. Yeah.

The Senator was another lieutenant. Tall—over six three—and distinguished looking in a preppy, yuppie way, he had a reputation as a ladies' man who could order the "right" wines and knew which fork to use. He was young and had been through training only recently. I figured he'd be good if we needed to infiltrate somebody as an executive. And if he didn't work out? Well, every unit needs cannon fodder.

That sounds cold, doesn't it. Well, it's a fact of life in the military. Every unit *does* need cannon fodder. The small SpecWar units that get sent behind the lines are cannon fodder—for battalions and divisions. Recon platoons are cannon fodder for the companies of which they're a part. Every man who takes the point on a patrol knows he is cannon fodder—expendable. The difference is, I told the men I was picking why I'd chosen them. I told them they were expendable—that we were all, ultimately, expendable. They came anyway.

Lieutenant Cheeks got his nickname because he looked like a squirrel hoarding nuts in his mouth. An ex-Marine, Cheeks had seen combat in Vietnam. I knew he was an aggressive son of a bitch, a guy I could count on to drop a tango before the tango dropped him—or me. He was married to a Filipino and spoke just enough Tagalog to make him sound authentic, which gave him the additional plus of a second language.

The Duke was another ex-white-hat, an enlisted man who'd seen his share of combat in Vietnam before attending OCS. Now a lieutenant, JG, he'd become an experienced training officer—something Six needed. That, plus the combat experience, was good enough for me.

I pulled Ensign Trailer Court right out of Officer Candidate School in Newport, Rhode Island. I took one look at his naive baby face and realized we could slip him in anywhere in the world as a high-school student. Clean-shaven (he never grew any facial hair—I don't think he was able to *grow* facial hair) and apple cheeked, he was our resident health nut, our jeep-driving Mr. Outward Bound—good at rock-climbing and skiing—who existed on nuts and twigs and other healthy things to eat. But deep down, there was another, more shadowy facet to Trailer's personality, a dark side. It was that aggressive undertone, which I somehow instinctively perceived, that led me to select him from the group of ensigns made available to me.

The last officer at the table was Ensign Indian Jew. To me, Jew personified the ideal SpecWar officer: he was a big, strapping, spirited ex-enlisted man who reminded me of me as a child. Except he is better looking, and I fight dirtier. I'd been his commanding officer at SEAL Two when he'd been an enlisted man. Six foot plus, dark haired, well muscled, movie-star handsome, I remembered Jew as a carefree guy who worked out on the weight pile every day, could press more than four hundred pounds with ease, and whose only real responsibility in life was his beloved blue Corvette.

Even as a kid, Jew had impressed me during field exercises. He'd always asked to be given the most demanding jobs, which he handled with aplomb. He was aggressive and bright, and not the sort I wanted to see finish his hitch and leave. SpecWar needed kids like Jew, and I wanted to ensure his career in the Navy, if he wanted one.

One evening I asked him what he wanted to do with the rest of his life. He told me he'd always dreamed of becoming an officer and making SpecWar his career. It was an obsession, he said.

I knew what Jew was talking about; I'd felt exactly the same way myself at about his age. So I took him under my wing, in much the same way I'd adopted Lieutenant Tom Williams. I was tough but encouraging. I convinced Jew to attend school and made sure he took the right courses for a degree that would further his Navy career. Then, when I moved to the Pentagon, I hand-carried Jew's personnel package through the bureaucratic maze myself. Between his determination, my greasing the wheels, and the help of a few enterprising officers, Jew ended up at OCS.

In the meantime, he'd married a young beauty named Denise, the girl he'd been dating since she was fifteen and he was eighteen or nineteen. Good-bye, Corvette; hello, station wagon. In my book that was a plus: the kid needed responsibilities.

After he completed OCS, I pulled more strings and got Jew detailed to SEAL Two. SEAL Team Six was being designed, and I wanted him as part of the package. By getting Jew assigned to Little Creek, he'd be on the shelf until Daddy Demo came home.

The enlisted men swapping stories at the club that night had backgrounds as varied as the officers'. I'd chosen them for youth and stamina, for combat experience, language specialties, and aggressiveness. A couple of the youngsters were picked because Six, like all units, needed cannon fodder.

Baby Rich was one of them. When I'd interviewed prospective SEAL Six members, I took one look at Rich's round, naive baby face, gangling, tall body, and ham-sized fists, and laughed. "What the hell makes you think you can cut it, junior?"

"I know I can, sir."

I shook my head. "You're a regular tyke, a cherry. If I take you, it'll be as an expendable, kiddo. If there's a rope to climb and it looks like it's gonna break, you're the one who goes up to see. If we need to throw a jumper out of the plane to check the wind—you're gonna be 'it.' " I gave him my Sharkman Crazy Otto look and wiggled my eyebrows. "How does that sound to you?"

"Sounds fuckin' ducky to me, Commander." He thumped my desk for emphasis. "Count me in. Shit, sir, I always wanted to be a fuckin' SEAL—and now that I are one, I wanna be the best fuckin' SEAL there is. So if that means getting myself killed in your unit, as opposed to sitting somewhere with my thumb up my ass, I say go for it."

Of course I hired him—who wouldn't have?

Others I chose because they were just plain crazy. I figured, if we were going to jump out of planes at thirty-five thousand feet, free-fall, then parasail another fifteen, craziness was a definite requirement.

You want crazy? Okay—there was Snake, popping the pop-top on his Coors. Snake was a dark-haired petty officer, third class. A former paratrooper from the Eighty-second Airborne and a qualified radio operator, Snake combined natural athletic ability with considerable strength and imagination. I liked him because he wouldn't try to outthink you—he'd simply outperform you every single time.

Pooster the Rooster was another PO3. Pooster was a spelunker from the Pacific Northwest whose specialties were shooting and women. He was deadly at both. Pooster got his handle from the Italians during SEAL Two deployments in the Mediterranean. He's got copper-red hair that stands up in a perpetual cowlick, almost like a rooster tail. The locals in Naples and Rome would point at him and exclaim, in pidgin English, "Mista Poosta-Roost." The moniker stuck.

Larry and Frank were my Gold Dust Twins. They'd met as swim buddies during BUD/S and become as close as brothers. Even though Larry was at SEAL Two in Virginia, while Frank had been posted to BUD/S in Coronado, California, they'd still start and finish each other's sentences seamlessly.

But talk about opposites. Gold Dust Larry had dirty-blond hair and a face that looked as if it had weathered one too many brawls. Gold Dust Frank was dark haired, and he looked like a bulkier version of the actor Mark Harmon. Larry was moody—when ecstatic, he looked as if he'd never had a happy day in his life. Frank was ebullient, with smiling eyes, the kind of guy who walked into bars and made easy conversation with the ladies.

Larry's skills included specialties in ordnance (he'd helped me build my wooden soldiers for the Iranian raid) and air operations—he could fly a plane. He'd seen combat as a Marine, so I knew he'd pull the trigger if he had to. Moreover, I'd been his CO for a short time at SEAL Two. He'd arrived just as my successor and I were exchanging command. I hadn't gotten to know Larry well, but he'd impressed me as steady and dependable—the first guy to show up, and one of the last to leave.

In fact, if there was one type of man I'd visualized whenever I thought of the archetypal plank-owner of SEAL Team Six, it was Larry. He was a sailor in the tradition of Ev Barrett, a PO2 who never stopped working with the men under him. Larry'd made the cut for Six before there *was* a cut.

Gold Dust Frank was an unknown quantity, so far as I was concerned. But during a beer-soaked night while I was conducting my personnel interviews at Little Creek, Larry had vouched for his buddy's skills, written his Gold Dust Twin's name on a soggy bar napkin, and stuffed it in my pocket. "He's workin' as an instructor at BUD/S, Skipper."

When I showed up at Coronado to do my recruiting, I had the napkin on the table in front of me. Frank walked in. "Name?"

He told me. He'd never met me before and didn't know what to expect. He got my crazy commander act. I picked up the soiled cocktail napkin and made a big thing of trying to read it. I turned it every which way, screwing up my face as I puzzled vocally over the ink blots. "Your name's not Fnnnnnunnk Fynnnnnnufff?"

"No, sir." He repeated his name.

I looked at him critically, then examined the napkin again. I shook my head. "Are you *sure* your name's not Fnnnnnunnk Fynnnnnnufff?"

"Yes, sir."

"What's your social security number?"

He told me.

"You're Larry's swim buddy."

"Yup."

I balled up the cocktail napkin and three-pointed it into a nearby wastebasket. "You got the job. Now get outta here."

"Uh, Commander . . ."

"Yeah?"

"What *is* the job?"

"You mean Larry didn't tell you?"

"No, sir, all he said was to show up, and if you asked if I wanted a job, say yes."

Frank turned out to be all right. He became a flier. And he helped us perfect our parachute work and sniping, as he was both an imaginative and accomplished jumper and a quick-eyed shooter. But I chewed his ass that first night at Little Creek. He showed up in a SEAL T-shirt. "Hey, shit-for-brains . . ." I grabbed him by the offending garment. "Can *you* say 'operational security'?"

Horseface was Paul's selection. A former state-champion wrestler, he'd left the Navy and was crop-dusting in Ohio when I called him and sketched out the possibilities if he'd reenlist. He was at Little Creek in a few days, smiling his trademark yard-wide, big-toothed smile. Large, strong, and intimidating, Horseface was one of those rare individuals who knew no fear. Best of all, there was nothing he wouldn't fly —from a Piper Cub to a 727, he'd climb into the cockpit and after a few minutes get us off the ground.

Fingers was a chief who'd known me long enough to call me Demo Dick and remember why. He didn't look much like your archetypal SEAL. He weighed less than 150 pounds soaking wet, had ears like Dumbo, big blue eyes, and a metabolism that ran so fast he probably burned a hundred calories every time he blinked. An EOD specialist, he could only count to nine using his fingers, which is how he'd received his nickname. And he had a mouth that never stopped moving. Fingers had at least one opinion about everything. Sometimes he had two or three opinions. Whether they conflicted or not didn't matter—after a while we figured he had multiple personalities. He was a shoot-and-looter; a combat workaholic who'd be graded D on style—he looked like a real dirtbag— but A-plus on results. He'd helped Mac and me design Six and was exactly the kind of AVIS asshole I was looking for.

SEAL Team Six would be permanently based about thirty miles from Norfolk. Our facility, however, would not be finished for almost a year. In the meanwhile, we needed somewhere to hang our hats, stow our gear, receive our phone calls, and put up our shingle. Little Creek was convenient and familiar ground for most of us, so we set up shop in two chicken coops located fifteen yards behind SEAL Team Two's HQ. At least I thought they looked like chicken coops— WWII wooden structures forty feet wide and eighty feet long built atop concrete slabs. One had been used as the Wives Club meetinghouse; the other was the base Cub Scout den.

Me, my XO, my operations boss, and my command master chief, Mac, all shared space in the same room. I appropriated the best furniture: a battleship-gray metal desk with three legs we salvaged from the junk pile, and a rickety swivel chair. Paul's ensemble was similar, but in worse condition. Our wall decorations were Cub Scout leftovers with the exception of a composite photograph some wiseass had made of my head atop the CNO's four-star body.

Our situation was not ideal—and not simply because the quarters were cramped and ill-suited to our needs. Our location was just too damn *visible*. We were, after all, an alleged top-secret unit. We wore civilian clothes; I'd ordered my men to remove the base stickers from their vehicles, keeping them instead on magnetic strips they'd attach just as they drove through the gates. We'd come and go at odd hours. Nothing about SEAL Six was military—and that's the way I wanted it. But less than a hundred feet away, SEALs from Two, dressed in their green fatigues, stared openmouthed as convoys of trucks rolled up to our sheds, unloading box after box of goodies. I'd look across the chain-link fence that separated the men from the boys and tsk-tsk them. "Thou shalt not covet," I chided.

There was a lot to covet, too. The inventory that was piling up in our sheds looked like a lethal, high-budget version of Outward Bound. Gore-Tex parkas and boots. Parachutes. Climbing gear. Helmets and goggles. Backpacks and ballistic nylon soft luggage. Skis. Aqua-Lungs. Wet suits. Camouflage for every environment from arctic to desert. Smith & Wesson .357 revolvers in stainless steel, so they wouldn't rust when we swam with them. Beretta 9mm automatic pistols. HK machine guns, with and without silencers. Stainless steel Ruger Mini-14s. Silenced .22-caliber automatics. Sniper's rifles. Stun grenades. C-4 explosive. Claymore mines. Radio-controlled remote detonators. And hundreds of thousands of rounds of ammunition.

We mounted antennas on the roofs and set up our own secure communications network. We used walkie-talkies, waterproof portable radios, SATCOMs, and mini satellite dishes. Each man was given a secure beeper. When it went off, he was expected to show up, prepared for deployment and fully equipped, within four hours. If the second hostage-rescue mission was mobilized, we'd be ready to go—even if we hadn't finished our training yet.

It took a couple of weeks to settle in. I brought Kathy and the kids down from Washington. All they knew was that the War College was out the window, and Daddy had a new job, which he couldn't talk about, but—golly, gee, Pop—your hair and beard sure are getting long. The men arriving from the West Coast, too, had to find housing, buy transportation, and get adjusted. Training, however, commenced immediately. I'd hinted we were going to do a lot of climbing, so the guys began going to the base gym and working on their upper-body strength. We started firearms workouts, too. Most SEALs believe themselves to be great shots. I, on the other hand, remembered how badly things had gone with Bravo Squad, Second Platoon, before we deployed to Vietnam in 1967, when me and my five Daniel Boones only put 2 rounds out of 360 in a six-by-eight-foot piece of slowly moving plywood.

The shooters of SEAL Team Six would have to be able to bring down their targets with one or two shots, under any condition. That meant our shooting had to be both instinctive and accurate. To achieve that end, I designed a program in which each SEAL in Six would shoot a minimum of 2,500 rounds a week, every week. That was more per week than most SEALs shot in a year.

There was bitching, but at my insistence we began with the basics. Every night, when the pistol range at the Armed Forces Staff College closed down, we'd run teams in and work from 1700 until 2300. During the first couple of days, we didn't even use ammunition. The men hung silhouette targets in each lane, then practiced acquiring a sight picture and squeezing the trigger of their stainless-steel Smith & Wesson .357 Model 66s. We started everybody dry-firing at three yards, then progressed to five yards, then seven, ten, fifteen, and finally, twenty yards. The exercise was rudimentary, starting slow, getting fast: acquire the sight picture, then fire. Acquire, then fire. Acquire, fire. Acquire/fire.

The third day we tried the exercises again, then repeated them with live ammunition. We examined each target carefully to see who was heeling, shooting high at one o'clock; who was squeezing too tight, which grouped the shots low and left or low and right; who was anticipating recoil; jerking the gun; or breaking the wrist too far up or down. Problems were noted and corrections made. In less than a week, the guys were shooting straight. Now all they had to learn was to shoot to kill.

We built doorjambs out of two-by-four and canvas. Once again, we began without ammo, teaching the men how to come through a doorway singly, then in pairs, then in groups of four, and finally, in groups of six. They weaved in a lethal, complicated choreography, until everyone had mastered the art of dancing through a door and entering a room without getting killed, or killing the man in front. We began discussing the tactics of clearing a room, of determining friend or foe. And as one set of SEALs worked on entry, another group two lanes down the range worked on firing basics, shooting round after round after round at silhouette targets.

Except now, I added a new twist. The men would paste a three-by-five index card on each silhouette, sometimes on the head, sometimes on the torso or shoulder or groin or neck. The score would count only if they hit the card. Any other holes in the target meant they had to start all over again. I also encouraged people to break into pairs and shoot against each other for beers. The Gold Dust Twins, Frank and Larry, were natural and vocal rivals. Mac and Fingers paired up, bitching at one another as they punched paper. XO Paul, whose white-wall, Marine-style short-crop was growing nicely into curly, Prince Valiant locks, shot against Jew. And Snake shot opposite Pooster. I could hear them over the gunfire ragging each other—and God help the poor asshole who missed the three-by-five.

The second week we began, very carefully, to send one guy at a time, moving downrange, using live fire. This was something new to everybody. It's one thing to acquire a sight picture and fire when you're looking at a silhouette. It is entirely different when you are moving toward it, crouching or running. By the end of the week, I was able to add the doorjambs to the scenario and watch as four SEALs at a time would "enter" an area and clear it with live fire.

The work was not without problems and hazards. The indoor range had no proper ventilation, so we had to break regularly to vent it. And concrete walls and floor made the place prone to ricochets. There were a couple of close calls, and my guys took a minor ding or two as we live-fired at angles for which the facility had not been designed. Still, it was all we had, so we used it.

Each night after we finished, we'd roll out of Gate Five in a convoy, cruise up to Virginia Beach Boulevard, hang a left, and three blocks later pull up in front of a decrepit, one-story storefront, painted an indeterminate and undefinable dark color. This was our permanent hangout, the bar we'd visited the first night I arrived as Six's commander, the FO Bar. It was an after-hours joint run by the Fraternal Order of UDT/SEAL. Inside two sparsely furnished, dimly lit rooms were pinball machines, card tables, a couple of bars, and a microwave for nuking sandwiches and pizzas; along with a friendly bunch of active and retired Frogmen, SEAL groupies, girlfriends, and even an occasional wife or two. The place was open all night, and if there was any single place SEAL Team Six's unit integrity was built, it was the FO Bar, during the first three weeks of September 1980.

Since we'd just been shooting, we all smelled of lead and primers—not as pungent as cordite, but it told people we'd been having fun. We'd be high from the exercises, and the guys from the East Coast would be playing head games on the West Coast SEALs and vice versa—kind of like the first day of kindergarten where the kiddies are deciding who gets to play in the sandbox first. The women were plentiful—and available. Also, we were the new kids on the block, and the old-timers wanted to test us. Testing was usually done with fists and chairs.

I watched as partnerships formed—who was marrying up with who; I sat at the bar, sipped my Bombay on the rocks, and made mental notes about who could handle his liquor and who couldn't. I noted which of my Six guys were aggressive, which ones were passive. When there were fights, I stood back and let them happen, only wading in and separating people if it looked like serious damage was about to be done. The harbingers were good. My men might fight among themselves, but as soon as outsiders stepped in, they'd turn on the strangers and stomp them into the floor.

While the Team got itself into physical shape, Paul and I honed the training schedule. By the fourth week of September, we'd done as much as we could at Little Creek. Most of the equipment had been delivered—what remained to arrive could be forwarded. Now the serious work was ahead: our first road trip to Florida, where, at a secluded corner of Eglin Air Force Base, we'd begin our training in earnest.

The press of events had been so tight, I hadn't even held a full team meeting yet. So, two nights before we left for Florida, I scheduled the base auditorium for the evening and assembled the Team. I put Paul and Command Master Chief Mac outside the doors to keep interlopers away.

Then I mounted the stage. Behind me, appropriately enough, hung a huge American flag. If this was going to be a SEAL Six version of the opening to the movie *Patton*, that's where the similarities ended. I was missing the ivory-handled revolver and the polished boots, not to mention the gleaming helmet. I looked like a wild man with my beard and long hair. And my mode of delivery was somewhat different than George C. Scott's throaty growl.

I looked out upon my troops, who were sprawled over the first dozen rows of the auditorium. "Fuck you all, cock-breaths," I said by way of introduction.

There were scattered laughs. I paced back and forth, searching out faces. I liked what I saw.

"Gentlemen," I said, "this will be a no-shitter."

There was a murmur of approval. "You know what we are here to do—counterterrorism. And what does counterterrorism mean? It means that we will fucking do it to them, before they fucking do it to us." A dozen of the men cheered. "Right on," I answered. "It's about goddamn time, right?"

I waved my arm over the assembled SEALs. "You are all talented SpecWarriors. You are all—as of now—gifted shooters. You all get a lot of pussy—" I was interrupted by laughter. "Now we're going to hit the road and make you prove those things all over again." Scattered applause and whistles. "But before we do, there are a few things I want to tell you.

"First. You do not have to like everything you do. Fact is, I don't give a shit whether you like everything you do or not. All you have to do is do it.

"Second. You are the system, gentlemen. You. The buck stops with each one of you. I bought you your own gear, and you will take care of it. You assholes have the very best toys money can buy. If your equipment fails, it's because *you* fucking failed—not it. So I will not accept any goddamn excuses—'The gear didn't work, sir' or 'I got the wrong lung, sir' or 'I didn't bring the right weapon, sir.'

"*You* are the fucking system. Failure is on your shoulders. I will accept no excuses. None.

"CNO Hayward sent me down here. You know what he fucking said, gentlemen? He said, 'Dick, *you will not fail*.'

264

"So I *will* not fucking fail, gentlemen, nor will *you* fucking fail."

I paced back and forth in front of the flag. "For SEAL Team Six, I am fucking lifting the rules. You've already seen that at the range. And now hear this: each of you will carry a weapon at all times. On duty, off duty, liberty—fat fucking chance of that—on the road, getting laid, whatever. You gentlemen are going to become the living embodiments of 'Have Gun Will Travel.' Why? Because the more you're used to the weight and position of the gun, the less obvious it will become. The less you will think about it. The more a part of you it will be. When we go clandestine, gentlemen—and believe me, we will fucking go clandestine—I don't want you playing with the jockstrap where you stowed your .38, so some numb-nuts, shit-for-brains, buck-an-hour airport-security monkey in Ouagadougou catches you carrying and tosses you into the hole. That will not fucking happen on my watch.

"Listen closely, gentlemen, because you will hear these words again: safety is out the window. We will train the same way we will fight—balls to the wall. That means some of you will get hurt during training. Some of you may die. That's a fact of life. But we will watch each other's back. We will take care of each other. If you screw up and waste your swim buddy, I will waste you. Believe me, it's easy to rig a fatal accident, and I *will* waste you. You will be history.

"Your loyalty must be first and foremost to your partner, your squad, your platoon, and the Team. I am the law, gentlemen—and my law is simple. There will be unit fucking integrity."

There was absolute silence. Good. I had their attention.

I hunched my back and slipped into my godfather mode, speaking in a passable Vito Corleone accent. "This command . . . will be like a friggin' Mafia. I . . . am the *Capo di tutti capi,* the *Padrone.* I make the offers nobody refuses. And I . . . I take care of everybody. What's more, we're a family. And you never talk family business outside the family. You got a problem—you come to me. Before you go anywhere else, you come to me first."

I walked to a covered easel stage right and threw back the black drape, revealing a large map of Iran. "We have been assigned a mission. We aren't even a unit yet, but we have a mission—which is par for the course. Okay, you see the map. You know where that is. You know who's still being held there. We are on call. Our number has been posted." I changed the display, showing a list of seven targets we had been assigned to neutralize while Delta Force went in after the hostages. I ticked them off, one by one.

"That's the mission, gentlemen. It's a shitty one, too—a real goatfuck, if you ask me. But guess what? We don't have to like our mission—we just have to do it.

"So, when the training gets hot and heavy and you think 'I'm tired' or 'The old man's pushing too hard' or you're scared because we're going too fast and it's gonna be a motherfucking meat-grinder, remember—you don't have to like it. You just have to *do* it.

"Now you know what our mission is. Every time you go through a training mode, I want you to think of how you're going to apply that training to these targets. Every time you think I'm being too tough on you, think of those targets. Every time you want to ease up, think of those targets.

"That's the whole goddamn story in a nutshell, gentlemen. It comes down to this: I'm giving you the tools. I'm giving you the opportunity. I'm giving you the support, and the backstops. If there is shit, I will take it for you. If there is flak, I'll absorb it for you. All you have to worry about is getting so fucking good at your jobs that you can fucking do anything. And leave those cocksucking, cunt-breath, pus-nuts, shit-for-brains, pencil-pushing Pentagon assholes to me. That's *my* fucking job. *I* don't have to like it, either. All *I* have to do, is *do* it."

Chapter

19

I'VE OFTEN BEEN ASKED IF I EVER FELT LIKE PLEADING guilty because I screwed with the system for so many years. Didn't I feel guilty for using so much profanity? Didn't I feel guilty about the strong-arm methods I used to get what I wanted? Didn't I feel guilty about making my superiors eat shit?

My answer has always been the same: guilty—absolutely. Guilty as charged. Guilty of putting my men before bureaucratic bullshit. Guilty of spending as much money as I can get my hands on to train my men properly. Guilty of preparing for war instead of peace. Of all these things am I indeed guilty. Mea culpa, mea culpa, mea maxima fucking culpa.

So, while my men flew off to Florida to start "dirty dozen" training at Eglin Air Force Base, I mud-wrestled the bureaucracy over how SEAL Team Six would be run, and where it fit in the chain of command. They got to throw themselves out of planes, fast-rope from choppers, and shoot until they were blue in the face. I got to fight the paper war, page by goddamn page. I didn't like it. But I did it.

On the charts, Six was assigned to the commander of the Joint Special Operations Command—JSOC—Brigadier General Dick Scholtes, who lived at Ft. Bragg. He, in turn, was responsible to the NCA—the National Command Authority—managed by the Joint Chiefs of Staff. My philosophical outlook about how this progression worked was simple: the president owns me, the JCS manages me, and JSOC tells me when I can break wind. So far as I was concerned, the Navy's administrative chain of command had only one function to perform for SEAL Team Six—the triple-S function, as in "Sit down, shut up, and shell out."

Organizationally, it was SURFLANT—SURface Force AtLANTic—that was my money manager. That's where all of SEAL Six's bills got paid. But according to the Navy's bureaucracy, SURFLANT and SEAL Six were not supposed to talk directly. Instead, an organizational interface was inserted. Why? That's a good question, to which I do not have an answer. One rationalization I came up with was that SURFLANT couldn't speak SEAL, and I allegedly couldn't speak Navy. Whatever the case, the interface assigned to come between us was NAVSPECWARGRU TWO, which was run by Commodore Ted Lyon.

Ted wasn't good at speaking either SEAL or Navy. But he was fluent in gibberish. To make matters even more pleasant, Ted had convinced himself he was a significant component of my chain of command.

We fought. He saw me as a recalcitrant junkyard dog who had to be brought to heel, so he yanked my chain at every conceivable opportunity. I saw him as a small-minded pismire, and when he tried to yank, I gnawed chunks out of him. He questioned virtually all the specialized equipment I purchased, memoing Washington that it was irregular and unnecessary. I ordered German-made Draeger bubbleless lungs for Six. Ted said we couldn't have them because one, they were foreign purchases, and two, we had current-model Emerson units available to us. I steamrolled over him and got the Draegers.

Next, I bought German Heckler & Koch MP5, 9mm submachine guns. He complained again. "Why foreign guns? We can get MAC-10s for a third the price."

"Because the HKs are better, Ted. They're more accurate. They're more consistent. They adapt well to our mission."

"I'm dead set against it."

He called his rabbis, and I called mine. SEAL Team Six got HKs.

The Navy leased us four Jeep Eagles as tactical-ops cars. We used them, but to be honest, they weren't going to be much help to us. For exercises in the States they were fine. But overseas, it's hard to find spare parts for Eagles. Besides, in the regions of the world we'd be playing, just driving an American car gets you undue attention. So, using a couple of contacts I had in Bonn, I finagled two customized, armored Mercedes 500-series sedans, and four Mercedes jeeps for $160,000, a discount of more than 60 percent. From the outside, the sedans looked like the big cars common to Europe, the Middle East, and all through the Americas. But on the inside they'd been customized for the German counterterror unit, GSG-9—with hidden firing ports, ram bumpers, concealed police-type lights, sirens, and communications packages. The jeeps had roof turrets and other goodies.

Ted went ballistic. But I shoved the Mercedes down his throat, closed his mouth, worked his jaws, and made him swallow.

In between bouts with Ted I'd drop in on my men as they progressed through the training cycle. By mid-October, everyone had qualified in HALO—High Altitude, Low Opening —parachute work (even Command Master Chief Mac, who had to be dragged off the C-130's ramp on his first jump). We'd also begun working on fast-roping, which was a way of putting six men on the deck from a height of sixty feet in less than four seconds.

The ropes we used were British—a reverse-weave, soft, twisted nylon line, which allowed us to brake ourselves with our hands. Unlike rappelling, which uses a line attached to a safety belt, fast-roping was simply a controlled fall. If, for example, we wanted to fast-rope onto the fantail of a moving ship, our chopper would make its approach at wave-top level from the rear so as to escape detection. Its sound would be masked by the ship. Then, at the last moment, the chopper would quickly rise or "flare" above the stern, hover as two ropes were kicked out and six men went down them, then perform a rapid turn and disappear.

The technique calls for split-second timing and first-rate flying. The chopper pilot must compensate for the weight shift as the lines are tossed and the men throw themselves onto them. He also has to move with the ocean swells. A five-foot sea can mean a nasty ten-foot drop at the end of the rope if the pilot screws up.

Shooting exercises were progressing, too: the Team was getting more and more accurate by the day. At first, I'd been able to hold my own with any of the men at Six. Now, it was me who'd end up buying the beer after a couple of hours on the range. The seven-man boat crews were shooting so much now—in the range of three thousand rounds per man per week—that some of the Berettas developed fissure cracks beneath the receivers and had to be modified so extensively by the manufacturer that SEAL Team Six in essence had custom-made pistols.

Not everything went smoothly. We had our first training fatality at Eglin. It happened during a live-fire, room-clearing exercise, and the victim was Six's one Chinese American SEAL, a youngster I'll call Donnie Lee.

In a remote corner of Eglin we built a series of four-by-four posts with canvas stretched between them to simulate rooms. The rooms, which could be configured any way we wanted them—big, small, rectangular, square, trapezoidal— also had doorposts and plywood doors. Inside the canvas walls, silhouette targets representing hostage-takers and their hostages would be set up. The object of the exercise was for pairs of SEALs to go into the rooms and "clear" them, killing the bad guys without harming the hostages. The drill was a common one for hostage-rescue teams. Indeed, Charlie Beckwith had used much the same technique in training Delta some years previously.

The goal was to build your shooters' speed and hone their intuition. An operator who can distinguish a good guy from a bad guy in a second is of no use whatsoever. Civilians can tell good guys from bad guys in about eight-tenths of a second. CT operators must act in hundredth-of-a-second increments —and their decisions have to be made both instinctively and correctly.

Hostage rescue is also a painstakingly choreographed exercise. Split-second moves have been rehearsed for months in almost every possible combination, so that if A happens, then the operators react instinctively with B. On this particular day, we'd begun by working with revolvers. This is significant, because we carried our .357s uncocked and fired them double-action.

After a break, the teams switched to Berettas. These are double-action semiautomatic pistols. For room-clearing, we carried them with a live round in the chamber and the hammer back, which made them into single-action guns. The amount of pressure needed to fire a pistol single action is significantly less than in double-action mode. Additionally, we reversed the order in which the men went through the door. Normally, a pair of SEALs would always hit the door in the same sequence. But sometimes we reversed them on purpose—because, in real life, Mr. Murphy's law applies. We wanted to be ready for what can go wrong—because it will, indeed, go wrong.

Donnie had been backup man all morning. Now he was first through the door. As his partner, whom I'll call Jake, followed, Jake stumbled, lurched forward, and squeezed off one round into Donnie Lee's back.

The wound wasn't fatal, and he was taken to the base hospital quickly. I arrived just after they'd wheeled him into the operating room. Donnie was a good kid—a little green, but his instincts were okay. He had a ready smile, and he'd do anything you asked him to do. What upset me so much about this screwup was that it had been done to him, not by him. Thoroughly depressed, I sat on institutional furniture holding a paper cup of vending-machine coffee and waited until the doctor came out to give me a verdict. It was optimistic. I was somewhat relieved.

After two days or so, we moved Donnie to a Navy hospital—where the doctors insisted on opening him up once again. After that second operation, the kid took a turn for the worse—who wouldn't have, after being slit open from stem to stern twice in a week. I was still upset about the accident, but had conditioned myself to accept the fact that SEAL Six would take fatalities during training. But I kept my word to the men: before twenty-four hours had elapsed, Donnie Lee's partner, Jake, was no longer a member of SEAL Team Six. In fact, Jake was no longer even a SEAL. I had him transferred to another branch of the Navy altogether. He had committed the ultimate SEAL sin—he had injured his swim buddy. If we had been on an actual operation, I don't think Jake would have survived it.

We flew Donnie Lee's mother in from Hawaii. The situation was toughest on her. She had no idea what Donnie had been doing and couldn't understand how he'd gotten hurt. What made it worse was that I couldn't tell her anything.

"How was he injured?" Mrs. Lee would ask again and again.

"In training."

"What kind of training?"

"I'm sorry, ma'am, I just can't say."

After about a week, Donnie developed a bad staph infection. Then he went comatose. Every day, I'd spend a couple of hours at the hospital, watching the kid on his respirator. I took to yelling at him. "Get the fuck up, Donnie," I'd shout.

Often, as I did that, he'd twitch. Mrs. Lee would get all excited. "He hears you—he hears you," she'd tell me.

She was a mommy: right until the end, she never gave up.

Donnie's death didn't interrupt the pace or intensity of our training schedule. I couldn't allow it to. In the real world, you don't stop and suck your thumb and talk and talk and talk. Not when there's a mission in front of you. All those Hollywood movies where some kid dies in training and his best friend goes into a funk and can't fly (*Top Gun* comes to mind) or do his job are utter bullshit.

If my men couldn't hack it, they knew they'd be gone. Not in months or in weeks or in days—but in hours or minutes. You don't give second chances in elite units; you don't coddle your men or spend a lot of time playing touchie-feelie with them. That's why they're elite units in the first place. Men volunteer for Delta Force or SEAL Team Six because they want to do things no one else has ever done. They do not volunteer for medals or glory or attaboys. They volunteer because they want to push themselves beyond any range of experiences they've known before—and either succeed or die trying. That is not hyperbole. That is simple fact.

So, death or no death, we kept working. It was important not to stop. I wanted SEAL Six to push the edge of the envelope—to be able to hit the enemy's back door in a way no one had ever done it before. I broke the team into two sections—Blue and Gold—and while Blue drove to Louisiana and practiced climbing oil rigs in the Gulf, Gold flew to Arizona, where I rented thirty miles of airspace, and we started HAHO—High Altitude, High Opening—jump exercises.

The technique made sense to me. You're a bad guy. You hear a plane. You look up. A bunch of pus-nuts asshole SEALs are dropping in on you. So you wax them as they float down. Fuck the *phoques*. But with HAHO, the plane is flying at thirty thousand feet, and maybe twenty miles away. You never see it. You never hear it. And then all of a sudden, it's "April fool, motherfucker, your ass is grass."

We began using our chutes as parasails; we bought mini-bottles of oxygen to keep us from blacking out, strapped lights to our helmets, and compasses to our wrists. We jumped at night from C-141 StarLifters flying so high that, without the compasses, we couldn't tell the lights of Phoenix from the lights of Tucson. During a day HAHO exercise, one of my better jumpers, a guy I'll call Nestle, malfunctioned at about twenty thousand feet. He tried to cut away—that is, release his bad chute, free-fall a couple of thousand feet, and then deploy his backup. He did the cutaway successfully, but his backup chute malfunctioned, too.

The death was listed as a sport-chute accident at the private facility from where we'd taken off, and Nestle's body was taken to the morgue. Then, within hours, a local reporter started asking questions about the forty or so "sport jumpers" who were renting an entire airpark and jumping out of big black birds that had no markings. That was us. I wasn't even on site, but Trailer Court and another of my fast-thinking officers spent a tense day. They ended up kidnapping Nestle's body from the local morgue and getting it to a military installation before the authorities and the press caught up with them. SEAL Six was not in a position to be questioned by anybody.

By the time I showed up, Gold Team had already resumed its HAHO training. The men knew they couldn't afford to break stride—so they didn't. Their quiet, fierce determination to go on made me proud—which is a simple way of saying a complex thing.

Let me explain. As a SEAL, you don't spend a lot of time philosophizing about what you do. Like the ad says, you Just

273

Do It. But those of us who have been SEALs know what "doing it" means—we know about playing with pain. We know that death is always a very real possibility. Those are facts of life. But we do not dwell on them.

Sports broadcasters—especially those who do NFL games—spend a lot of time talking about how players play through broken bones, or sprained or dislocated joints. The players themselves don't do a lot of talking. They just grit their teeth and hit the line. That's the way SEALs are, too.

With HAHO and HALO jumps under our belts, I began to ask how else we could hit bad guys through the back door. It occurred to me that a covert insertion could be performed effectively by jumping out of a commercial jet. All you need to do is get the jet moved off its scheduled course for a few minutes because of "engine trouble" or "cabin pressure malfunction."

For example: say we've been assigned to infiltrate Libya and blow up a chemical-weapons plant Qaddafi says doesn't exist, or hit a training camp deep in the Libyan desert and take out two dozen Abu Nidal terrorists. Solution: we commandeer—with the assistance of the local government, of course—a scheduled Egyptair or Royal Air Maroc flight that passes through Libyan airspace in the vicinity of the facility we want to visit. The authorities send the passengers away but get the plane off the ground on schedule—with us on board instead. Once it approaches the target area, the pilot calls in a flight irregularity and drops the plane from, say, thirty-nine thousand to about thirty-two thousand feet for a few minutes, and veers somewhere between fifty and a hundred miles off course. At the right moment, Six goes out the door. Then the pilot radios that everything's been fixed and resumes his course. Meanwhile, we parasail another forty miles, land, form up, hit the plant or kill the terrorists, then exfiltrate quietly. Doom on you, Muammar.

No one in the military had ever done that sort of thing before. So I leased us a 727 and two pilots from Braniff Airlines, and with Horseface in the copilot's seat, we flew over rural Arizona and practiced flinging ourselves out of the plane.

These exercises were no fun for Dickie, either. I'd made a commitment to the men that they'd never be asked to do anything I wouldn't do first. "I won't order you to fuck anybody I wouldn't fuck, and I'm not gonna order you to go anywhere I won't go," is how I put it. So I threw myself out of planes with Gold team, revived myself with Bombay and Ben-Gay, flew to Louisiana, and went oil-rig climbing with the Blues. Then I'd crawl back to Little Creek, where Ted Lyon used me as his personal punching bag.

He wasn't the only one. The secrecy surrounding Six affected my home life more than any other job I'd ever had. Kathy couldn't enjoy any of the perks or social bonuses a CO's wife usually enjoys, such as being near the top of the base's pecking order, enjoying the deference of the younger wives, and a lot of increased visibility. I was top secret. I was on the road. Not only was she cut out of the normal office gossip, but she was alone most of the time. When I'd commanded SEAL Team Two I'd been on the road a lot, too. But back then, she'd been able to share her troubles with other young mothers. Now she was older than most of the officers' wives, our kids were teenagers—and didn't need her as much—and she neither knew what I was doing nor was able to talk about the little bit she might have guessed at. The bottom line is that our relationship suffered.

We fought about everything. We grew apart. The house was a place to drop my bags, do the laundry, and stay a couple of nights. It wasn't a home. But I wasn't about to let my personal life affect my command. You can't let your feelings for your wife and kids intrude on getting the job done—if you do, you can get careless, and carelessness on my part could have caused fatalities.

It's not that marriages can't and don't survive the incredible stress commands such as SEAL Team Six place on commanding officers. Charlie Beckwith and his wife, Katharine, managed to get through the formation and deployment of Delta Force just fine. Paul Henley's marriage survived the formation of Six. But weak marriages, as mine had become, are probably doomed. And to be honest about it, I wasn't, at that time, a very caring husband at all.

I realize I gave my wife a hard time. I know I gave the Navy Excedrin Headache Number Six. The very fact that SEAL Team Six was a covert unit caused problems sufficient to give any admin officer a head of prematurely gray hair.

Officially, SEAL Team Six didn't even exist. I may have

been a commanding officer, but I didn't have a command. I was on the books as the director of a civilian research facility in the Tidewater area, about thirty miles from Norfolk. Second, Six traveled almost 100 percent of the time. No Navy unit had ever spent so much of its time on the road—staying, for the most part, at civilian facilities. We used—and abused—rental cars, flew commercial (smuggling our weapons on board), and booked ourselves into hotels and motels without benefit of military ID. We may have trained at Eglin, but we stayed at half a dozen motels in the area instead of at the base itself. The pencil-pusher dip-dunks whined. I told them to shove their complaints.

SEAL Team Six logistics became an administrative and bookkeeping nightmare. Imagine trying to keep track of roughly eighty guys, traveling twenty-nine days per month under assumed identities. There were huge numbers of receipts, piles of vouchers, and wads of claims to be audited. The confusion was compounded by the fact that we dealt mostly in cash, so as not to leave a paper trail (we were, after all, allegedly a covert unit). And when we traveled on military orders, we used fake IDs, nonexistent unit insignias, and signed receipts with all sorts of names—none of them ours. Those sorts of things probably gave Navy bean-counters a permanent case of the hives. I knew from personal experience they gave Ted Lyon Excedrin Headache Number Six.

Even when we didn't go commercial, we'd give the Navy problems. The Air Force was just beginning to deploy the gargantuan C-5A transport back then, and the giant plane could take the entire team and all our equipment in one load, whereas C-130 or C-141 travel required multiple aircraft, and we all had to arrive at the same time—unit integrity, remember? We practiced load-ins half a dozen times, then commandeered a C-5A and had the Air Force fly us to Louisiana, where we landed at a Naval Reserve station just outside New Orleans.

We didn't bother with advance warning or "permission to land, sir." The base found out about us when our C-5A—and it is a big goddamn plane—dropped in, taxied to a stop, the front end opened up, and more than half a dozen cars and trucks filled with long-haired dirtbags waving automatic weapons came pouring out, and drove right through the gate without so much as a hi-de-ho.

There was, of course, one asshole officer who ran down the tarmac to greet us and sign us in.

He huffed and he puffed and he waved his clipboard frantically. "Who are you? Where did you come from? Who said you could land here? Where are you going?"

I blew him a kiss, showed him some of the fake IDs I'd created, signed Dwight David Eisenhower's name to his paperwork, and told him to bug off. "Don't worry about it, Lieutenant." Then I put the pedal to the metal and disappeared. Somehow, word of our visit got back to Little Creek.

I created a cover for Six, Freeport Marine Corporation. There were business cards and letterhead, and we demanded the corporate discount when we checked into Holiday Inns and signed out rental cars. I made friends with a Louisiana State Police commander named Billy Poe, who ran the LSP SWAT team. Billy got us tags and driver's licenses, so we could switch the Virginia plates on the cars we flew down from Little Creek and check into hotels and motels with proper Louisiana ID. It may have been okay with the Cajuns for us to do what we did—but the Navy didn't like it at all.

Things came to a head in the last days of 1980. Ted Lyon and I had had our fair share of run-ins—battles over everything from purchasing to the chain-of-command structure, and I'd won every one of them. He'd gotten even in the way he knew best: on paper. As the commodore of NAVSPECWAR-GRU TWO, Ted wrote my fitreps. The one he composed for the fall and winter of 1980 was a work of art.

"*CDR Marcinko is an innovative gargorious* [sic] *officer who has accomplished a great deal in command of SEAL TEAM SIX*," Ted wrote. But it worried him, he continued, that "*Marcinko has, however, consistently displayed a trait which greatly concerns this reporting officer and our force commander; specifically he oftimes* [sic] *fails to observe the chain of command. . . . The relationship that exists between CDR Marcinko's fledgling command and others in special warfare could be described as 'We'll do as we wish,' or 'Who needs you.' I believe this to be a direct reflection of the man in charge.*

. . . CDR Marcinko must however conform to the Navy way and it is my intent that he do so."

Now, Ted summoned me again to his office, called me onto the carpet I knew all too well, and gave me another of his opinions.

"Dick, the appearance of the men under your command is a disgrace to the Navy."

I explained—patiently, I thought—that SEAL Team Six had been given permission to operate under modified grooming standards.

"There is modified, and there is unacceptable. Your team is unacceptable. I want you to get them cleaned up."

"And what about the civilian look they're supposed to have, Ted? They're supposed to be able to pass for blue-collar workers or students or—"

"Have them wear wigs," he interrupted.

"That's a great idea, Ted. Just one inspired notion. I can just see them free-falling from twenty-five thousand feet, unfurling their fucking wigs. Or—what about as they're fast-roping to pop through a window—' 'Scuse me, Mr. Terrorist, but I have to fix my wig before I can wax you."

"Dick—"

"What kind of dip-dunk shit-for-brains asshole idea is that, Ted? These guys have to be able to infiltrate foreign airports, or go through fucking border checkpoints manned by secret fucking policemen—and you want them to wear goddamn wigs? Are you out of your fucking mind?"

He bristled. "I'm talking about maintaining some kind of discipline. Your people are out of control." He frowned. Something on his desk was askew. Gingerly, Ted slid a cup of sharpened pencils half an inch, restoring it to its assigned position. Then he got back to me. "Look, Dick, I'm not talking about white-walls here. But modified grooming standards means hair that touches the ears, not Fu Manchu mustaches and ponytails. Those styles are offensive to the Navy. They make your men stand out too much. Which leads me to a second problem. I'm getting complaints from other commanders—they're beginning to have difficulties with their own men. SEAL Team Six is a bad influence and it's disrupting the whole base."

"Too bad, Ted. I seem to recall that when I commanded

SEAL Two, I had a hard-and-fast rule about no facial hair, and I made it stick. If the current CO can't handle his men, it's his prob, not mine."

Ted rolled his eyes and dismissed me. About a week later, I discovered he'd received a long memo from SURFLANT's commander, Admiral J. D. Johnson, complaining about Six's grooming standards, and demanding that Ted do something about it. I couldn't prove Ted engineered the admiral's complaint, but I had a pretty good idea he was behind it.

Well, there were ways to deal with Commodore Lyon. One of the first lessons I'd learned in Vietnam was, "Don't wait for the enemy to come to you—take it to the enemy." Of course, Commodore Edward Lyon III wouldn't know that tactic. He had never deployed to fight in Vietnam. Doom on you, Ted.

I called Brigadier General Richard Scholtes, the commander of the Joint Special Operations Command—JSOC—at Ft. Bragg. Scholtes was my true boss. Just as with Bill Crowe, I was on a first-name basis with Scholtes.

"General," I said, "I'm taking a whole bunch of flak from our asshole commodore down here, Ted Lyon. What about coming up for a personnel inspection? You're the operational commander, and if our hair's too long or our area's not policed, it's up to you to tell me to straighten up, not Ted."

Scholtes agreed and said he'd show up the following Saturday at 0900 hours.

Normally, uniform inspections would be done on the parade ground. But because Six was a clandestine unit, we held ours inside one of the two chicken coops behind SEAL Team Two. On Friday, the whole team policed the area—officers and enlisted men alike—raking up dead leaves and pinecones. I thought about adding an Ev Barrett border of beer cans to the walkways, but I decided that in this case, less would be more. Then we scrubbed down the chicken coops the best we could, although there wasn't much we could do to improve on what was basically a shitty situation.

On Saturday at 0700 I assembled my entire command in Class-A dress blue uniforms and medals. The officers wore swords and white gloves. We were an impressive group: one of my chief petty officers, Mikey T, had won the Congressional Medal of Honor in Vietnam. He wore it around his neck.

There were scores of other decorations, ranging from Silver and Bronze stars to various commendation medals, campaign awards, and Purple Hearts.

I've never been one for medals. In Vietnam, Drew Dix and Harry Humphries went out to rescue Maggie the Nurse and a bunch of other civilians during the battle of Chau Doc. The Army gave Drew a Medal of Honor for his actions that day; I recommended Harry for a Bronze Star, although when I learned what the Army had done for Drew I upped it to a Silver Star. So far as I was concerned, Harry was just doing his job as a SEAL, and medals be damned. Others, however, are impressed by commendations. So, we all wore every medal we owned. I had the Team snap to attention a few times just to get their timing down. The metal clanging on their chests sounded like fucking glockenspiels. We went over a few details, then I slipped over to the chicken coop in which I had my workspace and waited for Dick Scholtes to show up. I wanted a few minutes with him alone.

Dick Scholtes wasn't a Special Forces operator—in fact, although he'd graduated from SF school, he'd always refused to wear the blanket, the green beret. He was much more an old-fashioned soldier, a no-shit, gruff, grind-it-out conventional warrior who proudly wore his Eighty-second Airborne tie clasp and belt buckle whenever he dressed in civilian clothes. I'd always had the feeling that he'd been slightly disappointed at being given command of JSOC. He would have preferred to lead a parachute division. But if he was let down, we couldn't tell it from his leadership, which was supportive and kick-ass in its style.

At precisely 0900, General Scholtes arrived from Ft. Bragg, his big chopper setting down on the main pad at Little Creek. I sent one of my admin pukes to pick him up, explaining that I was in uniform and therefore couldn't be seen on the base.

To get to our chicken coops he had to walk through the SEAL Team Two area, which had not been policed very well. General Scholtes took careful note, then walked through the front door of my HQ.

I saluted. "Sir."

He returned the salute, eyeballing my uniform, sword, white gloves, Silver Star, four Bronze Stars, and Wolfman facial hair. "Nice beard, Dick. You always let your eyebrows grow down to your cheeks?"

"Only when I'm allowed to modify my grooming standards, or in the jungle, sir."

He shrugged. "Sounds good to me." He began to inspect his surroundings carefully, and his face screwed into a frown. "No rugs—nothing for the floors?"

"Nope."

"Nothing for the walls, either?"

"Sorry, sir."

"These desks look like crap."

"They are, General."

"Jeez, Dick, what a shithouse. Is this all they could give you?"

"I'm glad you noticed. This is the office I share with my XO, my ops boss, and my command master chief. If you'd like, I'll take you to see the two heads. They both flush on command at least fifty percent of the time."

"Pass on that," Scholtes said. "You got any coffee?"

"Yes, sir."

"So how's it going—aside from the accommodations?"

"Good." I poured him a mug and passed it over. "I don't mind this crap because we'll be moving to our permanent home base as soon as they finish building our facilities there. Besides, General, we're not here very much. If you look out at the backyard, there ain't a single oil rig to climb or ship to board. And OPSEC doesn't allow us to shinny the anchor chains down at the amphibious base. We go way out in the ocean to chase ships. We shoot in Florida, we jump in Arizona, and we climb in Louisiana. Besides, there's too many SEALs around here. They know us, we know them—that makes it hard on everybody."

"Agreed. And what about the chain-of-command bullshit?"

"I guess I'm just gonna have to live with it."

Scholtes nodded in agreement. "Large organizations," he said, "have trouble dealing with unprecedented efforts. They like going by the book. They live by a set of hard-and-fast rules. But in your case, Dick, there is no book. In SpecWar, there are no rules—or at least no rules that are comprehensible to anybody whose whole career has been spent thinking conventionally. Take Ted Lyon—"

"Do I have to?"

He laughed. "I think you're stuck with him. Look, Ted probably views you the same way staff officers look at anything or anybody who's out of the ordinary—as some rogue elephant trampling all over his turf. He deals with your requests the same way he handles memos about ordering more toilet paper or ballpoint pens. People like that have no vision—they can't see why the mission you've been assigned gives you any priority. They want you to wait on line with the rest of the assholes."

"I understand that, sir—intellectually. But it's becoming real hard to live with, day to day."

"Roger that," said Scholtes.

"Thing is, General, it's all a bunch of goddamn dip-shit numb-nuts nit-picking, like this grooming-standards bullshit that brought you here today." I told Scholtes about Ted's suggestion that Six wear wigs.

"This guy sounds like a real tightass," he said. "Look—I'll do what I can for you." He drained his coffee and stood up. "Well, Dick, let's get to it."

We walked across the breezeway between the chicken coops. At the door, I called out, "Inspection party arriving."

The door opened from the inside. Mikey T was holding it. The general looked back at me over his shoulder. "You son of a bitch," he said, a smile on his face. Then he saluted Mikey. Protocol says that all Medal of Honor winners get saluted. Mikey returned the salute, a big smile on his face. From inside, I heard Paul call out, "Attention on deck!" and the sound of the Team coming together as one man—bang.

I stood by General Scholtes's shoulder. "Sir," I said, "we are ready for your inspection."

So he moved up and down the lines, pausing by each man to inspect his medals and check out the grooming standards. No one wore earrings or ponytails, and everyone's hair was washed and combed. They didn't look pretty, but they were presentable.

After eight or ten minutes, the general had seen enough. He stood in front of the Team. "Have them stand at ease, Dick."

I nodded to Paul. "Team—at ease."

"I'm glad to be here," Scholtes said. "Glad because I'm

proud of you men—proud of how far you've come in so little time. Proud because you have dedicated yourselves to carrying out a tough mission, which I know you'll carry out as ordered. And proud because you look to be in super shape."

He cleared his throat. "I'm impressed by the medals you wear. It is obvious to me that you know your jobs and are good at them. I am saddened, though, at the conditions in which you live here. I will do my best to help your commanding officer rectify the situation.

"You gentlemen are building up an expertise that no one else in the world has—keep up the good work, and God bless you all."

The following week, I was told about a rocket sent from General Scholtes to Admiral Johnson. The gist of the message was: Dear Admiral, I'm happy to report that I held a successful personnel inspection of SEAL Team Six. The men met my grooming standards, given the clandestine, worldwide mission they have been tasked to accomplish. I was, however, appalled by the conditions under which they have been forced to live at Little Creek. I was further horrified by the sorry state of the SEAL Team Two compound, through which I had to pass on my way to visit SEAL Team Six. The number of soda and beer cans, cigarette butts, and other detritus on the ground was shocking and was grave evidence that details are not being properly taken care of by those in authority. It seems to me that instead of harassing SEAL Team Six, the administrative chain of command at NAVSPECWARGRU TWO under Commodore Edward Lyon III could better spend its time taking care of matters that truly concern it. Strong message follows. Love, kisses, and fuck you very much, your pals at JSOC.

Doom on you again, Ted.

In between training cycles, Paul and I ran head games on our beloved little boys. We'd spend the day, for example, twenty-five miles out in the ocean, running through 12-foot waves in our Boston whalers, working on boarding techniques. Boarding a ship under way at, say, twenty knots was simple. All we had to do was run our boats up behind a big humongous ship without being seen, hook a steel ladder on a 30-foot pole to the stern, and climb up. Of course, the waves were slapping our Boston whalers around like crazy, the ladder was cold and slippery, and we had to be prepared to shoot anybody who peered over the fantail as we were boarding. And if one of us slipped and fell, the propeller, which was going *whomp-whomp-whomp* between our legs as we climbed, would grind the poor unfortunate into hamburger.

So far as I was concerned, such activities were a piece of cake—if the men did it, I humped my body up the rope or out the hatch or into the water, too. Still, for reasons I could never explain, the guys would get back to Little Creek exhausted from these cheery, playful 14-hour excursions. So, I'd excuse them from CO watch at the Fraternal Order Bar —a fancy way of saying I was going drinking with them— and let them go home to see their wives and girlfriends for a couple of hours while Paul and I had a few beers alone.

Then, when we could almost hear the sounds of fucking and sucking, we'd beep everybody and see how fast they'd scramble back to the base. The men hated me for it, but it was a way of keeping them sharp—seeing who'd show up and who'd turned off his beeper while he was getting laid; or who would forget his weapons or chutes.

After half a dozen dry runs, the whole Team was pissed off at me for crying wolf when they thought they were entitled to a few hours of downtime. Too bad for them—the only way we'd get good at deploying in a hurry was to practice, practice, practice. They bitched and they moaned and they called me names even Ev Barrett never thought of. But they worked hard—and they stayed aboard. During my three years as CO of SEAL Team Six, the only men who left the unit were the ones I selected out. Despite the horrendous schedule, the lack of downtime, and the incredible pressure, my retention rate was 100 percent.

And we even had time for fun, every now and then. We took part in a shoot-off with Delta at Ft. Bragg and held our own. In fact, they selected their best shooters to compete, while I sent Paul and whoever else happened to be at Little Creek that week. Officially, the contest was a draw. But we won—and they knew it. The competition was good for both units because, in fact, there was no one else who came close to either of us.

Competition was natural: Delta was more than twice the

size of SEAL Team Six, and Charlie and I had argued endlessly over everything from my unit's size to the choice of
weapons (Delta used the .45 automatic as its basic sidearm,
while SEAL Six used 9mm and .357) to management and
tactics. I believed Delta had been overly influenced by the
formal administrative and training structures of the British
SAS; Charlie thought SEAL Team Six had been unduly influenced by the Marx brothers. We agreed to disagree, and
if the shooting competition proved nothing else, it was that
my frenetic, chaotic training schedule was as effective as his
more controlled and rigid one.

In one area, however, there was always total cooperation
and complete agreement between Delta and Six: the units
shared crucial information about ordnance. Bullet loads, specialized ammo, breaching charges, flash-bang and concussion
grenades—as soon as anyone from Six heard about anything
new, they'd call Delta to see if it had been tried over at Ft.
Bragg. And the men from Delta would do the same with us.

Although we'd practiced boarding ships under way, Six had
never staged a full-scale assault exercise on a civilian passenger liner that had been hijacked by terrorists. The scenario
seemed logical to us (and also to the Palestine Liberation
Front. The PLF, a terror group with ties to Iraq, Syria, and
Libya, would hijack the cruise ship *Achille Lauro* five years
later). So I rang up a friend of mine I'll call the Italian Stallion,
who was the executive officer of the FBI's Hostage Rescue
Team. Stallion and I had met when he was a weapons instructor at the FBI Academy at Quantico. He became a part
of the informal intelligence network I put together during my
years at the Pentagon. A no-crap former Midwest police officer with a bodybuilder's physique, a specialty in weapons,
and a terrific sense of humor, Stallion and I had become fast
friends quickly. Most of the FBI agents I'd ever met acted
like insurance agents. The Stallion was a weight lifter, a party
animal—a real pussy hound—and a damn good shooter. If
anybody knew where I could find a Love Boat for hire, it
would be him.

"I'll check on it and get back to you in a couple of days,
buddy," Stallion told me.

A few days later he called with good news: Norwegian

Cruise Lines was willing to loan us a Love Boat that was sailing empty between Jacksonville and Miami. Stallion said the ship's crew was willing to double as "passengers," his FBI agents would role-play the bad guys—a valuable lesson for them—and Six could be the cavalry.

We put together a full-scale operation, tracking the liner as it left Jacksonville and sailed into the southbound shipping lanes, listening in as the "terrorists" hit—the crew broadcasting a fake distress call and the terrorists grabbing the radio to state their demands. We set up a command-and-control unit, blanketed the area with discreet observation craft (we know they were discreet because Stallion's FBI guys looked for us but never saw us), and when we were ready, we did an intercept.

I was in the command chopper, supervising the boat crew that was to fast-rope onto the Love Boat's fantail, watching the action out the aft hatchway. I had communications that allowed me to speak, like the voice of God, into the earphones of all the players simultaneously. Paul, who had a new radio handle, PV, testimony to his Prince Valiant haircut, was in charge of six Boston whalers. Gunners in one of the whalers and snipers in two small choppers would pick off any of the FBI tangos who saw us coming. We'd kill them before they could warn their pals or wax the hostages.

We hit the ship at 2200, when visibility was best for us (we had night-vision devices) and worst for the terrorists (they didn't). Everything was planned down to the second. Every man knew his job. What no one remembered was that we were not alone on our mission: Mr. Murphy and his insidious law had also come along for the ride. Unless we were both careful and lucky, we were about to enter the TARFU Zone.

Okay, class, let's see how the *phoques* get fucked. I watched aghast as my small sniper choppers staged a near-collision because the pilots weren't talking to each other properly. I saw PV's boats approaching from the wrong angle—goddamn tangos picked them up right away. Then the Blackhawk I rode in flared above the Love Boat's fantail too soon, and my Katzenjammer Kidz went over the rails before the snipers were in position to protect them.

Katrinka fix. "Screw it." I threw off the headset, grabbed the thick nylon line, and went over the side myself. Just as I hit the rope, the Blackhawk put its nose up and began to swerve away from the ship. *Shiit*.

Mr. Murphy giggled. "Marcinko, you pus-nuts dip-dunk asshole geek: the goddamn chopper pilots saw six men go— they have no idea you're on the rope, too."

I looked down. There was deck below me, but not much of it anymore. I let go and fell the final twelve feet or so, bouncing ass over teakettle. I hit the deck on a swell, and as the stern fell, I slid toward the gunwales, my feet pedaling furiously to no avail. It was like sliding down a goddamn bowling alley.

"You shit-for-brains," gloated Mr. Murphy. "This is a cruise ship—it has waxed decks."

Mr. Murphy was right: we'd never thought about waxed decks. Navy ships don't *have* waxed decks.

We'd lost the element of surprise, so the "terrorists" were ready for us, too, and put up a big firefight. The question of who killed who was not a problem, as we'd loaded up with special Canadian training ammo—Simmunition FX cartridges filled with fluorescent red marking compound—so when someone was hit we'd know they'd been shot. The red dye also helped tell us whether all our target work with those three-by-five cards had been worthwhile.

Once we engaged, the situation improved. The SEALs moved in their prechoreographed "dances," clearing cabins and staterooms, rescuing hostages, and zapping bad guys. They looked like lethal demons as they swarmed over the ship in their tigerstripe-and-black fatigues, balaclava hoods, gloves, and blacked-out faces. Our communications systems worked, so we knew where everybody was, and what each team was doing. Our shooting was on the money—better by far than that of the FBI "terrorists." So despite the fact that we "lost" three SEALs, we wasted all the bad guys with well-placed kill shots. So far as I was concerned, three casualties was an acceptable rate for a first-time exercise.

We learned a lot from our Love Boat cruise. For example, while we'd killed all the bad guys who were shooting at us, we didn't have enough people on board to interrogate all the passengers and make sure there were no terrorist "sleepers" still around. There weren't even enough SEALs to secure the ship, much less deal with wounded hostages and interview hysterical passengers, all at the same time. I realized that if we ever did this one for real, SEAL Six would have to be bolstered by Delta, or the FBI.

After the exercise, Stallion and I did a walk-through to review where things had gone right, and where they'd gone wrong. He, for example, was concerned that SEAL Six hadn't preserved evidence, but moved everything around. "You can't do that, buddy," he insisted. "If you're gonna bring the boat back to U.S. territorial waters, the investigation's gotta follow Department of Justice guidelines, otherwise the scumbags walk."

"If they're alive."

Stallion smiled. "Gotcha."

Still, the fact remained that if we took down a ship in international waters and we were ordered to bring some of the terrorists back alive, we'd have to be pristine about the way we went about our jobs and handled both evidence and suspects. I made note and had the men memorize the Miranda warnings—although it was doubtful we'd ever utter them aloud. The only warning I wanted to give a terrorist was, "April fool, motherfucker."

In time, the "cry wolf" factor became something of a problem. Our training exercises were complicated by a number of false alarms in which we were scrambled by JSOC, then stood down. Once it was a plane hijacking. Another time it was a terrorist attack. Another time it was a pair of crazy Cubans. It got so that I'd assemble everybody and make a speech telling them this was it and we were going out to kick fucking ass and take fucking names, and fuck all terrorists and fuck all communists, and fuck the whole fucking world except for SEAL Team fucking Six. I'd really get myself worked up.

Then Prince Valiant would stand up and say, "What the CO really meant to say was . . . ," and he'd interpret my ranting and raving and explain that all we had were preliminary indications, and nothing had been decided yet, and so on and so forth, and stop me from chewing the carpet and making a damn fool out of myself. It got so bad that I'd call JSOC to complain about their goddamn yanking us back again and again. I didn't want any more exercises. I wanted Bravo Squad's first night on the river at Juliet Crossing. I wanted

Ilo-Ilo Island. I wanted Eighth Platoon at Chau Doc. I wanted SEAL Team Six to go out and kill us a bunch of Japs.

We wouldn't be doing any of our killing in Iran, either. A back-door deal had been made, and even as Jimmy Carter flew back to Plains, Georgia, on Inauguration Day, 1981, the fifty-three American hostages were being released by their Shiite terrorist captors. So much for our original mission as a part of a second hostage-rescue attempt. That left us our counterterror role.

I thought our time had finally arrived later in January 1981 when the Macheteros, a Puerto Rican terrorist organization, blew up a bunch of planes near San Juan. I got word from JSOC about a stolen nuclear device and a maritime environment—Vieques Island, where I'd trained as a Frogman. The situation looked good. All the signs were there: fresh intelligence from NSA; a real-time scramble and load-out—and a 56-man mass HAHO night jump and ten-mile para-glide onto our objective, something no unit had ever accomplished before.

We scrambled. We went. But Vieques, too, turned out to be yet another dry hump. An exercise—what they called a full mission profile.

It occurred to me, as Paul and I sat at the Fraternal Order Bar the day after we flew home from Puerto Rico, that it might be gratifying for the men, if ultimately unrewarding for our careers, to stage a live-fire hit on JSOC headquarters.

Paul drained his beer and called for another round. "Don't worry, boss—we'll get lucky soon."

Chapter

20

IT TOOK A LONG TIME BEFORE SEAL TEAM SIX GOT LUCKY. Despite repeated presidential rhetoric about terrorists being able to run but not hide, there were hundreds of terror incidents between October 1980, when SEAL Team Six was formed, and July of 1983, when I gave up my command—and the U.S. did little to interdict any of them. It wasn't that we didn't have the men, or the ability, to do the job. Moreover, SEAL Team Six could launch a preemptive strike against terrorists if there was hard intelligence an American target was about to be hit. The fact that there were so many attacks and no action by Six told me that either our intel apparatus was screwed up beyond repair and incapable of developing the hot information necessary to deploy a first strike, or the administration didn't have the guts, or the will, to act.

Additionally, Ronald Reagan saw terrorism through his own ideological prism, instead of viewing it through the warrior's clear glass. He viewed terror as a byproduct of the East-West struggle, another form of surrogate warfare waged by the Soviets against the West, not as the far more sinister struggles of anarchy against order, of culture against culture, of sociopaths against society—which would outlast the Cold War. He was mistaken.

So SEAL Team Six trained and rehearsed and drilled—all balls to the wall. But we did no actual counterterror. We played on trains and planes and automobiles. We drove up to Washington, D.C., and practiced rescuing hostages from a subway train—the nation's capital allowed Delta and Six to play in the city's new metro system after it had shut down one night. We visited Atlanta and assaulted various types of aircraft at Eastern Airlines' hub facilities. We commandeered a raceway in California and spent weeks perfecting stunt-driving techniques—every trick from bootlegger's turns to controlled head-on crashes.

We went to mountaineering school—the men got so good at climbing things that when we checked into hotels and I told them to go to their rooms, they often did so by scaling the outsides of the buildings. The Team traveled to Germany for joint exercises with General Ricky Wegener's GSG-9 commandos. We played war games and strategized with the Brits and the French and the Italians. But we didn't do a single thing for real.

Four of my boat crews (remember, there are two boat crews to a platoon. You will see this material again) spent six months in Egypt, where they taught some of President Mubarak's Army Rangers a few basic CT techniques. The sessions were only moderately successful. No matter how hard we tried, it was almost impossible to teach the Egyptians about specialized operations. Their capabilities were—to be tremendously kind—crude. Even though we worked with the most elite of their Rangers, we found their marksmanship unsatisfactory, their physical condition second-rate, and their motivation nonexistent.

One reason for these flaws was Egypt's military caste system. In Egypt—as in most Third World countries—enlisted men, who were basically peasants, were treated like slaves, while officers, many of whom were political appointees, were treated like princes. Often, the officers wouldn't even bother to show up for training—figuring that when it came to the crunch, the enlisted men, not them, would do the fighting. The concept of officers leading from the front was unknown;

the phrase *unit integrity* didn't translate from SEAL into Arabic.

I decided to motivate the officers in my own subtle fashion—by slapping a few captains and lieutenants around in front of their men when they couldn't, or wouldn't, do the work properly. That got the officers' attention. It also caused a couple of migraine headaches at the Presidential Palace, which rocketed the U.S. embassy. I was asked politely but firmly to desist slam-dunking Egyptians. I desisted. (I should have been allowed to continue my strong-arm methods, because at least they were working. As it happened, neither we, nor any of the other Special Ops units that visited Cairo to tutor, assist, inculcate, train, or educate, would do the Egyptian military much good. When it finally came to the crunch in 1985, and Egyptian "commandos" rushed a hijacked Egyptair plane in Malta, they killed fifty-seven of the passenger-hostages and destroyed the plane while trying to rescue it, as American Special Ops advisers watched in horror.)

Looking back on it now, my mood was probably not improved by the fact that I'd sustained a stress fracture of my right leg during a HAHO jump just before we deployed to Cairo. The whole leg was somewhat tender, and the Egyptians, who had a hard time controlling small boats under the best of circumstances, kept knocking my bad leg with their gunwales almost every time we rehearsed water-based infiltrations and extractions. Paul wanted me to see a doctor. I refused—I could live with the pain, and I was worried that, once I checked into a medical facility, the doctors might rule me unfit to jump, swim, and shoot with my Team. No jumping, swimming, or shooting meant no commanding—and I was not about to relinquish SEAL Team Six before we'd completed a real CT mission. So I suffered in silence, although my vile temper often betrayed my nasty physical condition. There were a number of black-and-blue Egyptian Army officers who could vouch for it.

On the positive side, our six months in Egypt gave us the opportunity to learn a little bit about the Arab mentality—at least the Egyptian Arab mentality. It was also a chance to sneak and peek at the ships in the Suez Canal, and to work on harbor assaults against actual hostile targets—unsuspecting foreign shipping at Port Said or Suez. All our findings went into dossiers. Who knew if we'd ever have to operate in Egypt covertly, or whether or not Egypt would stay friendly to the U.S. Besides, SEAL Team Six was on a diplomatic mission—and as I'd learned at the Defense Intelligence School back in the seventies, all military diplomats are spies—so, while we taught our students, we also built up our operational files and tactical data bases. And while we played, we watched as the Israelis and the Soviets played intelligence tag with us, trying to figure out what the hell a bunch of Navy assholes were doing in Egypt besides teaching Egyptians to swim and climb anchor chains.

Because of our international role, we trained with CT units all over the world. It was likely that, if we ever got called up for real, we'd be coordinating our actions with a foreign force, and the more we'd worked together in the past, the more comfortable the shooters felt with each other, the easier it would be when hostage lives were on the line. I respected them all—the British SAS, the French GIGN, the Italian GIS, the Norwegian Special Ops combat swimmers; they were all first-rate. But the unit to which we probably felt closest was Germany's *Grenzschutzgruppe-9* (GSG-9). It was commanded by a lean, mean s.o.b. of a brigadier general named Ulrich Wegener. GSG-9 had seen action in Mogadishu, Somalia, where it had rescued ninety-one passengers and crew of a hijacked Lufthansa 737 in October 1977. In 1979, elements of the unit flew to Saudi Arabia, where Shiite fundamentalists had taken hostages in the Great Mosque in Mecca. Wegener, then a colonel, advised the Saudis on tactics, although it was the GIGN, not GSG-9, that finally assaulted the site.

I'd gotten to know Wegener in 1979. He'd come to Washington to brief the JCS on counterterror operations, and I'd watched as he entered the briefing room ramrod straight, his Border Guard uniform impeccable, his confident, self-assured body language silently shouting, *"I knew what had to be done—and I fucking did it!"* The Joint Chiefs had been transfixed by his presentation. So was I—after twenty minutes of listening to Herr Oberst Wegener I was ready to goose-step through a brick wall and volunteer for his unit myself. Later, I'd wangled my way onto the guest list of one of the IHO (in honor of) parties hosted by various generals and assistant secretaries and met another Ulrich Wegener altogether.

This happy warrior called himself Ricky, not colonel. He was a sociable, sophisticated officer who held his wineglass correctly and charmed the panty hose off generals' wives. Later, when I'd managed to convince him to visit some of the Washington area's better saloons, I discovered that he loved pounding his cowboy boots on the floor while listening to country music, told jokes on himself, drank SEAL-like quantities of beer (complaining loudly that it was too light in character compared mit der gutt schtuff in Deutschland), and was eminently down-home approachable. He and I spent our all-nighter touring bars from Old Town Alexandria to George-town and promising each other it was love at first sight. By the time we shared double portions of ham and eggs, home fries, and good strong coffee, we not only still respected each other by dawn's early light, but we'd exchanged secret hand-shakes and decoder rings and vowed that, if we were ever given the opportunity to have a meaningful relationship to-gether in the future, we'd do it.

Which is how, in November of 1982, I found myself in the middle of the frigid-as-a-witch's-tit North Sea, clinging to the rail inside the fart-filled pilothouse of a seagoing German Navy tugboat at oh-dark hundred, more than thirty miles from the closest land, watching as 20-foot waves crashed over the bow, slapping my SEALs and Ricky's commandos silly as they tried to make sure the six Boston whalers we'd lashed to the deck weren't washed overboard along with forty-two happy warriors—a joint SEAL Six–GSG-9 strike force bound for Oil Rig B/44, fifty-eight miles northwest of Sylt Island, off the coast of Denmark. On board the rig (which would come to be known in the course of this morning's enterprise as the Dirty Name, in memory of the obscenely difficult, excruciatingly painful obstacle course that almost killed me during my UDT training), West German soldiers, playing the role of both hostages and terrorists, were waiting for us. Our goal was to assault the target under cover of darkness, wax the "terrorists," and free the "hostages."

Piece of cake, right? SEAL Team Six had assaulted oil rigs before. We'd trained in the Gulf of Mexico and off the south-eastern coast of Tasmania, Australia, where we'd developed effective climbing techniques and choreographed the best ways in which to take down the huge, skeletal structures. Piece of cake—*wrong*. Tonight was no balmy Gulf of Mexico water. We were facing not only icy weather, but the roughest combination of sea and wind I'd ever encountered.

God, how I hated the ocean at times like this. The 40-meter tugboat kept lifting out of the water and slam-dunking back with a series of keel-rattling, bone-jarring shudders. Every time we went airborne, I grabbed for a handrail. It was like getting kicked in the balls—no matter how hard you train to get kicked in the balls, it hurts every single time it happens.

Outside, the air was in the low thirties, with a wind-chill factor that put it below the teens. The whole tug was coated with ice. This was the coldest water I'd ever seen—and the most treacherous. The Atlantic has its long swells—lifting you out of the water just high enough to see the horizon, then thrashing you down deep and fast, making you grab the gunwale in momentary panic as you ride the roller coaster down, down, down. The Pacific, with its 60-foot-high walls of water and miles-deep trenches, has engendered respect from generations of sailors, me included. But no water was as nasty, as bad, as nut-numbing motherfucking sphincter-puckering cruel, as the North Sea. It was a masochist's delight: misery at its finest.

You want evidence? The manufacturers of Boston whalers state—categorically—that one cannot capsize their boats. Bullshit. Horse puckey. During our first day of trials off the German coast, the massive North Sea waves, treacherous currents, and powerful winds flipped and/or rolled our Boston whalers three times, leaving SEALs and GSG-niners frigid and swamped until they could right their boats and call for a tow. The boats had been lifted completely out of the water by the wave action, then turned like flapjacks as they were caught by wind-tunnel gales and wind-whipped water. Our frozen, wet, hypothermic kraut brethren thought we were flipping the whalers on purpose—some crazy *Amerikaner* initiation rite—until we explained it wasn't part of the script. Then they berated us for trying to pound square-hole boats in round-hole water.

The tug's captain looked disdainfully at my greenish complexion and lit his pipe, filling the already pungent wheelhouse with the foul odor of strong, black tobacco. He and his crew were taking professional pleasure in our obvious discomfort. I clambered outside and pulled my way aft of the superstructure. Trailer Court, Pooster, and Horseface, layered in thermal underwear, English-made dry suits with hoods and boots, over which they wore black SEAL load-bearing combat vests, were working on the lines that held the whalers down. Snake, icicles forming on his mustache, was double-checking the assault gear in the boats. He, Trailer, and Pooster were my lead climbers—and they knew they had their work cut out for them tonight.

I called down, "Everything okay?"

Snake gave me a thumbs-up. "Roger that, Skipper. But it's gonna be fuckin' cold shinnying up those goddamn stanchions and pipes."

"You volunteered to play with the grown-ups, asshole. You could have been a regular sailor."

Snake grabbed the rail at my feet, chinned himself up, and somersaulted over the rail to where I stood. "No way, Skipper. Who the hell'd want to be stationed aboard a fucking ship?"

He was right of course—six months without booze or pussy was the ultimate curse suffered by all fleet sailors, and Snake, former paratrooper, was not cut out for that kind of life.

So instead, he was waterlogged, half frozen, and ice encrusted, on a perverse training mission that Ricky Wegener and I had designed to come as close to the real thing as we could without causing undue fatalities. The GSG-9 commander and I saw eye to eye on *that* subject as well. He, like I, believed that unless exercises were performed at the very edge of the operational envelope, they wouldn't help the men survive in real-life situations.

We both carried the weight of having killed men in training. But—we'd talked about it in the past—there was no guilt, just anxiety and the teeth-grinding, migraine-engendering stress of leadership. It was an integral part of the responsibility we had volunteered to bear. Neither of us liked it—but we both did it.

We'd been under way almost four hours—although it seemed like a lifetime—and I struggled back into the wheelhouse where the captain told me we were almost at our launch position, three nautical miles from the rig.

"But *Fregatten-Kapitän*—Commander—we'll want to circle the target at least twice to verify it is the right rig, and also so you can see how the currents will affect your small boats, yes?"

"Affirmative." I wasn't about to contradict him. He knew these waters. I was a new cork bobbing in a strange pond. Once we saw how the currents were moving, we'd be able to decide which direction to insert from.

I went aft again and explained the situation to the troops. Their faces showed disappointment. Trailer Court spoke first. "Why the hell do we have to wait, Skipper? Let's just go."

The others agreed with him in a chorus of *ja*'s and right-ons. I saw their point. Anything was better than the beating we were taking on board the tug. But this was no time to improvise. We'd have to assess the currents and the winds before we inserted.

An hour and a half later we began launching the boats. That sounds easier than it was—in all, the launch took more than an hour. Getting the whalers into the water was difficult enough, without beating their hulls to shreds alongside the tug. Harder still was getting the forty-two shooters in—timing the swells, then jumping, laden with explosives, weapons, ammo, and climbing gear, hoping you weren't carried by the 50-knot winds into the water.

I went over the rail. Below me, the Boston whaler pitched and yawed. In rapid sequence, my mind ran over the possibilities. Which way would I leap/fall/swim if I missed the whaler? If I went in the water, should I worry more about the screws on the whalers or the gargantuan screws on the tug? If I got swept astern, would the force of the tug's props suck me down and turn me into hamburger? How much pain can I take? *What the hell am I doing here?*

As I jumped, it came to me with crystal clarity that Ricky Wegener—no fool he—had politely declined the boat trip in favor of playing observer aboard the rig. He'd choppered out during daylight. That's why he wore stars, and I wore scars.

After almost an hour we finally got all forty-two malevolent, spiteful shooters into the small boats—maybe not the ones they were assigned on paper, but at least they were off the damn tug and heading toward a target, which, when neutralized, would mean they'd get warm clothes and a cold beer—if they lived that long. In the last-minute shuffle on board the tug it had been decided that three men would stay with each whaler: one coxswain, one radioman, and one able-bodied shooter to return fire, pick up swimmers for rescue, and handle lines to steady the small boats alongside the rig and tug. That put the remaining twenty-four shooters in the loving North Sea—twelve swim pairs, two for each of the rig's six legs.

The sea was so bad that even at a thousand meters we lost sight of the rig often and had to rely on our ops people on board the tug, working from the transponders we carried and a radar screen, to vector us in. Under normal conditions, we usually approached oil rigs from multiple angles to ensure a successful clandestine hit. In this sea, though, we tried to stay within sight of each other so that no boat would get lost.

We tacked toward the huge rig—its lights still faint in the darkness. I checked my watch: 0145. It seemed like we'd been in the boats for hours, although when we debriefed much later we'd learn it had taken only fifty minutes to reach swimmer launch point.

How bad was it out there? Bad enough so that it was actually a pleasure to leave the whalers and slide into the icy water. At least in the water there was no wind whipping you. I adjusted my mask and went over the gunwale, a rope in my hands. Each pair of swim buddies carried one. The idea was to wrap the lines around the legs of the rig so we wouldn't drift off. I frown on MIAs.

I swam toward one of the huge hull columns from which we could reach the vertical braces that would allow us to climb up to the deck and living quarters. Above me, the platform loomed like a futuristic space station, a ten-story skeletal structure of concrete and steel. I reached for one of the massive columns but a wave washed me past it. Damn. I swam against the current. Now a riptide took hold of me, dragged me under the surface, and flung me against the barnacle-encrusted steel piling.

I breached the surface, spitting water. After two attempts I managed to loop the line around a brace. In doing so I realized that Mr. Murphy had come along for the ride in a big way: the entire metal surface of the rig was glazed with about an eighth of an inch of ice.

Quickly, I rounded up my best climbers—Trailer, Snake, Pooster, and Horseface—and explained the situation. They'd find a way up and then drop caving ladders, which would be secured with titanium hooks, so the rest of us could climb.

Pooster went first, wiggling his way up the slick cylindrical surface of the brace, cursing in a way that would have done Ev Barrett proud. The noise didn't matter—with the 50-knot wind, no one could hear anything anyway, and we were sure none of the terrorists expected us so soon.

I peered at my watch: 0225. Just slightly behind my schedule. I trod water. I mused about the existence I'd chosen for myself. I waited for what seemed an eternity.

"Fuuuuck!" Pooster's body came flying out of the blackness. He went into the water flat on his back five yards away with a sickening thwack.

I swam to him, sure he was dead or unconscious or that he'd broken his back. He lay in the water wriggling his fingers. Then his little red mustache twitched behind the mask. Finally, he groaned. "Shit. It's goddamn slippery up there."

He was okay. Thank God. I cracked a smile. I rolled my eyes skyward. *"Up,* asshole, up. You're supposed to go *that* way." I pointed over my head.

He rolled over, dog-paddled to the support, and began again—the little engine that could. This time he took off his rubber gloves. "My hands kept sliding."

"You'll lose some skin."

"So what—it'll give me traction."

Now, Snake and Horseface and Trailer went up, too. It was Trailer who finally got high enough to attach the first caving ladder, which looks like one of those things trapeze artists climb, and I signaled the first six men to begin their climb. Shortly, three other caving ladders, each wedged into the braces with titanium hooks, followed. I motioned for the rest of the team to start the assault.

The plan was a real KISS operation. We'd climb the caving ladders to breach the vertical braces. Then, once we reached the skeletal superstructure of the rig itself, we'd work our way up, go over the rail, and take down the bad guys. Twenty-four of us were enough to hit all major areas of the platform simultaneously.

I watched as two GSG-niners pulled themselves up the ladder Horseface had dropped. Twenty feet up they were smacked by a mini-tornado, and the hook pulled out of its niche. They dropped back into the water, still tethered by their swim-buddy line, sputtered to the surface, swam to a brace, and held on. The ladder was deep-sixed—shitcanned. I tried to calculate the cost. Each titanium hook equaled the price of a Concorde ticket from New York to London.

I waved the Krauts over to Pooster's ladder and signaled for them to go up. When I saw they'd be okay, I followed— the last one to climb. Halfway up I ran out of steam. What the hell is an old guy doing here? I hung suspended forty feet above the churning ocean and looked at my watch: 0518. It had taken more than three hours to get from initial launch to final attack position.

Wheezing and sweating despite the freezing air, I pulled myself over the rail and watched as everyone took their pre-planned positions in what I called the international-team mode—mixed shooter pairs. There was no movement on deck other than the normal sounds of wind and sea, and the hisses, groans, grinds, and wheezes of pneumatic, hydraulic, and electric equipment. Maybe, I thought, Mr. Murphy fell off the ladder and the son of a bitch drowned. I gave a hand signal. Trailer and Baby Rich, each with a German shooter partner, attached explosives to the main door. Another of my deadly shooters, an explosive little bantam cock I called Little Carlos, along with Snake, an armoire-sized SEAL I'd named Ho-Ho-Ho, Pooster, and their Kraut comrades, blocked the windows, escape hatches, and power stations.

This was too easy—not a sign of the bad guys anywhere. Were we being set up? Was this about to become goatfuck city? I flicked my transmitter on. *"Go!"*

It was the fucking Fourth of July, Bastille Day, and the Queen's goddamn jubilee all at once. *KA-BOOM!*—the charges breached the doors. *KA-BLAM!*—the guys rolled flash-bang grenades inside the control room and went in, quick and low.

I followed tight on Trailer's shoulder. His Smith was up

and ready. There was movement behind an electrical panel obscured by the smoke of the flash-bang.

Trailer swung his .357 around instinctively and squeezed off three shots of special dye-marker Simmunition ammo. "Die, motherfucker." Three red stars appeared on the chest of a bad guy. There was more movement to his right. Trailer's Kraut partner swiveled his HK P-7 and took the terrorist out with two 9mm wax bullets to the throat. Even with the padding he wore, that son of a bitch was gonna have trouble breathing for a couple of days.

"Clear," Trailer announced into his radio. Now Carlos, Snake, Ho-Ho-Ho, Rich, Horseface, and the others began their methodical, chamber-by-chamber sweep of the rig's main compartments. I got on the radio to the tug and the whalers and told them to converge. In the background I heard scattered two- and three-shot bursts from pistols and submachine guns.

"I got hostages—alive." It was Gold Dust Larry's voice on the radio. "But they're wired."

Shit. They'd been booby-trapped. Where the hell was the detonator? Was it electrical or radio controlled? Was it— Pooster's unmistakable voice broke in. "I got the cocksucker with the initiator—he was asleep and it was wedged under his mattress. Untie 'em, Larry."

We broke off the exercise at 0730. The umpires (three Germans and three Americans) totaled the scores: two bad guys killed, three wounded, eight captured. Two good guys wounded. Twelve hostages released, none injured. All in all, not a bad morning's work.

I found Ricky in the galley, working on a steaming bowl of oxtail soup, a wedge of black bread slathered with white German butter in his free hand, a mug of black coffee at his elbow.

"Enjoying yourself, Herr General?"

He looked up at me with a malevolent smile. "*Ja*, dickhead. It's been an interesting morning. Good progress." He paused and took a big spoonful of soup. "But these exercises—they always give me a big appetite." He gnawed at the pumpernickel. "And you?"

And me? I stood there in my rubber suit, with my dripping beard and my frozen, skinned fingers, and my aching joints.

I'd relieved myself in my suit—common practice during operations—and I smelled like a latrine. "You no-good son-of-a-bitch cockbreath dip-shit numb-nuts shit-for-brains hotsy-totsy fucking Nazi Kraut bastard. You sit there eating fucking soup and fucking bread and fucking drinking hot fucking coffee while I've been fucking freezing my fucking ass off in your fucking North fucking Sea and you ask me *that?* Fuck you, Herr General."

He roared with laughter. "Seems to me, *dickhead*, if you'll pardon my French, that this morning it's you who's the real *phoquee*."

The son of a bitch had a point. But then, he wore the stars, and I wore the scars.

Our visit to GSG-9 may have left us cold and sore as hell. But at least we got to play with people we liked. Shortly after we returned stateside, I was summoned to JSOC headquarters and told that a detachment from SEAL Team Six was needed for a clandestine operation in Lebanon. I liked nobody in Lebanon.

But there were American naval assets in Lebanon in the winter of 1982, part of the multinational force that had been sent in just after the massacres at Sabra and Chatila refugee camps, where Phalangist militiamen had taken revenge for the assassination of their charismatic leader Bashir Gemayel by murdering roughly a thousand unarmed Palestinian men, women, and children the previous September.

So JSOC and—grudgingly—the State Department had decided that two reduced boat crews from SEAL Team Six (twelve men instead of fourteen) would be inserted in Beirut clandestinely. Our mission would be to assess possible terrorist threats to American targets, survey the embassy and Marine positions, and suggest improvements. As had so often happened before, I deployed just before Christmas.

I made the selection carefully. I'd take Paul, of course, and the Duke. And I thought Indian Jew would fit in well. The Gold Dust Twins were included, as were Snake, Horseface, Fingers, Pooster, and the big, bearded son of a bitch I called Ho-Ho-Ho because of the way he laughed. I also took my favorite junior-junior cannon-fodder enlisted man—Baby Rich (I told him we needed him to volunteer in case we had to throw somebody to the wolves. He asked if he should bring his little red riding hood. "If it looks anything like a kaffiyeh," I said, "pack it").

The rains had come early to Lebanon the winter of 1982, and it was raw and cold as I pushed my way through the crowded terminal at Beirut International clad only in a light jacket and a turtleneck sweater. I slipped my rucksack over one shoulder, took my overnight bag in my hand, and let myself be carried by the human current toward the customs and immigration desks.

I'd flown from Norfolk to Washington, Washington to New York, New York to Paris. I overnighted in Paris and sampled some of the holiday cheer—I never did get her name, but she was Vietnamese and she was beautiful—then rose at five and took a cab to Orly airport, a half hour southeast of the city, from where the Middle East Airlines flights departed for Beirut. I was traveling light: carry-on baggage and a small .380 pistol that was easily concealed when I passed through metal detectors.

Our commo gear, heavy weapons, and specialized goodies were traveling with Duke, Larry, Frank, and Baby Rich. They had the easiest trip: a Military Air Command flight to Sigonella Air Base in Sicily, a restful night of cold beer, then an early-morning air shuttle aboard a Navy C-2 Greyhound COD (Carrier On-board Delivery) aircraft, which would drop them onto the flight deck of the USS *Independence*, just off the Lebanese coast. From there, my SEAL quartet would infiltrate by coming ashore with a Marine contingent. Then they would change clothes, lose themselves in the crowds, and make their way north to the city. I was to pick them and their booty up outside the airport terminal in seventy-two hours.

Paul, Horseface, Pooster, and Snake were scheduled to fly to Amsterdam, then make their way overland by train to Athens. They'd stay there a couple of days to make sure they were "clean," then fly to Cyprus, where they'd catch a ferryboat to Beirut. They would be at the Museum Crossing—one of the few places where it was possible to pass between East and West Beirut without getting sniped—in eighty-four hours. Jew, Ho-Ho-Ho, and Fingers had the most circuitous and dangerous route: London, Paris, Frankfurt—and Damascus. Once in the Syrian capital, they'd hire cabs and make their way to Beirut overland, then check into the Summerland Hotel, on the beach just north of the airport.

On this particular combat patrol, I was point man. I'd operate solo for a day or so, getting the lay of the land, arranging transportation, looking for appropriate safe houses, and watching out for—whatever. I smiled at the mustached official who'd stamped my passport for me. There had been a pastel pink and yellow, 50-pound Lebanese note folded neatly in my Irish passport before I passed through immigration. Now I had a two-month visa, and the fifty pounds had disappeared. "*Shukran*—thank you."

"*Aufwan*—you are welcome."

I walked up the ramp toward the outer doors. It looked as if there were a riot going on outside, but it was only the usual bustle, common to Third World airports from Cairo to Karachi. The difference in Lebanon was that here, everybody was armed to the teeth.

Three cabdrivers fought over me, and I surrendered to the winner, a small dark man with a single, thick eyebrow and a crooked smile below a badly repaired harelip. He guided me toward what might once have been a Chevrolet. I went along, watching him lope in front of me, shoulders rolling. We reached the vehicle. He paused. He turned. The massive eyebrow raised itself almost a full inch. "Where we go?"

"Commodore Hotel, Igor."

He gave me a thumbs-up. "*Sahafa*—press? Journalist?"

"Yes. *Sahafa. Irish Weekly Flagpole.* Heard of it?" I watched as he gave me what I assumed was a Beiruti's quizzical look. "No, mister."

"That's okay—no one else has, either." I climbed into the passenger's side, threw my baggage on the rear seat, and wrestled the door almost closed. "What's your name, *habibi?*"

"*Habibi?* You speak Arabic?"

"No—only a few words. I can tell you to go fuck yourself and ask where's the pissoir."

"That's enough." The driver turned to me, his grinning made all the more absurd by the condition of his lip. He pulled out, oblivious of the traffic careening on either side of us. "Call me Abu Said, *habibi.* Said Abu Said." He shook his head, reached behind himself, and tapped my luggage. "*Ya, habibi*—please not to do that—it is giving temptations. Putting them under your feet, please."

I restowed my luggage properly as the taxi swerved precariously out of the airport proper. We negotiated two Lebanese roadblocks and started north on the divided roadway running into the city. Two Volvos that appeared to be in a drag race a hundred yards ahead of us suddenly bounced off each other. One swerved precariously, did a 180, then pulled to the side of the highway. The other Volvo veered to the shoulder and skidded to a stop. Both drivers got out brandishing pistols. Abu Said put pedal to metal and sped past the gunshots. Welcome to Beirut.

We were waved through a Marine checkpoint, manned by apple-cheeked kids with unloaded M16s. One of the idiotic "rules of engagement" that had been promulgated by the bureaucrats in Washington was that Marines were not allowed to protect themselves. I looked back over my shoulder. They were sitting ducks. I turned back to see an urban sprawl of bombed-out, gutted ruins in front of us. "Bourj al Barajneh—Palestinian camp," Abu Said explained as we passed. "Israelis no like."

He swerved left at an intersection, then soon bore right around what remained of a traffic circle. A sign on a building to my left told me we'd just passed the Kuwaiti embassy. Now we passed what looked like a football stadium. "Sports center," he explained. "PLO used it for weapons. Israelis bombed. Syrians—shoot with tanks. Everybody—ka-boom."

We drove on. To my right, houses flattened like pancakes cluttered the landscape. "Chatila camp," the driver explained. "*Kataeb*—Phalangists . . ." He drew his finger across his throat. "Kill many Palestinian here."

We swerved left, then right, then left, following a small residential road lined with double-parked cars and apartment houses that seemed to have weathered the war without too much damage. We S-turned again, and I was suddenly presented with a remarkable expanse of green-blue Mediterranean on our port side. Even with all the destruction, the view was spectacular—this must have been an incredible city before the Lebanese decided to commit national suicide. I sat back and relaxed. After a few hundred yards, the cab was shaken by a huge thump and a tremor that was followed almost instantly by a dangerous-sounding explosion some-where behind us. I turned to see brown-black smoke coming from the residential area we'd just left.

"What was that?"

Abu Said pulled onto the sidewalk and stopped. He got out and looked back at the smoke. "Car bomb," he said matter-of-factly. "Dangerous."

"No shit."

He returned to the cab and hunched over the wheel, yanked the door shut, and put the car in gear. "No shit, *habibi*." We ground our way up a steep, narrow street that cut through a hillside urban canyon, then slalomed down the other side, threading the needle between pedestrians and parked cars as a pair of fire trucks, sirens screaming, came careening up the opposite direction heedless of oncoming traffic. Then came another, steeper hill. Finally, radiator smoking, the cab wheezed up in front of the hotel entrance. I gave Said Abu Said a hundred Lebanese pounds. He bowed and grinned. "*Shukran, habibi*. May you have a good stay—and a peaceful one."

"Thank you, Abu Said." I bent over to retrieve my luggage. "I will need a driver for a few days—are you available?"

He nodded affirmatively. "Three hundred American dollars a day—and fifty dollars more each time we cross the Green Line under fire."

I put out my hand. "Two fifty a day—and fifty each time we cross the Green Line under fire, without getting hit."

He laughed. "Done and done. Shall I wait for you now, *habibi?*"

"No—I'll see you tomorrow morning at eight. Today, I want to get settled, then I'd like to go sight-seeing on foot."

I picked up my bags, walked into the Commodore's lobby, and dropped them on the floor by the registration counter. Ahead and to my left I saw a comfortable-looking red-vinyl bar, and glass doors leading to what appeared to be a deck and swimming pool.

The Commodore had a reputation that was worldwide. It was a journalist's hotel in the Old World style: expense-account heaven. Bar bills became "Laundry"; restaurant tabs became "Telex" or "Long Distance." The same thing could be done with gold or jewelry—they could be bought for guests and billed as room charges. Even the wine cellar was re-nowned: the Commodore's sommelier could supply almost anything—so long as he had time to get a label printed up.

I checked in, dropped my bags in a shabby, rear-facing room, hit the bar, had a couple of Bombays, then went out for a stroll.

From the Commodore I walked to Hamra Street, the commercial heart of West Beirut. French paras patrolled the sidewalks, strolling in pairs with submachine guns slung around their necks. Their presence must have been reassuring: Hamra Street was humming. Cars and taxis honked shrill horns in a continual cacophony of caterwauling. Fast-food shops did a brisk business in crusty roast chicken, *shwarma*, and falafel. Juice bars churned out frappés. Storekeepers, long since bombed or shelled out of their shops, piled their wares and plied their trade on the sidewalk.

Despite the peaceful activity, the knots of young men in jeans, leather jackets, and not-so-well-concealed weapons who loitered outside various apartment houses and storefronts gave off the same kind of vibes I'd gotten while watching Mr. Charlie in the Mekong Delta more than a decade earlier. I bought an éclair at a bake shop and was amazed to see what appeared to be a bomb factory in the basement as the shop's cellar door opened fleetingly. A tick of information clicked into place. Beirut was just like Vietnam, where a peaceful hootch often concealed the entrance to a weapons cache in the secret tunnel below. Okay, Lebanese—doom on you. The Sharkman has arrived.

With the help of a map, I navigated my way toward the American University, wandered alongside the gates and walls, then meandered slowly past concrete-shard ruins where bou-gainvillea grew in clumps and occasional street cats, lean and mean-tempered, skedaddled, down to the corniche—the Avenue de Paris—to see where the seven-story American embassy faced the sea.

I walked past the embassy, a relic of the days when embassies were as open and unguarded as public libraries, paused a few minutes to sit and admire the relentless Old Testament sky, uncompromising and obstinately blue—and then re-sumed my stroll. It didn't take long to see that embassy security was a goatfuck. Sandbags had been piled high alongside the driveway to guard against firing from the street. But if terrorists came up the unprotected driveway with a car loaded with TNT, the explosion would be directed into the embassy instead of deflected away from it. And anybody could drive right up to the front door: there were no heavy-duty barriers to keep vehicles out, only lightweight barricades and oil drums filled with sand. Most of the Lebanese guards outside carried sidearms, but nothing more potent. The Marines and their shotguns were inside, where they were least needed.

The rest of the day I wandered the streets, getting the lay of the land between the embassy and the hotel, searching for apartments we could use as safe houses. Problem was, I couldn't read the Arabic "for rent" signs—or even tell if there were any. Dusk fell early, just after 1630, and as the streets got dark, I made my way back to the Commodore and its friendly bar. Up in my room I checked my luggage carefully: it had been searched. That was okay—there was nothing in it to tell anyone about me, other than the fact that I carried no razor, my paperback books were British editions, and I had a blank reporter's notebook. Downstairs, I hadn't even settled onto the stool before the bartender set a double Bombay on the rocks in front of me. My room may have had stained, threadbare carpeting, lousy plumbing, and a sway-back mattress, but the bar was strictly five-star. It's all a matter of priorities—and the Commodore had its priorities straight.

Abu Said was sitting in front of the hotel at eight the next morning, his motor thumping. I jumped into the front seat. "*Yallah*—let's go."

"Where?"

"Coffee. Take me to the best coffee shop you know."

"It is done, *habibi*." Abu Said grinned wetly through his mustache, stomped the accelerator, and wheelied down the hill toward the seafront.

We ran the Coast Road south to Khalde. *Ran* is an understatement. Abu Said drove like a SEAL. The highway was a divided road, and whenever the southbound flow was too slow for him, he jumped the divider, turned on his brights, hit the horn, and drove against the northbound traffic, feinting and weaving up the shoulder and passing lane as cars and trucks swerved to get out of our path. About six clicks south of the airport he turned onto a rutted dirt road, bounced another half click, then screeched to a stop in front of a small, anonymous storefront whose windows were shielded by a double row of sandbags.

"Best coffee in Beirut. My cousin's coffee."

"Terrific. Now, Abu Said, please be so kind as to join me. I need your assistance and your counsel."

That day, the ubiquitous Abu Said helped me find two apartments, one for my "news bureau," the other for my "photographers" and "technicians," who would be arriving the next afternoon. I paid a month's rent, plus another month in baksheesh, the all-encompassing bribe-cum-expediting-fee-cum-gratuity that greased wheels all over the Middle East, and took possession of two sets of keys. I checked out of the Commodore and dropped my bags in the larger of the two flats. And I hired another of Abu Said's endless supply of cousins as a second driver. That gave us two pseudo-Chevys, and two mustached drivers named Abu Said—so I promptly began calling one Taxi Alpha and one Taxi Bravo.

By dusk of day three, the team had arrived intact. I snatched Duke, Larry, Frank, and Baby Rich from the airport, picked up Paul, Snake, Pooster, and Horseface at the Museum Crossing, and trekked out to the Summerland Hotel, which sat near the beach due west of Chatila, and found Jew, Ho-Ho-Ho, and Fingers holding court at the bar. It took me almost two hours to separate them from three delectable young things who wanted to come along for the ride.

The safe houses—safe apartments, actually—couldn't have been better situated. One sat on the corniche not six hundred yards from the American embassy; a four-room flat on the third floor, it looked out onto the Mediterranean, facing north, with a view of Juniyah, the Maronite Christian stronghold. The second apartment was near UNICEF headquarters. It was smaller, but comfortable. It gave us good access to the embassy's back door.

Communications were important. Duke's group had brought a number of secure radios, and we set up three separate networks. One was rigged from apartment to apartment; another, using miniature transceivers, was for on-street use. There was even a portable satellite dish and a SATCOM, so we could talk to JSOC if necessary. Ever careful, Duke had brought a new toy—a hand-held scrambler. To use it, you punched in a scrambling code, then recorded your message onto a tape. You made your call on an open line—you could use pay phones, hotel lines, whatever—then played the tape into the receiver. The receiving party taped the message and used the same numerical code to unscramble the message. The combinations could be changed daily—or even hourly if necessary.

The parameters of our job were tight. The embassy knew a survey team from JSOC was going to be coming in, but the dip-dunk diplo-dinks wanted nothing to do with us. So far as they were concerned, embassy security was A-okay and there was nothing to worry about; 'twas the season to be jolly, and fa-la-la-la-la, la-la-la-la.

Screw 'em—we'd save them in spite of themselves.

I broke us up into two-man teams—swim buddies. Paul and Duke, Snake and Pooster, the Gold Dust Twins, Rich and Ho-Ho-Ho, and Jew and me. The mission was to see if there was a terrorist threat, and if there was, how it could be countered. We knew the Marines were already taking sniper fire from the Shiite slums facing the airport, so I sent Paul and Duke to recon the area from one side, and the Gold Dust Twins to take the opposite point of view for their target assessment. Snake, Pooster, Jew, and I would concentrate on the embassy. The other two pairs would do a general sneak and peek, assessing the mood of the city and trying to locate specific areas of concern.

Specific—shit, the whole city was an area of concern. The following morning Jew and I went for a quiet stroll along the neatly manicured paths that ran through the American University of Beirut, which sat behind the embassy. Jew carried an autofocus camera, and so far as any passersby were concerned, he was just another asshole taking occasional snapshots. What he was really doing, however, was classic target assessment: producing a visual "narrative" showing how unprotected the rear of the embassy was, and how easily it could be breached from every side.

We walked and talked and took pictures for about an hour, then decided to find a place and grab some lunch. Outside a small shop near Bekhaazi Street, Jew turned to me. "Smile . . ." He brought the camera up.

I waved. "Hi, Mom."

He snapped away, and we turned to continue down the street.

In a split second, six teenagers, four with drawn pistols and two with AK-47s, lunged at us from an alleyway, babbling in rapid-fire Arabic, pointing at Jew's camera, and signaling us to stop.

Jew started to react defensively. I stopped him with a flick of an eyebrow—we didn't want any trouble in broad daylight on a crowded street. I raised my hands and put my back against the wall. Jew did the same. "What's up?" I smiled at the gunmen reassuringly. No response. *"Parlez vous français?"*

One of the kids answered me in heavily accented French. "Who are you?"

"Je suis journaliste. Sahafa. Press."

He translated for his friends. They weren't impressed. The AKs pointed at our throats. I noted for the record that the weapons' selector switches were on full automatic fire, and the kids had their fingers on the triggers. I tried to remember how many pounds of pressure it takes to set an AK off. I decided it was a piece of trivia I didn't want to remember.

The French speaker turned back to me. "Your friend took a picture of a secret military installation."

I told Jew what he'd done. "Look ashamed, asshole," I chided.

Jew hung his head and muttered something under his breath. Then he opened the back of the camera, took the film, and pulled it out, exposing the entire roll. "Ask 'em if it's okay now—'cause if it isn't, I'm gonna waste the motherfuckers."

French speaker took Jew's film. The weapons were low-ered. "What installation did we violate?" I asked.

The kid pointed toward the storefront. "Militia live here. Murabitoun."

"That's a secret installation?"

The kid nodded seriously. "The whole street belongs to Murabitoun."

"And the next street?" I pointed west.

He shook his head. "Belongs to Amal—Shia militia," he explained.

"And there?" I indicated eastward.

"One street, Murabitoun. Next street, Syrian National Party." He pointed toward the slums beyond Hamra. "There Hezbollah—Party of God Shia militia."

I inclined my head graciously. *"Shukran. Merci beaucoup."* Jew and I turned and walked away.

"It's like the goddamn South Bronx," Jew said. "Every street is another gang's turf."

By the end of the first week we knew "they" were watching the embassy. What we didn't know was who "they" were. There were too many unhealthy patterns—the same cars coming by at irregular hours; the same bearded faces pausing as if to see how many guards were on duty; the same cabs and trucks probing the side gate and front entrance to test whether or not they'd be stopped.

I set up some patterns of my own. We watched the embassy twenty-four hours a day, using cameras, binoculars, and low-light glasses. Snake and Pooster, who had the graveyard shift, took to coming and going by climbing up and down the outside of the apartment house. That way, they wouldn't disturb the gunmen who often slept in the stairwell, and no one would hear the elevator as they came or went.

From what we could tell, there were roughly two dozen separate armed groups in West Beirut, not counting the MNF, the Israelis, the Syrians, or us. That included militias, private armies, street gangs, just plain thugs, and dyed-in-the-wool terrorists, so we had a full spectrum from which to choose our bad guys.

By the beginning of our second week in Beirut we'd heard half a dozen car bombs go off. We'd rushed to the scene a couple of times to see the extent of the damage. It was considerable. Pack a Mercedes with a hundred kilos of explosives and the same weight in nails and other scrap metal, set it off in a crowded neighborhood at rush hour, and you can do a decent amount of damage.

There is also something innately terrifying about the concept of car bombs. Any car can become one. They are designed to kill innocent people in a horrifying manner; they are almost undetectable without specialized equipment; and they can be set off either with a clock timer, by infrared signals, or with a remote-control radio device.

The array of weaponry available to the allegedly disarmed Beirut militias was awesome. But no tank, or rocket-propelled-grenade launcher, no mortar, or even howitzer, had the slam-bang, horrific impact of a car bomb.

Paul's forays to the shantytown slums of south Beirut also brought a pessimistic prediction. "The Marines are being dragged into a fight they can't finish," he said. Paul explained that the Marines faced Shia and Druse guerrillas. To the south, he said, the Israelis were conducting reconnaissance by gunfire against the Shia slums at Hay al-Sellum. The Marines held the low ground near the airport, while the militias held the high ground in the hills to the east. That in itself was crazy. But the ten-point rules of engagement under which the Marines operated, Paul concluded, were absolute lunacy:

—*When on the post, mobile or foot patrol, keep loaded magazine in weapon, bolt closed, weapon on safe, no round in the chamber.*

—*Do not chamber a round unless told to do so by a commissioned officer unless you act in immediate self-defense where deadly force is authorized.*

"The only instruction they didn't give those poor bastards is, 'When firing starts, bend over, put your head between your legs, and kiss your ass good-bye.' "

Marine security, Paul concluded, was just as bad as the embassy's.

We celebrated Christmas Eve by running our own sneak and peek against the embassy to see how close we could get without being noticed. The answer was not good: Fingers, Duke, and Baby Rich were able to set enough "charges"— we used plastic bottles filled with water—to turn the whole building into a pile of concrete flapjacks, and no one in authority saw or challenged them. Larry and Frank took a piece of plastic pipe the size of a bazooka and worked their way around the beach side of the building, leaving the plastic tube zeroed in on an office where we believed the CIA station was located.

Snake and Pooster climbed the back side of the embassy, edged their way around, and left a four-by-six Post-it note on the outside of a closed window. It read: *The boys was here and fuck you all*. Paul and I reconned the front door. If we'd been murderers, it would have been a slaughter. The Lebanese guards were asleep, the Marines were inside, and the embassy security detail was a joke. Even Egyptians would have done a better job.

We camped out on Christmas Day in the big safe house facing the sea, feasting on roast chicken, french fries, and beer, while the men debated how the tangos would hit the embassy.

"RPGs," Pooster said. "They're the weapons of choice for the region—every militia has hundreds of 'em."

"Plus," Frank added, "with an RPG you can hit from anywhere—break into an apartment anywhere in the neighborhood and zero in on the ambassador's goddamn office."

"Not *his* office," Paul corrected. "His secretary's office—that's the one with the outside window."

"Whatever, Skipper," Pooster said. "What I mean is, there're a lot of 'em, they're easy to use, and they're effective."

"You could coordinate an RPG attack real easy," Baby Rich chimed in. "Hit with twenty, even thirty at a time—that would cause confusion."

Fingers popped the top on a Heineken and took a long, slow swallow. He belched and sighed. "I don't see it."

"See what?" Pooster dipped a drumstick in garlic sauce and chewed.

"RPG attack, Poost. Seems to me, if you're gonna hit an embassy, you want to hit it hard."

"Guerrillas shot at the embassy in El Salvador with RPGs," Snake said.

"They use 'em in the Philippines, too. So what? That don't mean anything." Fingers was adamant. "First, they were guerrillas, not terrorists. Second, they didn't have anything heavier."

"So?" Pooster three-pointed the bone into a wastebasket.

Ho-Ho-Ho weighed in. "I think Fingers is right. RPGs are a possibility, but they got mortars here, too, plus Amal has a bunch of armored personnel carriers the PLO left behind, and a tank or two."

"Hezbollah's got tanks, too," said Duke. "And maybe even a howitzer."

"Shit," said Paul, "the damn Phalangists probably have as much armor as the Lebanese Army—but what does any of that prove?"

"It proves," said Jew, "this place is a frigging powder keg."

Gold Dust Larry sat on the corner windowsill, quietly sucking on a beer and communing with the Mediterranean. He swiveled to cast a melancholy glance at the rest of us. "I'm gonna let you boys in on a little secret," he drawled. "If I was a fucking tango, I wouldn't go around pissing away my tactical fucking surprise with any fucking RPG. You want to get somebody's attention, you hit the motherfucker dead between the eyes with a fucking two-by-four. You build the biggest fucking bang you can get for the buck—and that's a goddamn fucking car bomb, and that's the fucking truth, and that's all she wrote." He turned back to watch his ocean.

I guffawed. "Well, fuck you very much, Chief." I drained my beer. "Gentlemen," I said, "that's the longest comment we've ever heard from Larry—probably the longest observation anyone's ever heard from Larry. So it should be treated with respect."

"Well, he's right," Fingers said.

"Bet your ass he's right," I said. "Car bomb is what they'll use. So let's do some reverse engineering: they want to come in Uncle Sam's back door—and we want to keep 'em out. How do we do it?"

Five days later we had our answer. I'd called back to the techno-wizards on our SATCOM and explained the problem. They sent us two black-box gizmos, and a single page of instructions.

The concept was simple enough: radio-controlled bombs are detonated by sending a signal over a specific frequency. If you broadcast the range of frequencies used by radio-control devices, and you hit an active one, the detonator will activate, and the bomb will go off.

The black boxes had a 1,000-foot range. The question was, did they work.

There was only one way to find out. Paul and I each took one and packed them inside nylon rucksacks, then he and Fingers, and Larry and I, went for leisurely drives through

West Beirut. I drove with Abu Said Alpha; Paul took Abu Said Bravo.

We drove slowly. Larry sat in the backseat, an attaché case that had been specially fitted to hold an HK MP5K submachine gun resting easily on his lap. To fire the weapon, all Larry had to do was press a trigger on the attaché's handle. The attaché bore the logo of a TV news organization. I sat in front, the knapsack on my knees, the black box inside switched on.

We drove along the Corniche al Mazraa to the northern edge of Fakahani, the district in which the PLO had its offices during its long occupation of Lebanon. Now, the least-damaged buildings had been occupied by new tenants, Lebanese Muslims. According to Abu Said, many of them were poor Shiites. From there, we'd go south toward Bir Hassan and Bir Abed, two of the poorer Shia neighborhoods. It seemed a likely place for bomb makers to live.

"What you want first?" Abu Said asked.

"To show my colleague the old PLO offices," I said. "He is a television producer from America, a very important man. What they call a big gun." I said it with a straight face, too.

"Ah—big gun." The Lebanese grunted. "I will take you."

We turned off the Corniche, edging toward the warren of bombed-out houses, bunkers, and offices that had once been home to Yasir Arafat's legions. The streets, still strewn with debris and massive chunks of concrete, were nonetheless filled with people.

Abu Said pointed to a charred house on the right. "Here was one of Arafat's offices."

Larry grunted.

"And there—across the street—more PLO offices."

Larry peered through the open window. "Who lives here now?"

"Shia live here. Shia who lost their homes."

We circled the block while Abu Said pointed out more of the PLO's former sites. Then he turned south again, and we moved toward the old Sabra camp.

Two blocks ahead, a three-story building suddenly erupted like a volcano. A large red fireball consumed the house; the roar of the explosion was deafening; the shock wave kicked our taxi a foot in the air.

"Jesus—" Larry ducked onto the floor as a shard of concrete slammed into the car's roof.

"Turn the car around and wait for me here." I jumped out and ran in the direction of the explosion. Larry followed, briefcase at the ready. The closer I got the hotter it became. Flames were everywhere. Half a dozen autos had been tossed into the air like matchsticks; where the apartment house had been, a crater perhaps thirty feet deep now sat, filled with burning rubble. Dozens of Lebanese, some of them in pieces, lay in the street. Two men struggled to open the door of a burning station wagon in which two women were trapped. As the flames rose higher, they abandoned their efforts; people watched, sickened and repulsed but still unable to turn away, as the women were consumed.

Sirens and horns sounded in the distance. A pair of pickup trucks with 20mm Triple-A cannons bolted to their beds careened onto the street, two gunners dressed—somewhat bizarrely, I thought, for gunners—in short, padded black leather jackets and designer jeans, firing blindly into the air. They must have thought there'd been an Israeli bombing attack.

I grabbed Larry by the shoulder and we made our way back to the cab. "Was that real, or was it Memorex?" I said as we shouldered our way through the hysterical Lebanese.

"Does it really matter, boss?"

I paused to look back at the carnage. "Not anymore it doesn't."

My request for a meeting with a senior American official was granted, but grudgingly. To maintain operational security, only Paul and I would show up, and we'd try to change our appearance just in case the watchers were snapping pictures or videotaping the comings and goings.

We were shown into a huge office on one of the upper floors. After a few minutes the official and an aide arrived. He was another Central Casting diplomat: tall, gray haired, and distinguished looking in an aristocratic way. He clearly didn't want to be at this meeting, and he showed it.

Introductions were made. He gave Paul and me a cold handshake, then sat on a couch and waited for us to make our presentation.

I'd brought our black box, as well as some evidence we'd assembled about the state of the embassy's security. I got to the point right away: "Sir, my men and I have spent almost three weeks surveying your site, and we believe you're vulnerable to attack."

"If that is your opinion, Commander, I assure you I will take it under strict advisement."

"We've been keeping tabs on your security, and it has gaping holes."

He cleared his throat. "Somehow, Commander, this embassy has managed to withstand the Lebanese civil war, which has gone on unabated since 1975. We have endured the PLO, the Syrians, and the Israelis. We are still here. Now you have come and spent three weeks in country, and—instant experts that you are—you tell me that my security apparatus has 'gaping holes.' Let me remind you, Commander, that I know this country, and these people, and I know and trust my staff. The security of this embassy is airtight. That is my position."

"But the situation has changed in the past few weeks, sir. Our survey indicates that Americans are beginning to be seen as allies of the Maronites, not as honest brokers protecting all the Lebanese. There's resentment in the Shia, Sunni, and Druse communities, and—"

He cut me off. "I am well aware, Commander, of the political situation here. And while there is some flux in the situation, our security posture has no need of change."

"With all respect, sir, I think your situation is about to become all fluxed up."

The diplomat flushed. "Commander, there's no need—"

"Our survey indicates a strong possibility that the embassy will be the focus of a car-bomb attack in the near future. Therefore, I'd strongly recommend, sir, that you reconfigure the access to the embassy, bolster the armed presence on your perimeters, and employ devices such as these." I indicated the box.

"What is that?"

"It's a radio transmitter that broadcasts the frequencies commonly used to detonate car bombs. It has a range of about one thousand feet. We suggest that you set a pair of these on the roof. That way, any radio-controlled car bombs in the vicinity will detonate before they get close enough to do any damage to the embassy."

He looked at me incredulously. "You mean, we'd destroy the car bomb before it got to the embassy?"

"Yes, sir."

"But that would cause casualties."

"Well, yes, sir, but—"

"That is unacceptable," he said.

"What is?"

"Causing casualties. We can't cause casualties. Indiscriminate casualties would be bad for our diplomatic image."

"Pardon my French, but screw your diplomatic image. We're talking about keeping you and your people alive, sir."

"Not like that." The senior official looked at the black box distastefully. "Such things aren't . . . correct. That's not a proper way to do business, Commander. Such devices would be unfair to the Lebanese population, and I refuse to have anything to do with them."

He stood up. "Now, if you'll excuse me. Thank you for coming, Commander. I hope you and your men have a safe journey home."

Well, bugger him and screw all diplomats. That same day we packed our toys, drove through the Marine lines, flashed Navy IDs, ferried out to the USS *Independence*, and were COD'd to Sigonella, then back to Norfolk.

The senior American official wasn't one of the sixty-three people killed when, on April 18, about ninety days after we left Beirut, a suicide bomber driving a truck laden with explosives turned his seven-story diplomatic fantasyland into rubble. He escaped with hardly a scratch, which says something about the luck schmucks sometimes enjoy. Car bombs have backup radio detonators just in case the suicide drivers get cold feet at the moment of truth. Had our black boxes been on his roof, the bomb would, in all likelihood, have been detonated before it was driven through the pair of flimsy barricades and right up to the embassy's front door.

But as he said when we briefed him, our black boxes might have caused Lebanese civilian casualties. And God forbid that Lebanese die when Americans can die instead.

Chapter

21

I TURNED OVER COMMAND OF SEAL TEAM SIX TO CAPTAIN Bob Gormly on July 5, 1983. It was not my idea to leave, but I'd had a three-year stint (most commands run two years), and I began to sense through a series of subtle hints that the Navy wanted me elsewhere.

How subtle were those hints? One example. Letter ratings on fitreps are similar to school grades. A is the best, F is failing. Ted Lyon regularly gave me B's and C's. He shivved me with comments like, *"While still under my administrative control, Cdr Marcinko is under the operational control of the Commander, Joint Operations Command and it is the latter who can best say if the achievements of Seal Six are worth retaining a commanding officer who flaunts authority and impacts negatively (outside his command) on good order and discipline."*

Vice Admiral J. D. Johnson, the man who ran SURFLANT (SURface Force AtLANTic), had regularly taken Ted's side, until Dick Scholtes came for our uniform inspection. After Scholtes's visit, Dave Johnson's attitude changed. He became supportive and helpful—and for every nasty fitrep Ted wrote me, Admiral Johnson filed a dissenting report. *"SEAL TEAM*

SIX is a highly classified command with direct White House/ JCS interest," Johnson's response said. *"There is no other organization exactly like it. Thus its structure, procedures and training had to be conceived without benefit of role model. . . . He has had to overcome the inevitable inertia of a 'system' geared to less urgent requirements. He has often had to go outside the system to meet the stringent time requirements of SEAL TEAM SIX development. Inevitably, he has raised eyebrows. I know of no way he could have avoided this. Doers and talkers often disagree. . . . It is unfortunate that the highly classified nature of this project, coupled with a confusing chain of command, should have caused Commander Marcinko to be evaluated less than enthusiastically by his immediate superior."*

But all of Vice Admiral Johnson's praise couldn't help in the long run. The SEAL establishment wanted me gone. So, on my final fitness report as CO of Six, I received H's and I's—grades so low they were off the scale. You get an H if the chief of naval operations catches you making the beast with two backs in *his* bed, with *his* wife, on *their* anniversary. You get an I for deflowering the CNO's 14-year-old daughter on a pool table in the local saloon to the cheers of an appreciative crowd of horny SEALs.

I got my H's and I's because, by 1983, I'd done more than ride roughshod over Ted Lyon. What I'd done with Ted, I'd repeated with the NAVSPECWARGRU ONE commodores in Coronado, Dave Schaible, and his successor, Cathal "Irish" Flynn. By 1983, I'd pissed off, threatened, alienated, provoked, offended, and screwed with the SpecWar commodores on both coasts. So far as I was concerned, I'd acted justifiably—I'd had a mission to fulfill. In their view, I'd gone past the point of no return. I took their best men. While they scrambled for pennies, I—in their eyes—lighted cigars with hundred-dollar bills. I got all the nicest toys. Worst of all, I played havoc with their system. I treated my lowest-ranking seaman with more respect than I did most SpecWar captains and commodores. I ate and drank with my enlisted men and chiefs; I threw loud parties; I said "fuck" to flag-rank officers.

There were phone calls and memos and meetings. A decision was reached—and in June 1983, I was advised I was about to be replaced, and told who my replacement would be. I had always hoped Paul Henley would follow in my footsteps. It was not to be. Less than four weeks later, I was gone. I had no say in the matter. My departure had been decided by the Navy's chain of command, at the instigation of the SpecWar commodores and their chiefs of staff. I had no vote. Nor did I have any clout: my commander was an Army brigadier general. He could protect me while I was CO of Six. But he couldn't stop the Navy from removing me. Doom on you, Demo.

There were few of the usual celebrations that precede change of command, and none of the nostalgia, esprit de corps, and camaraderie. I received no plaques nor any of the other goodies usually given to departing COs because my troops didn't know that I was going in time to have them made up.

There was no red carpet, no chief boatswain's mate piping me ashore, no ship's bell, no white gloves, no swords, no spit and polish at my ceremony. I'd had the big parade ground and a Navy band serenading me when I left SEAL Team Two at Little Creek. This change of command was held behind closed doors at our top-secret facility at Dam Neck. I was in civilian clothes. I spoke for less than ten minutes, recapping some of the physical and bureaucratic hardships we at Six had been through together.

Then Bob and I read our orders. I lied when I came to the part where I said I was ready to turn over my command. It didn't matter. The words were said. The transfer of power was accomplished. It was over. I felt empty, alone, betrayed, enraged. All, I believed, with good cause: in many ways I'd spent most of my adult life preparing myself to command a unit like SEAL Team Six and lead it into action. I'd achieved a great portion of my dream—I'd conceived, designed, built, equipped, and trained what I believed to be the best group of warriors in the nation's history. But now I was being pushed aside before I was able to accomplish the goal I had always considered the most fundamental—leading my men into battle. I felt decapitated.

I took a handful of people to the Dam Neck O Club for a few cold drinks, and then—I was gone.

Yes, I am often abrasive and obnoxious. But even my enemies will admit that SEAL Team Six was the best-trained, deadliest, and most capable counterterror unit ever formed. Yes, we broke the rules. Hell—we shattered the rules and tossed them out the window. But the rules we threw out were rules that had been written for carrier battle groups and nuclear submarines, not seven-man squads. As SEALs we'd had to write our own book of rules—an improvised Bible of unconventional warfare doctrine. That had been hard enough in a system that has historically been harder to turn around than a battleship at full speed. The problem was compounded by SEAL Team Six, which not only rewrote the rules of the conventional Navy, but also revised the hell out of the SEAL book, too. SEAL Team Six didn't fit *anywhere* within the Navy's system. We were orphans, outcasts, pariahs—and I was the chief pariah.

Once I'd been moved aside, things started to change at Six. Bob enforced a Ted Lyons–style dress code: no Fu Manchu mustaches; no ponytails; no earrings. Hair could touch the collar but not descend below it. The men I'd selected for their dirtbag looks now began to resemble yuppie scum.

More crucial to the success of SEAL Team Six's mission, however, was the change in leadership style that Bob established. He was a passive, not an active, CO. I had always led from the front. Bob led from behind. He stayed in his office and sent his men to the field. He did not train with them. He did not drink with them. He did not socialize with them. Under Bob Gormly, unit integrity did not extend to the CO.

I heard about these unsettling developments, but from a distance. I had thirty days' leave coming, and I wanted to take it all. I couldn't remember the last time I'd had thirty days' leave. My wife was visiting her family in New Jersey, and I spent the month slapping a fresh coat of paint on our house. The exercise did me good—it helped work out some of the frustration I was feeling. Then, rested and tanned, I drove to Washington. The Navy still owed me a year at the National War College, and it was time to take them up on it.

Except, I wasn't going to be allowed to go to the National War College. No one told me I was about to be barred. As a matter of fact, if it hadn't been for some chiefs who whispered what was about to happen, I would have appeared at Ft. McNair to register and suffered the ignominy of being told publicly that the Navy had removed my name from the list of attendees. But my SEAL Team Six intelligence network was still operational. So I was warned, and I never showed up. Instead, I went to the Military Personnel Command and confronted a rear admiral I'd known for some years. I'll call him Dave. He didn't look happy to see me.

"I hear I'm not going to be allowed to go to the National War College."

Dave hemmed and he hawed and finally he spoke. "Well, Dick, policy is not to send people who don't have a ninety-five percent chance of promotion to captain."

"Does that include me?"

"It appears that way. You have an Article 15—an official letter of reprimand—on your record."

"I'm appealing it. I was reprimanded for an auto accident in which I wasn't even driving. My driver got into the fender bender, not me."

"The question of who's at fault isn't applicable. The letter says your driver had been on duty for more than eight hours—that's working him too long."

"We didn't punch clocks at Six, Dave."

"I know. But a rule is a rule. You broke it, and you got caught. Besides, that's all water under the bridge. Bottom line is that your appeal hasn't been honored. You won't attend the War College."

"That's funny."

"Why?"

"Because I haven't written my appeal yet. How the hell can they not honor something that hasn't been written?"

Dave smiled weakly. "Hey, Commander, it's above my pay grade."

"So screw me, right?"

He shrugged. "Listen, Dick, you have a super record. You punched good tickets. I can get you something great in Hawaii. Or Norfolk—snare you a staff job until 1988. Then you retire with thirty years on the job."

"Sounds real cushy."

"It'd be better—we're talking country club. Norfolk would be perfect. It's close to home for you. You can go in late and leave early—you'd be home sitting by your pool by fifteen hundred every day. Build a real estate portfolio. Get yourself set up for retirement."

"No offense, Dave, but fuck you. I'm not going home to die. Not yet."

"It's up to you. But if you were smart, you'd take my advice."

"Shit, you've known me for fifteen years and I've never been very smart, Admiral—that's my whole goddamn problem. I'm just one of those assholes who likes to work."

My old boss Ace Lyons had been transferred back to the Pentagon. For the past two years Ace, who had been promoted to vice admiral—three stars—had been commander of the Second Fleet, and his area of responsibility had run from the Caribbean to the North Sea. Now, he was given Bill Crowe's job as deputy chief of naval operations for plans and policy. Ace Lyons was, in effect, the ops boss for the entire U.S. Navy.

I went straight to his cabin and cried on his shoulder. He, sea daddy that he was, sat me down on his lap, patted my head, wiped my nose, and made sympathetic clucking sounds. Then he drop-kicked me in the ass and encouraged me to find some work to do.

By the fall of 1983, Ace saw to it that I'd been tucked safely away in a crowded corner of the Pentagon's Navy Command Center, a bustling, crowded series of rooms on the fourth floor D ring, where I worked as one of the sweat hogs who kept constant track of naval movements and tracked crises worldwide. One day in September, I glanced up to see a gaggle of intelligence squirrels come out of their SCIF and start poring over a series of nautical charts on the wall. A little red light went off in my head. Normally, these guys didn't leave their desks unless they'd just won the Super Bowl pool, or some DefCon Four international disaster was imminent. Being September, it was too early for Super Bowl.

I snuck around the room and bullied my way into the group. "Hey, guys! What country are we losing today?" My humor was not appreciated. But before I was shooed away, one of the squirrels screwed up, and I heard a word I wasn't supposed to hear: "Grenada."

I tried my version of witty repartee. "Grenada? What's going on there—carnival?"

No response.

RICHARD MARCINKO

"Come on, guys—if there's the slightest chance of pussy, I wanna be included."

Silence.

I departed with a polite "Up yours," directed at their backs, and headed for my desk—and the secure telephone thereon. They should never have put me in the command center with a secure line and a computerized directory that had priority calling. It made stealing information too easy. Three hours, seven chiefs, and a bunch of junior officers later, I had a pretty good idea of what was about to happen. We were going to invade Grenada—and SEAL Team Six would be part of the operation.

Shit! I'd relinquished my command less than ninety days before. I still considered Six *my* unit. Goddamn it—*I* had staffed it and equipped it. *I'd* trained the men. *I'd* honed them into the best shoot-and-looters in the world. And now, someone else would be taking them to war. That wasn't fucking right. There was no justice in the world.

Six minutes later I was in Ace's cabin begging for the opportunity to deploy in some capacity, any capacity—to help, advise, observe, report—anything other than sit on my ass in a windowless room and listen to reports coming over the radio. "I did that before, Ace—during Desert One, and I swore I'd never be stuck like that again."

Vice Admiral James A. Lyons, Jr., put it to me as delicately as I deserved: "Fuck you, asshole. You stay put. Five minutes after you got out the goddamn door, you'd start believing you were in charge and there'd be hell to pay. Goddammit, Dick, you're *not* in charge—you were relieved. You work here now—for me. So get your shit-for-brains ass back to the NCC where you belong."

Noting the humongous pout on my face, Ace lessened the blow. "Okay, okay—look, Dick, keep up to speed on this. I'll assign you as my primary briefer to SECNAV on Grenada."

Brief, schmief. Tail between my legs, I went back to my corner and glowered. But I also kept on top of things. The more I discovered about Grenada, the more I cringed. Talk about your world-class goatfucks.

How was it planned? Badly. As best I could reconstruct

326

it—and as I briefed Secretary of the Navy John Lehman—
here's what happened.

Where is Grenada, anyway, Admiral?

*Damned if I know. Get a map, Captain, I heard the name
once—maybe it's in one of our* Islands *Op Plans.*

*Yes, here it is in the atlas, sir, but damn—we don't have any
tactical maps, just nautical charts.*

*Well, go downtown to a travel agency and find some damn
tourist maps. They'll have to do.*

And that's what they fucking did.

*Here's the intel package, Admiral CINCLANT/CINC-
LANTFLT.*

*Damn. What the hell are U.S. citizens doing going to medical
school there? What the fuck are they learning, witchcraft? Voo-
doo? Hey—what the fuck are all those goddamn Cubans doing
there? Why didn't we know about them before? How did we
miss that? What a way to fuck up my weekend! Goddammit,
Captain, my wife and I were entered in the doubles golf tour-
nament, and that ain't gonna happen. I'm in deep shit at home.*

*Well, sir, there's another itsy-bitsy wrinkle, just developed,
too. Seems we believe these here Cubans are holding those
there students as hostages on that there island.*

Well, who the hell does hostages, Captain?

JSOC does, sir. Delta Force. SEAL Team Six.

*Well, get on the fucking phone and call them. Oh—and
Captain, call the Marines. They do islands, too. Iwo Jima,
Guadalcanal, Okinawa—you remember. As I recall, we've got
that Marine Amphibious Ready Group (ARG) just about to
head across the pond to Beirut. I got a great idea. Let's steam
'em down to Grenada and give 'em some action on the way.
Get mud on their boots. Let 'em piss in the bushes. Then they'll
be ready for those ragheads in the Med.*

In one glorious, frenzied weekend, a plan was dusted off,
shined up, squeegeed, and modified to include JSOC, and—
voilà—an engagement was born!

But on every C-141 StarLifter flying Army Rangers south,
on each EC-130 C³I command and control aircraft, on every
LSD and LST of the Marine ARG, on every U.S. military
plane, chopper, or ship, a malevolent stowaway had managed
to creep on board unnoticed. His name was Murphy, and his
word was law.

—JSOC was well organized and trained for hostage-rescue operations. JSOC units had special equipment, support assets, and best of all, their own secure communications network. *MURPHY: JSOC units couldn't talk to the conventional Task Force commander (afloat), or to the Marines.*

—SEAL Team Six was assigned an air-sea rendezvous with a U.S. naval man-of-war off Grenada. *MURPHY: no one told the pilot he wasn't over target when he signaled the drop. No one advised the SEALs that there were heavy surface winds and high waves. No one checked to see whether or not the ship was in the proper location.*

The result was that four highly trained members of my SEAL Team Six family drowned at sea. They weren't killed in action. In fact, what made their deaths criminal was that they didn't get a chance to kill anyone at all. They jumped with more than a hundred pounds of equipment into 12-foot seas and drowned. There is no fucking justice in this world. I briefed SECNAV Lehman on their deaths. I told him about Bob Shamberger, a SEAL Team Six plank owner. He was a chief, a team leader, a real father to his crew. He burped their babies, bailed them out of jail, helped them with personal and professional problems, and he died because of Murphy. And I told him about Kodiak, who'd just become a father. The kid was proud as a peacock that there was now an heir apparent, another future SEAL Six member. He, too, was dead at Murphy's hands. Two other shooters died with them. Four SEAL Six warriors now stand an eternal watch on the ocean floor, waiting for that next recall to muster for another war.

—Local island governments were advised of the pending action in advance, despite the fact that it was common knowledge that most of the island governments had been penetrated for years by the DGI—Cuban intelligence. *Señor Murphy got the word early and told the Cubans on Grenada, so they were ready for the gringos.*

—The CIA didn't have dedicated full-time agents or operatives on Grenada. But Christians in Action knew what to do. Murphy saw to it that the clandestine ops planning was taken over by a couple of veterans of the goatfucked Desert One operation—Lieutenant Colonel Dick Gadd, who had retired, and active USAF colonel Bob Dutton (both of whom would later go on to greater glory as part of the Iran-contra scandal).

Mr. Common Sense says, "The last time these guys tried to put an op together, it didn't work."

Murphy says, "Not to worry—they can handle it."

Mr. Common Sense says, "But they're Air Force officers and the Cubans are on the ground."

Murphy says, "Whaddya, whaddya—I told ya, they can handle it."

—On the primary airborne assault, the lead StarLifter, with armed-to-the-teeth KATN Rangers on board, screwed up its approach because the plane's CARP—Computerized Airborne Release Point—system malfunctioned. So Plane No. 1 circled, and the Rangers in the second C-141 jumped first. *MURPHY: the second plane was filled with the clerks and jerks—the Ranger support company, whose weapons probably weren't even loaded.*

—An Air Force general in charge of the delivery of the chopper support elements for Delta and SEALs apparently decided that he shouldn't violate the noise abatement restrictions on an adjacent island and leave before dawn. He didn't want to wake anybody up. Besides, the general probably figured, that way the SpecWarriors could assault their targets in broad daylight and see them better. The results, which Murphy loved, included large numbers of WIAs and damaged choppers.

—SEALs assaulted, and successfully took over, the island's radio station. After neutralizing the enemy-held site they radioed that their mission was complete, and where were the troops to whom they'd turn the facility over?

Troops? You want someone to come out and actually take possession of your objective? Sorry, Lieutenant, that's not part of the plan. Why don't you and your men disengage and get back to your ships.

And how should we do that, sir?

Why not swim, Lieutenant?

And that's exactly what they fucking did.

Even after the island had been secured, Mr. Murphy didn't quit. Somehow, he tricked the Task Force commander, Vice Admiral Joe Metcalf, into trying to ship home too many war souvenir AK-47 automatic rifles. Disclosure of Metcalf's gaffe in the press cost him his fourth star and forced him into premature retirement.

As I scored it for SECNAV Lehman, the primary victor in Operation Just Cause was Señor Murphy. Even though the medical students were freed without casualties, four SEALs died for no reason at all, command and control was a complete fiasco, the shooters from Delta and SEAL Team Six had been used as shock troops instead of surgical SpecWarriors, scores of casualties had been sustained through carelessness and stupidity, and the Air Force had functioned more like a trade union of elevator operators than a combat force of pilots. It was enough to make me sick.

Early in 1984, I was summoned to Ace's cabin. "You know what really gave me headaches at Second Fleet?" he asked.

"Visiting congressmen?"

"Don't be a smart-ass, Dick. I'm talking real headache material."

"No, sir."

"All right, I'll tell you. It was the fact that the Navy, as an institution, is so focused on the Soviet threat that we don't take the time or energy to deal with other, perhaps equally dangerous, potential adversaries."

I nodded. I hadn't been CO of SEAL Team Six for the past three years for nothing. "Terrorism."

"Bright boy." He drummed his knuckles on his desk. "We're a peacetime Navy, Dick, and we think like a peacetime Navy. That makes for liabilities when it comes to dealing with terrorism. The Germans, the Italians, the French, the Brits—they all deal with terrorism on a daily basis. The British Navy doesn't just study the Soviet threat—it considers the IRA threat as well. The French have to worry about Basque terrorists and Direct Action. The Germans—Red Army Faction and Baader-Meinhof. Italians? Red Brigades. Meanwhile, we just go blithely along. Then all of a sudden the shit hits the fan—some asshole blows up the embassy in Beirut, or we get intelligence that the Iranians are going to target the Sixth Fleet with kamikaze drones or remote-controlled boats, and we go ape shit, because we're not prepared."

"Well, Admiral," I said, "one of the biggest problems I

faced at Six was convincing the goddamn chain of command that counterterror was something the Navy needed."

"What was the usual reaction?"

"A lot of smoke and mirrors. Most COs were more concerned with my playing on their turf than they were about whether or not their HQ was going to be blown up by some raghead. It was as bad as Vietnam. You know, me and my platoon would show up at some Special Forces camp way out in the boonies, and the goddamn CO would start bellyaching about the fact that we were eating his rations and using his potable water, and God forbid we needed any bullets or frags. It was like, 'Are we fighting the same enemy, or what?' "

"Precisely." A wry smile came over Ace's face. "That is exactly the problem."

He stood up and began to pace. "The system," he said, "tends to be static, unmovable, inflexible. That is dangerous. We, as commanders, tend to react, instead of initiate. That, too, is dangerous. Why dangerous? Because those conditions lead to complacency. And complacency is the worst fucking enemy the military can ever have."

"Aye-aye, sir."

"You bet your ass 'aye-aye, sir.' " Ace put both hands palm down on his desk and leaned forward, a proud preacher behind his lectern. "The bottom line, my boy, is that we're not prepared. The Navy is not fucking prepared. The Navy has thirty fucking manuals about community fucking relations, but not a single fucking piece of paper about what to do if we're faced with the possibility of a suicide bomber, or a remote-controlled speedboat filled with Semtex. We stamp millions of papers Top Fucking Secret, but our most sensitive installations are open to attack twenty-four hours a day."

I began to see his point.

"Look," Ace continued, just beginning to hit his stride, "who's in charge of Navy security? Bureaucrats. Dip-shit idiots. They think of everything passively. 'How many locks do you have?' 'How many feet of chain do you use to secure your back gate every night?' 'How many checklists do you have?' That's no goddamn way to conduct security, Dick."

He pounded his desk. "You can't lead people to change their thinking about terrorism—you have to *push* them. That's why I want to shake up the whole system. That's why

I want to rattle the Navy's cage like it's never been rattled before. I want our base commanders to see how goddamn vulnerable they really are. I want to stick it to them—and have 'em *learn* from the experience, learn something they won't put in a file drawer and forget. I want an end to all the goddamn complacency. This threat is real. I know it. You know it. And it's about time *they* knew it, too."

He looked at me with the same ecstatic, sinister expression master chiefs get when they're plotting some new and malevolently insidious way to play mind games on unsuspecting officers. "Go write me a goddamn memo. Design me a unit to test the Navy's vulnerabilities against terrorists. Come back with it next month. Now, get the hell out of here and go to work."

I called it Red Cell, although it was formally on the books as OP-06D. It was originally classified somewhere above top secret. There were fourteen plank owners in the unit, three officers and eleven enlisted men—one platoon, two boat crews, seven pairs of swim buddies. It was a classic SEAL design.

Thirteen of us were from SEAL Team Six. The sole outsider was a baby-faced, red-haired New York Irish dirtbag named Steve Hartman, who'd won two Silver Stars on classified missions in Laos and North Vietnam as a Force Recon Marine. Hartman wasn't an operator in the formal, SpecWar definition of the word—he was neither Special Forces nor a SEAL. He was, however, an evil-minded mother whose talents included lock-picking, motorcycle racing, parachuting, and saloon brawling. He had black belts in three different forms of karate, and he'd had ample opportunity to put them all to good use.

Hartman was the only one of us except me who'd ever eaten raw monkey brain. He also had a Mark-1-Mod-Zero New Yorker's smart mouth, which he'd acquired in the proper way: sitting at his maternal grandmother's knee. Grandma Noel ran a cop's saloon in Jackson Heights, a neighborhood in Queens where they know how to bend an elbow. She kept a baseball bat behind the bar—and could use it.

You had to like Hartman. He may not have been a SEAL, but he spoke Marine, which meant he swore like a chief, and he'd been stationed on nuclear subs. That meant he could always take point—after all, he was the one who glowed in the dark. Best of all, since we maintained the old SEAL Six tradition of shooting for beers and lunch, he became (until his marksmanship improved, which took about a month) a constant source of food and drink for the rest of the men.

From Six, I stole Lieutenant Commander Duke as Red Cell's XO, and Lieutenant Trailer Court. I would have liked Paul Henley along for the ride, but he'd been assigned elsewhere and wasn't available. The enlisteds included Pooster the Rooster, Baby Rich, Horseface, Snake, Cheeks, Ho-Ho-Ho, Gold Dust Twins Frank and Larry, a guy I called Minkster, a wiseass known as Artie F, and my favorite corpsman-cum-weapons-expert, Doc Tremblay. They didn't have to be coaxed very hard to come play with me, either. Bob Gormly had turned Six into a bureaucracy. There were fewer hours training and more spent doing paperwork, getting haircuts, and playing touch football. The CO frowned on the Team's drinking and partying the way the guys were used to doing. Snake wanted to wear earrings again. Baby Rich, who thought all officers were assholes, complained loudly about all the paperwork. Word came back that if he was unhappy he could leave. He left—and floated right into my arms. The others heard I was putting a new unit together and drifted in, one by one—Daddy, Daddy, can I play, too?

It was a classic case of the ships deserting the sinking rat.

Besides, I had the perfect job for my favorite dirtbags. After almost a year of preparation, staffing memos, and bureaucratic infighting, I was able to assemble my troops and say the secret words: "We're gonna be terrorists." For these nonconformist warriors, it was the perfect assignment: except for maintaining their SEAL qualifications in diving, parachuting, and demolition, we were on our own. There was no formal training cycle, no organized program. Each man was responsible for keeping himself fit and capable.

My personal situation was sweet, too. Regardless of the H's and I's on my fitreps, I'd finally been frocked for captain in February 1985. My record—over which there was some controversy—was scrutinized by Ace Lyons's legal aide, Captain Morris Sinor. Sinor spent hundreds of hours over virtually five months examining my fitreps, balancing out my pluses and minuses. In his view (and despite intense, antagonistic lobbying by the East and West Coast SpecWar commodores, as well as a large contingent of captains and one- and two-star admirals I'd wrangled with) I'd earned the right to be promoted. Ace, going by the book, sent Sinor's findings to Admiral Ron Hays, the vice chief of naval operations, who, after his staff concurred with Sinor's findings, approved my promotion. Later, Ace would tell me, "Dick, this is probably the one time in the past few years when the system absolutely worked to your benefit." He wasn't far from wrong, either.

Temporary or not, I was a four-striper. And I had clout: I worked for Ace Lyons, and—through him—for the CNO. I interpreted that to mean that I took no orders and brooked no shit from anyone else. Full of myself—as immortal as before Risher's death—I felt my unit was immune to the apparatchiks, the bean counters, and that virulent strain of assholia that affected much of the Navy. So far as I was concerned, there wasn't a one-, two-, three-, or four-star admiral except the CNO who could lay a glove on us. My friends accused me of living in a fantasy world—which suited me just fine.

Red Cell was assigned to the Pentagon, but our real headquarters was a bar on Duke Street East called Shooter McGee's, where the platoon assembled almost nightly to drink, brawl, and play head games with each other. There was little else to do: by 1985 my wife and I had separated. It was the right decision. Kathy and I had grown apart. We didn't have anything in common anymore. I was focused entirely on my work, which meant I traveled most of the time. When I finally went home to Virginia Beach—Kathy had refused to make another move to Washington—I preferred the company of other SEALs to my wife's companionship, so I'd find excuses to come home late and leave early. I spent a lot of time at the half dozen Virginia Beach bars where SEALs hung out. Indeed, dinner at the Marcinko household—the few times I was around—was eaten in awkward, painful silence. Our being together was so abysmal that Kathy probably welcomed my absences. The kids were grown and could accept the rift.

We talked it over, and I moved out. She kept the house in Virginia Beach and saw all our old friends. I moved into a studio apartment in Old Town Alexandria and began a bachelor's existence. The place was small, but it was convenient to the Pentagon—and to our informal HQ at Shooter's. Snake and his wife, Kitty, even rented an apartment directly across Duke Street from Shooter's, a two-bedroom penthouse, which they shared with Pooster the Rooster. Most nights, Pooster and Snake would scale the outside of the building to get home. The climb often became a race on which the rest of us would bet as we watched them scramble from the Shooter McGee parking lot. If Snake and Pooster were coming home at what Kitty determined was an unacceptable hour—which was often—she'd increase the level of difficulty by locking the terrace doors, which forced them to hang outside by their fingers while they jimmied the windows. When that happened, volunteers would sometimes make the climb to help out the hapless SEALs.

If Shooter's was Red Cell's HQ, the world was our playground. We could act like real terrorists: travel incognito, smuggle our weapons aboard commercial flights, scope out the targets before we struck, then buy the materials for our bombs at hardware stores or steal what we needed from Navy bases, improvise the demolition charges, and build the bombs ourselves. Finally, when we were ready, we'd phone a series of threats to the installation and stage our strikes. (Playing terrorists is nothing new for Frogmen. The very first class of them, at Ft. Pierce, Florida, in 1943—they were called S&Rs, or Scouts and Raiders, back then—staged a "graduation" infiltration exercise in which they kidnaped the admiral in charge of the Seventh Naval District Headquarters in Miami. And that was during a full *wartime* alert!)

Occasionally we would use military transportation to get to our target. But for the most part, we'd be like Chairman Mao Tse-Tung's revolutionary guerrillas, "moving through the masses like a fish through water." In fact, one of Chief of Naval Operations Admiral James Watkins's major concerns was whether or not we could carry enough equipment with us on civilian aircraft. There was no need for him to worry. I proved it late one autumn afternoon. I had just returned from Los Angeles, where I'd been doing a quick security survey, and Ace ordered me to get myself up to the CNO's cabin double time.

I appeared in my jeans, workshirt, blazer, and running

shoes and was ushered inside immediately. Admiral Watkins was sitting behind his desk. Ace sat facing him.

I saluted. "Sir?"

Watkins looked up at me. "I'm concerned about your OP-06/Delta group flying on commercial airlines, Captain. The new security arrangements at most airports would preclude your being able to move the Cell efficiently, especially as Ace tells me you'll be carrying weapons and equipment."

"I don't think so, sir."

"Why not?"

"Well, Admiral"—I reached into the crotch of my jeans, retrieved a loaded, snub-nosed .38-caliber revolver, and laid it on the CNO's desk. "It so happens I just now flew commercial from L.A. . . ." Now, I removed my belt. Concealed in the buckle was a three-inch dagger. "And I was carrying"—from my back pocket I produced a pair of handcuffs—"all of this." I slipped a collapsible, spring-loaded sap from my jacket. It joined the pile of goodies on the desk.

Admiral Watkins looked at me wide-eyed. "You carried all *that* on a commercial flight without being stopped?"

"Aye-aye, sir."

He laughed. He looked at me. "Dismissed, Captain. Don't forget your toys." He turned toward Ace. "Ace, I'm glad the boy's on our side."

I'd learned in Vietnam that the back door was the best way to hit Charlie; now I'd get to *be* Charlie and hit the Navy through its own back door. Red Cell's mission, just as Ace and I had conceived it, was to test the vulnerabilities of base installations, command and control facilities, operations centers, and naval assets. They were actually going to pay us to mud-suck people—it was too good to be true.

Despite my cavalier speeches to the men, Ace had formulated a thick book of guidelines to make sure Red Cell did its job according to the rules. A Navy lawyer traveled with the unit to ensure that we operated within the law. Each scenario was developed carefully to expose a base's weaknesses, then approved—first by Ace, then by VCNO Hays and his staff, and finally by the CINC of whatever theater in which we'd operate. Ace knew all too well my predilection for improvisation: "Stray from what we've agreed on, and you and your boys are history," he warned me. I believed him. And—most of the time—I followed his orders.

Each of the base commanders would also be briefed in advance on precisely which targets we would hit, and when we would hit them, so they could beef up security. If it was necessary, umpires would be used to rule about the number of casualties in exercises where we used bombs directed against personnel. And to help each base fix what was wrong, every exercise would be videotaped. Using low-light equipment and former SEAL operators as cameramen, we would provide televised object lessons in how not to deal with terrorists. The video would also provide hard evidence that the Cell did what we said we'd done—no base commander could dispute where we had or hadn't been.

"The idea," Ace growled, "is not that you assholes shoot and loot like a bunch of crazies. The idea is that we teach the Navy how to make life difficult for terrorists. They're like goddamn burglars. If a terrorist group is doing target assessment against two bases, and one of 'em looks prepared, he'll hit the less prepared base instead. That's what we want our base commanders to understand."

Early in the spring of 1985, Red Cell pulled a dress rehearsal in Norfolk. The turf was familiar, so the operation didn't require much advance work by the Cell. The real work was discovering ways in which to integrate the camera crews into our terrorist "attacks." After all, not only did my men have to get through the security cordons—each op had to be taped as well. Fortunately, a trio of former SEAL Team Six sailors had been hired as cameramen, and they could sneak and peek almost as well as Red Cell. In the space of only a few days we managed to wreak havoc on the Second Fleet and LANTFLT headquarters with bombs, booby traps, and smoke grenades—and get most of it on tape.

After Norfolk, I called a Cell meeting at Shooter's. I toasted my boys with Bombay. "Okay, cockbreaths, we've gotten our act together—now it's time to take it on the road."

CNO Watkins was a nuclear submariner. So where better to start our series of hop-and-pops than New London, Connecticut, home of the Trident- and Boomer-class nuclear submarines. I visited New London and briefed the appropriate commanders, who were not happy about our imminent arrival. Despite their lukewarm reception, we worked out a series of scenarios, which were "chopped" up and down the chain of command. Finally, early in June, we drove north to pay 'em a visit.

The base—two bases, actually—sat on the bank of the Thames River about six miles north of Long Island Sound. An upper facility contained the usual Navy creature features—BOQ, commissary, movie theater, PX, and barracks, as well as the command-and-control functions for both bases. More significantly, there was an ordnance compound —where tactical weapons such as torpedoes and more esoteric, nuclear devices, were kept. Below, on the river, were the pens where the Boomer-class subs were tied up (Tridents, which were too big to sail under the U.S. I-95 highway bridge, were moored elsewhere).

We set up shop in Groton, Connecticut, just down the road, and began to probe. The base, it didn't take long to discover, was wide open.

How wide? It had no real front gate, only an entranceway. There were train tracks running on a north/south axis between the upper and lower bases. The chain-link fences to keep people from wandering from the right-of-way onto the base were rotted and eroded. Along the easternmost perimeter of the upper base, there was no fence at all—only a 100-foot schist cliff dotted with scrub, bayberry, and thistles. At its foot was the ordnance facility, surrounded by a single chain-link fence eight feet high.

We prepped for three days. Cheeks went to an Ace hardware store and bought three bags of goodies, which he turned into incendiary devices, bombs, and booby traps. The bombs were wired with flash paper; the booby traps and incendiaries had flashbulb "explosives."

I rented a small plane, and Horseface flew us under the I-95 bridge, wetting our wheels in the Thames as we swooped low. We buzzed the sub pens. No one waved us off. We rented a boat and flew the Soviet flag on its stern, then chugged past the base while we openly taped video of the subs in their dry docks, capturing classified details of their construction elements. The dry docks were exposed and unprotected—if we'd decided to ram one of the subs, nothing stood in our way.

We scouted the local bars. Hartman, who'd served on nukes

based out of New London, provided a list of the best ones. Terrorists—especially the middle-class Eurotrash variety that make up such groups as the Red Brigades, Baader-Meinhof, or Direct Action—love to scout bars. That's where they overhear base gossip, pick pockets, and steal IDs. An enterprising terrorist can go to a bar where military folks hang out and come away with IDs for himself and his car, safe combinations, which are often stored in wallets, believe it or not, even operational schedules, which people toss unthinkingly into their briefcases. We discovered the bars frequented by Navy guys, and the places that folks from the General Dynamics shipyards—where they built Tridents—hung out. It was tough work, but we never complained.

Then Minkster—who did the best Arab accent—phoned in the first threat. He called New London's main number.

"Naval Submarine Base, may I help you?"

"Yeah," Minkster said, "this is the Movement for the Free Ejaculation of Palestine. Free all our prisoners or you Zionist infidels will suffer." Then he hung up, just as the poor operator was going, "Whaaaaaa?"

That night, the base was on full alert. Marine guards patrolled the fence line near the main entrance. Naval Security pickets manned the side gate where a single road ran to the base hospital. The motion sensors deployed around the ordnance facility were turned on. But the sensors protected only two sides of the building. After all, who'd be rude enough to hop and pop from the rear?

Ricky's Raiders is who. As Cheeks and I watched from the top, Frank, Larry, Snake, and Pooster quickly lowered themselves down the cliff, moving silently through the wide-open "back door."

I nudged Cheeks. "It's like Ilo-Ilo Island all over again. Everybody's watching the front door—and we shoot and loot up the back."

After the quartet of SEALs made a secure infiltration, we lowered the camera crew, which positioned itself to catch the action.

Roll tape. Larry and Frank burrowed under the chain-link fence and snuck around one side of the ordnance facility; Pooster and Snake went the other way. A sentry carrying a shotgun with no round chambered challenged them. Before he could react, Snake "shot" him with a silenced pistol and he went down. An umpire ruled him dead. Then the fun began. Pooster booby-trapped a pair of propane tanks. Then he and Snake picked a side-door lock and positioned a timer-detonated explosive charge next to a nuclear weapons prep area. More IEDs—Improvised Explosive Devices—were hidden among the torpedoes.

To add insult to injury, Larry and Frank hung a huge sign made from a bedroom sheet on the ordnance building. It said, "KA-BOOM! Love and kisses, the Movement for the Free Ejaculation of Palestine." Then everybody climbed up the cliff, we jumped into the cars we'd parked in plain sight at the side of the road, and we drove away.

A passable night's work under our belts, we went out for some serious terrorist partying. At one of the bars we'd scoped out, we picked up a pair of General Dynamics' better-looking female employees. While they were dirty-dancing with Pooster and Gold Dust Frank, I stole their ID cards.

Doom on you, ladies.

We'd hit the upper base with no problem. On Day Two, we scored hits on the hospital, communications center, and HQ buildings, all with no resistance. The reason was apparent from the very beginning: submariners are very orderly people. They work from checklists. Once something has been checked, it is crossed off the list and not checked again. Terrorists do not work from checklists, they hit targets of opportunity. So we'd wait until a location had been visited by security, then we'd hit it, confident that no one would be waiting for us.

The same thing proved true for the sub pens. Also on Day Two, I sent Minkster, Baby Rich, Horseface, and Wiseass Artie upriver about a quarter mile to a yacht basin. There, they changed into wet suits, put their clothes in waterproof bags, and swam down to the sub pens. They climbed the pilings, changed clothes again, hung the bags off the pier, and went to work. First, they found the sentries—who were secure in their shacks drinking coffee—and silenced them. Then, they concealed explosives behind the diving planes of one nuclear sub. They boarded another Boomer sub and placed demolition charges in the control room, in the nuclear-reactor compartment, and in the torpedo room. When they were challenged, they talked their way out of the situation by claiming to be maintenance people from GD. No one asked them for IDs—and if they had been asked, they had the cards I'd stolen the previous night. They'd have flashed them—thumbs conveniently covering the pictures—and no one would have been the wiser.

The SEALs finished their work, climbed back into their wet suits, and swam upriver to the yacht club, where we picked them up.

Then we all went out and partied again.

The base commander, a captain, was not happy when we showed him the tapes. His boss, a two-star squadron commander I'll call Admiral Cocksure, was even less enthralled.

"Captain," he said, "this exercise wasn't fair, and it shouldn't count. You people didn't play by the rules."

"What rules, sir?"

"Well, you climbed down the cliff to raid my ordnance facility. You never told me you'd do that—you only said you'd attack it. You swam downriver and came up the docks when you attacked the submarines. If we knew you'd come from that direction, we'd have been waiting. We can't have people watching everywhere."

"I'm sure that Abu Nidal or the Popular Front for the Liberation of Palestine will take your views into account if they decide to stage a hit on your base, sir."

"Don't smart-ass me, Captain."

Moi? Dickie? "No, sir. Wouldn't even think about it, sir."

The base commander glared at me. "Your so-called terrorists called and said they were going to hit the PX. We were ready, but they didn't."

"No, Captain, we attacked the communications center instead."

"That's not right."

"Look, gentlemen, let me lay it out for you. Terrorists don't operate by any rules. You have a nice neat base here, and it probably runs very efficiently. But so far as security is concerned, you are extremely vulnerable. You don't show any initiative. The tapes, which the CNO will just love to see—because, as you know, he's a nuclear submariner—show how I blew up two of your nuclear subs, and if I'd wanted to, I could have blown 'em all up."

Admiral Cocksure bristled. "That's another thing, Captain, your men weren't authorized to board nuclear submarines. They don't have the clearances."

"Then why didn't you stop us?"

"That's not a fair question."

"Admiral, fair has nothing to do with it. We agreed the subs were fair game. The best defense against enemy subs is to keep 'em in port. So, all the bad guys need to do is bend one shaft or screw up one diving plane or alter one screw—and your fleet of multimillion-dollar nukes is bottled up."

I tossed the ID cards we'd stolen onto Cocksure's desk. "You may want to return these."

"Jesus," he gasped, "that's—"

"Admiral," I interrupted, "the Marines that look after your main entrance don't have the same radio frequencies as the rent-a-cops you use to patrol the perimeter of the base. The rent-a-cops can talk to your security office, but not to the NIS men on the pier. Nobody carries loaded weapons. Nobody challenges intruders. Your perimeter chain-link fences are only six feet high. And anybody can sail right up the river into the sub pens. Security here sucks."

Cocksure got all huffy. "Don't be insubordinate, Captain."

He was beginning to piss me off, but I held my tongue. "Admiral, I'm not being insubordinate. The deputy CNO for plans and policy is worried about your installation's security. I believe he has good cause for concern, too, because the security here does suck—and that's exactly what I'm going to say in my report."

As I left, the good admiral was already writing Ace a strong letter of complaint. It was to be the first of many Ace would receive about me.

We'd done a good week's work. We'd illustrated the sub base's glitches and given the security people something to think about. We'd even managed to piss off the admiral—something I took as a compliment. I would have liked to continue terrorizing him through the weekend, but a locally sponsored regatta on the Thames forced us to cancel our plans. Ace was firm about certain procedures: we could screw around with the Navy, but not with innocent civilians. Still, it was too nice a weekend just to go home. So, instead of returning to Washington, we drove north to Massachusetts for a two-day clambake.

One of our civilian film crew was a plank holder at SEAL Team Six—a tall former lieutenant known as the Senator. His Navy career had been cut short by a training accident at Six in which he'd lost an eye. Now, he worked with the defense consulting firm that was coordinating the videotaping of Red Cell's attacks.

The Senator's parents had a big house right on the beach in southern Massachusetts, about forty minutes outside Boston, and that's where we went. We bought enough beer to sink a skiff and spent the weekend eating corn, lobsters, and steamers, all cooked out on the beach in a 48-hour nonstop party.

Party? It turned into Mardi Gras. As the celebration grew louder and more boisterous, neighbors began showing up. Women ogled muscular SEALs. SEALs ogled shapely women. Pooster fell in love. We wrestled with each other and tossed anybody we could get our hands on—especially pretty young things—into the surf. We played SEAL volleyball, which is a full-contact sport. We made neat little Everett E. Barrett rows of empty-beer-can pathways to show off our talents in landscaping.

And we prepared SEAL foods. We built a huge, seaweed-lined pit in which we steamed our lobsters, clams, corn, and potatoes. Later, after enough beer, the six-foot bed of coals would be suitable for fire walking.

One of us preferred to prepare his own unique rations. The Senator's parents watched in fascinated, horrified amazement as Gold Dust Larry really *laissez*'d *les bons temps roulez*. He got himself worked up on Coors into a quintessential Gold Dust Larry funk, then went wandering off by himself down the beach. Sometime later—no one could be precise—he returned, carrying a dead sea gull. He stood silent, morosely watching the fire we'd built, and bit the bird's head off.

"What is that chap doing?" Poppa Senator wanted to know as he watched Larry chaw and chaw.

"He's making sea-gull tartar," Duke explained patiently.

The rest of the team had to be physically restrained from embarking on a scavenger hunt to find more dead creatures for Larry to eat. It was a long, long night.

Sunday morning, after everyone resumed consciousness, we rented a lobster boat, stocked it with five or six cases of beer, and spent the morning cruising the coastline. After about case three, Snake decided he'd ride in the punt the lobsterman was towing. He worked his way down the towline and settled in with a couple of six-packs.

The rest of us were content to lie in the sun, looking at the huge houses that sat above the distant beach. Then Trailer Court had a bright idea: "Cast and recovery," he shouted. "SEALs in the water."

An order is an order. Lead by example. Without waiting, I threw myself over the bow rail and into the Atlantic, diving headfirst and swimming away from the port side of the boat underwater. Ouch—the water was goddamned cold enough to make my balls go "pop." I kicked toward the surface and began treading water just in time to see Snake's big, muscular arm coming at me like a club. He grabbed me by the throat and swung me easily into the punt.

"Thanks," I wheezed.

"Anytime, Cap." Snake pointed as Gold Dust Larry went off the bow headfirst. "Better move it, Cap—Larry's about to be recovered."

The bottom half of my body dragging in the water, I worked my way hand over hand up the fifty feet of towline back to the boat. Before I finally hoisted myself over the stern rail, I'd lost my tennis shoes and one of my socks in the prop wash. Exhausted, I groped my way forward on hands and knees.

"How was it, Cap?" Pooster asked.

"Oh, it was peachy-keen ducky, Pooster. Why don't you try it, too?"

I lay on my back on the lobster boat's foredeck, cold, wet, and salty. My wallet was squishy. My shoes were flotsam. Snake's fingerprints were visible like five hickeys on my neck where he'd one-handed me out of the water. My Adam's apple throbbed in pain. But the sun was bright, and the sky was blue, and somebody was standing above me, dribbling beer into my open mouth.

I thought, God put me on this earth so I could be here and do this, with these men—*my* men. It was absolutely, totally, incontrovertibly, completely, utterly fucking perfect.

Chapter

22

IN CIVILIAN LIFE, LABOR DAY SIGNALS THE END OF SUMMER vacation, the time when, even though the seasons haven't actually changed yet, there's this ineffable feeling of permutation—a visceral sense that something is about to happen. That's the way it was for Red Cell on Labor Day weekend of 1985. We'd had a good spring and a great summer, shaking up commands and embarrassing COs all over the country.

Best of all, I felt as close to the men in the Cell as I had to my first command in Vietnam, Bravo Squad, Second Platoon. Except that instead of Patches Watson, Eagle Gallagher, Ron Rodger, Jim Finley, and Joe Camp—who were as crazy a bunch of shoot-and-looters as I'd ever known—I now had fourteen guys who could shoot and loot with the best of 'em—*and* fly their own planes and choppers, *and* HAHO jump from seven miles up, *and* come equipped with a selection of goodies we hadn't even dreamed of in Vietnam, *and* screw around with admirals in ways heretofore unknown in naval history.

But change was definitely in the air. Ace Lyons had just received word he was being promoted. He was about to receive his fourth star and be sent to Hawaii, where he'd become

CINCPACFLT—Commander-IN-Chief, PACific FLeeT. The implications of that move were immense. A quick scan of CNOs or vice CNOs showed that many of them served with the Seventh Fleet, headed the Pacific Command, or were appointed CINCPACFLT. There was a possibility, therefore, that Ace's move would ultimately lead to his selection as CNO.

In hindsight, however, the promotion was, in fact, an efficient—even insidious—way to get Ace out of town and out of the power loop. He was perceived by much of the Navy establishment, which was mainly peopled by bureaucratic nuclear types, as a troublemaker, a rabble-rouser, a hard-liner. Ace may have been able to represent the Navy ably at the 1984 Incidents at Sea talks with the Soviets in Moscow, but at home he represented a hardheaded, seemingly intractable point of view that other four-star admirals found difficult to digest.

What they found most unsettling about Ace was that he had a warrior's mentality. He was audacious and unconventional. He could swear like a chief, he respected the men who served under him, he insisted on shaking up the system, and he wasn't afraid to call a spade a spade. This combination made him too much of a threat to too many others. So, Ace was promoted out of his staff job at Plans and Policy, where he didn't command a lot of men—but what he said and did had a substantial impact on the entire U.S. Navy, twenty-four hours a day. Instead, he was shipped off to Honolulu, where he commanded more than 250,000 personnel and managed an annual budget of more than $5.5 billion, but was safely removed from the political mainstream.

More significantly, so far as I and my little Red Cell operation were concerned, Ace would now be six thousand miles away from being able to protect Demo Dickie's rear end.

Of course, the dire implications of Ace's transfer didn't hit me right away. Not by a long shot. Indeed, if my senses about getting ambushed had been as keen in 1985 as they were back in 1967, the hair on my neck would have been standing straight up and I would have stalked the Pentagon corridors with my M16 locked and loaded. But that didn't happen. I was having too much fun. Me and the boys were about to spend Labor Day weekend, 1985, with Ronald Reagan. Well, we weren't actually with the president, but with his plane. Air Force One was housed at Point Mugu Naval Air Station, about 125 miles south of the president's ranch in Santa Barbara, whenever the Reagans vacationed there. With all the extra security around, it seemed like the perfect opportunity to play our unique brand of fun and games.

The base commander at Mugu was a Navy flier named Gordy Nakagawa. Gordy had been a POW twice in his life: first as an internee during WWII, then as a Navy pilot, when he'd been captured by the Viet Cong. I liked and admired Gordy. Unlike most base commanders, he took security seriously. He'd even formed a Pt. Mugu SWAT team—it was unusual in that it contained both men and women—which he lovingly called his Rambo and Rambette SWATs.

Gordy Nakagawa was a world-class marksman and a game-player, and he loved the prospect of his people getting the chance to rock and roll with Red Cell when Air Force One was on the ground. The Secret Service had a different point of view. "We don't play games," they said. "Period."

I shrugged. Whatever. Just because they wouldn't play with us didn't mean we couldn't play with them.

We took the entire Cell to California, with the exception of Hartman, who was left behind to hold down the office, something for which he has never forgiven me. Luckily for him, Shooter's was open Labor Day.

Gordy and I had settled on that particular weekend because, even with Air Force One on the tarmac, the base would resemble Sleepy Hollow. *Function* is not in the Navy lexicon during weekends—especially long holiday weekends. *Alert* has never been a proactive word on Navy Sundays, when everybody sleeps late. It's historic: remember Pearl Harbor?

The Cell arrived ten days before the festivities were to begin, filtering in on commercial flights to Los Angeles and Santa Barbara. The guys rented half a dozen vehicles ranging from Cadillacs to pickup trucks. We drove to Mugu and checked into the same motel used by Air Force One's Secret Service and Air Force security details. That would allow us to keep an eye on the opposition. Meanwhile, the heavy equipment and camera crews arrived aboard a Navy jet that flew into Alameda Naval Air Station.

Once settled in, Red Cell began to scope out the base. I stayed in the background, playing the Abu Nidal role, allowing the Cell to function at its own speed. The men knew our goal was to test every element of the base security apparatus. The question of exactly how they did that was up to them. I might suggest a few specifics or design a particularly evil operation I wanted to see mounted in a distinctive way. But for the most part, they were on their own.

My major role was to observe, so I could help make suggestions after the exercise. So I spent time with Gordy, to see what his people were up to, or went out on patrol with Bob Laser, Mugu's security chief, to show him the sorts of things he might want to watch for. Most of the time, however, I floated between my teams, watching their preparations, keeping them on a long leash as they discovered new and cunning ways in which to have their perverse forms of fun.

Pooster the Rooster (I always thought we should have called him Pooster the Booster) "borrowed" a ten-speed bicycle and cruised every piece of road alongside Pt. Mugu. His meanderings brought him to a seldom-used back gate behind the flight line. He found, much to his delight, that the wide gates were secured with a simple lock and chain. He bought a bolt cutter, snipped the chain, deep-sixed the lock, and replaced it with his own lock and chain.

Duke, meanwhile, rented a boat from a local marina. He and Larry trolled offshore, looking for women sunbathing topless. They also scanned the Pt. Mugu shoreline for likely ground-sensor positions. Through field glasses, they also kept track of the base's SWAT team, rent-a-cop patrols, Navy security sweeps, and Marine guards as each detail made its predictable, by-the-clock rounds. The terrorists took copious notes, just like real bad guys do.

To ensure its own unit integrity, Red Cell checked out the local bars and saloons en masse. Once again, we gleaned valuable information. Who drank where? What was the gossip? What kinds of badges did people carry? Often, whilst the point men were inside, forcing themselves to become part of the crowd by imbibing cold beer, Bombay gin, or other assorted beverages of quality, two or three laggards stayed behind in the parking lots, peeling base stickers off windshields and bumpers so the Cell could use them on our own rental cars.

By Friday afternoon, we were ready. The Cell had probed the base, searching for weaknesses. Many had been found. It was child's play to get someone over the fence—even in broad daylight and right next to the main gate. How? Horseface drove by the gate, honking and cursing at the guards, tossing a couple of cartons of milk in their direction as he went past. Yoo-hoo—everybody watch Horseface.

Meanwhile, ten feet away, Ho-Ho-Ho and Doc Tremblay were vaulting over the eight-foot chain-link fence and jogging away. Doom on you, gate guards.

That was basic. We also broke into junction boxes and tapped phones. We monitored police radio frequencies with Bearcat scanners. We made our own tactical maps, complete with shortcuts, back doors, and escape routes. Targets were assessed, selected, and prioritized.

Air Force One was already on the ground and parked in a remote corner of the field, surrounded by Secret Service dip-dunks and Air Force blue-blankets—security personnel in blue berets. It didn't matter to us whether there were twenty men guarding the plane or two hundred. We'd deal with 'em as our grand finale.

Then, we went to work. For a base that was allegedly on full alert, the place seemed to be barely breathing. The sentries watched TV in their sheds. The flight line with its F-18 Hornets was deserted. The rent-a-cops came and went by rote. Nobody was taking care of business. Even the telephone operator who took Minkster's threat from the Movement for the Ejaculation of Palestine wasn't running on all her cylinders.

"This is the Movement for the Ejaculation of Palestine. If the Israelis do not free one hundred and seventy-three of our political prisoners within two hours, your facility will be bathed in American blood. The mother of all wars will begin on your accursed Zionist-loving territory."

"Could you spell that name for me again, caller?"

"That is *E* as in ejaculation, *J* as in ejaculation, *A* as in ejaculation, *C* as in ejaculation, *U* as in ejaculation . . . ," Minkster droned in his very best Yasir Arafat accent.

Ah, yes, Pt. Mugu was just like a sleepy little southern-

California town in the hours before the Labor Day weekend began. Which is precisely why my very own MEP guerrilla, Lieutenant Trailer Court, wearing a purloined commander's uniform instead of black pajamas and a kaffiyeh, checked in at 1900 Friday evening. He drove up to the gate and explained to the guards he was supposed to report for work Tuesday, but had arrived early so he could spend the weekend at the BOQ and not pay a motel bill. Trailer carried an ID card we'd stolen at a bar two nights before, but it wasn't necessary: the screwups in Navy Security let him in without checking a thing.

He went straight to the BOQ, jimmied his way into an unused room, and unpacked the weapons, night-vision goggles, radio equipment, and explosive devices we'd had him smuggle onto the base for us. Then he used his vest-pocket scrambler to call us on the phone in his room to report the coast was clear. Great. I dispatched Ho-Ho-Ho, Horseface, and Baby Rich, dressed in fashionable basic black, over the fence. No one saw or stopped them. They went to Trailer's room, changed into work clothes, picked up their explosives equipment, and went out to steal a weapons carrier we'd spied sitting by the motor pool the previous day.

The trio drove the WC to the ordnance warehouse, broke in, jump-started a forklift, and stacked the truck with a pallet-load of bright blue, dummy 500-pound bombs they found there. They rigged the bombs with remote-controlled detonating devices and booby traps, covered the bulky load with a camouflage tarp, and drove the whole consignment back to the BOQ parking lot where Trailer could keep an eye on it. Then, looking as innocent as Huey, Louie, and Dewey, they ambled out through the main gate, waving at the rent-a-cops as they went.

Meanwhile, Frank and Snake had slipped into wet suits for their own version of a quiet evening of infiltration. Pooster drove them to a location on the Pacific Coast Highway just above a wildlife refuge that ran alongside the north end of the base. Accompanied by a former SEAL Six teammate, our cameraman named Neil, they swam about a mile down a small river until they reached the marshy wildlife preserve. The men tried to infiltrate straight across the preserve, but were stymied by four-foot-deep mud. So they reversed course and took the land route, working their way around the game refuge's perimeter, moving southeast in a methodical, painful belly crawl.

About eight hundred yards of slow crawl later, as they came through a culvert that security had forgotten to blockade with bars or screens, the terrorists ran into a Rambo/Rambette patrol. A quartet of SWATs, in black fatigues, was patrolling the perimeter of the base.

The SEALs lay silently in foot-high marsh grass as the cops' boots passed inches from their noses.

One of the SWATs squatted down on the edge of the culvert and lit a cigarette. Another joined him. Meanwhile, Frank, Snake, and Neil kept themselves busy trying to ignore the ants crawling on their faces and up their wet suits. After what seemed a lifetime, the Rambos and Rambettes finally resumed their patrol, but not before one of the cops unknowingly left his bootprint on Frank's blacked-out hand.

Alone again, they resumed their mission. Moving slowly, Snake, Frank, and Neil crept up a ditch alongside a taxiway. Snake and Frank broke into a hangar, changed into coveralls they found, then walked onto the flight line and stuck explosives inside the air intakes of half a dozen F-18 fighters. Neil got it all on tape, using a low-light lens. The mission complete, they marched straight to the back gate, unlocked it, slipped out, and relocked the gate. Pooster was waiting for them—after all, it was Miller time.

Minkster and Cheeks didn't make Miller time. They were my first-day cannon fodder. I needed a diversion to ensure that Frank and Snake would get onto the flight line. So I sent them to the fuel farm at the other end of the base, where they made enough noise to elicit a response.

That was important: I wanted to see who would answer the alarm. Would it be rent-a-cops, Department of Defense police, or the Rambo/Rambettes who'd come a-calling? And when the cops captured bad guys, how would they deal with them?

We monitored the authorities' progress on our police-band scanners. Trailer, sitting with a pair of night-vision binoculars on the roof of the bachelor officers' quarters, was able to give us a running commentary on who was moving, and where they were going. It was like a travelogue.

The DOD police caught up with Cheeks and Minkster just as they were "planting" explosives. They'd given themselves away by purposely walking across a sensor-rich area. The cops surrounded my boys and took 'em down. Then, they were quickly frisked, cuffed, thrown into the back of a car, and taken to the DOD police station, which was located outside the Pt. Mugu base perimeter.

Except, they hadn't been frisked very carefully. Cheeks had a handcuff key in his pocket, and a pistol in a crotch holster. He was frisked by a female, who was understandably reticent about giving his groin a businesslike grope, especially when Cheeks ragged her about it—"Hey, baby, how about a lube job—come on, just put your hand down there where it's hot and hard."

Big Mistake One. Cheeks was armed and he was dangerous. He used both key and gun to good advantage once he was inside the station. First, he freed the Minkster. Then, the pair of them took all the rent-a-cops, as well as their station, hostage. The rent-a-cops now had to call the SWAT team for help.

Meanwhile, Duke and Snake "blew up" Pt. Mugu's main radio antenna. All communications between Rambo/Rambette headquarters and the rest of the emergency-response people ceased, as the umpires ruled Red Cell's bombing had caused sufficient damage to kill the police command and control functions. The "explosion" also brought out the base fire department, which was already being harassed by a series of Red Cell–generated false alarms, thoughtfully provided by Pooster. So much for opening night.

At first light, another security glitch became apparent. We terrorists were fresh—we'd all gotten some rest. The security forces, on the other hand, were beginning to tire—there was no plan for them to rest in shifts. Gordy had built himself a team—but he had no bench. Everybody had been scrambled at once, and everybody was still on duty.

That was Big Mistake Two. A tired policeman is a careless policeman. Just after daybreak, Ho-Ho-Ho, Rich, and Horseface captured half a dozen early breakfasters—including women and kids—at the Mugu cafeteria, which was located off-base, just down the road from the main gate. They blindfolded their captives and turned them over to the Gold Dust

Twins to use as human currency. Now the cops were between the proverbial rock and hard place: it was common practice not to trade for cop hostages, but women and kids were another case altogether. A deal was made with the exhausted police negotiators, and just after 0900, Minkster and Cheeks were freed from the police station.

We knew the cops were planning a roadblock half a mile from the station because we'd eavesdropped on their conversations and phone calls. So we did the unexpected. The Gold Dust Twins exchanged their hostages for our men. Then Frank hightailed it in the one direction no one had anticipated: right through the main gate—*onto* the base.

We listened to screams of frustration on police radios, then—after the initial confusion—we heard ecstatic celebrations. They now believed Red Cell had screwed up royally—because the getaway car was headed straight for the flight line, from which they knew there was no escape.

Frank and his rent-a-car, followed by three jeep-loads of Rambos and Rambettes, led everybody along a merry chase all across the base. He careened through back alleys, slalomed the wrong way up one-way streets, and doubled back to play "chicken" with his pursuers. He lurched onto the flight line and drag-raced the length of the main runway. By the time he wheelied up to the back gate in a cloud of dust and a hearty "Heigh-ho, Silver," he must have been doing 150.

"Hey," said Cheeks, "how the hell we gonna split?"

"No sweat," Frank answered. *"Voilà."*

Cheeks peered through the windshield. Who was standing by the back gate? Meesta Poosta Roost, with his ten-speed bike and his cold-steel chain and his Medeco lock and key.

Pooster bowed. Frank drove through. Pooster locked the gate. Everyone drove away. We got wonderful video of the Rambos and Rambettes trying to bust the lock and chain. Which was impossible, of course. The SWAT team had not been issued bolt cutters, and they were unwilling to drive through the gates and ruin their jeeps, not to mention damage government property. Once again, it was Miller time.

On Sunday, we played "Chester Chester Child Molester" with the local police. Horseface, Doc Tremblay, and Ho-Ho-Ho went scrambling through the hallways of an enlisted family housing complex about half a mile outside the main gate. The appearance of three evil-looking guys in black T-shirts, jeans, and balaclavas, carrying machine guns, brought real screams from mommies and daddies. Dozens of people called 911 to report the incident. We used the complaints to tie down the local police, a crew of FBI agents who'd shown up to play, the DOD police, and two jeeps of Bob Laser's Rambos/Rambettes. It looked like a police convention outside the housing complex: a dozen cars with gum-ball lights flashing, while the quartet of law-enforcement organizations argued long and loud about who the hell was in charge here.

We, of course, didn't give a rat's ass who *they* thought was in charge. We knew who was in charge—us. So, while the cops argued, we set off smoke-grenade explosives in the main HQ building, the power generating station, Gordy Nakagawa's prized weapons locker, and the fuel depot.

Doom on you, cops.

The ensuing explosions brought the local fire department onto the scene. It also caused a six-mile backup on the Pacific Coast Highway, which ran outside the base. Why were unhappy vacationers and Sunday drivers cursing the constabulary? Because the security people had shut down traffic so that each and every car in the vicinity could be checked for terrorists. Meanwhile, Pt. Mugu's medical facility was now being stretched to overload. Base hospitals are designed for everyday ailments—they specialize in earaches, nosebleeds, and sprained ankles. Now they were dealing with dozens of "shock-trauma" victims, "critically" wounded and "dying" patients, and the doctors began going, "Whoa—I didn't sign up for this."

Gordy Nakagawa surveyed the chaos from his office with a wry smile. "The problem," I told him, "is stovepipe organization."

"Huh?"

"Think of your base as a series of parallel stovepipes—chimneys—all surrounded by the perimeter fence. Your security chimney reports to one organization—NIS. Your medical chimney reports back to another: Bethesda Naval Hospital. Your personnel chimney reports back to BUPERS. Your air wing reports to Naval Air. They may all be located on your base, and they may all answer to you, but they each have separate command authorities. As a terrorist, I use that system against you. I pit each sector of your base against the other sectors, and the results"—I pointed out the window toward the raucous gridlock—"are truly glorious to behold."

Gordy thought about it. "Cunning devil, aren't you?"

By Monday morning we'd taken Pt. Mugu Naval Air Station way past chaos, all the way to anarchy. We had blown up most of our targets without resistance. The local cops were so tired they were walking into doors. The fire department was bouncing off the walls. The doctors were on the verge of staging a sit-down strike. The FBI had picked up its toys and gone home because no one was playing fair. Only the Coast Guard was steaming unconcernedly off the coast without so much as a flutter.

Gordy was delighted with the exercise because he'd been able to see where his vulnerabilities lay. Bob Laser was happy because he'd been able to let his Rambos and Rambettes go balls and boobs to the wall. Their mistakes would be corrected, and the next time around they'd be much improved. I was euphoric because my guys had worked hard, played hard—and had fun. A couple had even managed to get laid, which was more than I could say for myself.

It was almost time to go home. But one succulent, irresistible target remained—Air Force One, which was scheduled to depart about midday. It was just too tempting to ignore. Dressed in mechanic's coveralls, Frank and Cheeks climbed into the weapons carrier that had remained parked all weekend in the BOQ lot and drove it over to the far corner of the field, where the president's 707 was being fueled and serviced. They climbed out and activated the explosives rigged to the pallet-load of 500-pound bombs. Just to be extra thoughtful, Cheeks set another charge: he booby-trapped the weapons carrier's driver's seat.

Their job completed, Frank and Cheeks sauntered back to the BOQ and changed clothes in Trailer's room. The three of them packed the car and got ready to leave. Then they went up onto the roof of the BOQ to watch the results of their handiwork.

As a parting gesture of friendship, we'd also rigged explosives in the SWAT team's emergency response truck. When Minkster telephoned our threat against Air Force One to Bob Laser, virtually every one of Bob's Rambos and Rambettes headed for the truck, which "exploded" in a cloud of smoke. The umpires ruled ten dead, ten injured. Doom on you, Rambos and Rambettes.

When the SWAT survivors finally discovered the weapons carrier (it took them more than an hour to work their way onto the lot adjacent to Air Force One), they approached it with great caution. You could see the apprehensive looks in our long-lens video shots. They were going to do this by the book.

They sealed off the area. They called for EOD—the demolition team. It arrived and there were fifteen minutes of consultation. Then, carefully, the explosives in the rear were disarmed wire by wire. With the bombs safely defused, a Rambo climbed into the cab to drive the vehicle away.

Ka-boom—our smoke-grenade booby trap went off and exploded the whole pallet-load of 500-pound bombs. It was a Frogman's dream come true—a living centerfold from the *Blaster's Handbook*. Trailer radioed me that the view from the BOQ roof was spectacular.

"Skipper, the only thing missing was the caption 'The End—a Dick Marcinko Production of a Red Cell Scenario.' "

I roared. "Wait till they see the goddamn sequel!"

The season changed from warm and friendly to frosty and cool shortly after we got back from Mugu. At a farewell party for Ace Lyons, I met his successor, my new boss at OP-06, a gaunt, balding vice admiral named Donald Jones. I knew Jones slightly. As a staffer working out of the Joint Chiefs, he'd helped me transfer a one-eyed ops officer from Coronado to SEAL Team Six. Jones was an integral part of the Coronado Mafia, which included officers who liked me—such as Bob Stanton, the captain who'd taught me to write memos when I started my first staff job at COMPHIBTRALANT—and officers who didn't, such as Cathal "Irish" Flynn, the mean-tempered son of a bitch who'd been commodore of West Coast SEALs when I was forming Six. Jones was also friends with Flynn's successor, Ch-Ch-Ch-Chuck LeMoyne, who liked me even less than Irish did.

It was bad enough that Irish was about to be appointed to run NIS—he was, in Ace's opinion, too rigid and small-minded to be given the responsibility. But now, OP-06 was being turned over to a pleasant but by no means aggressive admiral, an antisubmarine-warfare aviator whose deferential personality was exactly the opposite of what the job called for. Ace's raison d'être had been to rattle cages. Jones was less prone to make waves.

Ace's party was held at the Fort Myers Officers' Club. We'd put together some gifts—Red Cell's parting shot to Ace was a booby-trapped bottle of vodka—which were presented with much fanfare. After the presentations and the speeches, it was time for the ritual backslapping and the hot hors d'oeuvres.

I was reintroduced to Vice Admiral Jones. He reached out to shake my hand. His grip was dead fish. By way of greeting, he said, "I'm surprised you're not in jail yet."

If I'd been perceptive, I'd have realized that working for this guy was not going to be one of life's great pleasures.

I, however, smart-assed an answer and went back to my Bombay.

Strike one.

About a month later, I'd forgotten all about Vice Admiral Jones's greeting. "Anybody feel like a European vacation?"

Duke's hand shot up. So did Baby Rich's and Hartman's.

"Too bad, cockbreaths. I got the list already. The Gold Dust Twins and Ho-Ho-Ho. It's gonna be a short trip—so we're traveling light."

We flew military. Hop one was to London, where we transferred onto a small, twin-engine jet for a two-stopper: Sigonella, then Naples. I made another friend on that flight, a two-star, who thought he had the plane all to himself. When he saw Larry and Frank and Ho-Ho-Ho and me—dressed in jeans, with long hair and Fu Manchu mustaches and no "Aye-aye, sir" in us at all—he went ballistic.

An aide inquired, as aides are wont to do, who we were.

"I'm performing a function for the CNO," I said. "Goodbye."

A minute later he was back. "Where's your authorization?"

I displayed my middle finger. "Here. Ciao."

A minute later he was back again. The admiral wanted to see our ID cards.

"If the admiral wants to see my fucking ID card, I'll be

happy to fucking come fucking forward and show it to him. But as for the rest of my team, who they are is none of his business.''

I gave the aide Vice Admiral Jones's name and address. "Please send all inquiries there. Now, will you please be a good boy and bugger off?"

The two-star didn't ask any more questions. But Jones got a letter. Unlike Ace, he didn't round-file complaints. He hung on to them.

I may have sounded capricious when I told the men we were going to Naples. The reason behind our visit, however, was anything but frivolous. There was a real terrorist threat in Italy. In 1981 the Red Brigades kidnapped Brigadier General James Dozier in Verona. He was held forty-two days before being freed by Italian counterterror forces. In 1984, they assassinated Leamon Hunt, the American director general of the multinational force that monitored the peace agreement between Israel and Egypt. Those acts, and others, caused Ace Lyons great concern about the vulnerability of the U.S. Navy admiral in Naples, a three-star I'll call Mott.

Even though Ace had become CINCPACFLT and no longer oversaw Red Cell, he'd wanted me to take my unit to Naples—and I had agreed. When we arrived, I saw that Naples was just as busy as I remembered it. I thought about visiting some of the haunts where I'd played on my one-year tour when I worked for Big FUC, or the bars where Ev Barrett had taken Second Platoon of UDT-22. But we only had five days, so we got right to work.

We rented two cars and a motorbike and drove to the admiral's home to stake it out. We toured the streets leading to the admiral's house, dodging Neapolitan taxis, cars, buses, and cycles as we went. We circled his home a couple of times to get the layout. Then we rang the doorbell.

Mrs. Mott answered the door. She was an attractive woman in her late thirties with a confident smile and an easy manner about her. I introduced myself, Larry, Frank, and Ho-Ho-Ho and explained who we were and what we were doing. She seemed relieved.

"I've been telling the admiral we're vulnerable," she said. "What with all the Red Brigade activity, and the Mafia kidnappings, I've been a little nervous. And now, with that ship hijacked—the *Achille Lauro*—who can tell what'll happen next. But NIS says we're very secure here. The house has a high wall, we've got two humongous guard dogs, and an armed driver takes us everywhere."

"That seems like a good start. We'll see what we can do to help."

The admiral came downstairs and greeted us warmly. "Let me show you around," he said.

He led us outside. "We're on top of a hill, which is good," he said. "And we're part of a compound—there are Navy people all around us, so if something happens, we can call for help."

"Maybe," I said.

"Huh?"

I walked to a gray box attached to his wall and opened it up. It had a power switch. I turned the switch off. From inside the house, I could hear Mrs. Admiral wail, "What happened to the lights?"

I turned the switch back on. "So much for the electricity."

"NIS never noticed that," the admiral said.

"Scenario one: they pop your power. You come out to fix it. They grab you, toss you in the trunk of their car, it's five minutes to the *autostrada*, and—ta-daa—you're another General Dozier."

Admiral Mott's face took a definite downturn.

Ho-Ho-Ho was jimmying a manhole cover that sat directly in front of Admiral Mott's front gate. He pried an edge up and lifted the steel disc as if it were papier-mâché.

Larry and Frank poked flashlights into the darkness. "Scenario two: ten kilos of plastique to surprise you when you come through your gate." The admiral's face fell another inch. "Your water pipes are down there, too. Easy for them to be tampered with. Maybe a little spritz of bacteria in the tap water."

"Shit," the admiral said. "NIS never told me about that, either."

"Frank," I said, "show the admiral how easy it is to pay him a visit."

Frank scaled the wall with no problem, loped across the front lawn, climbed a grape arbor, and was through the admiral's bedroom window in about thirty seconds. He waved at us.

"But NIS put broken glass on top of the wall so no one could go over it."

"I guess they forgot a spot or two."

"Well, the dogs would stop anybody coming over the wall."

"Larry . . ."

Larry produced a silenced 9mm automatic from his shoulder bag. "Hollow-point, subsonic ammo," he said matter-of-factly. "Deadly against dogs."

Admiral Mott's brow furrowed. "What do you suggest, Captain?"

"I'll draw you up a long list of suggestions, sir, after we've done the complete survey—five days from now. But for now, why not put everyone on full security alert and have NIS button up your house. Meanwhile, we'll try to take you hostage. And that way we'll test some of the other security arrangements NIS has in place."

He shook my hand. "Sounds great, Captain. I'll be awaiting your report with interest. I hope to see you and your men before you leave."

"I think you can count on that, sir," I said with a knowing smile.

Both the NATO base and the Navy's Neapolitan facility were already at full alert because of the *Achille Lauro* incident, which was under way while we were in Naples. But security was still a joke. We kidnapped Admiral Mott that first night. He made a well-received speech at the NATO base Allied Officers' Club—the event was publicized on television, no less. His wife looked on proudly. We shadowed him so heavy-handedly that even Egyptians would have sensed something was amiss. NIS saw zippo. We took pictures; we asked questions; we made pests of ourselves. Nothing. Not even a nibble.

Admiral Mott's armed-and-dangerous driver never saw us either. We bullied our way into the O Club without benefit of ID cards by talking tough and acting as if we owned the place. The guards let us through.

We followed Mott's car off the base, and just as it turned into the hills, we ran it off the road, pinning it against some trees.

Larry and Frank jumped out, balaclava hoods over their faces and guns drawn. They subdued the armed driver, pulled the admiral through the door, hog-tied and blindfolded him, then tossed him unceremoniously into the trunk of their car. Mrs. Mott went absolutely bonkers. This was not a diversion she'd signed on for.

Ho-Ho-Ho waved politely as he wheelied and sped away. "Ciao, Mrs. Mott," he called out.

They drove the admiral to his house—he actually arrived before his wife did—and dropped him off. Larry told me that he was shaken, but smiling gamely, and muttering evil things about NIS as he staggered through his front gate.

That night, Larry and Frank staked out Casa Mott, hidden in trees well inside the high walls. Larry even dropped into the front yard and made friends with the two huge bullmastiff watchdogs. He tied notes around their necks as evidence he'd played with them.

Then, precisely at 0730, the admiral's car pulled up to drive him to the office. The driver honked. Admiral Mott came out his front door and walked toward his gate.

Larry dropped out of the tree. *"Bon giorno, Ammiraglio."*

"Oh, no—not again."

"Sì, Ammiraglio, ripetutamente." He stuck a pistol in the admiral's ribs, and they marched out toward the car in lockstep. The driver and a Navy Security man were sitting in the front seat. Larry was polite. He and the admiral chatted. No one noticed anything askew.

Together, they rode to the naval base, through the gate, past the Marines, and up the elevator into the command center. "Now we open your safe and I get to see all the operational codes," Larry suggested.

"Would you settle for an excellent cup of espresso instead?"

Larry shook his head. "Nope, sir. But do you have any sea gulls?"

Later in the day, Frank and Larry "assassinated" officers. Navy personnel were constantly being warned about the dire consequences of wearing uniforms to work and using NATO license plates on their cars. But uniforms were cheaper than civvies, and NATO plates meant easy parking in restricted areas.

So, Larry and Frank took their motor scooters and waited by the Navy Base gate. They followed cars with NATO plates or cars driven by men wearing Navy tan jackets—rank and all—over their civvy shirts. They'd pull up at a stoplight and slap a paper sticker on the driver's-side window. Then they'd roar off into traffic. The stickers had bullet holes and the legend, "You are one dead Navy asshole, sir. Love and kisses, the Red Brigades." They were hell to peel off, too.

We had a productive five days. But talk about agitated admirals. By the time we flew out of Naples for London and home, Admiral Mott had reamed his security people new sphincters and sent a barrage of rockets to NIS headquarters about the idiots allegedly sent out to provide for his safe-keeping. He may have been happy with our work, but the officer in charge of those "idiots" at NIS, on the other hand, was decidedly less than enthralled with our performance. And as luck would have it, the officer in charge was none other than "Irish" Flynn—the old and dear pal of our new boss, Admiral Jones.

Strike two.

My career died the day Ace left for Hawaii, but I didn't know it. Others did. But not me. Besotted with my own immortality, I kept playing my own version of hardball. My marriage had come unraveled, and Red Cell was my life, my existence, my reason for living. Besides, I had it all: I wore four stripes. I'd assembled what I believed to be the best team of unconventional warriors in the world. We worked where and how I wanted to work; we did what I wanted us to do. For the first time in my career, no one was yanking my leash; no one muzzled me or tied me down.

Then, Ace left to become CINCPACFLT, and the thick, protective wall that had been protecting my back and flanks was gone.

Ace's former executive assistant, Phil Dur, tried to tell me, but I wouldn't listen. I hadn't been back from Naples more than a week when I ran into Phil as I was sailing the corridors outside OP-06, trying to find something or other. I hadn't seen him in a while—at least since Ace had left for Pearl Harbor.

I liked Phil. A big, moon-faced guy who moved like a

Polack pulling tackle from Penn State, he'd worked hard and loyally for Ace. He slammed me on the shoulder and asked how things were going. I gave him a two-minute dump on our op in Naples that had him in stitches. The fact that we'd kidnapped Admiral Mott twice in twelve hours brought a roar to his throat.

Then he drew me aside. "Dick, do yourself a favor."

"Sure."

"Get out of town."

"What—"

He flicked a thumb toward the OP-06 doorway. "They don't want you around anymore. You're an embarrassment. You give them grief. Admirals write letters of complaint, and the new guy takes them seriously. Ace could cover your ass. Now—it ain't gonna happen."

"I'm a big boy, Phil."

"They're gonna get you. They're beginning to put an investigation together—initiated by your old 'pals' from the West Coast."

"That's a load of crap. Besides, I've got nothing to hide. I can take anything they throw at me."

He backed me up against the corridor wall. "You could be the biggest man on the whole frigging campus, and it won't mean a goddamn thing. Believe me, Dick, they're gonna hang you out to dry."

"Bullshit."

"It took a long time for you to get your four stripes. Want to keep 'em? Get the hell out of town."

But I knew better. "Screw 'em all," I told him. "I'm staying."

Strike three.

Chapter

23

I SHOULD HAVE TAKEN PHIL DUR'S ADVICE. BECAUSE, WHILE Red Cell blithely played Peck's Bad Boys all over the world, NIS, under "Irish" Flynn, was stealthily organizing its own guerrilla attack—on me, and on SEAL Team Six.

NIS code-named its operation Iron Eagle. The investigation first became public when John B. Mason, one of Six's plank owners, was indicted on thirty-seven counts of filing false travel claims and making false statements. (In September 1987, Mason finally pleaded guilty to four counts of falsifying vouchers, and stealing $3,800 in scuba-diving equipment in 1983 and 1984.) Additionally, two enlisted men, both of whom came to SEAL Team Six after I'd left, were court-martialed for filing false claims and vouchers.

Bob Gormly, who was CO of Six when the two court-martialed sailors committed their crimes, was promoted. *I* was the one NIS investigated.

Ultimately, Iron Eagle became a witch-hunt that took up six hundred man-*years* of NIS's time. According to the GAO—the General Accounting Office—one hundred man-years costs the Navy roughly $10 million. So the Navy spent somewhere in the region of $60 million to investigate me—and came up with nothing.

Well, not quite nothing.

If it was NIS's intention to ruin my career, the operation was a complete success.

Doom on you, Sharkman.

—On April 3, 1986, I was summarily dismissed from Red Cell. The new OP-06B (this is Navyspeak for the mouth-filling title Director, Politico-Military Policy and Current Plans Division, Office of the Deputy Chief of Naval Operations for Plans, Policy and Operations), Rear Admiral Roger Bacon, ordered me to "report to the Commandant of the Washington Naval District by 1600 today. You are under investigation." As instructed, I reported to the Washington Navy Yard. The CSO—Chief of Staff Officer—"welcomed" me aboard, then curtly dismissed me "until further notice." I spent the next six months sitting in my studio apartment in Old Town waiting for that further notice. The time wasn't a total loss: I caught up on my reading. I also got back into the habit of polishing both the tops and the soles of my shoes. Once a geek, always a geek.

—On July 22, 1986, after only twenty-five days in office, the newly appointed secretary of the navy, James Webb, somehow found the time to read my entire file, after which he administratively removed me from the promotion list to captain. Webb's legal adviser was a captain named Rudy—the same Rudy who had argued against my promotion when, as a commander, he was VCNO Ron Hays's legal adviser eighteen months previously.

—On May 20, 1986, I underwent a 17-hour interrogation by NIS. The transcript was immediately classified, and I was denied access to it. It was not the only document I wasn't allowed to see. NIS ultimately pulled sixty-four cartons of records from SEAL Team Six, which filled three safes full of classified materials; filing cabinets were crammed with thousands of receipts, vouchers, notes, memos, and memorabilia. I was allowed to see none of it. Secrecy, however, didn't deter NIS sources from leaking stories within the SpecWar community about the "evidence" that was piling up against me.

NIS took the pistol I'd been presented—months after I left the CO slot at Six—by my former SEAL Team Six teammates, as well as one of two sterling-silver belt buckles they'd designed and had cast for Paul and me. Despite the fact that all the men interviewed by NIS swore under oath that they had each contributed $20 toward the gifts and they were not purchased with government funds, NIS still has my pistol and buckle. They confiscated Paul's buckle, too, although we can't figure out why.

—In September 1987, SECNAV James Webb forced Ace Lyons into retirement. Webb's predecessor, John Lehman, described Ace's firing from the CINCPACFLT slot as "the revenge of the nerds."

—I retired from the Navy with the rank of commander on February 1, 1989, after thirty years, three months, and seventeen days of active duty. Despite being under investigation for more than two years, I was never charged by NIS with any impropriety.

—In July 1989, I was "invited" to take part in a grand jury hearing relating to the alleged overcharging on specialized grenades used by SEAL Team Six, Delta, and other elite units, by an Arizona company in which a former SEAL, John Mason, had a financial interest. Mason was serving five years probation after he had pleaded guilty in September 1987 to falsifying travel vouchers and stealing $3,800 worth of scuba-diving equipment in 1983 and 1984, while he'd been at SEAL Team Six. Mason had been given probation instead of a jail sentence on the condition that he cooperate in other investigations—notably the one against me. After the hearing, the U.S. Attorney in Alexandria, Virginia, decided to press conspiracy charges against me.

—In September 1989, I was instructed by Bob Gormly (he and I had served together during my first Vietnam tour in 1967 when he was a lieutenant and I was an ensign; then, in 1974, when we were both lieutenant commanders, I had succeeded him as CO of SEAL Team Two. In 1983, he was a captain and I was a commander, and he succeeded me as CO of SEAL Team Six. Still a captain, Bob headed the Plans and Policy branch of Navy SpecWar) about what I could and could not say regarding my Navy career. Many of my previously *unclassified* fitreps were now arbitrarily classified by the Navy. It was crucial to my defense that I be able to explain what I'd done as a staffer at OP-06, and as CO of SEAL Team

Six. But the Navy ruled that most of my activities between 1977 and 1985 could not be described.

—After I was muzzled by the Navy, my case went to trial. In November 1989, I was tried on three counts of conspiracy. John Mason, now a convicted felon who wanted badly to make a deal with the government, was the prosecution's main witness against me. I was acquitted of one charge, with a hung jury on the other two counts.

—A second trial was held January 16–24, 1990. I was acquitted on one of the two remaining counts and convicted on the final count of conspiracy—but not before the judge broke the hung jury by giving it new and specific instructions that led it to convict me.

—I was sentenced on March 9, 1990, to twenty-one months in prison and a $10,000 fine.

—On the morning of April 16, 1990, the Monday after Easter, I surrendered myself at the Petersburg, Virginia, Federal Correctional Institution. It was as tough a thing as I've ever had to do. Not because I feared prison—God knows I can take care of myself, and heaven help the man who lays a hand on me—but because I knew I'd been railroaded. I was furious with the system for what it had done to me, and with myself for being incapable of making things turn out better.

I didn't check in alone, incidentally: my old friend Mr. Murphy came along for the ride. As it was Easter Monday and many of the staff had taken the day off, I was not sent to the camp right away, but held in the maximum-security prison across the street for a day and a half until I could be signed in. Since I hadn't been properly processed, I was given food—but no utensils. I didn't mind eating pasta that way (after all, in my Geek days I'd sucked it through my nose), but the oatmeal presented a certain extraordinary challenge.

When I crossed the street to Camp Swampy, with its five-story dorm, outside gym, and six-tenths-of-a-mile cinder track, things improved. I've been in worse places. The chow's about the same grade as the O Club at Little Creek. My fellow campers, a mixture of white-collar criminals, dope dealers, and snitches, most of whom have no idea who I am and what I've done, remind me of some of the folks at the Pentagon. No one bothers me—guards included (they're known colloquially as hacks, which stands for Horse's Ass Carrying Keys)—and I keep mostly to myself.

Life is certainly passable. There's CNN on the cable TV, and HBO, too. I've read more than sixty books since coming here. I work out two or three times a day. My weight has dropped from 235 to 195; my waist from 36 to 31; I press 500 pounds on the bench and crunch 190 on the gut machine. I make a whopping sixty-six cents an hour at my prison job—gardening, landscaping, and doing maintenance chores at the prison's UNICOR factory, which makes everything from electrical cable for the military to desks for government offices. Half my salary goes to pay off my fine. I sit in my third-floor living space, which I share with a biker/dope-dealer named Jesse, as I compose these words.

I've also had a lot of time in these months to think about the past—and the future. One of the most gratifying aspects of my incarceration has been the mail. I've received scores of letters from the SEALs and Frogmen with whom I served. Ev Barrett, now retired and living in Florida, scribbled me a couple of notes, telling me to keep my blankety-blanking nose clean, and that he was thinking of me. Patches Watson sends constant bulletins from the UDT/SEAL Museum in Ft. Pierce, Florida, where he is now assistant curator. Even Paul Henley, who hates writing anything, managed to post a couple of letters my way. Dozens of the SEALs I picked for Six—some of whom are still there, others who have retired or gone on to other assignments—have written, telling me to keep the faith, passing on a bit of gossip, or reminding me they're thinking of me whenever they have a cold one. The mail from the guys at Six is all the more significant because some of them were warned that contacting me could mean the loss of their security clearances or their jobs at Six, and they wrote anyway.

Fact is, sitting here on the inside, it would be easy to turn inward and become bitter, to say "What the fuck—" all the time, and curse the world. But those cards and letters have pumped me up, kept me going, given me strength. I'd always preached about unit integrity. Here, behind bars, those words came back to me at mail call, and I knew I'd achieved something great.

The SEALs I selected and trained, after all, are my real

legacy. And despite the Navy's attempts to eradicate much of what I designed, that legacy lives on. Sure—things have changed. Six is much more conventional than it was in my day. It's a huge command now—more than three times the size it was when I ran it—and it is as cumbersome to move as Delta Force. Red Cell is still in existence. But the emphasis has been shifted from "show me" to "tell me." They don't do as many live exercises—and when they do 'em, the scenarios are geared to allow the base commanders to win more times than they lose.

But the men I selected and trained are passing on what I taught them to a new generation of SEALs. Some of the kids I picked for junior-junior cannon fodder are now senior-senior chiefs, lieutenant commanders, and commanders. And, like guerrillas, they're working quietly, within the system, to build SpecWar units the way I taught them to do. They keep me apprised of their progress. And they learned to do it my way. When my SEALs develop their ops plans today, they don't plan Mustins—they plan *Marcinkos*.

As to what's ahead, I'd always joked about taking SEAL Team Six commercial. "You Call, I Haul." KATN, Inc.— Kick Ass Take Names, Incorporated.

It's not so farfetched. The U.S. government has guidelines that ordain assassination unacceptable as national policy. It has rules, which say that hostile targets, such as chemical-war plants, nuclear facilities and weapons, can only be hit during bona fide military strikes. But what happens when a superpower such as the United States is faced with a Muammar Qaddafi, a Manuel Noriega, or a Saddam Hussein?

The Israelis have the ability to launch preemptive SpecWar strikes against specific targets, as they did when a combined Mossad–Israeli Army commando unit assassinated the PLO's number two terrorist, Abu Jihad, at his home in Tunis in April 1988. Other nations, including France and Great Britain, also have hit targets—both human and otherwise—covertly. The Soviets have an active campaign of clandestine operations. The United States, however, has always been reluctant to wage similar shadow wars against its enemies.

One way for the U.S. to strike back and still retain plausible deniability would be to subcontract its covert hits. So, instead of launching a complicated, costly, major military operation against Muammar Qaddafi, for example, let Demo Dick's KATN, Inc. do the job instead. Just call 1-800-SEAL R US.

Think about it: I have friends, now retired from SEAL Team Six, who can fly anything from a Cessna to a 737 to an HH-53H. I have my own intelligence network. I can get hold of specialized equipment. All of those elements are easily recreated outside the military framework. Personnel is no problem either: the hardest chore would be selecting the few who'd make my final cut.

KATN could do the job lean and mean. Two platoons at the most. Four boat crews. Fourteen pairs of swim buddies. Helping each other according to Barrett's Law. Infiltrated two by two, or four by four, via sea or air or land. As in SEAL. Living off the land. Going in the back door, just like Ilo-Ilo Island. Developing intelligence, just like SEAL Team Six. Watching the patterns, just like Red Cell.

Then, when we're ready, we hop and pop. We shoot and loot. We slip out the back door. If we're caught? Too bad— we knew the risks. We're cannon fodder—expendable assets. And the government still has plausible deniability. You want one or two of Qaddafi's chemical plants blown up? You need Manuel Noriega snatched? You want to vaporize the Iraqi nuclear facilities in Baghdad?

Well, Mr. President, Mr. SECDEF, Mr. Chairman of the Joint Chiefs of Staff, Mr. CNO—you call, I haul. Oh—half the fee up front, please.

It's not so farfetched. Believe me.

Over Christmas of 1990, I was given a five-day furlough from prison. I spent it at my studio apartment in Old Town, visiting with friends I hadn't seen in months, cooking copious amounts of spicy food, savoring my first sirloin steak in eight months, enjoying the freedom of keeping my own totally unsupervised schedule, and delighting in the holiday spirit.

On Christmas Eve, I had a visitor. I'll call him Tony Mercaldi. Tony works for one of the shadowy agencies that don't list telephone numbers in any of the government directories. He is one of those people spy novelists write about but never get to meet. I've known him for some years and can vouch for the fact that he's good at what he does.

Merc is a large man, but deceptively so. If you looked twice at him—which you wouldn't be prone to do—he'd appear unremarkably ordinary. Brown hair, not too long, not too short; a round face that blends in; a physique that says nothing about the man. This is exactly what makes him so effective. People don't remember him when he operates.

I took Tony's coat, poured him a drink, grabbed a Diet Pepsi for me—we're not allowed any booze on furlough—and we settled onto my couch.

He toasted me. "Merry Christmas, Demo."

"Thanks. It's nice to be out for a few days."

"I'll bet."

We talked awhile, gossiping about old friends and laughing about things we'd done together in the past. It was good to see him.

Then, Tony got serious. He turned the volume on my FM radio up until it became uncomfortable and moved closer to me. "How'd you like a permanent vacation from Petersburg?"

"Only if there's lots of pussy involved."

"I'm serious."

"So am I. Besides—I don't know, Merc, I'm making good money and I'm learning a trade. By spring I'll be a hell of a gardener."

He laughed. "You already have a trade."

"Which one?"

"Breaking into key installations. As I recall, you made quite a nuisance of yourself."

"Ah, *that* trade."

"That trade." His voice got lower. "We've got a problem, Dick. You follow the news. You know what's happening in Iraq. There's gonna be a war—and people are gonna get killed."

"So?"

"How'd you feel about helping out?"

"Depends," I said.

"On what?"

"On the conditions. And on the problem."

"The problem is, we've identified a number of potential targets in the Baghdad area that need to be verified and eliminated—"

"Eliminated?"

"Either they get brought out—which seems impractical to

me, but you know how screwed up the guys who draft options get—or they get destroyed where they live."

I nodded. He wasn't asking the impossible. "Okay. What's the probs and stats?"

"The war-gamers are talking eighty percent casualties if they send Six."

"That's awful damn high."

"Things have changed since you were CO. It's a lot more cumbersome to do business. Plans go through layers of management—they get screwed up."

"So you want me to go instead."

He nodded. "There are those of us who figure you can keep the casualties to forty percent."

I smiled wryly. "It's nice to know some people still care enough to send the very best. Under what conditions would I operate?"

"Since you'd be going after legitimate military targets, the best condition is, you put your old uniform back on. That way, everything's official—we're talking military targets, after all."

"Three-word answer: screw you, cockbreath. No way. This asshole shit-for-brains geek has learned the hard way. The Navy spent millions trying to screw me once. I'm not gonna give it a second chance by going back into uniform."

Merc held up his hand. "Understood, Dick. I knew that's what you'd say, but I was under orders to ask." He sipped his drink. "So—under what conditions would you consider taking the job?"

I thought about it for a while. "My choice of men, my rules. Unlimited budget. You tell me the objective. You give me the timetable. Then you leave me alone."

"I'll carry the message back." He reached forward and turned the radio volume down, stood, stretched, and retrieved his coat from the chair where I'd tossed it. "Keep the faith, bro. We'll be in touch."

My furlough ended the night of December 26, when I surrendered myself to the convivial and ever-amusing Federal Bureau of Prisons facility at Petersburg. January 15 came, and went. Operation Desert Shield became Operation Desert

Storm. I'm still behind bars. But things may not be as far-fetched as they seem: Tony did finally get back to me.

A Valentine's Day card with familiar handwriting made it through the prison system. The cryptic message inside was short and sweet. "Dear French Fuck—Cease," it read. "But always remember what Tommy H told you." It was signed "Until We Meet Again Under Better Conditions." I shredded the card and deep-sixed it down the head.

In phonetic French, "Fuck Cease" becomes *Phoque Six*—SEAL Six.

And Thomas Hayward was the chief of naval operations who gave me my command. It was he who told me, "Dick, you will not fail."

And "better conditions"? Oh, I liked that thought a lot.

So, doom on you, Navy—strong message follows. I'll be back . . . but not in uniform. And I will not fail.

Glossary

ALUSNA: Air Liaison, U.S. Naval Air (naval attaché for air).

Baader-Meinhof: also known as Red Army Faction (RAF); operations are primarily in the Federal Republic of Germany.

balaclava: a knitted hood commonly used by CT operators to conceal facial features.

Bearcat: radio-frequency scanner, available at Radio Shack, etc.

black: synonym for any covert or clandestine activity.

BlackHawk: H-60 Army chopper (troop transport).

Boomer class: U.S. Navy strategic nuclear submarine.

BUPERS: BUreau of PERSonnel.

C-130: Hercules turboprop transport aircraft, originally made by Lockheed in 1951 and still flying all over the world.

C-141: Lockheed's StarLifter, a jet transport with a range of up to five thousand miles.

C-3: a yellowish, solid plastic explosive of pre–Vietnam War vintage, used in Mk-135 satchel charges.

C-4: white plastic explosive. It is so stable you can ignite it and nothing bad will happen. Just don't stamp on it to put the fire out.

C-5A: no explosives here—this is the Air Force's biggest transport plane.

Christians In Action: SEAL slang for Central Intelligence Agency or its personnel.

Chu-hoi: (Vietnamese) defector. Chu-hois were often used in Provincial Reconnaissance Units (see PRU).

CINC: Commander-IN-Chief.

CINCLANT: Commander-IN-Chief, AtLANTic.

CINCLANTFLT: Commander-IN-Chief, AtLANTic FLeeT.

CINCPAC: Commander-IN-Chief, PACific.

CINCPACFLT: Commander-IN-Chief, PACific FLeeT.

CNO: Chief of Naval Operations.

cobra feast: Cambodian ceremony that makes snake-eaters eat beaucoup snake.

cockbreath: what SEALs call people who only pay lip service.

COD: Carrier On-board Delivery aircraft.

COMNAVSPECWARGRU: COMmander, NAVal SPECial WARfare GRoUp. There are two of these: ONE, based at Coronado, California; TWO, based at Little Creek, Virginia.

COMPHIBTRALANT: COMmander, AmPHIBious TRAining Command, AtLANTic.

CSO: Chief of Staff Officer.

CTJTF: CounterTerrorist Joint Task Force.

DCM: (State Department) Deputy Chief of Mission.

di-di-mau: (Vietnamese) get outta here.

dip-dunk: nerdy asshole (see NILO).

diplo-dink: cookie-pushing diplomat apparatchik type.

dirtbag: grungy blue-collar look favored by SEAL Team Six.

DOD: Department Of Defense.

doom on you: corruption of Vietnamese phonetic for "go fuck yourself."

Draeger: German-manufactured oxygen rebreather unit (it produces neither bubbles nor sound and is therefore perfect for clandestine SEAL insertions).

du-ma-nhieu: (Vietnamese) go fuck yourself (see DOOM ON YOU).

dumbshit: expression of affection used by chiefs to describe their favorite people.

E-5: an E-2 is an airplane. So is an E-4 (the military designation for a 747). But an E-5 . . . is a Navy rank, equivalent to an Army or Marine sergeant.

EC-130: A C-130 configured by the Navy (or Air Force) as a command/control/communications (C^3) aircraft.

Ekernforde: home of the German Frogmen.

EOD: Explosives Ordnance Disposal.

ERA: (Equal Rights Amendment) Marcinko's philosophy about people: Treat them all the same—JUST LIKE SHIT.

F-111: Air Force aircraft that can kick ass wherever there is air.

F-14: Navy aircraft that can kick ass wherever there is air, *and* land on a carrier.

Fakahani: the district in West Beirut where the PLO made its headquarters.

flat: configuration of parachute (it glides and sails).

four-striper: U.S. Navy captain (equal in rank to a colonel).

frags: fragmentation grenades.

FUBAR: Fucked Up Beyond All Repair (see GOATFUCK).

FUC: Female Ugly Commander.

GED: General Equivalency Diploma (high-school equivalency).

geek: dumbshit (see MARCINKO).

GIGN: *Gendarmerie Nationale (Groupement d'Intervention de la Gendarmerie Nationale)*. French counterterror unit.

GIGO: computerese for Garbage In/Garbage Out.

GIS: Italian carabinieri CT unit *(Groupe Interventional Speciale)*. Known as grappa drinkers.

goatfuck: FUBAR

GSG-9: *Grenzchutzgruppe-9*, West German CT unit.

HAHO: High Altitude, High Opening.

HALO: High Altitude, Low Opening.

HH-53H: a Sikorsky H-53 Sea Stallion helicopter outfitted for SpecWar operations.

GLOSSARY

HK: Heckler & Koch weapon, usually a 9mm submachine gun.

hop and pop: this is what you're about to do if you're a SEAL carrying an HK and going out of an aircraft.

HUMINT: HUMan INTelligence, gathered by an agent or agents.

hush-puppy: silencer (suppressor) for a weapon.

Hydra-Shok: extremely lethal hollow-point ammunition manufactured by Federal Cartridge Company.

IBL: Inflatable Boat, Large.

IBS: Inflatable Boat, Small.

IED: Improvised Explosive Device.

Intelbabble: bureaucratic gobbledygook often used by NILOs.

JSOC: Joint Special Operations Command.

JTF: Joint Task Force.

jumpmaster: the operator responsible for the safe conduct of parachute operations.

Kampfschwimmerkompanie: (German) combat swimmers (equivalent of SEALs).

KATN: Kick Ass and Take Names.

KC-135: USAF flying gas station.

KH-11: NSA spy-in-the-sky satellite.

KIA: Killed In Action.

KISS: Keep It Simple, Stupid.

Langley: CIA headquarters.

LANTFLT: AtLANTic FLeeT.

LDO: Limited Duty Officer (or, in SEAL slang, Loud, Dumb, and Obnoxious).

LSD: Landing Ship/Dock (amphibious ship).

LSP: Louisiana State Police.

LURPs: Rations used on LRRP (Long Range Reconnaissance Patrol) missions.

LZ: Landing Zone.

M16: basic .223-caliber weapon used in Vietnam.

M60: a machine gun that fires 7.62mm ammunition.

MAC-10s: submachine guns favored by drug dealers.

MAC: Military Air Command (also known as trash haulers —you call, they haul).

Marcinko: see DUMBSHIT.

Marvin: SEAL rhyming slang for Army of the Republic of Vietnam (ARVN) personnel.

MC-130: USAF special operations aircraft.

Memcon: MEMorandum of CONversation written by intelligence or diplomatic officers after meeting with any contacts.

MEP: Movement for the Ejaculation of Palestine.

Mini-14s: Ruger's ubiquitous .223-caliber semiautomatic rifle.

MNF: MultiNational Force

MOB-6: MOBility-6. SEAL Two's counterterror unit, a precursor of SEAL Team Six.

Mossad: *Mossad Letafkidim Meouychadim*, or the Central Institute for Intelligence and Special Duties. Israel's foreign-intelligence organization.

MP5: an HK submachine gun favored by CT units including SEAL Team Six and GSG-9.

Navyspeak: redundant, bureaucratic naval nomenclature, either in written nonoral, or nonwritten oral, mode, indecipherable by non-military (conventional) individuals during interfacing configuration conformations.

NCA: National Command Authority. The top-level chain of command consisting of the president and the secretary of defense.

NCO: NonCommissioned Officer.

NILO: Naval Intelligence Liaison Officer (see DIP-DUNK).

NIS: Naval Security and Investigative Command (see SHIT-FOR-BRAINS).

NMN: Navyspeak for No Middle Name.

Nung: Chinese mercenary.

NVA: North Vietnamese Army.

OP-06: Deputy Chief of Naval Operations for Plans, Policy, and Operations.

OP-06B: Assistant Deputy Chief of Naval Operations for Plans, Policy, and Operations.

OP-06D: formal Navy designation for the Red Cell.

OPSEC: OPerational SECurity. Very important in black ops.

GLOSSARY

PBR: Patrol Boat/River. The Jacuzzi-powered plastic battle-ship used on the Vietnamese rivers.

Peary, Camp: CIA training facility near Williamsburg, Virginia, also known as The Farm.

pencil-dicked: a no-load, bean-counting pain-in-the-ass.

phoque: (French) seal.

phoquee: he or she who gets screwed by SEALs.

plastique: plastic explosive (see C-4 and SEMTEX).

PLF: 1. Parachute Landing Fall (how not to bust your ass). 2. Palestine Liberation Front. The terrorist group led by Muhammed al Abbas that hijacked the cruise ship *Achille Lauro*.

plink: discriminating single shot, usually a kill shot to the head.

PLO: Palestine Liberation Organization.

PO: Petty Officer. According to Ev Barrett, petty officers are petty until they become chief petty officers. Then they rule the world.

PO2: Petty Officer Second Class (same as a staff sergeant).

PO3: ditto, but Third Class (equivalent to a corporal).

PRC-101: man-portable satellite communications.

PROCOM: PROvincial COMmander. An ARVN officer who was nominally in charge of a specific province.

prowl and growl: see KATN.

PRU: Provincial Reconnaissance Unit (Vietnam). U.S.-led, Vietnamese-staffed hunter/killer unit that liked to prowl and growl.

PSC-1: Portable Satellite Communications terminal.

PT: physical training. Hoo-yah!

Quantico: home of FBI Academy and base of their Hostage Rescue Team (HRT).

recon: reconnaissance.

RFPF (Ruff-puff): Regional Force/Provincial Force (Vietnam).

RH-53D: PAVE LOW special operations chopper.

rock and roll: fun and games, usually with a shitload of hot lead flying.

RPG: Rocket-Propelled Grenade (Soviet-made).

RVN: Republic of VietNam.

GLOSSARY

SAS: British Special Air Service. Motto: Who dares, wins.

SATCOM: SATellite COMmunications.

SBS: British Special Boat Squadron (a unit of the Royal Marines).

SCIF: Special Classified Intelligence Facility (spook talk). A secure bubble room.

SDV: Swimmer Delivery Vehicle.

SEALs: the Navy's SEa-Air-Land units. The most elite special operations force in the U.S. arsenal. When they were created in 1962, there were only fifty SEALs. In SEAL slang the acronym stands for Sleep, EAt, and Live it up.

Seawolves: USN chopper gunships in Vietnam.

SECDEF: SECretary of DEFense.

SECNAV: SECretary of the NAVy.

Semtex: the Czech version of C-4 plastic explosive. If it goes off prematurely, you end up with a canceled Czech.

SFOD-D: Special Forces Operational Detachment–Delta (Delta Force).

shit: what happens.

shit-for-brains: a real numb-nuts pencil-dicked asshole; or: anyone from NIS.

shoot and loot: the SEAL version of rape, pillage, and burn.

SIGINT: SIGnals INTelligence.

Smith: a Smith & Wesson pistol, generally a .357-caliber Model 66 stainless-steel revolver with four-inch barrel.

SNAFU: Situation Normal: All Fucked Up.

SNARE: horse-collar loop used for snatching SEALs from the water into an IBL.

SOF: Special Operations Force.

SOSUS: underwater listening-device network deployed to detect hostile submarines.

SpecWar: Special Warfare.

SR-71: high-flying intelligence collector (spy plane).

STAB: SEAL Tactical Assault Boat.

SURFLANT: SURface Force AtLANTic.

SWAT: Special Weapons And Tactics.

TAD: Temporary Additional Duty. (In SEAL slang: Traveling Around Drunk.)

TARFU: Things Are Really Fucked Up.

GLOSSARY

TAT: Terrorist Action Team.
TECHINT: TECHnical INTelligence.

UDT-21: Marcinko's first home away from home.
UDT-22: Marcinko's second home away from home.
UDT: Underwater Demolition Team. (In SEAL slang: UnderDeveloped Twerp, or Urinal Drain Technician.)
UNODIR: UNless Otherwise DIRected.
USNR: United States Naval Reserve.
USS: United States Ship.

VC: (Victor Charlie) VietCong.
VCNO: Vice Chief of Naval Operations.

W.G.M.A.T.A.T.S.: Unofficial SEAL Team Six motto: We Get More Ass Than A Toilet Seat.
WIA: Wounded In Action.
WPs: (Willy-Peters) White Phosphorus grenades.

XO: Executive Officer.

Zulu: Greenwich Mean Time (GMT) designator, used in all formal military communications.

Index

* All entries preceded by an asterisk are pseudonyms.

INDEX

INDEX

ADD THESE

ROGUE WARRIOR®

BOOKS FROM RICHARD MARCINKO, AND JOHN WEISMAN TO YOUR COLLECTION

Echo Platoon

Option Delta

Seal Force Alpha

Designation Gold

Task Force Blue

Green Team

Red Cell

Rogue Warrior

AND FROM RICHARD MARCINKO

Leadership Secrets of the Rogue Warrior

The Rogue Warrior's Strategy for Success

The Real Team

Visit www.SimonSays.com/rogue

POCKET BOOKS
A VIACOM COMPANY

2378-02

Visit the

ROGUE
WARRIOR®

at
www.SimonSays.com/rogue

where you can read excerpts
from his books, find a listing
of future titles, and learn more
about the Rogue Warrior®
and his mission!

2377

Don't miss these riveting thrillers from Pocket Books!

Joy Fielding
CHARLEY'S WEB

An ambitious South Florida journalist is in a heart-pounding race to save her children and herself from a killer's deadly designs.

Robert K. Tanenbaum
ESCAPE

District Attorney Butch Karp takes on a controversial defense in the courtroom, as a deadly terrorist plot unfolds in the heart of Manhattan.

Robert Ferrigno
SINS OF THE ASSASSIN

Radical forces battle for control of a nuke-ravaged nation...the land once known as America.

Bob Reiss
BLACK MONDAY

A worldwide epidemic—affecting not humans, but oil—causes civilization to descend into chaos.

John Connolly
THE REAPERS

A chain of killings is obscurely linked over a long passage of years, and it is time for the blood debts to be settled.

Available wherever books are sold or at www.simonandschuster.com

20474